C
AS
DEATH

COLD
AS
DEATH

T. J. MacGregor

PINNACLE BOOKS
Kensington Publishing Corp.
www.kensingtonbooks.com

For Tony Janeshutz,
the best dad anyone could ask for.
10/20/1913–9/25/2005

Special thanks to:

My husband Rob & my daughter Megan,
& to Kate Duffy & Al Zuckerman.
You make all things possible!

Between the idea
And the reality
Between the motion
And the act
Falls the Shadow

Between the conception
And the creation
Between the emotion
And the response
Falls the shadow

—T. S. Eliot, from "The Hollow Men"

PART ONE

Vision

We live in "nonlocal" reality, which is to say that we can be affected by events that are distant from our ordinary awareness.
—Russell Targ, from *Limitless Mind*

I

Hill House

The hillside looked as if a giant in the midst of a temper tantrum had torn across it, knocking down trees, ripping bushes out by the roots, trampling everything in its path. Here and there, Mira Morales passed pines or banyans that still stood, but most of them had been stripped of needles and leaves and their trunks had been sheared of bark. On one area of the hill, a dense copse of pines had survived the hurricane relatively intact, trees huddled together like orphans, the top branches leaning left, blown that way by the wind.

On the street below her, piles of debris waited at curbsides to be hauled away—vegetation, broken fences, sheets of aluminum, chunks of concrete. Some of the piles stood five or six feet high and included mattresses, doors, sofas, chairs, rolls of moldy carpet, broken refrigerators, stoves, tables. Even now, five weeks after Hurricane Danielle had roared in, her winds in excess of 155 miles an hour, Tango Key still looked like Hiroshima, but without the bodies.

Mira paused to catch her breath. The air was so still that birds didn't sing, branches didn't stir. The speckling of clouds in the vast blue field of sky resembled tiny white sailboats stuck in the doldrums. The air smelled scorched, as if an iron had been held too long to a wardrobe of shirts. The extreme heat and humidity caused her T-shirt to cling to her. Her denim shorts, soaked through with perspiration, felt like they weighed fifty pounds.

She pulled her thick black hair behind her head and snapped an elastic band around it, getting it off her neck. She was tempted to pour her bottle of cold water over her head, but decided she was much too thirsty to waste it. She twisted the cap and drank down half of it.

Question: Why had she ventured out on a morning in late July when the temperature already stood at a muggy ninety and it wasn't even seven yet?

Well, that was easy. She couldn't stand the reality of what she faced, another day of struggling to piece her bookstore back together. The boxes of books she had salvaged were now housed in the yoga room at the back of the store. Each day, she opened boxes and checked each title against a master inventory list. She figured she had saved only a third of her entire inventory, but remained absurdly hopeful that the statistics would improve.

Hurricane Danielle had crashed ashore at high tide. The water had exploded upward through the wooden slats of the Tango pier, collapsed the concrete pilings, and swept through the downtown with the power of some ancient, enraged god. At its peak, the water at the front of her store had reached six feet and when it receded, it left behind a soggy beach of mud, sticks, stones, and shells. As the mud dried, creatures crawled out of that dark, erratic landscape: fire ants, snakes, skinks, spiders, roaches, worms, mice, rats, a regular zoo.

For some reason, the yoga room at the back of the store, separated by a wall and a metal door, had remained relatively dry. The books she had stored in there and those she had taken to her house were all that remained of her inventory.

The exterior of the store had sustained major damage—

holes in the roof, dry rot setting in to the wooden front door and the floor, trees still down, the fence collapsed. The storage shed, crushed like a tin can, still had an uprooted banyan lying across it. The work crew that was replacing most of the store's roof would be hammering and pounding today, another crew would be laying tile on the eastern side of the store, and someone was coming out to remove the banyan and the remains of the shed.

Yet, her store and home could be repaired and rebuilt. Other people had not been as fortunate. With nearly a third of the buildings on Tango completely destroyed, hundreds of people were homeless and dozens of businesses had been wiped off the map. On her bookstore's block, only two buildings out of ten remained: her bookstore and Mango Mama's, a restaurant that had withstood hurricanes since the early 1940s. The Tango bridge, the island's connection to the rest of the world, had lost six miles of concrete and steel and wouldn't open again for another year. The only ways to or from the island were by air or ferry.

Since eighty percent of the island was still without power, they lived under a curfew and what amounted to martial law. For looting, they were told. To keep people safe, the officials said. No alcohol was being sold on the island as long as the curfew was in effect, so a black market now flourished. On a given day, a bottle of ordinary California red wine—five bucks at your local grocery store—could be had for thirty to fifty dollars a bottle. A six-pack of beer was going for about fifteen bucks. A bottle of hard liquor—any hard liquor, regardless of its quality—began at about seventy-five dollars.

Generators were also in great demand. For a basic unit that would power a refrigerator, a few lights, and maybe a TV, the standing price was $1,200 cash. Without gas, though, generators were useless and only one gas station on Tango presently had power. Most mornings, its supply was sold out before breakfast.

You could leave the island to buy any of these items, but

only if you had enough gas to make it somewhere. Forty percent of the power in Key West had been restored, yet it was as sporadic and unpredictable as true love. Most of Sugarloaf Key, fifteen miles north of Key West, supposedly had gone back online four days ago. But according to the grapevine, *dependable* power, *continuous, uninterrupted* power there was a pipe dream. Between Sugarloaf and Key Largo lay an electrical wasteland where life languished in the Dark Ages.

To find anything being sold in the black market on Tango, you had to drive two or three hours to Miami. Only the courageous, the stupid, or the owners of VWs, hybrids, or other models that got great gas mileage even attempted the trip. In a state where SUVs, Hummers, Suburbans, and other gas-guzzlers proliferated like mosquitoes in a swamp, she figured that maybe five to ten people on Tango were making it as far as Key Largo or Miami for liquor, food, generators, and gas. Even though there were laws against price-gouging in the aftermath of a hurricane, no one in Key Largo, the nearest place with steady supplies of gas, had been arrested for charging five bucks a gallon.

Here on Tango, people whose homes had been torn apart had banded together to keep watch over each others' properties because looting was still a problem. And, like tribes of old, they also shared supplies, food, and water. In this regard, Mira considered herself fortunate as well. While the extensive reconstruction of her home was under way, she was living in a trailer on her property that belonged to two of her long-time clients and friends. Until the hurricane, Ace and Luke had been evening street performers on Tango's pier. With the pier gone, they now did odd jobs on the island and had become her extended family while her daughter, grandmother, and three cats were staying with friends in Miami, where there was power.

Unplugged from the grid, life in the Florida Keys and especially on Tango Key had screeched to a halt. All the rules had changed. It was a whole new universe.

In the weeks since Danielle had turned Mira's life into a parody of survival and a search for the most basic items—ice, bottled water, canned food, gas, propane—she had forgotten who she was. The *who* had become irrelevant. *What* she could do and *when* she could do it were all that mattered. And so, during those times when she couldn't face the stink or the mess in her store any longer, she went walking.

Every day, at various times of the day, she ventured to a different part of the island and invariably discovered areas on Tango she had never seen before. Neighborhoods tucked away in the hills, coves on the west side of the island where dolphins frolicked, old buildings that had withstood time and hurricanes. On these walks, she understood what had driven men like Magellan.

And on these walks, she thought a lot about global warming, the gradually rising temperature of the planet's oceans, the shrinkage of the ice shelf, the wetlands that the current administration had opened to developers, the loss of barrier islands that once had provided buffers from monster storms. There would be more storms, bigger storms, monstrous storms that would make even Danielle look insignificant. And then the coming global oil crisis would bring about the collapse of an era of unbridled greed, lies, and corruption.

She walked faster, as if to outdistance this line of thought. Right now, she had to focus on her little corner of the world.

Her thighs and calves had gotten tan, lean, hard as rock. She had dropped eight pounds. Freckles now dotted her cheeks and crossed the bridge of her nose. Physically, she felt stronger and healthier than she had in years. She supposed her psyche was healing too, but she had some serious doubts about her heart.

Five years with Wayne Sheppard had ended in the bleak hours when Danielle had moved on, ended out there in a wind-ravaged grove of trees. The door had slammed shut with resounding finality shortly afterward, when he had moved out of her place and in with his partner, John Gutierrez. Annie, her teenaged daughter, was furious with her. She loved Sheppard like a father and as far as she was concerned, the whole thing was Mira's fault.

If you weren't so weird, Mom, if you weren't always so certain you're right . . . In other words, Mira thought, bend like a straw and you can keep your man. Never mind if you have to compromise yourself or what you know to be true. Five years might be just spit in the huge cosmic soup of things. But it was five years of loving the same man, of being accustomed to the solidness of his body next to you in bed at night, five years of habits and quirks and memories that were tough to obliterate. She and Sheppard had hit dry patches before in their relationship, but never had come upon something that felt as final as this did.

Mira started climbing again, moving more quickly now to escape the pity party her thoughts had become. She realized the hill was steeper than she'd thought, strewn with fallen trees, uprooted vegetation, the old trail obscured. She kept climbing; the air grew warmer. She spotted a lizard dozing on top of a rock in the hot sun. As she passed it, the little thing opened its eyes and watched her. Lizard, lizard. What message did the lizard have for her?

Camouflage. Slow down the pace of your life. Be still, watch, observe.

Yes, okay. That fit.

Nadine, her grandmother and business partner, understood completely what had happened between her and Sheppard. She never came right out and said Mira was better off, but Mira suspected Nadine was thinking it. Nadine and Sheppard rarely agreed on anything. *There will be other men,* Nadine assured her.

Oh? That was supposed to console her? She considered herself lucky to have loved twice—Sheppard and her husband, Tom Morales, dead now for eleven years. She had invested so much of herself in these two relationships that she doubted she had the fortitude to go through yet another.

Forty-one and your sex life is over.

Mira finally reached the top of the hill and sat down to drink in the view. The Gulf of Mexico spread out far below her, an unbroken vastness a deeper shade of blue than the sky. The heat released the sweet scent of grass, the thick humidity of the July air.

Distantly, like a voice in a dream, she heard someone screaming for help, a woman. Her voice—wild, frantic, desperate—hammered the stillness. Mira shot to her feet, listening hard, and heard it again. She ran toward the voice, arms hugging her sides, hands fisted. Her vision turned strange, blurry one moment, clear the next; then she was racing through a world as black and white as a photographic negative. She tore around a pile of dried bushes and gnarled branches, crashed across a collapsed wooden fence, and finally saw it, there on top of the hill, a burning house.

Flames leaped from the windows, tongues of fire licked at the roof, fat plumes of dark smoke curled toward the dome of gray sky, swollen with thunderheads. And she saw it all like a negative. A woman stumbled down the driveway, waving her arms frantically, her clothes on fire. Before Mira reached her, an old Buick raced away from the side of the house, tires kicking up dust and gravel.

The car was between Mira and the woman. Even in this strange black and white world, it shimmered and quivered like a mirage. Mira shouted and waved her arms wildly, trying to flag down the driver. She jumped a low hedge and ran fast across a lawn, trampling recently planted flowers, and reached the driveway just yards in front of the car.

She saw a boy's face pressed to the glass, his eyes wide, dark, horrified. He clawed at the window, his mouth opened wide in a scream she couldn't hear. The car didn't slow. It bore down on her at an alarming speed—and then passed through her, ghostlike.

Mira felt the car's passage through her blood and bones. It shocked her so deeply that she looked down at herself like some actress in a bad movie, almost expecting to see a huge hole in her abdomen. She was intact, but her knees buckled and she went down.

It seemed she lay there for half a lifetime, her face in the dirt, the gravel biting into her forehead, her cheeks, her heart hammering, the center of her chest seized up. *Heart attack. I'm in cardiac arrest and just hallucinated all that.*

Something wet and warm slid up the side of her cheek. She raised her head and there sat a fluffy Himalayan cat, its soft blue eyes regarding her with frank curiosity. Mira rolled onto her back, sat up, and the cat scampered off.

Color had returned to her world, but she didn't see a car. Or a woman on fire. No burning house or terrified kid. Her ticker was still ticking. Only one explanation fit: She was locked inside a full-blown mental meltdown.

Jesus God, she was a mess. Mira got shakily to her feet, feeling disassociated, not quite here, as though she'd left part of herself back in the vision of the fire, the fleeing car. She turned slowly in place. Tasted dust in her mouth. Felt it caked on her hands, her face. The light was bright, the sky wasn't overcast. The house looked peaceful and serene and different.

What's going on? Had she seen something from the past? The future? A probable future? What? Just what the hell had she seen? And why had she seen it in black and white? As far as she could remember, that hadn't happened before.

Who lived in this house?

Where's the woman? The car? The kid? The cat?

Mira moved hesitantly up the driveway and toward the house, slapping her shorts free of dust. Her face hurt. She'd lost her bottle of water. A sudden terror gripped her. Maybe recent events in her life had caused her grasp on reality to unravel. Stress. Sure. Stress could cause it. Category-five hurricane. House no longer habitable, living in a trailer, store closed, no income, lover of five years gone, her family elsewhere. Rootless.

She pressed the doorbell, listening for that sonorous ring,

that melodic *hello,* but didn't hear anything. Of course not. No power, no doorbell. She rapped sharply. *Run,* whispered a soft, inner voice. *Run now, while you still can.*

The temptation to take off nearly overpowered her. She didn't want to straddle two worlds anymore—this one and something *other.* But given the clarity of the vision and the discrepancies with what she saw in front of her—that the house wasn't on fire—and the fact that a child was involved, she had to check. At the very least, she needed to find out if a child even lived here.

Mira started to knock again, but realized the door wasn't shut tightly. She touched it with the toe of her shoe and it creaked open slightly, releasing warm air from inside the house.

Goose bumps broke out along her arms, the skin along the back of her neck tightened. Mira hesitated and finally nudged the door with her foot again. This time, it swung wide open.

She called out once more, her voice echoing through the cavernous house, and crossed the threshold, calling out again. She glimpsed the cat as it vanished into a room off the hallway. Then a figure appeared at the end of the long hall, a portly woman in a blue flowered dress. She stared at Mira, hands on her teapot hips.

"I'm sorry to bother you," Mira said, speaking loudly, as though the woman were deaf. "But I was . . ."

The woman seemed to motion for her to come in, then moved quickly through a doorway on her left and out of Mira's sight.

"Ma'am?"

No answer.

Yeah, okay. What did that mean? *Come in but don't talk to me?* Mira went inside and hurried down the hall, past an exquisite display of island art, then an original Salvador Dalí, a pen-and-ink Picasso, an original Andy Warhol. An art collection already worth more than everything she owned.

She paused in the doorway of the largest kitchen she had ever seen. Light spilled through a pair of skylights and a double bay window that overlooked a large screened pool with a curved slide, a Jacuzzi at one end and an explosion of colorful plants at the other. The woman stood at an island in the center of the kitchen, looking around with an expression that revealed profound confusion.

"Listen, I'm really sorry to intrude like this, but can you tell me if a child lives here?" Mira asked.

The woman didn't hear her. She ran her hands over her face, then smoothed them over her dress, and suddenly thrust out her plump, fleshy arms. She turned them this way and that, examining them, her confusion deepening. She lurched forward with sudden, shocking swiftness, crossed the kitchen—and dissolved into the wall.

Aw, shit, she looked so real. Who was she? Not the woman from the vision.

Mira pitched forward and ran into the room on the other side of the wall through which the ghost had vanished. Mira glimpsed her moving down a hallway, the blue flowers on her dress bright and vivid enough to attract butterflies. Mira's internal alarms shrieked. The muscles in her legs, her shoulders, her jaw had gone tight, tense. *Leave,* the inner voice warned.

The woman melted through a door at the end of the hall, on the north side of the house. Mira loped after her, shoes pounding against the tiled floors, and threw open the door. In a single, sweeping glance, she determined the bedroom belonged to a teenaged boy with some unusual interests—poster-sized photos of dolphins and whales covered one wall, a large model plane hung from the ceiling, the ceiling looked like outer space. The only hint of normalcy lay in the movie and music posters that covered another wall. The ghost in the blue flowered dress stood completely still, staring down at a woman in voluminous pajamas who was sprawled on the floor. Blood stained the front of her pajama top; her eyes gazed vacantly at the ceiling.

The Himalayan raced past Mira's legs, screeched to a stop like a cat in a cartoon, its back hunched, fur going up. It started hissing.

"That's me," the woman gasped. "I'm dead." She looked at the cat. "Dolittle sees me." She raised her eyes to Mira. "You see me." Her mouth quivered. "I . . . I . . ."

Static filled Mira's head. She understood she wouldn't be able to see the woman much longer, that their connection was breaking down. "Who did this?" she asked quickly.

The temperature in the room dropped so rapidly that the next intake of breath hurt the inside of Mira's chest. Frost formed on the mirrors, the metal surfaces. The closet door began to glow a luminous blue. The young woman Mira had seen in the driveway emerged from the blue, stepping out of it with a dancer's grace. She wasn't on fire now, wasn't shouting or frantic. She had a beautiful face and wore loose, khaki-colored pants, a rose-colored shirt, sandals. The cat—Dolittle—apparently saw her too, and took off, a blur of speed. The young ghost slipped her arm around the shoulders of the older ghost, then glanced deliberately at Mira, as if aware of her only now. Both women vanished and the blue glow winked out like a candle.

During this entire episode—which lasted maybe twenty seconds—the room had grown as cold as death. Mira's teeth now chattered. She blew into her hands to warm them. Her knees creaked and complained as she sank to the floor beside the dead woman. Mira gently shut the corpse's eyes. Her fingertips tingled, a sure sign that if she opened herself a little more she would be able to pick up information about the woman. But she already knew more than she cared to know.

She rocked back onto her heels, noticing that the room was warming as quickly as it had chilled, and struggled against a tidal wave of emotions. Sadness for the woman, deep regret that she herself had gone against her own judgment and entered the house at all. But she had chosen. Only a single option remained. She pulled her cell from her back pocket and punched out Wayne Sheppard's number.

It rang and rang. Either it was turned off or Sheppard refused to take her call. She left him a message. Just as she snapped her phone shut, an explosion of noise and shouting erupted from the front of the house.

"Adam? Gladys?" The man's voice boomed and echoed through the rooms.

"Back here," Mira shouted, getting to her feet.

The man loped through the doorway, breathing hard, blinking rapidly, and looked at her as though she were—what? A thief? A serial killer? "Who the hell are you?" he demanded. "Where's my son? What . . ."

The sight of the corpse eclipsed his raging monologue. "Gladys," he whispered, and his eyes darted back to Mira. "My son, where's my . . . son?"

"I . . . I don't know. When I came in here, the body was on the floor, the . . ."

"Don't you fucking move," he yelled, wagging one hand at her and pulling out his cell phone with the other. "I'm calling the cops."

"Hey, for all I know, *you're* the one who did this." Mira, still clutching her cell, stepped forward.

"Stop," he hissed, and whipped out a gun and pointed it at her. "Stop right there."

The sight of the gun triggered an inchoate, elemental dread in Mira. She patted the air with her hands, backed away from him, tried to speak calmly, as though she were dealing with a recalcitrant two-year-old who had found Daddy's gun. "Okay, okay, I'm sitting down, see?" She lowered herself to the floor beside the dead woman.

He backed up to the door, shut it, leaned against it. "Yes, hello," he said urgently. "There's been a murder . . . my son's gone . . . A woman . . . broke into my house and . . ." His voice cracked and he started to sob. "I . . . I don't know . . . At home . . . I'm at home . . . I . . ."

The temperature in the room started dropping again and the ghost in the khaki tunic pants stepped out of the wall and looked directly at Mira.

Say something, Mira pleaded silently.

Her skull filled with so much static that her head pounded.

In moments, the room felt like the Arctic again. Mira scooted back until her spine was up against the foot of the bed and pulled the end of the quilt around her shoulders. The man, no longer talking on his cell, looked around anxiously, murmuring, "What the hell. Why's it so cold in here? Did the power come back on or what?"

Mira didn't say anything. She was afraid that if she explained there was a ghost in the room, a young woman standing over by the closet, he would lose it completely and start shooting. So she brought her legs up against her chest, pressed her forehead to her knees, and hoped that the cops got here before she froze to death.

2

Spenser Finch

Sugarloaf Key

Spenser Finch caught himself grinding his teeth and immediately stopped. The last dentist he'd gone to had told him that if he didn't stop the grinding, his teeth would be stunted in about five years. Not acceptable. His teeth were his best feature, still perfectly straight, strong, and healthy. In his thirty-some-odd years, he'd had only three cavities, one when he was in his teens, two when he'd worked in Silicon Valley. No root canals, no crowns, no caps. He even had his wisdom teeth. But his old man had had rotten teeth, an upper bridge, all sorts of problems. Go figure.

He held his jaw still and gazed down at the kid. Every detail he had tended to in the last year had paid off. Right now, he thought, he should be feeling elation. Joy. Pride. Instead, a deep unease gripped him, as if he had forgotten some small but vital detail that might catch up to him tomorrow or next week. Even worse, he didn't have a clue what to do with the kid once he came around. He didn't know squat about kids. Couldn't stand them.

At the moment, Adam Nichols lay flat on his back on the bed in the spare bedroom, sleeping off the shot of Valium Finch had given him after he'd hauled him out his bedroom window and carried him to his electric golf cart. He'd gotten the Valium from a pharmacist he'd met in one of the Key West bars who was into heavy downers. He didn't know how long it would last before Adam came to, and worried that he hadn't calculated the dose correctly. Suppose the kid died? What then?

No, that wouldn't happen. He *knew* he had calculated the dose correctly. Details were his specialty. He was so anal about details that he had an entire notebook and a massive folder on the computer devoted to just Adam and his family. Finch had studied them the way biologists study a particular species.

He knew, for instance, that Adam was a lacto-vegetarian, a computer whiz who also played the piano by ear. He occasionally smoked pot with his buddy, Jorge, an older rich kid who lived up the block. He was a voracious reader, was tops on the school track team. Finch knew that his mother's accountant saved her more than two hundred grand in taxes last year and that his old man had a mistress. He felt such intimacy with the Nichols family that they were like his extended family. In that context, he merely had borrowed Adam, nothing more.

Borrowed. Considering that he had studied and spied on the family for months, broken into their home and nabbed their kid, shot him full of downers, loaded him into his houseboat, and brought him here to his place on Sugarloaf Key, *borrowed* was a stretch.

On the bed, Adam stirred, groaned, and rolled onto his side, hands tucked between his knees. Finch moved closer to the boy, studying his face. He definitely was his mother's son—the same beautiful bone structure that had graced movie screens for twenty years, the blond hair, the wiry body. Yet he was small for his age, maybe five and a half feet tall and a hundred and twenty pounds. When Finch was his age, he had reached his full height of six feet one and had lurked around with hunched shoulders, his head perpetually bowed, trying to look smaller, shorter, invisible. It really wasn't a fair comparison, though. Finch's childhood had been shit. Adam's was the American dream.

He noticed a stray bit of electrical tape stuck to the corner of Adam's mouth and quickly picked it off. With any luck, he wouldn't come around until this afternoon. Regardless, Finch had prepared the room well. The double bed was deliciously comfortable, with two down pillows, fresh towels in the bathroom, and some of Adam's clothes tucked in the drawers. For entertainment, he had a DVD player and a library of several dozen movies, including some of his mother's. The satellite TV gave him access to more than three hundred channels. Hell, he could watch news from Russia and cartoons from Japan, if he wanted to. The Xbox games were the newest on the market, the PC was equipped to the hilt with everything except Internet access. There was also a library of e-books, all selected with Adam's tastes in mind. Finch figured that a busy teen would be less trouble.

He had kept the hurricane shutters on the windows. Here and there, a dusty, muted light filtered through. The shutters prevented Adam from knowing exactly where he was. Kept him somewhat off balance. It also meant that even if he found a way to break the glass—damn unlikely—he still wouldn't be able to escape.

The windows were fiberglass-reinforced and consisted of three layers—two heat-treated glass sheets with a thin layer in the middle that was made of polymer reinforced with glass fibers. Finch knew what they could withstand because he had conducted the same tests that the glass industry did. He'd fired a two-gram bullet that struck the glass at 160 miles an hour, at the exact same spot until the glass broke, and then did the same test on a standard glass panel. The standard panel broke after about forty shots. The fiberglass-reinforced panel could withstand at least a hundred shots before it broke.

He had done his homework. That was how you won the game.

And this game had been a long time in the making. A dozen years. When he thought back to that time, the exact sequence of events and dates got all mixed up in his head. But he knew he had gone to Hollywood when he was eighteen, a self-taught computer guy with a GED, good-looking, talented, but still a wannabe, determined to become the next Big Name. He had given himself five years to seven years to make it.

Thanks to the computer work he'd done on the side, he never had to depend on his acting to pay the bills. He didn't have to wait tables, tend bar, or do any of the other usual and awful things that wannabes were forced to do. It had freed him. And within three months of his arrival, his cocky charm had paid off. He had landed print and commercial gigs because, as one photographer had confided, the camera loved his face. Other opportunities had followed—the role of a leading bad boy in a short-lived TV series, then several small parts in movies. And just when he'd been poised to make a leap into the big time, Suki and Paul Nichols had entered his life and had caused him to fail at the one thing he had loved above all else.

If she had been a different sort of woman, *if* she hadn't had the clout she'd had when their paths had crossed, *if* she had gotten sucked in by his talents or his smile or some other goddamn thing, the entire course of his life would have been different. But that wasn't the way things had turned out. So now the entire course of *her* life would be different because of *him*.

Karma.

Finch stood there watching Adam as he slept off the drug, and couldn't help feel a bit sorry for him. The kid was just a pawn in some vastly complex game that even Finch didn't fully understand. After all, other people in his life had screwed him and he hadn't gone after *their* kids, now had he? But only a few people held the defining power over the cross-roads in your life, he thought. His old man had held that sort of power over Finch. And he was dead. Suki Nichols had held that kind of power too, and before he was finished he would make her wish that she were dead.

He pulled the sheet up over Adam's body, suddenly terrified that if the kid got sick here—from the cool air that poured out of the AC vent, from stress, fear, a virus, bacteria—what the fuck would he do then? Aspirin, vitamin C, echinacea: He had only so many options for sickness.

Finch's old man had believed that a shot of whiskey could cure anything. So by the time he was twelve or thirteen, Finch had downed more shots of whiskey than he could count. In his milk, his hot chocolate, sprinkled over his pancakes and scrambled eggs. He rarely drank now and when he did, it was nothing more than a cold beer or a glass of wine. He enjoyed an occasional joint and considered leaving a couple for Adam. To take the edge off. But if he left behind joints, he would have to leave matches or a lighter. Either of those could be a potential weapon.

Suddenly, Adam bolted upright, his dark eyes widening, darting about frantically, and then he started shrieking. Nothing intelligible issued from him, just a relentless, high-pitched noise that clawed at Finch's nerves a million times worse than fingernails scraped across a chalkboard.

He watched as Adam leaped off the bed and ran to the door. He jerked wildly on the handle, but the door was controlled electronically and the remote-control clicker was in Finch's back pocket. *Scream away, kid. Go for it. Get it all out.*

Adam kicked the door savagely, repeatedly, and kept right on shrieking. Then he ran over to the window and beat his fists against the glass. He spun around, eyes burning, face bright with rage. *"Let me outta here, you can't do this, it's kidnapping, it's . . ."* He threw himself at Finch.

He wasn't ready for it, didn't anticipate it, and the assault nearly knocked him off his feet. Adam clawed and kicked, hit and bit. For such a small fry, he was surprisingly strong, rabid, wild. Finch grabbed him by the arms, lifted him up, up into the air, and tossed him onto the bed.

"No screaming, hitting, clawing, biting," Finch shouted.

Adam fell silent, his face as bright and shiny as a new penny. "Why . . . why're you wearing a mask?"

"So I don't have to kill you."

That shut him up. The power of language, Finch thought with satisfaction. But the kid's silence lasted about ten seconds.

"Alien masks are so, like, retro. Especially ones like yours, where the aliens have those huge, shiny, black wraparound eyes and a slit for a nose and an asshole for a mouth."

"How poetic, Adam. Let's get something straight. You're going to be here for a while. The more cooperative you are, the better you and I will get along. In return for your cooperation, you can use whatever is in this room." Finch threw his arms out, indicating everything he had assembled here for the kid. "And you'll get three square meals a day and as many snacks and so on as you want. I'll leave a Styrofoam cooler in here filled with water, soda, whatever else you drink. We clear?"

"I don't drink soda."

Right. How careless of me. "And you don't eat meat or chicken. Occasionally, you eat fish, eggs, cheese. Your preferences are salads and fruits."

His eyes widened. Finch could see that Adam was starting to get it, to realize how much planning had gone into this.

"What . . . what else do you know about me?"

"Everything I need to know. You've got an I.Q. of one-forty-eight. You've been in gifted programs all your life. You're a very bright kid, so I expect you to follow my few basic rules."

"I have a medical condition, I bet you don't know that."

"Bullshit." *But hey, good try.* "I bet you saw that in *Trapped*. The kid had asthma."

"Actually, it was in one of my mom's movies."

"Yeah? What movie was that?" Finch had seen all of Suki Nichols's films.

"*Romancing the Raven.* It was the first thing she ever did, a twenty-minute video when she was in college."

Clever little shit. He'd caught Finch on that one. "I haven't followed her career that far back." But the hidden camera in the room was catching all of this and once Finch ran it through his computer, editing out anything that would compromise him, it would make a compelling piece of documentary.

"Do I get to shower and use the bathroom?"

"That's why the bathroom's here."

"It's so dark. Can you take the hurricane shutters off?"

Hurricane shutters: That would have to be edited out of his little documentary, he thought. "No. But you'll have plenty of lights." He slipped the clicker from his back pocket, pressed a button, and every light that wasn't already on blazed brightly. The press of another button turned on the television and PC and released the remote control on both. "Is there anything else you'd like?"

"My mom."

"Sorry, I didn't bring her."

"You killed Gladys."

He spoke in a hushed voice, but without tremors. That was good. Rage was understandable, but a crybaby, especially in a teenage boy, would piss him off. "She got in the way."

"You want something, but Friend says it isn't money."

"What friend?"

"Friend. That's her name."

"You're a little old for an imaginary playmate." It seemed that a sly smile tugged at the corners of Adam's mouth, a reminder that Finch didn't know everything about him.

"So what do you want?" Adam persisted. "Sex? Are you a pervert? Are you looking for publicity, because of who my mom is? Is that it?"

"You watch too many Lifetime movies, Adam."

"Lifetime is for women and teenage girls. I don't watch Lifetime."

Hey, I stand corrected. "I don't want money or publicity and I'm not a pervert. As we get down the road a bit, we'll talk about what I want. But for right now, how about something to eat?"

"Okay. Do I have any clean clothes?"

Finch gestured at the bureau. "In there. Clothes from your closet. In the bathroom, you'll find everything you need—towels, soap, shampoo. How about scrambled eggs and toast?"

"Are the eggs vegetarian?"

"Yes. And the bread is whole wheat, with organic butter and some organic strawberries on the side."

"No meat byproducts?"

"None. I'll be back in a while."

Adam nodded and remained on the bed, watching Finch, his vivid blue eyes filling with contempt. As soon as Finch shut the door, Adam screamed, "You perverted fucker!" He started kicking the door, banging his fists against it.

This would be simple to remedy. Finch aimed the clicker at the door and pressed the button that turned off all the lights.

The temper tantrum abruptly ended.

"See what happens when you don't cooperate, Adam?"

No answer, just soft, choked sobs.

"Now you'll have to sit in the dark for a while."

* * *

And suddenly the room goes dark and the bogeyman moves around under his bed, a soft rustling like leaves. Then he hears that small, evil cackle and knows that the bogeyman, emboldened by the darkness, is coming for him. He screams and screams and the door to the room flies open. The man marches in, slapping a leather strap against his open palm.

"You pipe down in here, boy, or I'll really give you something to scream about."

"It's under my bed, get it out, help me, help me. . . ."

Finch staggered against the weight of the memory or whatever the hell it was, and fell against the wall, breath exploding from his mouth, heart slamming against his ribs. These images, their *presence,* were nearly too much to bear. Gasping for breath, Finch slid down the length of the wall. Shudders whipped through him. *I'm dying.*

After several moments, his heartbeat stabilized, he sucked air in through his teeth. His perfect teeth. Upper teeth met lower and started to grind. *No, don't do that. Don't grind them.*

Relax the jaw. There. Good, very good.

Who was that kid cowering on the bed and screaming about the bogeyman? It felt like a memory, but he didn't think the memory belonged to him. The boy was young, maybe five. Was it him?

Couldn't be.

His first clear memory was of speeding across a desert with his old man, the hot sun beating down against the windshield and burning his legs. While it was true his old man was a mean bastard when he was drinking, mean enough to punch Finch around, he never had locked him in a dark room, never had hit him with a leather strap.

Guilt swept through him, and he struggled to his feet and pressed the button on the remote control that turned on the lights in the kid's room. No torture chamber. Christ, what the hell was wrong with him?

That wasn't in his game plan.

It wouldn't be in the video.

As he snagged the alien mask over the hook next to the door, a snowstorm of light exploded in his peripheral vision. Panic tore upward from the pit of his stomach. He knew he had about a minute to reach his meds before the light became a full-blown migraine.

He stumbled into the kitchen and poured what was left of the morning's coffee into a mug and gulped it down cold. Cuban coffee, thick, heavy, loaded with caffeine. He followed this with two homeopathic remedies for migraines that Eden had given him. She was a former nurse who had studied alternative therapies. She knew about these things.

He barely made it to the table and collapsed in a chair directly under the AC vent. Cold air poured over him. He went utterly and completely still, eyes shut, the cold air blowing down over his head, face, his aching temples.

He didn't know how long he sat there, his mind blank. But when he opened his eyes again, his vision was normal. No aura, no blurring, no brightness.

He pressed his forehead against the surface of the cool table, absurdly grateful that he had averted a migraine that might have lasted two days. *I got lucky.*

This time.

3

Body Heat

The cop stood near the screen door that led from the porch and swimming pool to the back of the property. Just to his left, Mira saw that panels of screen were missing and that the inner struts that held up the structure of the porch looked new. Destruction and repair, that was the rule of life on Tango now.

Now and then, the cop glanced Mira's way, as if he expected her to bolt any second. No one had said the cop was keeping an eye on her. No one had to. She didn't have to be psychic to know that she was the primary suspect in a homicide and in the disappearance of a teenage boy.

For years, Nadine had drummed into her that when she psychically read anything or anyone, she was opening a door to herself and that object or person. At no time in her forty-one years had this adage been driven home so completely. It occurred to her that she maybe she should call an attorney, but she didn't know any criminal attorneys. She had read for physicians and politicians, for scientists and teachers, for celebrities and con men, for judges and killers and rapists, for artists of every type, for directors and CEOs, FBI and

CIA agents. But she never had read for a single criminal attorney, except Wayne Sheppard, who had practiced law between his stints in the FBI. But he didn't count because she hadn't read for him when he had practiced law.

She knew plenty of people who knew criminal attorneys, so she could make some calls and get a name. The question was whether she wanted to open *that* door and what would happen if she needed to open that door—and didn't.

Mira eyed the apple on the table in front of her, probably left by someone who had sat here earlier. Fresh food and vegetables generally didn't convey anything she could read psychically. Give her metal, wood, ceramic, fabric, glass, plastic. Sometimes even fabric and paper retained emotions and psychic residue that she could read. The best conduit was the human body.

Okay, so the apple was safe and the plastic bottle of water beside it, set here moments ago by Sheppard's partner, probably wasn't. She picked up the apple, bit into it, put it down and tucked her hand inside the bottom part of her shirt, and grasped the bottle of water. Nothing. The fabric between her hand and the bottle blocked any impression. Goddamn. She was on a definite roll here. She twisted off the top, drank.

Behind her, the sliding glass door opened, shut. John Gutierrez stepped out. "You need anything, Mira?"

"Yeah, Goot. An honest answer."

He pulled out the chair across from her and sat down, an earnest man who was not only Sheppard's partner, but his closest friend. Cuban-American, the grandson of a renowned Cuban *santera*, he understood her abilities nearly as well as Sheppard did. His wide, dark eyes regarded her with an openness that belied his body language—fidgety, uncomfortable, tense.

"Shoot," he said.

"Hey, relax. My question isn't about Shep. Do I need a lawyer?"

Goot rubbed his hand over his unshaven jaw and glanced

toward the local cop at the screen door. Mira followed his gaze. Beyond the cop, a line of police officers with dogs fanned out across the fields, looking for the missing boy.

"I'm supposed to say it would be premature." His voice softened. "But yeah, it'd probably be a good idea, Mira."

"You think I *killed* that woman? That I kidnapped some kid? Jesus, Goot."

He looked as if she'd punched him and leaned forward. "Do *I* think that? C'mon, Mira. We know each other better than that. But it doesn't matter what I think. The boy is missing, the housekeeper is dead, and the guy who owns the house found you next to the body."

"And this man is who exactly?"

"No one told you?"

"He sure didn't pause long enough in his rantings to introduce himself."

"Paul Nichols, movie director and now a visiting professor in that film program at the University of Miami. Married to Suki Nichols, the actress who . . ."

Uh-oh. "I know who she is." What were the odds? "I've read for her."

"You did? When?"

When the universe brought her my way. Maybe, she thought, the portal had been opened then, during that first reading. "Before Danielle hit. It must've been in late May."

"Did you pick up anything about her son? About the housekeeper?"

Had she? Late May seemed like lifetimes ago. She squeezed the bridge of her nose, struggling to conjure up the day that Suki Nichols came up to one of the registers at her bookstore with a stack of books. She had a psychedelic print bag slung over her shoulder with a yoga mat rolled up inside it, wore workout shorts, a T-shirt with TANGO FRITTER written across the front of it, and sandals. Mira hadn't recognized her at first. Her sunglasses, the short, curly style of her blond hair, her clothes: She could have been anyone. Then she spoke.

Mira would recognize the voice anywhere, soft but firm, throaty but whimsical, a voice that made spoken language sound like music.

Who do I see to schedule a reading?

Me, Mira replied, and rang up her sale.

Suki Nichols. Four years ago, she'd won an Oscar for her role in *Acid Trip,* in which she'd played a Sixties hippie looking for meaning in a world gone mad. Since then, her film presence had soared and moved her into the same stellar circle as Kidman, Thurman, and Diaz. And yet, she had done only two films since her Oscar win and one of them wasn't slated to come out until next year. Mira didn't know what, if anything, that meant.

With more than twenty films to her credit, Suki's roles were as diverse and unpredictable as the character in *Acid Trip.* Angel and prostitute, vampire and soccer mom, gay woman, senator, dork, psychic, computer nerd: There was no neat and tidy category into which she fit.

They had gone outside to the garden and settled at the metal table in the shade of a banyan tree the hurricane had toppled several weeks later. Even before she began the reading, Mira had sensed Suki's churning anxiety. But she couldn't tell if it was due to some underlying problem in her life or to her nervousness about getting a reading.

Do you use cards? Do my chart? Read my palm? What?

Mira considered using cards just to focus, but in the end, asked to hold her wedding ring. Big mistake.

"What I remember from the reading is that her husband was having an affair and she was considering divorce," Mira said finally. "Look, get her out here. She'll remember me, Goot."

"She's in New York on business and is supposedly on her way back."

"And where the hell was the father last night?"

"He claims he was returning from his class at the University of Miami, but got out of there so late that he knew he wasn't going to make curfew here. He didn't think he'd be able to make the last ferry out of Key West."

Mira rolled her eyes. "The last ferry leaves at eleven. That's plenty of time to get home before the midnight curfew. C'mon, it sounds fishy to me."

"I'm just telling you what he said. He checked into a motel on Big Pine. Has the receipt to prove it. He says he called the housekeeper and told her he wouldn't be back until this morning. We've got proof of that too."

Meaning what? Just what was Goot really saying? Before she could ask, the sliding glass door opened again and Charlie Cordoba, the new chief of police, stepped out. A young man, this Cordoba, with thick hair the same shade as his chestnut-colored eyes, a quick, easy smile, plenty of charm. He was a runner, lean and compact, had two young kids and an American wife who practiced law in Key West. Solid Cordoba.

So solid, in fact, that two or three years ago when he was just a beat cop in Key West and his wife was having problems in her pregnancy, he had stopped by Mira's house and asked her to read for him. He had come in the dead of night, parked his car three blocks away, and asked that she never tell anyone that she had read for him.

"Hi, Mira," he said pleasantly. "How's it going?"

"How's *what* going, Charlie?"

The smile faded and he pulled out the other chair and sat down. "Do you have an attorney?"

"No. Do I need one?"

"For starters, Mr. Nichols is pressing charges for trespassing."

"I thought someone in the house was in trouble, that's why I came in. And the door was open. And trespassing is a misdemeanor. I don't need an attorney for that."

He rubbed his chin, folded his hands on the table, and leaned forward. "Let me put it this way. You were found next to the housekeeper's body, you were the only person in the house, the front door was wide open when Mr. Nichols got here, his son is missing, and the housekeeper is dead. We've got thirty men out there now looking for the son. Another twenty are on the way. Right now, you're the primary suspect, Mira."

"For murder and possible kidnapping," she said, and forced herself to laugh. "And what's my motive supposed to be?"

"You tell me."

He really thinks I may have done this.

"Knock off the bullshit, Charlie," Goot snapped.

"You don't have to answer that question, Mira." Sheppard ducked as he came through the door. At six feet four inches tall, he had to duck through most doors. "You're outta line, Charlie."

Cordoba rolled his eyes and sat back. "Lancelot to the rescue. Gimme a break."

Sheppard picked up a stool from the poolside bar, brought it over to the table, and set it down between Mira and Cordoba, as if to use his body as a shield. Gallant, Mira thought, but considering that she hadn't seen him for weeks, it seemed beside the point.

She thought his face looked thinner, that his beard was grayer. But maybe that was what she wanted to see, an aging, haggard Sheppard, evidence that he suffered in his new life without her. He wore cotton chinos the same beach-sand color as his hair and a print shirt she'd never seen before. The shirt was like a punch in the stomach. It meant his life had gone on without her—he shopped, went to restaurants, had Cuban coffee, read the morning paper, went jogging, probably had found a new honey. He was carving out a new life for himself—without her.

Never mind that she knew that was what "split up" meant

and that her life had gone on as well. But her life hadn't moved on in the same ways. She mourned for the demise of the relationship, mourned every time she passed a landmark they had shared, found a book they had discussed, or came across a new mix of delectable coffee that she knew he would enjoy.

She didn't want to sit here any longer. Didn't want to be near him. But she had a feeling she wouldn't be allowed to leave just yet.

"Okay, next question," Cordoba said. "What prompted you to come into the house?"

"You can answer that." Sheppard glanced at her.

"Oh, you're her lawyer now?" Cordoba asked.

"If necessary."

Right. Sheppard hadn't practiced criminal law in years, but now he was her attorney. Was this a macho thing or what?

"I walk every day," Mira said. "And this morning my walk brought me here. As I approached the top of the hill, I heard someone shouting for help." She went on from there, and noticed the odd expression on Cordoba's face as she described the woman on fire, the kid's face pressed to the glass, the car that passed through her. But Sheppard understood immediately.

"So was this a future event or something that had happened in the past?" Sheppard asked.

"I'm not sure." But as the scene replayed in her head, she realized it was like a hologram, vividly real and yet not real at all for her. It was as if she had stumbled into a memory loop that belonged to the house, the property. Was that what the black and white images meant? A new twist in her abilities, here but not here? Where in time did the hologram belong?

"You said the woman was on fire." Goot now, leaning forward, intense, needing to nail down the details. "Why was she on fire?"

"The house was on fire," Mira replied. "I assume her clothes had caught fire."

"Can you describe the car? The driver? The woman?" Sheppard asked.

"The boy was young, the driver was a blur. The car looked like an old Buick. I don't know what year or model."

"How about the color?" Sheppard asked.

"I saw all of this in black and white, like a negative. The woman wasn't Suki Nichols. Anyway, I came up to the house to find out if a boy lived here, if there had been a fire. The door wasn't shut all the way, so I nudged it open and called. A woman in a blue floral print dress at the end of the hall waved for me to come in. She, uh, turned out to be the housekeeper's ghost."

"A ghost." Cordoba smirked, then burst out laughing. "Sweet Christ. I've heard a lot of reasons for trespassing, Mira, but never that one."

Go pound sand, Charlie. "It's what happened."

Cordoba held out his hands, the reasonable man attempting to use logic on his FBI counterparts. "Gentlemen, please. This is such a crock of shit I can't begin to tell you. She has a vision, a ghost invites her into the house, and it turns out to be the spirit of the dead woman. How convenient."

"Excuse me, Charlie." Mira resented the way he addressed Sheppard and Goot, as though she weren't present. "But you weren't quite as quick to dismiss a ghost when I told you the problems with your wife's pregnancy were because of a malign presence in your house."

Color flooded his neck and cheeks and for seconds, his eyes held hers, their message clear: *I told you to keep that reading between us.* She glared back at him and he quickly looked away.

The good ole days are gone, Charlie. Attack me and I'll bite.

"It'll never stand up in court," Cordoba said lamely.

"Whose court?" she shot back. "Yours?"

He shook his head. "Look, I'm just doing my job."

Mira leaned forward and hooked her finger at Cordoba, who also leaned forward. "How's your hearing, Charlie?"

"My hearing? It's good. Very good. Why?"

"Fuck you," she whispered, and pushed to her feet. "I'm done here. Whenever you decide to arrest me, you know where to find me."

"Hey, hold on a minute," Cordoba called after her. "I've got more questions."

She kept right on walking. "Talk to my attorney."

She crossed the massive living room and was halfway up the hall when Paul Nichols came barreling through the front door, his cell pressed to his ear. He saw her, stopped, and ended the call, his body blocking her exit.

He was a big man—about six feet tall, slightly overweight, but mostly stocky, like a wrestler, with massive shoulders. His dark hair was going gray and starting to thin and his paunch attested to a fondness for dark lager beers. He stabbed a finger at her.

"I'm pressing charges against you."

"So I heard. Excuse me, please. I'm on my way out."

"Fifty people are out there now, looking for my son. You . . . you . . ." His voice cracked.

Mira didn't intend to stick around for his breakdown. She sidled past him, careful that her body didn't brush up against his, but Nichols grabbed her arm, whipping her around. "You can't just walk into a person's home," he hissed, his cheeks burning with patches of bright pink, his hand still gripping her forearm. "You can't just . . ."

There he is, humping a woman whose face she can't see, his hairy, massive body covering the woman completely. He sweats, grunts, and growls like some sort of beast, and the woman's thin, tanned legs tighten around him and . . .

Mira jerked her arm free. "You lied, Paul," she said softly.

"You were with the other woman and if you'd been home, your son would be here this morning."

His body seemed to convulse, then to shrink in size, and he stepped quickly away from the door, from her. Mira slipped outside, into the scorched summer air, and hurried down the driveway. In her haste to get away from the house, from Nichols, Sheppard, Cordoba, the whole stinking mess, she stumbled over her own feet, lost her balance, and fell.

Her knees struck the ground first. She started to laugh, then rolled onto her side, rubbing her bruised, skinned knees. *Losing it, you're losing it, c'mon, fast, get out of here.*

Mira rocked back onto her heels, and saw the Himalayan watching her from under nearby bushes. *You a ghost cat? Or just wish you were? Are you the boy's cat? Is that it?*

The cat blinked and edged back farther under the bushes, out of sight.

Mira got up and made a beeline for the ravaged hill she had followed up here hours ago.

Her cell, tucked in her back pocket, played the 1812 Overture. She slipped it out, saw Sheppard's number in the window. Forget it, she thought, and turned her cell off and ran for the sanctity of the undamaged pines.

4

Car Talk

Sheppard's fury at Cordoba was nothing compared to what he felt when Paul Nichols stormed out onto the porch, shouting, "She left and you jerks are standing around looking at your dicks? Go arrest her. Take her in. Something."

Cordoba appeared to have been zapped with a paralyzing spray. Goot stood up, as though Nichols were a judge or royalty, but couldn't seem to find anything to say. Sheppard snapped his cell shut, marched over to Nichols. "We know where to find her, Mr. Nichols. Please have a seat."

"Listen here . . ." His eyes darted to Sheppard's badge, looking for his name. "Agent Sheppard. I want her . . ."

"Sit. Down."

He blinked, started to say something, and thought better of it. As he sat down, he said, "I've already answered questions. I've given my answers."

"You haven't answered *my* questions." Sheppard remained standing. "When was the last time you saw your son?"

"Yesterday morning, when I drove him to camp. Gladys picked him up and they got home around two. I spoke to him then by phone."

"How long has Gladys worked for you?"

"Two years. Since we moved here. We trusted her implicitly."

"In the past few weeks or months, Mr. Nichols, have you felt at any time that your home was being watched? Did you get hang-up calls? Weird e-mail or letters? Did your son ever tell you he was followed? Approached by strangers? In other words, has anything out of the ordinary happened?"

"Look, Mr. Sheppard." He sat forward, his large hands folded on the tabletop. Earnest. Soft-spoken. Mr. Intensity spouting what was supposed to be logical, reasonable. "Given the nature of my wife's fame, there are always e-mails, letters, calls, and what have you from every imaginable sort of crazy. But nothing that has involved or even alluded to Adam."

Cordoba finally roused himself from his celebrity torpor or whatever had afflicted him. "Who besides Gladys knew you were going to be late last night?"

"No one, unless Gladys called her daughter, but she wouldn't have any reason to do that because her daughter lives in Tulsa."

"You didn't notify your wife?" Goot asked.

"My wife was in business meetings in New York. There was no reason to contact her."

How quickly he replied, Sheppard thought, and made a mental note to ask Suki Nichols what sort of arrangement she and her husband had about glitches in child care. "I hope you've contacted her since all this happened."

Nichols looked pissed now, nostrils flaring. "Of course I called her. And she's on her way back. I resent the implication that I'm hiding information from my wife, Mr. Sheppard."

You said it. I didn't. "We're going to be setting up a special unit here in the house to monitor calls in the event that you receive a ransom demand."

"We'll . . . we'll pay whatever is asked."

"We'll see what unfolds."

Cordoba butted in now. "The FBI handles the missing-child part of this investigation, Mr. Nichols. But the Tango County PD handles the homicide investigation and the, uh, trespassing charges against Ms. Morales."

"She's your primary suspect, right? In both instances?" Nichols asked.

"It's too early to charge anyone with anything," Sheppard said before Cordoba could reply.

Nichols stammered, "But she trespassed, she . . ."

"And you intend to file charges about the trespassing." Cordoba again. He seemed eager to establish Paul Nichols's intentions while Sheppard and Goot were present.

Nichols rubbed his jaw. "I think I'd like to, uh, discuss this with my wife before we decide what to do."

Interesting switch, Sheppard thought, and wondered if he and Mira had exchanged words when she'd hurried out of here.

"But I don't want her leaving the island," Nichols added quickly.

"She's not going anywhere," Sheppard said.

"How can you be so sure of that, Mr. Sheppard?" His tone had grown increasingly hostile while he'd sat there, and now sounded downright nasty.

"Because she owns a business and a home here. Because I believe her story."

"So you're biased."

You're goddamn right, moron.

"He's not biased," Cordoba replied. "He has an opinion."

"Did you know your wife got a reading from Ms. Morales?" Goot asked.

"A reading? What's that mean?"

Goot and Sheppard glanced at each other, thinking the same thing, that Nichols didn't have a clue. "Mira is a psychic," Sheppard said. "She also owns a bookstore in downtown Tango."

"A *psychic*? You mean, like . . ." He shook his large, dimpled hands. "As I come into your vibration . . ."

"Not exactly," Goot snapped. "She's worked with the FBI, local police departments. . . ."

Nichols sat forward, elbows resting on the table. "Look, I don't give a good goddamn what you call her." His eyes went to Cordoba. "If I have to file charges to prevent her from leaving the island, then I'll do it right now."

Cordoba shook his head, suddenly switching sides. Again. "Talk it over with your wife, Mr. Nichols. Right now, Ms. Morales is our primary suspect in a homicide and that's enough for us to keep an eye on her."

"If she's your primary suspect, then arrest her, for Chrissakes."

"We don't have any evidence," Cordoba said. "But you have my word, Mr. Nichols. She won't leave Tango Key."

Just then, the forensics team arrived. Nichols stood up. "I'm going to join the search party. You have my cell number if you need me."

As soon as he left, Sheppard muttered, "What an asshole."

"Hey, Shep," Cordoba said. "Maybe you need to recuse yourself from the investigation, given your relationship with Mira."

"We don't have a relationship anymore. So there's nothing unethical going on here, Charlie."

With that, Sheppard headed into the house to talk to the forensics team. He felt Cordoba's eyes burning large, black holes through his back.

Sheppard walked around the property, getting a sense of its size, how far it was from the main road, the distance from the house to the trees behind it and along the north side. At one time, a fence had surrounded the property. But it had collapsed during the hurricane, except where the fence was iron—the gate at the end of the driveway and the fence just to either side of it. The gate was electronic, but wasn't connected to the generator, so he had to push it shut.

He headed into the woods where Mira had walked earlier this morning and kept glancing back at the house, at the windows of Adam's room, to measure the distance. Thanks to the lack of leaves, the room was visible until the ground sloped downward. Sheppard followed the twisted path down through the bent and damaged trees, skirting piles of dead branches and debris, and emerged on Mango Drive, at the opposite end from where Mira's store was located. Had Mira inadvertently followed the kidnapper's path up the hill to the Nichols's place? Or had the man approached from the back, where the woods were denser and filled with Australian pines?

His cell rang; Mira's cell number appeared in the window. Typical, he thought. She had refused to take his call when she'd stormed out, but now *she* was calling *him*. Whatever.

"Hey, Mira. What's up?"

"Are you still in the house?"

"I'm on Mango Drive."

"Where on Mango? I don't see you."

He stepped out from the trees and glanced down the sidewalk. Mira pedaled toward him on her bicycle, black hair flying out behind her, a shiny veil. He waved.

"Okay, I see you."

She disconnected and, moments later, stopped in front of him. She wore dark sunglasses that reflected twin images of his face. He would rather see her eyes, where everything she felt would be naked, obvious. Without that visual cue, he was clueless.

"I wanted to tell you the rest of what I picked up, but without anyone else around," she said.

"I was hoping for something like that. How come you didn't answer your phone when I called?"

She shrugged. "I just wanted to get away from the place."

"You were pissed."

She tilted her glasses back onto the top of her head, revealing her magnificent eyes. "Yeah, I was. I mean, don't get me wrong, Shep. I appreciate that you went to bat for me as an attorney. But after weeks of us not even talking to each other, it seemed, well, sort of beside the point."

"I just wanted to make it clear to Charlie that he wasn't going to pull any bullshit."

"Oh, he'll still try. Charlie's eager for recognition. Sort of like Dillard was, you know?"

Leo Dillard, Sheppard's former Bureau boss, had been indicted several weeks ago as a result of information Sheppard and Goot had uncovered during those endless hours during Hurricane Danielle, when they had been confined to a cellar with Dillard and former Chief of Police Doug Emison. Sheppard figured he must have karma with corrupt authority types like Dillard and Cordoba. Well, maybe not Cordoba. Maybe the man was just misguided. He wasn't sure yet about him.

Mira pointed off toward the right. "He came from that way, on an electric cart, and followed the same path that I took when I hiked up the hill. He left the cart at the edge of the trees and got in through the utility-room door. Once he was in Adam's bedroom, the housekeeper surprised him and he shot her. He then took Adam out through his bedroom window. If I were you, Shep, I'd keep the utility-room part of this out of the press."

He nodded, slipped a notepad from his shirt pocket, and scribbled the basics. He actually had a good memory for detail, but needed an excuse to look away from her. Up at the house, he had noticed that when he looked at her, he remembered touching her face, running his fingers through her luxurious hair, making love to her—memories that disturbed him.

"Anything else?" he asked.

"Paul Nichols was with his mistress last night. I don't know who she is, couldn't see her face."

"And you picked this up when?"

"In the hall, as I was leaving. Paul Nichols has got some major screws loose. Also, I think the house is haunted."

Here we go, he thought. Back into the weirdness of Mira's world. "You mean, by the housekeeper?"

"No. The woman I saw in my initial vision. She helped the housekeeper cross over."

In his head, some little gremlin whistled the refrain from *The X-Files.*

"When she was in the room, with Nichols holding a gun on me, the air turned to ice. He felt it. I also picked up a phrase. *Car talk.*"

"What's that mean?"

She shrugged. "Beats me."

"When did you pick it up?"

"When I was hiking back down the hill. It was, like, I don't know, a residue, an echo, something connected to that first vision."

After five years of working with Mira on various types of investigations, Sheppard knew enough to pay attention to everything she said. He knew what questions to ask. Hell, he knew the drill better than anyone. What might seem inconsequential or silly often turned out to be the very thing on which the entire investigation turned.

"Is that it?" he asked.

"It's all I can remember now."

He put his notepad back into his shirt pocket. "I thought you weren't going to do this anymore."

It was a loaded remark and he knew it. But he was curious. Mira dropped her sunglasses back onto her nose, hiding her eyes again, and mounted the bike, one foot on the pedal, the other still touching the sidewalk. "This one sort of found me. And it involves a child."

"So how've you been, Mira?"

As soon as the words were out of his mouth, he regretted them. He hadn't wanted to make any of this personal. He'd gotten along fine without her for the last four weeks and really didn't want to know about her, her personal life, her daughter, the dog, the cats, none of it. Hell, he'd even gone to a movie with another woman, a relative of Goot's girlfriend, Graciella. A looker, a federal attorney with whom he'd had zip in common. He'd been bored out of his mind. But it was a start, right?

"Oh, I've been fantastic. Life right now is really grand, you know? Met a couple of interesting men . . . well, one of them needs a dentist and the other wears white socks and needs a fashion consultant, but hey, how shallow am I?"

He laughed. Even to him, though, the laugh sounded false, a bit too loud, too quick, too forced. "Bad teeth and white socks. Sounds promising."

"Hmm. And that's the rah-rah-cheerleader version."

"What's the Morales version?"

She tipped the shades forward and peered at him over the rims. "No electricity for—what? Five weeks now? Six weeks? My car's scraping empty in the gasoline department, so to conserve, I walk or ride my bike to the store or Ace or Luke give me a lift into town. Annie, Nadine, and the three cats are staying in Miami, with friends who have electricity, there's about fifty grand worth of damage to the bookstore, half that for the house, my insurance company hasn't issued shit, FEMA is a joke, and most of the work that's being done is paid for from loans or goes on credit cards. But I've got great credit. Anything else you'd like to know, Shep?"

He instantly felt guilty. Not once in all these weeks had he offered Mira help or support. He had moved out of her place with his self-righteous indignation and cut her off completely. "I can get you gas through the Bureau, Mira. I can get you a generator, a curfew pass, whatever you need. Just ask."

"Look, you made it pretty clear you don't want to see me

again, period. And that's fine, it's your choice. So don't expect me to ask for your help, Shep. In fact, the missing boy
is the only reason I called you. Have a great day."

With that, she poked her sunglasses higher onto the
bridge of her nose, turned the bike around, and pedaled away
from him, moving like the wind.

A huge, swelling tide of regret swept through him.

5

Paradise

Finch had a weakness for redheads. Eden Thompkins's hair was long, thick, rich with waves and texture, a flamboyant copper mane that his fingers begged to touch, comb, caress. The freckles scattered across her cheeks with such wild abandon seemed delicately beautiful and yet strange, as though nature were experimenting with her genes. Her body was luscious enough to gobble whole, round and full in all the right places, but with a flat tummy and hips as sharp as knives. Finch had met her in a bar.

Before the hurricane, she'd tended bar at Pepe's Restaurant fifty hours a week. But with tourism in the Keys now dead, her hours had been sliced in half and she had a lot of spare time. So they spent much of that spare time in bed.

As far as beds went, this one was first-class—Swedish, made of some mysterious material that molded itself to your body. No creaking, squeaking, rusty springs. As they rolled across it, the silence of this bed enveloped them, swallowed them. She was naked, her skin a cool silk against his. He wanted to sink into those cat-green eyes and confess about Adam. Or brag about how he'd pulled it off. Or both. But he didn't. Couldn't. Not yet. Maybe never. He wasn't sure where or if she would fit into his life in the future. And until he knew, Adam would remain his secret.

Eden often accused him of being secretive and complained that she knew almost nothing about his past. The truth was that her knowledge of his life consisted of the colorful fictions he had told her, that he was a computer consultant, on the road a lot, that he lived and worked on the houseboat where she'd visited him on numerous occasions. She didn't know about the house on Sugarloaf, his early acting career, or that he'd been forced to flee Hollywood, a castoff, a reject, a failure. She had no idea that he'd made a killing on stocks when he'd worked in Silicon Valley and had left California as a millionaire. He had wrapped himself in so much secrecy that at times it nearly smothered him and left him feeling lonely, isolated, and desperate for the kind of companionship she provided.

Back in the early weeks of their relationship, when Eden had her own secrets, she had told him he reminded her of an actor she'd seen years ago on a TV series. A sliver of cold had licked at his spine. *Yeah? What series was that?*

I can't remember the name. It was about this family with two sons and one of them was really a rotten guy.

Couldn't have been me. I never did TV, he'd said with a laugh.

Even in the unlikely event that the ten episodes ever went into reruns, he thought, she wouldn't recognize him. No one would. As the consummate chameleon, he had remade himself half a dozen times since Hollywood, each time immersing himself in a new role, a new persona. He was the ultimate method actor and, like Brando, Paul Newman, and Al Pacino, a follower of Lee Strasberg's techniques.

"How long can you stay, Spense?" Eden whispered, nibbling at his ear.

"For another hour or so." *I need to get back to the house, to Adam.* "I've got an appointment with a client at five-thirty, then need to move the houseboat to a marina for some minor repairs." Covering his ass for what he foresaw to be an absence of at least several days and perhaps as long as several weeks. "Do you work tonight?"

"Yeah, I got a couple of hours because someone else called in sick. Pepe's is still running off generators, but we've got a limited menu and people still come in to drink. The bars are the only places where you can get booze. Listen, if you need a place to stay while the houseboat is being repaired, you know where the key is, Spense."

He moved his body over hers and brought his mouth to her forehead, her cheeks, her breasts, murmuring, "You talk too much."

Every time he was inside her, he felt a secret thrill—he was where Paul Nichols had been. In the beginning, when he had watched the Nicholses to learn more about them—their routines, passions, all the minutiae that made up any family's life—he didn't know Eden even existed. Then he followed Paul one afternoon when he headed off to Miami to teach a class. He taught the class, all right, but on the way there he stopped at a motel on Big Pine Key. And didn't come out for hours. The only thing that could mean was a woman who was not Paul Nichols's wife.

At the time, Finch couldn't understand why any man would cheat on the likes of Suki Nichols. Then he saw Eden as she and Nichols emerged from the motel that evening. She looked like a goddess fallen from Olympus. Right then, he knew he had to refine his plans, that she was his missing piece.

Does she suspect me?

Doubtful. She was too trusting and he was very good at what he did.

Afterward, they lay side by side, stroking each other. His fingers slipped and slid over her damp skin, through her beautiful hair. Finch arranged her hair on the pillow so that it fanned across the fabric, copper against the blue, with her pale face as the sun. Her eyes watched him and crinkled at the corners as she smiled, amused. He sometimes wondered if, when she was a nurse back in North Carolina, her patients had hungered for her in the way that he did.

"What do you think about when we make love?" she asked.

This was how they talked during these long hours in her first-class bed. "How beautiful you are. What do you think about?"

"I don't. When we make love, my mind goes totally blank."

Finch lifted up on an elbow and with the tip of his finger, circled her belly button, a nipple, and connected them with an imaginary line. His fingers crept lower, her eyes fluttered shut, the lids as pale and translucent as eggshells. Her right arm came up over her head, fingers closing over the railing, grasping it as he moved his hand between her thighs.

It was uncomfortably warm in her bedroom. Her generator was just large enough to power the window AC unit, her fridge, and a light or two. The air conditioner struggled against the thick torpor of the afternoon heat. But he didn't want to interrupt the flow to get up and turn on the fan. He stroked her slowly, watching the minute changes in her expression, the way her breath quickened with her excitement.

Leaning forward, he slid his tongue across her lower lip and whispered, "What did you do in bed with him?"

Her eyes opened, she frowned. "What a weird question."

Finch's hand stopped moving. But she brought her hand over his and said, "Don't stop."

Then tell me what I want to know, Eden. He touched her in a certain way and she gasped and gripped the sides of his head. He hated being constrained and snapped his head free. "Did he do that to you?"

"Never. It seems like he barely touched me at all. It was usually over in about forty seconds. He liked the seduction part of it."

The foreplay.

"Sometimes he couldn't get it up, and then he would make it sound like it was. . . . my fault . . ."

"What pleasure did you get out of it?"

"I . . . I guess my pleasure came from who . . . he is."

Finch couldn't compete in that department and he blamed both Paul and Suki Nichols for that. But he could drive Paul Nichols out of Eden's mind and reward her for answering his questions. In moments, paroxysms of pleasure shuddered through her, her hands twisted the sheets, she cried out.

Now he really couldn't take the heat in here any longer. He got up to turn on the battery-operated floor fan.

"I'm sorry I canceled our dinner last night," she said.

"Don't worry about it."

"You haven't asked me how things went."

"I figured you would tell me if you wanted to." He returned to the bed, stretched out beside her, and pulled the sheet up over them. "What happened?"

"I met him at the motel, after his class, just like he wanted. And I let him buy me dinner and we had some wine and I told him we were done. He really lost it."

Finch smiled at this, the image of Paul Nichols losing it. He wasn't used to being dumped by the women he messed around with. When Eden called to cancel their dinner date last night, she said she was meeting with Paul, to end it once and for all. Finch already knew that Suki was out of town, and Eden's call had assured him that Adam would be in the house alone with the housekeeper. Thanks to all his planning, he was able to make his move. He had been ready to make that move for a year.

"I left around eleven and by then, it was too late for him to leave and make the ferry back to Tango, so I guess he stayed at the hotel all night." She giggled, a small, girlish sound, and pressed her hand over her mouth. "He had already called the housekeeper to tell her that he wouldn't be back and he couldn't very well rush home, now could he?"

"So how do you feel about it?"

"Wonderful." She rolled onto her side, stroking his face, then whispered, "Make me come again."

Entering paradise, he worried about what would happen when Eden heard about Adam's disappearance. She was his only connection to the Nichols family. What would she do? She undoubtedly would blame herself, reasoning that if she had refused to meet Paul last night, he would have gotten home and he would still have his son. But would her guilt consume her? If she called Paul Nichols, the cops might find out he had a lover and would track Eden down.

No, no, none of this would happen. Eden would live with her guilt. She would keep her secrets secret. He would make sure of it.

6

Suki

Thanks to a bomb threat that turned out to be bogus, her plane from New York was delayed five hours and she didn't touch down in Miami until seven that evening. She was frantic with worry. With her cell dead and the plane idling on the Miami tarmac, she was isolated from the people who might provide information she so desperately needed.

The flight attendant moved through first class, apologizing in her soft, breathless voice and passing out glasses of champagne as consolation prizes. Suki shook her head at the proffered glass.

"Can I get you anything else?" the attendant asked, flashing her fluoride smile.

"Yes, a phone that works."

"Did you try the phone on the back of the seat in front of you?"

"It's as dead as my cell phone."

"Oh." That annoying smile shrank.

"What's the holdup?" Suki asked.

"I don't know." She patted the pockets of her uniform, pulled out a cell phone, handed it to Suki. "Use my phone."

My God, Suki thought. Redemption. "Thanks very much. I'll pay you for the call."

"No, that's okay, Ms. Nichols."

No wonder she was so nice. Four years ago, when Suki had been nominated for—and subsequently had won—an Oscar for *Acid Trip,* people had started recognizing her more frequently when she was in public. She still wasn't comfortable with it and hated it in situations like this, when her preferential treatment usually meant the other person expected something in return—*read my script, get me a callback, give me an interview.* She was treated like royalty and yet she'd done nothing to deserve it. Even though she'd been outspoken against the war in Iraq and had been a vocal critic of the current administration's military policies, she never had fought an insurgency, saved a country, or brought peace to her corner of the world.

She quickly punched out Paul's cell number and reached his voice mail. She tried the house number, lost the signal, punched it out again. Paul answered on the second ring, his voice quiet, cautious. "Paul Nichols."

"It's me. Did—"

"My God, Suki, where the hell have you been? You haven't answered your cell, the—"

"Stop it," she hissed. Their son was missing and he was giving her the third degree. "Did Adam come home?" As though he had wandered off, taken a walk, and gotten lost. "Is there any news?"

"No. Not yet."

A huge rift opened in her heart. "Jesus, Paul." Her voice cracked and she turned her head toward the window. The plane had stopped at the gate.

"Suki, we'll find him. The press is going to be all over the story soon. Someone's meeting you at the airport and—"

"It happened on your watch," she snapped, and disconnected before he could defend or excuse himself and before she could find out who was picking her up.

The flight attendant came down the aisle again and Suki returned her cell phone. "Thanks very much."

"Not a problem. The, uh, captain says you're supposed to get off first. The FBI is here to pick you up. Did you check your bag through?"

The FBI? Why? Adam was only missing, he hadn't been kidnapped or anything. This wasn't serious enough for the FBI, was it? "No, I've just got a carry-on. I'll get it."

Suki quickly retrieved her bag from the overhead bin and followed the attendant to the door of the cabin, where a Miami Dade cop waited. His eyes widened when he saw her. He seemed flushed and nervous when he spoke.

"I'm, uh, supposed to escort you out to the tarmac, ma'am. We'll go up the ramp here just a ways, then out a side door so we can avoid the crush of passengers at the gate."

"Why the tarmac?" she asked.

"There's a plane waiting for you."

Moments later, they passed through a side door, down a flight of stairs, out onto the tarmac and into the oppressively warm Miami evening. A tall man paced pack and forth in front of a twin-engine Cessna, a cell pressed to his ear. When he saw them, he snapped the phone shut and hurried over.

"Agent Wayne Sheppard." He extended his hand.

He hardly looked like an FBI agent: bearded, jeans and a T-shirt, running shoes. But the ID tag clipped to his shirt pocket looked real enough. "Why the plane?" she asked.

Sheppard ignored her question, looked at the cop. "Thanks again for your help, Sergeant."

"Sure thing, Agent Sheppard. Ms. Nichols, me and the wife, we're big fans of yours. Could I, uh, have your autograph?" He held out a pad and pen.

Suki asked for their first names, so she could personalize the autograph. He thanked her profusely, his gratitude embarrassing her. She felt relieved when Sheppard took her bag, touched her arm, and urged her toward the plane.

She got into the passenger seat. Sheppard ducked into the back. "Suki Nichols, Ross Blake," Sheppard said.

"Nice to meet you, ma'am," the pilot said, and handed her a headset. "Put this on. It'll make it easier for us to talk while we're in the air."

Suki noticed that he was missing a finger and suddenly linked that fact to his name. "You own Tango Sea and Air."

Blake—blond, blue-eyed, nearly as tall as Sheppard— looked surprised. "If we've met and I don't remember, then I must be well on the path to dementia."

"My husband, Paul Nichols, has used your chartering services from time to time. I remember him mentioning you."

"Maybe dementia has arrived already. I want you to know how sorry I am about your son. If I can be of any help, just let me know."

"Thanks. I appreciate it."

"There's no better pilot around," Sheppard piped up from the backseat.

Blake started the plane, ran through his checklist, and radioed the tower. While he waited for a response, Sheppard leaned forward and tapped her on the shoulder. "If you turn the dial to COM 3, we can talk without disturbing Ross."

She did as he asked, slipped on the headset, and Sheppard got right down to business. He gave her a detailed rundown on where the investigation concerning Adam now stood. The search of the property and surrounding woods hadn't yielded anything. No ransom demands had been made, but the phones in her house were nonetheless wired in the event that a kidnapper called.

"Why're you assuming he was kidnapped?" she asked.

Sheppard's silence caused her to turn around. They were airborne now and in the glow from the cockpit, his expression made it clear that Paul hadn't told her the full story. "It's possible that he ran away, but right now, we're treating this as a kidnapping because your housekeeper's body was found in his room."

"Gladys is *dead*?"

Her eyes filled with tears and she turned quickly around, struggling with emotions that nearly overwhelmed her. Gladys had been their housekeeper since they had moved to Tango two years ago, when Paul had been invited to teach film courses at the University of Miami. Adam had adored her. The fact that Paul hadn't told her about Gladys meant he was covering up something.

And what is it this time? Another gambling debt? A drunk? A woman? What? "Who discovered Gladys's body, Agent Sheppard?"

"A woman who was out for a walk," Sheppard replied, and told her the rest of it.

She sat there in stunned silence, her thoughts scrambling around like hungry mice, and tried to make sense of it. "Mira the psychic? The owner of One World Books? *That* Mira?"

"Yes. Your husband is considering charges against her for trespassing, but decided to wait and discuss it with you."

She spun around, livid. "We will *not* be pressing charges. And where was my husband?"

"He got caught by the curfew on his way back from Miami."

Right. Sure, he did. "What else do I need to know, Agent Sheppard?"

"I've told you everything *we* know. But I need to ask you a couple of questions."

"Sure. Anything. Please."

"In recent weeks, have you gotten any odd phone calls or e-mails? Anything threatening or out of whack?"

"Not that I recall."

"Have you hired anyone new to do your lawn or do work on the property or in the house?"

"Before the hurricane, we had a lawn service. Now Paul pays one of the neighbor kids to do it. The two of us managed to fix our porch so it's at least livable, but we haven't been able to find anyone to repair it correctly. So I doubt if there have been any new people working on or around the house."

Blake clicked into COM 3 and asked, "Have any deliveries been made to the house that you weren't expecting?"

"No."

"Does your son have any allergies or medical conditions?" Sheppard asked.

She bit her lip, fighting to keep back tears. "No medical conditions. But recently, he's been adamant about keeping his door open at night. It embarrasses him, but he seems afraid. He has an imaginary friend too who he claims . . . protects him." A desperate yearning to touch her son, to hold him, swelled inside her and her voice cracked. She paused, cleared her throat.

"Has he mentioned anything to you over the past few months about being followed?" Sheppard asked. "Or strangers talking to him? Anything like that?"

"Nothing. Before the hurricane hit, he was going to a summer camp on Tango. One of us usually drove him. Occasionally, we carpooled with another friend of his, a boy who lives just down the road from us. But that family left before Danielle hit and they haven't been back. Adam's most constant friend is in Boston for the summer."

Blake glanced over at her. "What else can you tell us about Adam?"

"He's a lacto-vegetarian, very resourceful and bright. His interests are . . . oh, hell. He's a forty-year-old man in a thirteen-year-old's body." And unable to hold back her tears any longer, she covered her face with her hands.

Sheppard gave her shoulder a quick squeeze. "We'll find him."

They sat in the living room, where the air had grown hot and stale because the generator wasn't powerful enough to accommodate the AC system. Two battery-operated floor fans whirred quietly nearby, stirring the humid air. Suki just wanted to go to bed, but apparently sleep and bed wouldn't happen for her any time soon.

"The Bureau will reimburse you for any expenses you incur while we're here monitoring the phones," Sheppard was saying.

Paul's head bobbed up, down. Suki just sat there, numb and stricken, mulling over the fact that if her husband of fifteen years had been home last night, Adam might be here now.

"We'd like to release a photo of your son." This came from Sheppard's partner, John Gutierrez.

"Isn't that premature?" Paul asked.

No, it isn't, Suki thought, and went over to one of the wall photos. She chose a black and white picture of Adam taken two months ago, when they had gone away for a long weekend in the Bahamas. Because of Adam's passion for dolphins, they had rented a house on a beach where the mammals were known to congregate. While she and Adam had spent their evenings swimming with dolphins, Paul had sulked in the house because he didn't want to "swim with fish." In other words, Suki and Adam should do what *he* wanted to do.

Not exactly a great *family* outing.

"Here, use this one." She handed Sheppard the photo of Adam.

"C'mon," Paul snapped. "If we release this now, the media will be jammed in the street out front by dawn."

"I don't care," she replied. "Send it out, Agent Sheppard."

"Are you willing to go on TV shows?" Gutierrez asked.

"About this? No. The picture's enough. I'll give a statement to the press if I have to. But no TV. No John Walsh. No *Extra*. Nothing like that." She sat back down, her body wooden with exhaustion.

"Other than the questions I asked you on the flight down here," Sheppard said, "is there anything else you can tell me that would help us out here? Is there anyone . . . anyone at all . . . whom either of you have angered so badly that this person would take your son?"

If you only knew how many people we've pissed off, Suki thought. How many sweet young things had Paul alienated over the years? How many directors, producers, and other actors had she pissed off? Dozens. But would any of them do something as vile as kidnap Adam, the one person on whom her world pivoted?

Doubtful.

"No one," Paul said, and pushed up from the chair and walked out of the room.

End of discussion. Good-bye, FBI, good-bye, good-bye.

Suki sat in the middle of Adam's bed, the bedside lamp on, his pillow bunched in her lap. His Himalayan cat, Dolittle, was curled up beside her. He usually spent most of his time outside, but since the hurricane had been staying closer to home and sleeping inside at night. He seemed to understand something had happened to Adam because every so often he lifted his head and drew his warm, rough tongue over Suki's arm, as if to offer comfort.

Now and then, she pressed the pillow to her face and inhaled the scent of her son, that strange sweetness of childhood with its private thoughts, its teenaged secrets. And when she couldn't stand it anymore, she wandered around his room, as restless as a ghost, studying the wall posters and touching everything, as though the touch would bring him back to her.

The model airplane that hung from the ceiling had been a gift from her father the year before he passed away. She could still see five-year-old Adam, working diligently at piecing it together, painting it, his little hands as deft as an adult's. The odd cuckoo clock on his dresser had been a gift from Paul's mother, and it was cuckoo, as Adam used to say, because it never gave the right time. His collections of DVDs and music CDs were as diverse as his hundreds of books and more than a thousand wildlife photos he'd taken, many of them of whales and dolphins. Adam, genius.

In New York, he had been in a private school for gifted children. Here on Tango, he was in a gifted program in the public school and it was better for him. He had more friends than he'd ever had in New York, and this year even had three girlfriends. He had gotten involved with two after-school clubs—one on the environment, so that he could indulge his passion for marine life, and the other in computers and software development, at which he excelled. In another week, he would turn fourteen, and in the fall would enter the tenth grade, a year ahead of the friends he'd left behind in New York.

And now he's gone. Some maniac had broken into her home, killed Gladys, and stolen her son.

"Stop," she hissed.

"Suki?"

Shit, no, she didn't want to talk to Paul, not with feds still in the house. But she had nowhere to hide. "In here," she called.

He came to the doorway, a man now pushing fifty and a decade older than she was. When she'd met him on the set of her first movie, which he was directing, his thick hair had been the color of pine bark. It was still thick, but now it was gray and thinning. His eyes were now pinched, with deep laugh lines at the corners. He had gained weight over the years, twenty pounds or so, and although he wore it well enough, he didn't do anything about it. No gym, no runs, no moderation in his diet, nothing at all.

Paul didn't do much directing now either. Ten years ago, his directing career had flatlined and her own career had begun to shine. But Paul, forever resourceful, had written two bestselling books on screenwriting, gave seminars several times a year on his techniques, and now taught three

classes in the film department at the University of Miami.
Everything about him was excessive.

"I just got off the phone with Agent Sheppard," he said,
stepping into the room. "He's going to hold off a bit on releasing Adam's photo. He's really pushing for you to go on
John Walsh's program, that . . ."

She didn't hear the rest of his pitch, and that was what it
amounted to. Paul pitching, always pitching—a script, an
idea, a concept, even to her. She suspected that Paul, not
Sheppard, was the one pushing for her to go on Walsh's program, perhaps because their sons shared the same name.
Dramatic irony. Good TV fodder. Great publicity. Yada, yada.

"I'm not going on Walsh's program, Paul. I'm not going
on *Extra* or doing an intimate thing with Stone Phillips or
Katie Couric or Barbara Walters, got it? If and when the
press converge, I'll make a statement."

"Look, now that you've given the feds Adam's picture,
you need to use your fame to get as much coverage as possible."

Dolittle jumped down from the bed, hissed as he trotted
past Paul, and scampered out of the room. The cat didn't like
Paul, never had. The feeling was mutual.

Suki went over to the window and gazed out into the
darkness. Sheppard told her they believed the kidnapper had
come in through the utility-room door and had escaped
through this window. She didn't feel anything one way or another about the utility-room door, but the window felt right
to her. In the aftermath of the hurricane, without enough
juice from the generator to run the AC, all the windows had
been open, even at night. Especially at night.

"Where were you last night, Paul?" She turned, facing
him. "You promised me that while I was in New York, you
would be home with him every night."

"I didn't get off campus until—"

"That's a lie." Suki glared at him. "You were with whoever the current lady is, Paul. A little tryst in the afternoon

that held you up so you couldn't get back here before curfew, before the ferries stopped running. Or maybe she lives somewhere between Miami and Tango and you had the best intentions to get home before curfew, but oops, she was just *so* intriguing. Whatever it was, whoever she is, this is your fucking fault."

His face burned with phony indignation. "You want receipts, Suki? You want proof? You want the cell records so you can see when I called Gladys to let her know I wasn't going to make it? I stayed in a goddamn hotel, for Chrissakes. By myself."

"Sure, just like you did when you were having your little fling with . . ." She waved her arm in the air. "Whatever her name was, you know who I mean. That aspiring screenwriter who salivated over every word you uttered. Or what about that female director who wanted you to work with her on a script she was supposedly writing for *me*? What about that, Paul? You think I'm *blind*? I know what's been going on and right before Danielle hit, I did something about it. I went to an attorney. We're done, you and me. I'm bailing and Adam is going with me."

For months, she had tried to talk to him about their failing marriage, her suspicions, all of it. And for months, he had walked out every time she had raised the subject. But he wasn't walking now. He stood there like a grizzly bear that had run into a wall, shaking his head, his eyes seeming to slide around in their sockets as if they had torn loose from tendons, muscles, bones, whatever had held them in place.

"Jesus," he whispered. "I didn't realize you hate me so much."

The trump card, it always worked. Now came the wounded eyes. She couldn't bear to look at him and turned back to the window, where she saw her own reflection, her short blond hair looking as though it hadn't been combed in weeks, her eyes red and swollen, her mouth set in a grim, stubborn line. Hardly the movie version of Suki Nichols.

"There hasn't been anyone else since that horrible stretch when Adam was two. You were off on shoots most of the time, my career was crashing, and we had a kid who . . . who was . . ."

"Never a problem," she said quietly.

"But who needed parents who were together, a unit, and we couldn't do it. We fucked up big-time."

We. How she hated a plural used in that particular way. And how vastly their memories—and their versions of reality—differed. When Adam was between the ages of two and eight, she had taken him with her on her shoots, to every set, every far-flung corner of whatever continent. He was written into her contracts. Paul was never saddled with the responsibility and Adam had tutors when he needed them. And he had her, always.

Only Paul was absent.

She couldn't do this now, couldn't deal with any more of this conversation, of Paul and his lies. "I'm going to bed," she murmured. "I can't keep my eyes open any longer."

But as she started past him, he reached out and grabbed her hand, pulling her to him. "Don't do this," he whispered. "Please. Don't do this. He's my son too."

And there in the emptiness of their son's bedroom, she weakened. Their pain merged. Adam was gone and they were both to blame. She knew that. Yes, she had tried to be present in the way a parent is supposed to be present. But bottom line, Adam had been an accident, unplanned, unanticipated, and inconvenient. He had been a toddler when Paul's career had spiraled downward and hers had been racing upward, and if she didn't work, the bills weren't paid.

When Adam was born, when he had been very young, she had been more interested in herself and her career than in her son. Dear God.

She tightened her arms around Paul, he clutched at her, and they stumbled back, back, and fell onto Adam's bed. Paul ripped off her tank top, she tore off his shorts, and they fucked like there had never been any hope for any tomorrow, anywhere on the planet. And when it was done, she lay there in her sweating heap of flesh, her face turned toward the wall, and hated herself for what she had become.

7

Ghosts

The silence wrapped around everything. Mira couldn't hear herself breathing and pressed her fingers to the underside of her wrist, feeling for her pulse. Okay, she was alive. She pinched herself to make sure she was awake. Yes. Then how come she was standing on the stoop outside the trailer in the gym shorts and T-shirt she'd worn to bed? And it must be morning, she thought, because she could see the thinnest threads of gray light seeping through the trees to the east.

Question: If it was so close to sunrise, why weren't the birds singing?

She curled her bare toes against the cool concrete. It felt real enough. And the mist that swirled across the ground also looked real. But where had the mist come from? In five years here on Tango, she couldn't recall having ever seen anything like this.

Was it mist? Maybe she was developing cataracts or had a detached retina or something. She walked down the steps. The mist swirled around her feet and swallowed them to the ankles. It didn't seem to move at all now. She glanced at her watch; the hands had stopped.

And when she looked up, Tom emerged from the mist and the silence as if it were all perfectly natural that they should meet like this. *The watch, right?* She spoke to him, but her mouth didn't move. *When the watch stops, that's how I know I'll see you?*

Sometimes the watch, sometimes the mist, sometimes a combination. He put his arms around her. He felt solid, warm, real, completely human. *Let's walk,* he said.

Let's not. She stopped, stepped back from him, folded her arms against her. Her dead husband looked as she remembered him, the same thick, chestnut hair, warm brown eyes, a quick, engaging smile. He even wore regular clothes— shorts, T-shirt, sandals. It seemed odd to her that every ghost she'd seen wore human clothes.

What do you expect, Mira? White robes? Tom asked. *I create an image based on your memories. That's all.*

Tell me why you're here.

He took her hand. *I'll show you.*

And suddenly she was in another place, a room where a teenage boy sat in front of a computer monitor, clicking through photographs. As they moved closer, Mira realized the person was Adam Nichols. The photos apparently upset him; tears coursed down his cheeks. She tried to see the details of the photos, but it was like trying to read a book in a dream. She took in other details about the room, noticed the shutters on the windows, then said to Tom: *Okay, he's alive, but where is he?*

He didn't answer. Mira spun around—and fell out of the dream, onto the floor. Ricki, the golden retriever, licked her face and whined. Someone rapped at the door.

"Mira?" Ace called. "You okay?"

"Yeah, fine. I fell out of bed." She got up and opened the door. Ace's face was skewed with worry. "See? All here."

"Jesus, girl, you scared me. It's five-thirty in the morning and I hear you arguing with someone."

"Tom."

"Tom?" Ace's brows shot up. "You mean, like, *the* Tom?"

The Tom. Yes. The same Tom who, years ago, had defended Ace in a trumped-up drug charge and gotten him off. The same Tom who had fathered Annie, who had helped buy Mira's first bookstore in Lauderdale, the same Tom who had taken a bullet during the robbery of a convenience store on the night of Annie's third birthday. The only Tom she'd ever known.

Ace poked his head through the doorway, glancing around. "He was here?"

"I don't know. Maybe. Or maybe I was just dreaming. I wish this would stop happening to me."

Ace leaned against the door frame, a tall, gangly black man with hair as tight and wiry as a Brillo pad and deep, soulful eyes. He stuck his hands into the pockets of his psychedelic shorts. He wore a blazing red T-shirt with the words SUNSET PERFORMER screaming across the front of it in brilliant yellow. He and his partner Luke probably owned two dozen such T-shirts, free advertising for their routines on the Tango boardwalk—Ace as an escape artist, Luke as a tightrope walker.

She had seen Ace free himself from chains and straitjackets that would leave Houdini in knots, and had watched Luke do flips on a tightrope forty feet up, without a net beneath him. Ever since Hurricane Danielle had washed the boardwalk away, thus ending the boardwalk performances, they had been picking up odd jobs on the island, and were overseeing the reconstruction on her house. They also had invited her and the dog to stay in their trailer until the house was habitable again.

"What'd he say?" Ace asked. "I mean, was it, like *'Hey, Mira, how's it going?'* "

"No, it was more like, *'Let's go for a walk.'* "

"Ghosts *walk*?"

"I don't know, Ace. I don't know what the hell ghosts do. I just see them. I hear them. I watch them help dead people cross over."

"You need strong coffee and breakfast," Ace said. "Coming right up."

She didn't know what she needed. A lobotomy. A windfall of money to pay for the mounting bills on the reconstruction of her house, her bookstore. She needed a new life. *Pity party, pity party.* Ricki seemed to sense her mood, and trotted out of the room as if to distance herself from the negativity. Who could blame her?

When Mira came out of the bedroom a few minutes later, Ace had let Ricki outside and spread out a feast on the table. Luke, already seated, eyed everything with obvious delight. "If you don't hurry up and sit down, Mira, I'll eat your portion too," Luke said. "So I understand our trailer is haunted."

"Just briefly."

Luke was as tall as Ace, about six feet, but more muscular, with broad shoulders and powerful arms and hands that looked as if they could snap steel. Both men were in their mid-forties and in their eighteen years together had remained more committed to each other than most heterosexual couples she knew.

"Ghosts haunt briefly?" Luke asked.

"They drop in for visits," Ace said, setting a platter of biscuits on the table. "Like the woman at the Nicholses' place, right?"

Luke leaned forward, his blue eyes narrowing, and whispered, "Is anyone here now, Mira?"

"Yeah, actually, there's a woman leaning over your shoulder, trying to read the newspaper."

"What?" Luke shot to his feet so fast his chair tipped back and crashed to the floor.

Mira laughed. "Just kidding."

"Very funny," Luke groused, picking up his chair.

Ace chuckled. "I mean, c'mon, man, what self-respecting ghost would visit you?"

Outside, Ricki started barking. Golden retrievers licked, wagged their tails, sought to please, but rarely barked, she thought. Ace, who was closest to the window, parted the slats in the blinds with his hand and peered out. "Company."

"Not for us," Luke said. "Our friends don't get up this early."

"Wait, false alarm," Ace announced. "The car's making a U-turn in the cul-de-sac. It's a Mercedes, one of those spiffy jobs worth sixty or seventy grand."

"Oh, well, then. They're definitely in the wrong neighborhood," Mira remarked. "It's probably Charlie Cordoba, here to arrest me."

"Cordoba in a Mercedes?" Luke laughed. "Please. The man drives a rusted piece of shit that bears an uncanny resemblance to his brain."

Ricki continued barking, but the tone of the bark changed. This sounded like a warning, the kind they had heard a lot in the days right after Danielle, when the looting had been bad. Ace and Luke noticed it as surely as she did, and Ace stood quickly and retrieved his rifle from the broom closet. Luke, peering out the window now, said: "The car pulled into your driveway, Mira."

She pushed to her feet. "Okay, let's check it out, boys." She felt like Annie Oakley.

Ace went out first, the rifle cradled in the crook of his arm, with Luke and Mira right behind him. The Mercedes still stood in her driveway, headlights on, bright against the garage door. Ricki, no longer barking, sat back on her haunches near the car door, waiting for the driver to get out. Mira whistled for her. Ricki glanced her way, then back at the darkly tinted driver's-side window, then reluctantly returned to Mira's side.

"Stay," Mira said softly.

"Can we help you with something?" Ace called out.

The car door opened. The woman who stepped out wore denim Capris, a red tank top with a cotton shirt over it, sandals, and a baseball cap with the brim pulled down low over her eyes. She had a straw bag slung over her shoulder. When she took off the hat, Ace breathed, "Holy crap."

"Oh, my God," Luke muttered. "You might've shot her."

It was Suki Nichols. "Mira?"

"Suki. We thought you might be a looter. Sorry about this."

"I wasn't sure of the address. The trailer threw me." She strode toward them now, with Ricki the first to greet her, tail wagging.

Mira made the formal introductions. Ace and Luke, their eyes the size of pancakes, acted like tongue-tied groupies meeting a rock star.

"I've seen you two perform," Suki exclaimed. "You're terrific."

Ace looked like he might pass out from the praise and Luke seemed embarrassed.

"How about some coffee?" Mira asked.

"And breakfast," Ace added. "If you haven't eaten already. We were just about to eat."

"That sounds wonderful," Suki replied, and they all went inside.

If she found the trailer too humble or cramped, she certainly didn't show it. She acted as if she were among friends, comfortable enough to comment on Ace's rifle, on the delicious breakfast banquet, and to ask about the reconstruction on Mira's home. By the time light appeared in the windows, Ace and Luke were questioning her about how she chose her roles and memorized lines and what it was like to work with Spielberg on *Acid Trip*.

In a brief lull in the conversation, Suki said, "Mira, I'd like to hire you to find my son."

"We'll leave you two ladies alone," Luke said, getting up to clear the table.

"No, please, it's fine with me as long as it's okay with Mira," Suki said.

"I don't have any secrets from these two," Mira told her.

"Hey, we've got a gig in Key Largo in three days," Ace said. "We need to practice."

Suki pointed at Ace. "Escape artist." Her finger slid through the air to Luke. "Tightrope walker. Do I have that right?"

"Perfect," Ace replied.

"And just where do you figure you're going to practice around here?" Mira asked.

Ace grinned. "On your lawn, girl. And don't worry, you won't have to call nine-one-one. We'll be safety-conscious."

"He's lying," Luke added. "We're rarely safety-conscious." He whistled for Ricki, who trotted after them.

After they'd left, Mira said, "Look, I know Adam's alive, but I can't promise you that I'll find him."

"How . . . do you know he's alive?"

"I saw him." Mira described her dream, minus the part about Tom. "He was clicking through photos on a computer and seemed upset by it." She shut her eyes briefly, conjuring up the rest of what she'd seen, the details that hadn't registered at the time. "There was also a photo album sitting next to the computer with newspaper clippings in it. Stuff about you. I saw a Styrofoam cooler off to one side, a TV, all sorts of electronic games."

"So whoever took him is keeping him amused and comfortable."

"It seems that way."

"Adam's photo is going to be released today. Once that happens, the press and paparazzi are going to be camped outside my house. Paul is pushing me to make the round of talk shows, to use the media, but that seems pointless. Adam's picture will be out there, widely circulated even if I never do anything more than issue a cursory statement. Paul has his agenda, the cops have their agenda, and I need someone in my court."

"All I can tell you is what I pick up."

"Yes, I understand that."

"Do you?" Mira leaned forward. "How blunt and honest do you want me to be, Suki?"

She held Mira's gaze for a moment before speaking. "I know Paul is seeing someone, if that's what you're referring to."

"He was with her the night Adam was taken."

Suki nodded, but something in her eyes seemed to come apart, crumble, dissolve. She looked down at the tabletop. "I suspected as much."

But you made love to him anyway. Mira sat back, hands wrapped around the coffee mug. "Do you know who she is?"

"I have no idea." She paused, then added: "There have been a lot of women over the years, most of them groupie types who think he walks on water."

Mira rubbed her hands over her face, wishing there were some other way to do this, that she could wave her magic psychic wand and voila—Adam's location would appear to her, complete with address, geographic coordinates, and the name on the mailbox. A man she knew who had worked in the government's remote-viewing program had an eighty-five-percent success rate in finding anyone, anywhere, in any time frame. Mira had seen Joe McMoneagle locate a Japanese man who had been missing thirty-five years and yet he was given nothing more than the man's name and birth date in a sealed envelope. McMoneagle was the crème de la crème, a genuine anomaly whose abilities worked in a highly specific way. She wasn't at that level, would never be there. She read emotions, issues, *stuff,* and if anyone had handed her an envelope with a name and birth date inside and asked her to locate a missing person through nothing but that, she wouldn't be able to do it.

"Can you help me?" Suki asked.

The plaintive note in her voice, the desperation in her expression, the fact that she was here at all, prompted Mira to extend her hand, palm open. "I don't know. Put your hand in mine."

Suki didn't just put her hand in Mira's palm; she laced her fingers through Mira's and held on like a drowning woman clutching a life preserver. Mira altered her breathing, practicing what Nadine had taught her years ago. She inhaled deeply through her right nostril, exhaled through her left, repeated it three times and switched nostrils. She went through the process again and again, until she felt herself sinking deeper, deeper.

The first thing that popped into her awareness was the figure who stood next to Suki, a man holding a model airplane. "Anthony or Anton," Mira said. "He's holding the same model airplane that's hanging from the ceiling in Adam's room. Who is he?"

"My God," Suki breathed. "Anton is my dad. That was his birth name. He never went by that name. He's been dead for nine years."

Okay, she was on the right track. *Thank you, Anton. You can go away now.*

And he did. He was sure a lot more cooperative than Tom.

More breathing. Going deeper. Another person appeared next to Suki. As the woman became clearer, Mira thought, *Yeah, right.* It was Katharine Hepburn, looking very much as she had in *Love Affair*, a romantic comedy remake of the original Cary Grant/Deborah Kerr movie, Hepburn's last film role before her death in 2003. Mira couldn't remember much about the film except that it had a great cast—Warren Beatty, Annette Bening, Kate Capshaw, and Pierce Brosan.

What could she possibly say to the ghost of Katherine Hepburn?

You don't have to ask me anything, Hepburn said. *Just tell her I'm still here. Repeat my words exactly.*

"What?" Suki asked softly, leaning forward. "What is it?"

"This is going to sound nuts. But, uh, Katharine Hepburn said to tell you she's still here. She was very firm about my repeating the exact words. *Tell her I'm still here.*"

Suki looked shocked. "That's what she used to say to me

any time we got together. *I'm still here, Suki,* and then she would sort of laugh like it was all some big cosmic joke."

"How well did you know her?"

"Not well. I met her when she was filming *Love Affair.* I got onto the set and into her dressing room to tell her how much I admired her. We ended up talking for a long time. Every time there was a knock at the door, she told whoever it was to go away. It was one of the peak moments of my life. Several months later, she came over to the house for dinner. I think Paul was trying to get her to sign up for a film he wanted to direct. But she was more interested in Adam. He was just a toddler then and they got along great. From time to time over the years, we would get together for lunch or coffee and she always made a point of asking me to bring Adam. Maybe that's why she's here. Because of her affection for Adam."

Hepburn continued to stand just behind Suki, her head cocked to one side, as though she were listening to something. *Thank you,* Mira thought at her.

She smiled and was gone.

Suki had long since reclaimed her hand, so now Mira touched her arm again, focusing, silently asking, *Please give me more.* And then she had it, the core issue, at least for Suki. But she hesitated. Was this ethical? Did Suki really want the full truth? "Paul isn't Adam's blood father."

Suki sucked in her breath. "That's true."

"It may come out. Are you willing to live with that?"

"Yes."

No equivocation. And no explanation. "Could Adam's real father be the one who took him, Suki?"

"No. No. He was a producer for one of my films. Married. Not a very nice guy. Paul caught me on the rebound, and only later did I realize I was pregnant. Adam doesn't know. Paul doesn't know. No one knows."

"At some level, Adam has always known. That's why he and Paul don't get along well."

Suki nodded, folded her hands together, struggled not to cry—and failed. She broke down completely, her sobs so wrenching and devoid of pretense that Mira finally got up and sat down beside her. She put her arms around this woman whom she barely knew, hugging her tightly. Too tightly. Something new crept into her awareness. "Suki, does the word *kismet* mean anything to you?"

Suki drew back, her surprise as obvious as thunder. "How . . . I mean, yes. Kismet was the name of the production company Paul and I started shortly after we got married. It was mostly a tax write-off, but we produced four or five independent films. Why? How's it important?"

"I don't know. It means fate, right?"

"Fate, destiny, fortune, karma."

Mira didn't know why this particular word had come up, but now that it had, she would let it gel for a while. "We'll find Adam," Mira told her, and hoped she would be able to fulfill this particular promise. "I'd like to start by reading Adam's room. I would rather do it without your husband around."

"There are feds upstairs, monitoring the phones. Will that be a problem?"

"No, it shouldn't be."

"What else do you need?"

"Access to Adam's things—games, computer, whatever he touches a lot."

"Forensics has gone through his room, but otherwise it's just as it was."

"Did they take anything of his?"

"No. But they touched everything."

That might be a challenge. "I'll meet you at your place around ten or ten thirty. I have to go by my store first."

"That'll give me a chance to get Paul out of the house." She reached into the touristy straw bag, brought out her wallet, and handed Mira a check. "Is this enough?"

Mira glanced at the check and nearly swallowed her

tongue. Two hundred grand? "I think there are too many zeros, Suki. I can't take this. It's too much." She set the check on the table.

Suki looked horrified. "Mira, this is *my son.* I'll pay whatever it takes to get him back. I can afford it. And if I can't use my money to find my son"—her voice cracked. After a moment or two, she went on—"then what good is it?"

After Suki had left, Mira picked up the check and stared at it, turned it over and over in her hands, shook her head, rubbed her eyes, and looked again, certain that three of the zeros would be gone. She never had been paid anything like this for her psychic work. Up until now, her occasional consulting work for the Bureau was her best pay and at the most, they had paid two grand. This check would pay off her reconstruction bills, with money left over to stash into Annie's college fund and to restock her store.

But as soon as she thought this, she felt a terrible weight against the back of her neck and across her shoulders. She knew what it meant. Once she deposited this check in her bank, the pressure to succeed at this, to find Adam, would become almost unbearable.

8

On the Beach

Wayne Sheppard ran hard and fast across the island's north beach, following its gracious, wide curves with a kind of athletic lust. Hurricane Danielle had devastated the other two beaches where he used to run. Even though North Beach tended to be rocky, so that he had to wear shoes, he preferred it to the jogging path in the Tango park. It was more private.

But all of that aside, he ran here now because it marked a change in his usual routine. And change, he reminded himself, was good. Change was what he was after. The more easily he embraced it, the better off he would be. Every change he made, no matter how small, placed more distance between his former life with Mira and his present situation.

A faint mist clung to the surface of the water and drifted inland, deepening the mystique that always had surrounded Tango Key. Over the years he had lived here, he had heard most of the myths and legends that existed about the island: buried treasures that dated back to the days when pirates roamed the Caribbean, hauntings, mermaids, UFOs, wild dolphins that sought interactions with humans, a Bigfoottype creature that lived in the preserve. Then there was the black water mass that formed periodically offshore, nature's time tunnel.

Since he had experienced the mass last summer and had gone back thirty-five years in time, he couldn't discount the veracity of the other legends. If nothing else, his years on Tango had turned his worldview inside out and shaken loose every preconceived notion he'd held about how the universe worked.

Mira speculated that Tango was located at a critical juncture on the planet's energy grid of ley lines, so that it was a power spot like Stonehenge, the Mayan ruins, Machu Picchu, Tikal, the Egyptian pyramids. She felt this theory explained why her psychic abilities were heightened on Tango. Sheppard didn't know squat about any energy grid or ley lines, but he certainly knew about Mira's abilities.

He swiftly severed this line of thought.

Here and there, scattered haphazardly across the sand, lay the lingering evidence of Danielle's wrath—plastic bottles, aluminum cans, trees, mounds of garbage that had washed up during the storm, flattened beds of sea oats, the remains of a wooden canoe half buried in the sand. The dunes that once had graced this beach were gone and the half-dozen docks that had jutted out into the water had collapsed or been washed away. Just ahead of him, a landslide filled with trees and brush blocked his way.

Sheppard slowed and walked out into the shoals of the tepid Gulf. As he leaned over to splash water on his face, his arms vanished up to the elbows in the mist. Its air was cooler than the temperature of the water and felt oddly pleasant against his skin, like small, delicate kisses. Celibacy, he thought, could do that to you.

He waded out more deeply, cooling himself off from his run. The mist now reached to his waist. Spellbound, Sheppard barely heard the first soft, *whooshing* sound and didn't con-

nect it immediately with anything unusual. Then he heard it
again, louder and closer, accompanied by a lot of splashing,
and slowly raised his eyes.

Four dolphins emerged from the mist, water shooting from
their blowholes, the air filled with their clicks and whistles.
They arched gracefully, so close to him now that he could
see their faces, mouths like playful smiles, their small, wiz-
ened eyes. The clicks and whistles became another sound, a
kind of music that rose and fell with the beating of his heart,
the rush of blood through his veins.

The dolphins turned, two of them moving to Sheppard's
left, the other two to his right, and circled him in opposite directions. He turned too, watching as they dived, surfaced,
dived and surfaced again and again. Their music swept
through him, one wave after another, and he knew they were
scanning him with their sonar, gathering information about
him.

Years ago, off the coast of Venezuela, he and his mother
had gone swimming with wild dolphins. A pod had surrounded them and taken an inordinate interest in his mother,
bumping up against her, clicking and whistling as if to communicate something to her. A few days later, she'd found out
she was eight weeks pregnant. She believed the dolphins had
known because they'd zapped her with their sonar, the dolphin equivalent of ultrasound.

But he sure wasn't pregnant and didn't think he had any
kind of tumor—another detail that a dolphin's sonar had
been known to pick up. He wondered if dolphin sonar could
read loneliness. Or a broken heart.

Don't go there.

Maybe they were just having fun, trying to engage him in
a dolphin game. One of the two smaller dolphins suddenly
shot toward him and as she passed within inches of his body,
water exploded from her blowhole, drenching him. She
whipped away, clicking wildly, a noise that sounded suspi-
ciously like laughter.

Sheppard flopped back into the water, kicking his legs, splashing his arms, and whistled long, joyful notes. The dolphins picked up speed, their powerful tails whipping the water into a white froth. One of the dolphins bumped into him, startling him. He grabbed onto its dorsal fin and the dolphin sped away, pulling Sheppard along.

Exhilaration whipped through him. He tried to pull his legs in toward his body so they didn't create such a drag in the water, but the dolphin was moving too fast. He squinted against the assault of the salty air that stung his eyes, the muscles and tendons in his arms and hands now screaming for release. The dolphin abruptly turned again, with her companions gleefully turning on either side of her, their collective clicks now so loud that the noise threatened to burst open Sheppard's skull. The dolphin dived, water rushed into Sheppard's mouth, burned a path up through his sinuses, and whatever exhilaration he'd felt collapsed into fear that he could drown out here.

He released the dolphin's fin, but the vortex created by its rapid movement sucked him down, down. His ears popped from the pressure change. It was as if a plug had been pulled in the floor of the Gulf and he was swirling down through it like yesterday's bathwater. His feet touched bottom—how deep? Fifty feet? Seventy? He propelled himself upward, arms moving frantically, eyes pinned to the murky light very far overhead.

The salt water clawed at his eyeballs, his lungs pleaded and screamed for air. His foot caught on something—a tangle of branches and refuse, he wasn't sure, couldn't see clearly. He jerked his leg back and forth, up and down, fighting to get his foot loose. His lungs swelled, threatening to burst. It was the ultimate claustrophobia, blackness encroaching at the edge of his vision, his head spinning.

Sheppard doubled over, desperately clawing at the branches and the tangle of seaweed and fishing lines that trapped his foot. But the whole mess of whatever it was had caught on rocks. If he could work his foot free of the shoe, if he could get the goddamn shoe off, if he . . .

The last of his oxygen exploded from his lungs, panic seized him. *No air, no air* . . . As the blackness swam closer and closer, something shot into his rapidly narrowing field of vision. He couldn't make out exactly what it was—dolphin, shark, sea monster. The strong current whipped a huge, tangled veil of pale seaweed in front of and to the sides of the shape. He tore frantically at the netting and lines, his fingertips now raw and bleeding.

For a brief instant, the tangled stuff parted and Sheppard glimpsed the impossible. The seaweed looked like hair. He suddenly knew his oxygen-deprived brain was coughing up near-death visions of a woman's face—beautiful, delicate, pale—with luminous green eyes. *I'll get you out of this mess,* she promised.

Then water rushed into his lungs and the blackness seized him.

"Shep, hey, c'mon."

A woman's voice. Hands rolling him onto his side. Water surging up his throat. He started coughing and half the Gulf exploded from his mouth. He rocked back onto his heels, wiped his arm across his mouth, and looked into the face of Tina Richmond, the M.D. who headed up the Tango bureau's latent-fingerprint unit. A fellow runner.

"You all right?" she asked, kneeling beside him.

"I . . . I think so." He coughed some more, wiped his arm across his mouth. "What the hell happened to you, Shep?"

I saw a mermaid. "I nearly drowned." He knuckled his burning eyes. "What're you doing here?"

"I started running on this beach after the hurricane." She pulled a towel and a bottle of water out of her pack and handed them to him. "Take small sips. I saw fog rolling in off the water and covering this area of the beach. When I ran into it, I nearly tripped over you."

"Did you see the dolphins?"

"I heard them. They were thrashing around out there like crazy, stirring up the fog. This fog is weird. I've never seen fog here before."

If it was fog. "Me either." Sheppard rubbed the towel over his face and arms, sipped from the bottle of water. The muscles in his arms and legs twitched and trembled from the exertion.

"You lost a shoe," she remarked, pointing at his bare left foot.

He felt like he'd lost his mind. He told her about the dolphins, about getting trapped at the bottom. He didn't mention the other thing he saw. "I blacked out down there."

"How do you feel now?"

"Not quite here."

"Where's your car?"

"Three miles down the beach."

She sank to the sand beside him. "Let's sit a while, then I'll walk back with you."

"I appreciate it, but don't interrupt your run."

"You're saving me a phone call. Let's talk about the bullet that killed the Nicholses' housekeeper. I got the autopsy and ballistics report late last night. She died from a single nine-millimeter to the heart. The firing-pin marks and the ridge on that cartridge came from a Walther P99. They ran the gun print through the ATF and FBI databases, and didn't come up with any match for other crimes."

Not too surprising, Sheppard thought. Even though computers and other technological advances had moved ballistics light years beyond what it had been during his first stint with the Bureau twenty years ago, matching a single bullet to other crimes remained an imprecise science. With between 238 and 276 million firearms owned in the U.S. alone, the databases of the FBI and ATF held fewer than a million images of fired bullets.

"There's always a chance he hasn't shot anyone before."

"Sure, Shep. About as much of a chance as a UFO landing on the lawn of the White House. He shot her from a distance of five or six feet, probably just as she came into the bedroom. The bullet was a semi-jacketed, so the internal damage was extensive. She died instantly."

"What about latent prints?"

"The only latent print we found that doesn't belong at the house was Mira's."

"She found the housekeeper's body."

"Oh-oh."

Sheppard told her what had happened.

She just shook her head. "Frankly, I think Charlie Cordoba is way too eager to get involved in a high-profile case. It won't matter to him if Mira is the last person on the island who would kill anyone. He'll dig up a motive and try like hell to make it stick. She'd better be careful, Shep."

"Yeah, well, I'm the last person she'd seek out for advice."

Tina gave his arm an affectionate squeeze. She knew they'd split up. Everyone he worked with knew it. As long as they had lived on Tango, their names among friends and coworkers had been uttered as one: *MiraandShep*. It was a tough habit to break.

"Any ransom demand yet?" she asked.

"Not as of one this morning when I finally crashed in my office."

"Maybe the kid ran away after the intruder shot the housekeeper, Shep."

"Wouldn't he be home by now?" Sheppard shook his head. "It doesn't feel like that. I think this guy had been watching the family for quite a while. He knew what he was doing, where to enter, where to exit, who was home and who wasn't."

"He?" Her glance chastised him for being sexist.

"A generic term, Tina. Really."

She slapped his upper arm with the back of her hand. "Hey, lighten up, okay? That was a joke."

He reminded himself that Tina was married to an attorney for whom nuance was an art form. "Statistically, most kidnappers are male."

"Screw statistics. What's your gut say?" she asked.

"That the abductor is male."

"His motive?"

"Money is the reasonable answer. And the Nicholses have plenty of it."

"If we remove money from the equation, what's left?" Her index finger shot up, as if testing the direction of the wind. *"Revenge."* Her middle finger snapped up. *"Desire.* You have something I want. I covet your wife, kid, life, house, career, whatever the hell it is that draws TV and movie viewers to celebrities and elevates them to the status of royalty." Now her ring finger joined the parade. *"Random madness.* The guy sees a kid, decides he wants him."

They walked along the beach now, Sheppard holding his lone shoe in one hand, the bottle of water in the other. He noticed that the fog had dissipated completely. "In the desire category, maybe it's a matter of projection," he said. "You're famous and beautiful, so if I take something that belongs to you, I'll become famous and beautiful."

"He's after publicity?" She nodded. "That's possible. Or Paul and Suki Nichols are after publicity."

He could believe that of Paul Nichols, but not of Suki. If Paul Nichols wanted publicity and had arranged the kidnapping of his son to get it, then he was a monster, not just a publicity hound. Despite the man's short fuse and outrageous behavior, Sheppard couldn't connect him to the monster category. Not yet anyway.

They reached the parking lot. Sheppard heard his cell phone ringing inside his Jetta and hurried to answer it. As he opened the door, a blast of hot air rolled over him, scorched, crisp, with a thick scent of leather. He plucked the cell off the passenger seat. The number that came up in the window identified the caller as *Tango PD*. That meant Charlie Cordoba or one of his pals.

"Agent Sheppard."

"Shep, it's Charlie. The kid's photo was released to the news services two hours ago and now we're about to have a major situation."

"I didn't authorize that release," Sheppard said. His target time had been eight A.M. "Who did?"

"We don't know. But the paparazzi and the press are all over it and there are more on the way. I got a call from one of the ferry captains. His six-A.M. run was so jammed with press vans that the company had to bring out a second ferry just for commuters."

A logistics nightmare, Sheppard thought. That was what this would be. Was becoming. *Is.*

"There're only two hotels on the island that have full power restored—the Hilltop Inn and Tango Motor Lodge, and their rooms are filling up fast. We don't have the capacity right now to support all these people. We have one functional gas station that's usually out of gas by eight in the morning. Our public restrooms haven't reopened. What the hell are we going to do? Tell them to camp in the preserve? Even the preserve is a mess. Worse, the Nicholses lost the fence around most of their property during the storm and all that stands between them and the press is the gate and a strip of iron fence."

"Did you notify Mayor Dawson?"

"Yeah. He said that since the missing kid is a potential kidnapping and falls in the fed domain, I should call you. With the island still under curfew and emergency management, he can order them off the island by dusk. For those who choose to stay on Tango, there will be rules they'll have to follow—or they'll face deportation."

"Deportation is what they do to illegal immigrants, Charlie."

"You know what the hell I mean. Dawson will be meeting us over at the Nicholses' for an emergency meeting. Gutierrez, too. Thirty minutes. Be there."

Not likely, at least not in thirty minutes. He was drenched, had only one shoe, and needed to shower. "Hey, Charlie."

"Yeah?"

"I don't take my orders from you."

Sheppard disconnected before Cordoba could reply.

9

Developments

Finch, sitting in front of the PC in his den, went through the video feed, editing, enhancing, cropping, zooming, a wizard working the magic of digital technology. He ran the edited feed once again, fine-tuning it, disguising his voice, playing with shadows, light, textures, deleting anything that might give away the location, his identity, or his purpose. He added background music, a score stitched together from music straight out of his favorite films. If anyone paid attention, they might pick up a few hints from it all. Then he burned two DVDs.

Afterward, he sat back with a mug of rich Cuban coffee and watched the finished product, seven minutes and seven seconds of edgy drama. It excited him. There was just enough to terrorize but not inform, to seduce but not consummate. It would make Suki and Paul Nichols feel the way he had as a wannabe, waiting desperately for a callback.

He doubted if either of them would connect these events with him. Even if they thought back far enough, it was unlikely they would remember him, the tall, thin, twitchy guy who had auditioned for the male lead in *Bluff,* their produc-

tion company's antiwar film. In the final auditions, it had
come down to him and the man who eventually got the part.
No one had bothered to tell him when the selection had been
made; he'd heard it on the ubiquitous grapevine. He had
been so certain the part was his—he deserved it, it would
make his career—that no other Hollywood rejection had felt
quite like this one had, as if he were still trapped in his teens,
back in that Seattle trailer park, his old man's whipping boy.

He'd gone over the edge for days after that, moving
through a thick, red fog, driven by rage and bitterness. He
had stalked the casting director, Priscilla Branchley, an arrogant woman with pursed lips and glassy eyes who wore de-
signer clothes and carried a clipboard with her wherever she
went. One night he had slashed her tires; another night he'd
made repeated obscene calls to her home. Then he finally
got her alone, in her car, a knife at her neck, and instructed
her to drive into a particular canyon and pull off the side of
the road.

By the time she stopped, she was hysterical, her swollen
eyes beet red, great, heaving sobs exploding from her mouth.
She swore she had wanted *him* for the part but that Suki and
Paul had overruled her. When he pointed out she might be
saying that just to save her own ass, she told him to look at
her clipboard, the paperwork was still there. So he did.

*Suki says he has homicidal eyes, Paul thinks he's un-
hinged.*

But the truth had not set Priscilla Branchley free. Finch
had knocked her out, doused her and the inside of her car
with vodka, set fire to it, and rolled the car over the lip of the
canyon.

He'd fled Hollywood that night—not out of fear of getting caught, but because he knew he could never audition
again for anything. That he and his Hollywood dream were
finished. His enormous sense of failure brought back all the
years of living in abject fear of his old man, feeling like less
than nothing.

For weeks afterward, he had saved newspaper articles about the death of Priscilla Branchley and photos of her funeral. When *Bluff* was released the following year, the rave reviews often mentioned Branchley's brilliance and tragic death, believed to be an accident caused by alcohol. *Bluff* won some minor awards, had a respectable showing at the box office, and had catapulted the leading man from Nobody to Somebody, into a career that should have been Finch's. Suki and Paul had become the new darlings of Hollywood. Ultimately, it had brought all of them to this moment in time.

Kismet, he thought. Karma. Yes indeed. He loved the idea that because of his actions, Suki, Paul, and the cops were scrambling to figure out the 5Ws. In the movie business, these were the essential tools in understanding a character. *Who* was this character? *Where* was the action taking place? *When* did it happen? *What* was the dramatic conflict? *Why* did the character do what he did?

Finch put the edited scenes on a third DVD and switched screens to the live webcam in Adam's room. The kid sat at the laptop, his hair damp from a recent shower, a can of tomato juice open on the desk. On the floor around him lay clothes, towels, sheets he'd stripped from the bed. The cooler had been flipped on its side and the containers of juice and the few remaining snacks and pieces of fruit were on the windowsill. Dirty dishes and plastic utensils were piled on the floor, the bureau.

Goddamn slob, Finch thought.

Suddenly, Adam lifted his right hand and flashed a bird. He scooted away from the laptop, revealing the message on the screen in a 24-inch font: FUCK YOU ALIEN PERVERT VOYEUR.

How's he know I'm watching him? "Ditto, you little shit." Finch decided to make Adam wait a little longer for his breakfast and a refill on the cooler.

He packaged one DVD and put the other two into a storage tower with dozens of others in his collection. Rather than entrust the DVD to a postal system severely disrupted by the hurricane, he decided he would deliver it in person. But how and to whom? He wasn't sure yet.

Finch returned to the kitchen, disengaged the three locks, and stepped out onto the wraparound porch. A suffocating heat had seized the air, so thick and impenetrable that nothing moved—not a palm frond, a bird, an insect. It was as if a crippling torpor had infected everything. The water in the lagoon the house faced and in the canal at the side looked as flat, featureless, and shiny as aluminum foil and held the perfect reflection of the early morning sky, a blinding blue, cloudless. Not a boat or a plane in sight.

He headed quickly down the length of the porch, trotted down the stairs, and stopped between his two cars, a VW wagon and a Honda hybrid. Each was registered to a different fictitious person who had a credit history, Social Security number, address, and driver's license. In short, each phony person had *a life*. In the days before computers, when he and his old man had fled across the country from whoever his father had pissed off most recently, obtaining a new identity had been complicated, time-consuming, expensive. But somehow, his old man had managed to do it.

By the time Finch had fled Hollywood and needed a new identity, the world had changed considerably and he had the computer knowledge and the means to hack into systems to find ideal candidates. Then, while he worked in Silicon Valley, the birthing of home computers and Internet access for the masses had facilitated the process. Greedy hackers these days stole data on hundreds of thousands of clients from a single company, thus tipping off the feds. His thefts involved just one name from here, another name from there, not enough to alert anyone.

Spenser Finch paid off his phone bill and DSL connection every month. He paid taxes. He owned a small home in Miami, the VW Wagon, and, as far as the IRS was concerned,

was a computer consultant who earned about forty grand a
year. This amount was about what Finch took in for various
computer consulting jobs that he did throughout a given
year, for bogus offshore companies. Finch had no criminal
record. *Kevin Birch* owned the hybrid and a home in Wyoming
and was retired. He had a few investments on which he paid
minimal taxes each year. The Sugarloaf house was owned in
a corporate name.

He tucked the DVD into the visor of the hybrid so he
would be sure to take it with him to Tango, then hastened
back upstairs and into the blissfully cool house. As he prepared Adam's breakfast, he turned on the small TV set in the
kitchen. He had channel-surfed until one this morning, looking for news about Adam, but hadn't found anything. Maybe
seven hours had changed all that, he thought, and went to
CNN.

"We have a breaking story this morning," announced a
younger version of Connie Chung. Her perfect hair, flawless
skin, and red blazer testified to the power of correct choices
in fashion, dentists, nutritionists, and trainers. Finch turned
up the volume. "The thirteen-year-old son of Oscar-winning
actress Suki Nichols is missing and we're waiting for a live
press conference that is due to begin shortly. The story now
from Luz Hernandez, at our Miami affiliate."

A pretty Latina appeared, standing outside the Nichols
home on Tango Key. "This morning, the press and paparazzi
began converging on this tiny barrier island off Key West
that was damaged so severely in Hurricane Danielle. Ms.
Nichols and her husband, director Paul Nichols, and their
teenaged son, Adam, have lived on the island for the last two
years."

Pan of the house on the hill, tennis courts, swimming
pool, the ravaged trees at the back of the property. "The police believe that Adam disappeared sometime between eight
P.M. on July 26th and seven A.M. on July 27th, when a local

resident discovered the body of the Nichols housekeeper, Gladys Levereaux, who was shot in the chest."

A photo of Adam appeared next to a picture of Gladys, then the camera cut to the Asian woman in the CNN newsroom.

"Who was the resident who found the housekeeper's body, Luz?"

Back to Luz, who gripped her mike more tightly and tucked her shiny black hair behind her ears. "A businesswoman, Mira Morales. She's also a psychic who has worked with the local police and the FBI in the past. Her relationship with the family is unclear."

A psychic?

His mind scrambled back through all the material he had collected on Adam and his family, but he couldn't remember anything about their acquaintance with a psychic. Then again, he supposed big Hollywood types usually had psychics tucked away among their massage therapists, yoga instructors, gurus, and body trainers.

"We're going now to the press conference," Luz said, and the camera cut to the house, where Suki Nichols walked down the driveway to the gate, Paul at her side. Behind them were Mayor Dawson and a tall man whom Finch guessed was a cop.

Suki wore the clothes of a regular person—cotton skirt, blouse, sandals. Her thick blond hair, straight and struck through with sunlight, was windblown. But otherwise, she looked humbled, scared, uncertain of herself. When the camera zoomed in on her beautiful face, Finch saw that her eyes and mouth were pinched with fatigue. It delighted him.

Yet, as she stood at the mike, she pulled herself together in the same way that he'd seen other professional actors do. It was the subtlety of it all that he admired—a slight adjustment in expression, a quick brightening in the eyes, the suggestion that despite what was going on for her personally, she knew she had to get her message across. She was no longer an actress but the victim of a tragedy. You couldn't learn this, Finch thought. You either had it or you didn't. And maybe he never had had it.

"Good morning and thank you all your patience. Like so many others on Tango, we've been without power since the hurricane and keep our windows open at night. It's believed that Adam's kidnapper took him out his bedroom window. Our housekeeper apparently heard something, and when she went into Adam's room to investigate, the intruder shot her. I would like to ask that you respect our privacy during this difficult time. I'm going to turn the microphone over to FBI agent Wayne Sheppard and to Mayor Dawson."

Before she turned away from the mike, Suki flashed a thumbs up at the camera and mouthed something. *A-Okay*. That was what it looked like. Finch wondered if it was something she usually did during a live appearance, rather like Carol Burnett's tug at her earlobe at the end of her show, a signal to her mother that the show went well. Was this her signal to Adam?

Even if it was, so what?

The fed stepped to the mike first and said he would take several questions. Had there been a ransom demand? Where were the Nicholses at the time of Adam's disappearance? Were there any suspects yet? What was Mira Morales doing in the house when she found the housekeeper's body? This last question interested Finch, too, and he was disappointed when the fed replied that he wasn't at liberty to say. In fact, the fed didn't provide any new information, and Finch started to turn off the TV when the mayor stepped up to the mike.

He looked like a typical bureaucrat, except that he was dressed for the heat in olive-green chinos and a guayaberra shirt instead of a coat and tie.

"Since Hurricane Danielle, Tango Key has been operating under emergency management. Only fifteen percent of our power has been restored, just two hotels and one gas sta-

tion are open, we have no public restrooms, and only a hand-
ful of restaurants are open for business. In short, we can't accommodate several hundred reporters and journalists, their
vans and cars, and basic needs. So, all press people who don't
have accommodations must leave the island by six P.M. To
remain out here during the day, you will need a pass and to
get that pass, you'll have to show press credentials and ID."

Murmurs of protest went up from the crowd. Reporters
started shouting questions. A chopper flew past overhead,
sweeping in very low, and Sheppard and the mayor both
glanced up. Sheppard said something to the mayor, who
shook his head; then the fed walked some distance away
from him and got on his cell phone. Finch guessed the chopper belonged to the press, and wasn't surprised when it disappeared from view a few minutes later.

"If I may have your attention, please," Dawson went on.
"Passes can be obtained from the courthouse at the north
end of the island, on Toucan Street in Pirate's Cove. It's right
off Old Post Road. One member of each press party can ob-
tain passes for other members, as long as you have the
proper credentials to show for them. At the end of each day,
these passes must be returned at the docks, if you're taking
the ferry back to the mainland, or at the airport. They'll be
collected each evening, and new passes will be distributed
each day at both the docks and the airport. Any questions?"

"What about those of us who have reservations at the hotels?" asked one burly reporter.

"You'll still need a pass and you have to give the name of
the hotel and the room number. If you've flown in, we'll need
the make and model of the plane and the call numbers. You'll
have to wear your press pass around your neck at all times. If
you're caught on the island after dusk and don't have a place
to stay, the city jail will be your home for the night."

Finch smiled. Mr. Mayor was making this rather unap-
pealing for the press. But that was the point.

Finch's cell rang and Eden's number came up in the window. She probably was watching the same thing he was. He hesitated about taking the call. If he didn't answer now, though, she would call every five minutes until he did.

Get it over with. "Hey, hon, what—"

"Spense, Jesus, have you seen the news?"

"I just got up."

"CNN. Paul's son. He's missing." Her voice cracked. "He disappeared . . . around the same time I met Paul at the motel. He . . . they're saying he was kidnapped and my God, my God, I feel so responsible. If I . . ."

Hysteria, rising in her voice. "Calm down, Eden. You're not responsible for anything." *I am.* "You didn't cause this." *I did.* "You . . ."

"And this psychic they mentioned?" Eden rushed on. "I've heard about her. She's supposed to be incredibly good. I know people who have gone to her, who . . ."

"Psychics are bullshit."

"No, you're wrong about this woman. I've heard her name so many times I can't tell you."

"Look, even if she's as good as you've heard, so what? You're not guilty of anything." *But I am.*

"I . . . I guess I just feel guilty, you know?"

"I know. I understand. But there's nothing you can do about it, Eden."

"You're right. I know you are."

"Look, I've got an appointment in an hour and need to get ready. But let's talk later today. Maybe we can get together tonight or tomorrow."

"I've got to work for a few hours tonight. Call me before seven or after ten, okay?"

"Right."

"Love you, Spense."

"You too."

He had calmed her down, but had he convinced her of anything? Even if he hadn't, what could she do that might put him at risk? Nothing. Yet the conversation nagged at him.

Outside Adam's door, he grabbed the alien mask off the hook, slipped it on. Okay, so it had been a stupid idea, more fitting for a five-year-old than a teen. But it served its purpose.

He pressed the button on the clicker, the door opened, and he stepped inside. The chaos he'd seen on the webcam looked even worse here in the room. Adam was sitting in front of the television, watching CNN. "Hey, Mr. Alien. You believe in psychics?"

Finch laughed. "So you saw the broadcast too. I hope you're not banking your hopes on this Morales woman." He set the tray down next to the monitor. "Here's your breakfast."

"I need more ice and could use some more fruit. So you think all psychics are frauds?"

"Let's just say I maintain a healthy skepticism."

"Have you ever had a reading with a psychic?"

"Once. A man. He wasn't right about a damn thing."

"Well, skeptics walk away from readings with Mira with their brains dribbling out their ears."

"Really. And just how would you know that?"

"My mom had a reading with her and she was, like, blown away."

Interesting. He hadn't known this. The connection between the Morales woman and Suki disturbed him precisely because he hadn't known about it. "If she's so good, you wouldn't be here."

"Psychics aren't gods."

"So she's a fraud."

"You're not a god either, does that make you a fraud?" he spat.

Insolent little shit, he thought, and grabbed Adam's jaw, forcing the kid to look at him. "Let's be clear about a couple of things, Adam. You're here until I decide otherwise. That makes me God in your corner of the universe."

The kid stared at him, his mouth puckered up, cheeks sinking where Finch's thumbs dug into the flesh. When Finch was sure he'd gotten Adam's attention, he released his jaw. Adam didn't make a sound—not a gasp, sob, nothing. He lowered his eyes, swiveled his chair around, and raised the volume on the television, barricading himself behind a wall of noise.

Finch spent a few minutes straightening up, the blare of the TV filling the silence. He set out fresh towels and sheets, stuffed the dirty laundry into a pillowcase, tossed the clean sheets on the bed. Then he lowered the volume on the TV.

"Fresh sheets and linen. If you've got dirty laundry, dump it by the door. I'll bring in a fresh cooler."

"I do my own laundry at home."

"Good try, Adam. But you're not leaving this room. If you want to do your own laundry, you can do it in the bathroom sink and hang the clothes up in the shower."

"How come there are so many pictures of me and my family on this computer?" He jerked open a desk drawer and brought out one of the photo albums that had been stored in the closet. "And in this album?"

Excellent. Adam had searched the computer and the room. Finch had hoped that he would. Anything that kept a teenager engaged was good. And a teen on a quest for information was even better. He had removed any potential weapons before he'd taken Adam and knew he had been exceptionally thorough in that regard. Everything that remained in the closet provided fodder for the kid's search.

"Because I did my homework."

"And you're still spying on me." He stabbed a thumb behind him. "I figure back there somewhere you've got a hidden webcam set up."

Finch didn't confirm or deny it. Adam looked at him, his eyes glinting with something Finch couldn't read. "I know as much about computers as you do."

"I doubt it."

Adam clicked on the pictures file and brought up a photo of his father and Eden. Even though her face wasn't fully visible, it was obvious the woman wasn't Suki. "Who is she?" Adam asked.

"His lover." Finch took a certain satisfaction in saying it, rubbing it in that the Nicholses definitely lacked in the storybook-perfection department. "Her name's Eden."

Adam laughed, a harsh, grating sound. "Awesome. The lovers in the Garden of Eden. He's had a lot of lovers. That's what he does. Sneaks off with lovers and gambles and blows his money on fast cars and booze and that's why he can't direct anymore. He thinks my mom and I don't have a clue. So now he writes and teaches about directing because he doesn't know what else to do. He's pathetic."

The lack of emotion in his voice surprised Finch. "So you've got a dysfunctional family."

Adam shrugged. "Just a fucked-up old man." His eyes narrowed pensively as he glanced at Finch. "Like you."

"You don't know anything about me, Adam."

A sly smile shadowed his mouth, that indecipherable quality came into his eyes again. "You plan well. You researched everything before you brought me here. You're smart. And you really know computers, but you're not as smart with them as you think you are."

"Uh-huh. So you said. Give me an example."

Adam thought a moment, then rattled off a programming algorithm that left Finch speechless.

"You rewrote a lot of the programming code on this system," Adam went on. "You've got remote access to some other computers, like maybe my mom's? Or my dad's? The motherboard is a custom job, a really beautiful custom job, so I figure you work in the computer industry. Or used to work there. Or should work there."

Holy shit, Spense, he's got you nailed.

"I don't think you read many books, but you've, like,

studied my tastes enough to know what kinda stuff I read and what amuses me. You're obsessive-compulsive, have a thing about clutter. I could feel your reaction to the mess in here and I bet if I walked out into your kitchen, I'd find that every dish, every piece of silverware, every pot, every little fucking thing in your pantry has its place. I'm betting you've got some sort of fixation or obsession about a part of your body too. Compulsive types like you need to order their personal environments because their childhoods were total chaos."

Adam Nichols was sharp, for all the difference it would make in the long run. "Anything else?" Finch asked.

"Friend says your father did terrible things to you and now you're paying the price."

"So we're back to your imaginary playmate." Finch rolled his eyes and laughed.

"Since you don't believe I really have a friend, she's going to show you."

"Uh-huh. And exactly how is she going to do that?"

"I don't know."

"Of course you don't. It's all bullshit."

But as soon as he said this, Finch realized the room had gotten cooler. He wondered if the AC unit had malfunctioned. Since the hurricane, everything in the house was off-kilter. He went over to the closest AC vent and held his hands up to it. The air didn't feel any cooler than usual. "Something's wrong with the air-conditioning. I need to check the unit," he said.

"It won't do any good." Adam got up from the chair, pulled the blanket off the bed, wrapped it around his shoulders, sat down, and began eating his breakfast. "Friend's doing it. If you're going to stay in here, you'd better grab a blanket or a sweatshirt or something."

Finch ignored him and hurried over to the thermostat on the wall. It read forty-seven degrees, about twenty-five degrees colder than where he usually kept the thermostat.

Impossible. He jacked the thermostat to eighty—and the temperature abruptly dropped another five degrees.

This isn't happening.

He hastened toward the door, pressing the button on the clicker, but when he pulled on the handle, the door wouldn't open. He yanked again, kept pressing the clicker. Nothing, nothing. Adam now huddled on the chair, knees up against his chest, the blanket wrapped tightly around him. How cold did it have to be for your breath to be visible? In the thirties?

No fucking way this is happening.

Teeth chattering, hands trembling, his mind slamming against a wall of impossibilities, Finch struggled to think. He couldn't escape through the windows because the shutters were still in place, and the bathroom had no exit, except the skylight, which he couldn't reach. Yet, he knew there had to be a way out of here. He wouldn't be this careless.

Think, think, c'mon, you know the answer to this.

He ran back over to the thermostat. The temperature now registered a crisp twenty-nine degrees. Frost was forming on the windows. Adam had drawn the blanket over his head. Finch's own head began to ache, to throb. Already, an aura nearly blinded him, a visual white noise. He blinked, shivered. He knew what it meant. Knew what was coming. Finch fumbled with the clicker and stared at the keypad, trying to make sense of it.

Each button was coded to something. Number 1 for the door to Adam's bedroom, 2 for the lights, 3 for the computer, 4 for the DVD player and the Xbox, 5 for the front door of the house, 6 for the garage door, and 7 for the AC, 8 for . . . "Yes," he hissed, and pressed 8, the override that would allow him to open the door manually.

Finch weaved toward the door, feeling as though he were drunk or stoned. The lights in the room went nuts, flashing off and on quickly, like strobes. Music blared from the computer, voices blasted from the television, and every sound pierced his temples like knives.

He didn't know what was happening in here. All he wanted to do was escape it.

He pulled on the handle and stumbled out into the warmth of the hall. He jerked the door shut behind him, pressed 8 once more to cancel the override, pressed 1, and heard the telling click. He stumbled into the kitchen. Nausea gripped him, his stomach churned, he tasted bile in the back of his throat. The pounding in his temples spread across the top of his skull and then increased tenfold.

It's gonna be bad, real bad.

The peripheral vision in his left eye went south. He winked it shut and studied the bottles lined up ever so neatly on the counter. Which one held the real meds? The prescription meds? He couldn't remember and couldn't see well enough to read the labels.

You know the answer to this. Everything the kid said about you is true. Your kitchen is an anal-retentive's wet dream. Then his body remembered, his hand reached. Second bottle from the left. He was supposed to take two tablets at the onset of any migraine symptoms. He'd gone way beyond symptoms.

He gobbled three pills and fell onto the futon where he'd awakened earlier. Cool air flowed over him. AC air, not *weird* air, not whatever was going on in Adam's room. Then the agony seized him, clutched his skull in a vise, paralyzing him, and he was gone.

He is sick, feverish, and a hand touches his forehead, a light touch, loving and concerned. "Fever's going down, Spense honey. It's breaking."

"Stay with me," he whispers, and of course she does. She slides into bed next to him, fixes the covers over them, slips her fingers back through his hair, massages his scalp, his temples, and tells him a story.

"Once upon a time, there was a princess in a garden. She

was very small, this princess, no larger than a flower, and she wanted to leave the garden and see what else there was in this huge and magnificent world. So she went to the king and asked for his blessing, but the king wasn't happy about the thought of his only daughter venturing out into the larger world alone. . . ."

When Finch came to, he was crying.

10

Adam's Room & After

"What do you need?" Suki asked Mira.

They stood just inside the doorway of Adam's room, where *everything* had been disturbed since his disappearance. It wasn't just that forensics had touched and rearranged every object in here, but that Suki too had been here, that she and Paul had fallen back onto this bed and made such desperate and violent love. Would Mira see all that? Would Mira see her weeping over the gray bear? Would she see her argument with Paul and all that had followed?

She didn't care. She only wanted to find her son.

"I need something that's important to him emotionally," Mira said. "A stuffed animal, a T-shirt, book, DVD, anything personal. Metal and fabric are both good."

Suki opened the toy chest and brought out the gray bear. The Fids Bear, a toy that had been part of Adam's life since he was a year old. Her cousin, an eccentric man whom everyone in the family referred to as Fiddlesticks, had given it to him. The bear looked his age—one ear hanging by a thread, his gray fur worn almost smooth along the back, an eye gone.

"He got this when he was just a baby. Every year, the Fids

bear has moved down farther on the bed. When Adam turned eleven, the Fids went into the toy chest. But it holds a lot of emotional history." Suki set the bear on top of the toy chest, now filled with spare linens. "I don't know if it's useful to you, but one of the things Adam and I always say to each other is 'A-Okay.' Then we flash a thumbs-up."

Mira mouthed the words, nodding. "A mother/son mantra. I like that." She sat down on the chest, next to the Fids bear, and looked around. "Tell me something, Suki. Yesterday morning, when Paul found me here and called the police, the air in here turned bitterly cold. Did he tell you that?"

One more sin of omission. "No. He didn't mention it. What do you mean that it got cold?"

"The temperature plunged. I could see my breath when I exhaled. Frost formed on the windows."

"How's that possible? We still don't have electricity."

"Have you ever felt a presence in the house?"

"You mean, like, a ghost?"

"Yes."

"The house is haunted? Is that what you're saying?"

"It seems to be." Mira slipped off her sandals and walked barefoot around the room, describing yesterday's events. As soon as Mira described the blue flowered dress that Gladys's ghost had been wearing, goose bumps broke out on Suki's arms. She murmured that she would be right back, and hurried into the room where Gladys had slept whenever she stayed overnight. She threw open the closet door, rummaged through the clothes, and plucked out a hanger with a dress on it. She practically ran back into Adam's room. Mira now stood at the window, her fingertips sliding along the frame.

"Is this the dress you saw?" Suki asked. Pale silk, with delicate blue flowers on it. Suki had bought it for Gladys's last birthday.

Mira turned. "That's it."

"It . . . was Gladys's favorite."

"The woman I initially saw outside came through Adam's

closet door and helped Gladys pass over. She's the ghost here. The presence. And she may be connected somehow to what happened with Adam. She looked to be in her late thirties or early forties. I don't know if that's the age she was when she died or what. Anyway, when your husband was in the room, holding a gun on me, that woman returned."

Suki didn't know what shocked her more—that a ghost had come through her son's closet door or that Paul had pulled a gun on Mira.

"I don't understand," Suki said.

"Neither do I. But I think you should research the house, Suki. Find out who has lived here and who was living here when there was a fire. May I hold Gladys's dress?"

Suki removed the dress from the hanger, handed it to Mira, and tossed the hanger on Adam's bed.

Mira drew the fabric across her cheek, ran her hands over it, shut her eyes, and stood very still for a several minutes. It seemed to Suki that she hardly breathed. "She had bad arthritis in her knee," Mira said finally, and rubbed her own knee. "The right knee."

"Yes, that's right."

Now she dropped the dress and reached for the Fids bear. She pressed the stuffed animal to her chest, sat down on the bed, and stretched out, the bear cradled in the crook of her arm. Suki noticed that Mira's breathing changed. It deepened, slowed, and she flipped onto her side, one leg thrown over the other, a perfect copy of the way Adam slept most of the time.

"I'm dreaming," Mira said quietly. "It's a good dream. Then I hear something, a noise. Is it in the dream?"

Mira snapped forward, suddenly started screaming, then slammed back against the mattress as if someone had pushed her. She grunted, kicked, shrieked, writhed as though someone held her down against the bed, pinning her there, a butterfly under glass.

Suki realized she was seeing a reenactment of what had happened to Adam and stood there, horrified.

Mira's legs jerked in toward her body, then shot outward, as though she had kicked someone. She rolled across the mattress, her shrieks erupting in gasps for air. Suki pressed her knuckles to her mouth, powerful, almost crippling emotions sweeping through her. Then she rushed forward, toward Mira, and wrenched the teddy bear out of her grasp. "Stop. Please."

Mira blinked, the wildness gradually bleeding from her eyes, her face, and swung her legs over the side of the bed. She was rubbing her neck. "He injected Adam with something." Her arm came up, pointing at the door. "Then Gladys hurried into the room and . . . he shot her."

The bedroom door suddenly slammed shut, the bureau drawers snapped open and shut again, and then the bureau skated across the floor with such speed and power it left dark scrapes on the tile. A chair snapped backward and crashed against the floor. The closet door swung back and forth, a wooden pendulum.

"Sweet Christ." Suki scrambled onto the bed next to Mira. She pulled her legs up onto the mattress, whispered, "What's happening?"

Mira wrapped her arms around her legs, hugged them to her chest. "Stay still."

The closet door slammed open, crashing against the wall as if an invisible person inside the closet had lunged out into the room. The hangers trembled, shook, banged against each other, and clothes slipped to the floor. Mira grabbed the top edge of the quilt and pulled it around them. The bureau drawers kept shaking and rattling until they crashed to the floor, the closet door slammed open and shut, the screen in the window suddenly popped loose and fell outside. The window itself slammed shut so hard the glass cracked, fissures racing through it until it looked like a spider's web.

Now stuffed animals leaped from the toy chest and, like miniature supermen, took flight, soaring, dipping, then crashing into walls, diving into the closet, bouncing off the doors. The cord that held the actual model airplane in place abruptly snapped and the plane took off, soaring silently through the air, wings dipping one way, then the other. It swept in low over the bed and vanished through the open window.

The room crackled with energy that made their hair stand straight up, as though a tremendous charge of static electricity filled the air. When they pulled the quilt more tightly around them, static sparks jumped from the quilt's fabric.

The sparks seemed to trigger a chain reaction of events. A tremendous humming swelled in the air, a sound that grew in intensity and pitch until Suki could feel it in her teeth, the back of her throat, inside her skull. Everything that was still airborne abruptly dropped to the floor, the fissured glass in the window exploded inward, and the shards strewn across the floor lifted en masse, like a horde of shimmering locusts, and shot straight toward them.

Mira jerked the thick quilt over their heads and shouted for Suki to cover her legs as well. But she wasn't fast enough. Dozens of sharp missiles stung her lower legs. Mira threw herself toward the open toy chest, and pulled out more blankets and quilts. She tossed one over Suki's legs, pulled the other over herself. The humming reached a higher note. Suki gritted her teeth against the sound, but found it nearly unbearable. The inside of her skull felt as though bones were splintering; her eyes ached and burned and teared.

"Get out!" Mira shouted.

Suki leaped off the bed, holding the quilt over herself, and tore toward the door. Glass struck the quilt, her feet, her ankles, and seconds before she reached the door, it sprang open and she raced into the hall.

The door slammed, she heard the lock click into place, and she spun, realizing that Mira hadn't made it. Behind the door, the humming now rose to a fever pitch. Suki banged on the wood with her fists, kicked at it, shouted for Mira. But the door held fast, Mira didn't answer, and the humming now throbbed in Suki's head.

"I'm going to get help!" Suki hollered.

She dropped the quilt and took off up the hall, her ankles and lower legs bleeding from dozens of pricks in her skin.

For seconds after the door slammed shut, Mira stayed motionless beneath the quilt, her body braced against the assault of sound. The humming seemed to rattle inside her bones, in the fillings of her teeth. She stuck her fingers in her ears, but the sound penetrated the pores in her skin. Her entire body vibrated in rhythm with the humming, muscles and tendons strummed faster and faster by invisible fingers.

She never had intended to flee the room. She thought she could deal with this energy if Suki weren't present, but wished now that she'd run like hell. Mira frantically scooted back on the mattress, working her way toward the headboard and the open window, her closest exit. The intensity of the humming increased until her head throbbed, her ribs rattled, her larynx felt like it might explode.

Her back hit the headboard and she pushed up against it, felt something squish into the small of small of her back, and pulled it out.

The gray teddy bear. *Help me, Adam. This whole display is about you, so help me out here.*

The horrendous humming escalated to a shrill shriek that threatened to burst her eardrums. Mira leaped off the bed, the teddy bear clutched in one hand, a pillow in the other, and a brilliant light exploded directly in front of her, nearly blinding her. It elongated rapidly, like some special effect in a movie, and stretched and stretched until it narrowed into a horizontal funnel that shimmered and danced with pale green and blue light.

The same sensation she'd experienced outside in the driveway yesterday morning swept over her again. Was she in the throes of a massive breakdown? Was this a mirage? A hallucination? Was she dreaming awake? Was the funnel a physical or a psychic construct? She had no answers. So she approached it cautiously, and noticed that the intense cold and shrieking noise immediately diminished. Her teeth and bones stopped vibrating.

She held her hands in front of her, right hand still gripping the teddy, and touched the light. It felt warm and solid, yet when she exerted just a little pressure, her hands passed through the light—and into the long funnel. It felt strange, as if she had thrust her hands into a bowl of chilled Jell-O. Alarmed, Mira jerked her hands back toward her body, tucked the teddy under her arm, and extended her right leg. She allowed her foot to slide through the wall of light. Same sensation.

Hands again. This time, they vanished up to the elbow and she experienced an overpowering urge to step completely inside the light.

As she did so, she felt an excruciating pressure against her head, pressing down against her skull, squeezing at her temples, tightening along the seam of her jaw. Her ears popped, as if the barometric pressure suddenly had changed, the pain in her head eased, and she saw him.

Adam Nichols.

He was fiddling with something, but she couldn't see what it was. Mira shouted his name. He didn't look up, apparently couldn't hear her. *Am I unconscious? Tranced out? Is this physical? What?* She moved a little farther into the funnel and her vision expanded.

Details: a large room, with shuttered windows. Hurricane shutters? A laptop, bureau, bed, cracked bureau mirror. She sensed the building was on or near water. *Let me see it from the outside.*

Her ears popped again, she felt a rushing sensation—and

immediately found herself standing barefoot in warm sand, her toes digging into it, and a vast, shimmering expanse of water stretched out in front of her. Ocean? Canal? The air smelled salty, but it smelled that way everywhere in the Keys. The sun was so bright it burned away details. Mira turned and drank in the sight of the house. It stood on stilts, had two stories above it, lots of vegetation in the yard. *Address, I need an address, c'mon, please . . .*

Before anything could happen, she felt that bizarre rushing sensation again, but seemed to be hurling backward through time, space, dimensions. The funnel vanished, the air whooshed from her lungs, and she found herself flat on her back on the ground, blurred faces hovering above her.

MiraMiraMira . . . The sound of her own name echoed, rising and falling with the scent of grass, heat. She lifted up on her elbows and the faces around her snapped into clarity. Sheppard, Goot, Suki. Behind them stood Charlie Cordoba and Paul Nichols.

"I want her off this goddamn property," Nichols barked.

"Back off, Paul," Suki snapped. "I invited her here."

The only possible way she could have ended up on the ground outside Adam's bedroom window was if she'd dived through it. She didn't remember doing it. Didn't remember anything. One moment she was outside a waterfront house and the next moment she was on the ground. No memory connected these two events.

Mira sat up straight, knuckled her eyes, tasted dirt in her mouth. She pressed her hands to her thighs and tried to stand up, but her head spun. Sheppard helped her to her feet. "You okay?" he asked.

"I need some paper. And a pencil."

Off came his pack and out came a number-two pencil and a small sketch pad that was exactly the size she needed. "You just happened to have a sketch pad?"

He shrugged. "Old habits die hard."

Meaning: He had monitored her so often in the past that

he now included a sketch pad and pencil in the provisions he carried in his pack. "Thanks," she said.

She got shakily to her feet and weaved away from him, from everyone, and rounded the corner at the back of the house. She went inside the screened porch, kicked off her sandals, and sat at the shallow side of the pool where there was shade. Mira dropped her tired feet into the water, set the sketch pad on her lap, and began to draw what she recalled of the house.

She sketched with her eyes half-closed or shut altogether, her hand seeming to move of its own volition. She realized that in memory, she could see through the glaring brilliance of the sun glinting against the water. She could see a seawall, a dock that jutted out into a canal, trees and tropical shrubbery in the yard, wooden fences. She sketched all of it, and when she looked up from the pad, there was a bottle of water in front of her, a bowl of fresh fruit. And the gray teddy bear. Suki stood nearby, biting at her lower lip, arms pressed to her waist.

"You've been sitting there for ten minutes, so lost in what you're drawing that you didn't even hear me say your name, Mira."

Was she saying this because she wanted an answer? Mira wondered. Or was it just an observation? "Suki, from the time you left the room to when you and the others were standing over me, how much time passed?"

"Maybe five minutes, probably less."

Mira held out the sketch pad. "This is where Adam is. It looks like a house in the Keys." It looked, she thought, like every house in the Keys. "It's as specific as I can get right now. He's okay, I saw him again." *Saw him from inside the funnel of light.* But she knew how that would sound and didn't say it. "I can get more, but not right now. I'm spent." She pushed to her feet.

"Can I give you a ride somewhere?" Suki asked.

"Thanks, but I've got my bike." Right now, all she wanted

to do was get out of here. "I'll give you a call when I'm ready for the next round. In the meantime, let me know if you hear anything."

Suki accompanied her outside, neither of them speaking until the screen door banged shut behind them. "What's this bastard want, Mira?"

"I don't know. Like I said before, look into the history of the house, that's the most I can tell you right now. We'll talk," she said quickly, and hurried off to find her bike.

It was on the front porch where she'd left it. As she mounted it, Charlie Cordoba came around the corner of the house. "You can't leave by the road. The press will descend on you."

"I'll go through the trees."

"And make sure you don't leave the island unless you give me a call first, Mira."

She burst out laughing, couldn't help it. "Right."

Cordoba hooked his thumbs inside his belt and stood straighter, taller. But even straighter and taller didn't make him tower over Mira. A badge, a gun, and hubris: That was the sum total of his authority over her. "I'm serious, Mira."

"I know. You see an opportunity for publicity on a high-profile investigation that might boost your own status. That's pathetic, Charlie."

Color flared in his cheeks. "I could arrest you right this second on suspicion of murder."

Good God, what was with this guy anyway? "Okay. So arrest me. Where's my murder weapon? What's my motive?" *And who's my attorney?* "Suki hired me. The press will have a field day with that one. You want to fuck with me, Charlie? Then, great, take me in. Haul my ass in." She leaned toward him. "And watch your entire case go down the tubes in seconds."

Just then, a balding man with hunched shoulders took shape off to Cordoba's right. He wore a red Ralph Lauren shirt, riding jodhpurs tucked into shiny black boots, and clutched a riding crop. *You tell him Graham said he's ashamed of him,* the man said to her.

"And by the way, Charlie, Graham is standing next to you in his riding clothes and says to tell you he's ashamed of you."

Mira didn't have any idea who Graham was, but Cordoba did. He looked around uneasily, then gave a quick, nervous laugh. "Yeah, right. Sheppard buys your ghost bullshit, Mira, but I don't."

Graham spoke again. Mira listened, nodded. "Graham wants me to remind you of what happened the summer you went to stay with him in Coeyman's Hollow. Something about the sound of the train and that eerie green light moving along the tracks that night."

Blood drained from Cordoba's face and he wrenched back from Mira, stammering, "You're a . . . a . . . carny show, Mira, that's what the hell you are."

Graham was trying to butt in, urgently tapping Cordoba on the shoulder with his riding crop. The crop kept passing through Cordoba. Mira thanked Graham and asked him to go away, please. Cordoba was oblivious to all of it. He shook his finger at Mira, babbling threats.

Mira ignored them both and interrupted Cordoba. "Here's the deal, Charlie. Boy is missing. Housekeeper was killed by same guy who has boy. Simple, right?"

Then she pedaled away, leaving Cordoba and Graham in a cloud of dust.

The path through the pines and ficus trees at the back of the house wasn't meant for bikes. Within the first few moments, the bike hit the huge remains of an uprooted ficus tree, a booby trap. The bike skidded, she lost her balance, went down, and knocked the air from her lungs. She lay there, struggling to catch her breath, the wheels on the bike spinning noisily in the hot, still air. A bluejay flitted past, twittering with annoyance at her intrusion.

Why was it that every time she tried to leave this property

she fell? She rolled onto her side, drew her legs up to her chest, and tried to reconcile her performance in the house with the check for two hundred grand from Suki. She wasn't so sure her abilities were worth that kind of money. She couldn't perform on demand. The information was either there or it wasn't, and none of it came with guarantees. How could she justify what Suki was paying her?

She heard sounds behind her and glanced around to see an electric cart bouncing down the path, Sheppard at the wheel. Light and shadow ebbed and flowed across the planes and angles of his face. "The path isn't fit for bikes," he said, pulling to a stop beside her. "You okay?"

"Yeah, thanks."

"How about a lift to the store?"

"That'd be great."

Sheppard swung out of the cart and beat her to the bike. He pulled it upright, pushed it over to the cart, lifted it into the backseat. Mira climbed into the passenger seat, careful not to touch anything that might hold a residue of Sheppard or of anyone else who had been in the cart. She kept her hands pressed to her thighs, puzzled about his real motive for following her into the woods. It wasn't just because he was worried about her taking the path on a bike.

"Suki said she hired you," Sheppard said as he got in and started the cart.

"And you disapprove?"

"Me? No way. But I imagine that right about now, she and Nichols are arguing about it and Cordoba is scrambling to figure out what you know and how he's going to deal with all this."

"It'd be better if Charlie just got the hell out of the way and let you and Goot do the job. But he won't do that. He's going to be trouble for you, Shep."

"Did the room turn cold like it did yesterday when you and Nichols were in there?" he asked.

"No. I didn't see anything this time, but this presence,

this spirit, seems really pissed off. It was like she was having a temper tantrum."

"Suki showed me the sketch you did of the house. She's going to give me a copy. Whatever information you give her, Mira, we need it too."

"I'm working for her, not you, Shep. It's her choice to share it or not."

His glance was sharp, quick, annoyed. "What the hell does that mean?"

"Just what it sounds like. *She* paid me, not the Bureau."

He seemed a little shocked by this, that her abilities weren't available to him just for the asking. Maybe, she thought, this moment for Sheppard was the equivalent of what she'd felt yesterday morning when she'd realized he was wearing a shirt she'd never seen before. Her life *was* moving forward, after all. It buoyed her spirits, and she suddenly felt more generous toward Sheppard.

"I don't see why Suki would refuse to share my insights, Shep. She wants to find her son."

Then, out of the blue, he blurted: "Mira, have you ever seen a mermaid?"

Of all the questions he might have asked just then, this one never had crossed her mind. "Uh, no. Why? Have you?"

"Yeah, I think so. I think a mermaid saved my life this morning." He stopped the cart and the story spilled out.

Mira sat there in complete shock, her left brain coughing up all sorts of reasons that Sheppard might imagine seeing a mermaid: breakdown, sorrow, trauma, all of it related, naturally, to their split and the abrupt change in his lifestyle. Wishful thinking. Whether Sheppard had imagined the mermaid or actually had seen her smacked of some profound inner shift in his belief system. And quite frankly, she felt a bit envious that he had seen something, experienced something, that she never had.

"What do you think it means?" he asked.

Was he asking her as a psychic or as an ex-lover? Did that

distinction even matter? "It reminds me of that movie called *Whale Rider.*"

He nodded, remembering. "Last spring. Yeah, you, Nadine, and I watched it."

"It's like you've ascended into myth or something, Shep."

"It felt more like a plunge than an ascension." He tapped his fingers against the steering wheel. Sunlight streamed through the treetops and lit up his beard like a Christmas tree. Around them, crickets chirred for rain. "On the island of Chiloe, in Chile, the belief in mermaids is so widespread, Mira, that it's part of the culture. You see images of mermaids on ashtrays, restaurant walls, coffee mugs. The local fishermen believe that when they see a mermaid facing out to sea, it means the fish are running and the day's catch will be good. When she's facing the shore, the fishing will suck."

Only Sheppard would talk about mermaids in Chile, she thought. "We don't live on Chiloe."

"But we live on an island where mermaids are part of the local mythology. Like the Loch Ness monster in Scotland. Or the Mothman in West Virginia. Maybe I just tapped into Tango's cultural belief system or something. Didn't Jung say something like that was possible?"

Jung had said a lot of things about mythology, but she didn't know enough about the specifics to comment. What struck her most about Sheppard's confession was his obvious need to place his experience into some sort of context that would reassure him he had not gone off the deep end. That was new. And disturbing. Despite all the weirdness they had experienced in their five years together, he never had doubted his own experiences and beliefs about what was real.

"If it were a dream, how would you interpret it?" she asked. "What would the images suggest to you?"

"That the investigation into Adam's disappearance is about to take me into unknown territory." He paused, thinking, frowning. "That I'm diving deeper into an unknown world." He looked over at her. "Into your sort of world, Mira, where the unthinkable is actually business as usual."

"You believe I live in an unthinkable place? Thanks a lot."

"You know what I mean."

"No, Shep. I don't know what you mean. Explain it to me." *Talk to me.*

His large, beautiful hands tightened on the steering wheel. "Consensus reality says that mermaids don't exist. But I know what I saw, what I experienced. It's the same thing for you. When you intuit something the rest of us can't see, you don't doubt your impressions. Like with Tia Lopez."

Okay, she'd been waiting for this one, a reference to the final blow to the relationship. Lopez, who had killed five abusive men, including her husband, had been busted out of jail by the same man who had broken into Mira's home during Danielle, allegedly seeking a refuge from the storm. He and his girlfriend, Lopez's cell mate, had inflicted such chaos and damage on Mira and her family that it was inconceivable to Sheppard how Mira could side with Lopez in the end and allow her to escape.

"Excuse me, Shep. But Lopez saved my life, Annie's life, Nadine's life. She put her ass on the line for all of us."

He ignored what she said and rushed on. "Because of something you saw about Lopez, you were absolutely certain that she deserved to go free," he went on. "Fuck legalities. You were right and everyone else was wrong." He sounded angry, looked angry. His nostrils flared. "Well, that's how I feel about this. I *know* what I saw. A mermaid saved my ass."

So doubt about his own experience—his sanity—wasn't the issue, she thought. Anger at her was the issue. "Why're you so pissed off? I'm not passing judgment on your experience."

"Because I don't want to know about the weird and the strange, Mira. I don't want mermaids and things that go bump in the night."

In other words, he didn't want *her,* that was what he was

really saying. She digested this and all its implications, then swung her legs out of the cart. "Thanks for the lift. I'll take the bike the rest of the way." She pulled the bike out of the back, knew at a glance that she wouldn't be able to ride it the rest of the way downhill, and started pushing, fuming. She just wanted to get away from him.

"Mira, hey, hold on," Sheppard called after her.

Mira ignored him and kept on walking, faster, faster. Moments later, Sheppard caught up to her. "What'd I say? What is it?"

He didn't get it. "I feel like walking."

He caught her hand. "Stop, okay? Just stop and talk to me."

The moment he took hold of her hand, circuits opened up between them and images of his life without her rushed into her. She jerked her hand away. "She's drop-dead gorgeous, that woman you had dinner with."

Sheppard was taken aback—she saw it in his expression—but recovered quickly. "She was a cousin of Graciella's, an opinionated jerk, and by the end of the evening I told her off. And I really wish you wouldn't do that."

"Do what?"

"Peer into me like that."

"Hey, *you* touched *me*." She threw out her arms, the bike crashed to the ground. When she continued, she heard the fury in her voice. "This is what I am, Shep. I'm sorry that you think it's weird and strange, but I can't turn it off to suit you."

He looked so miserable and confused that when he suddenly put his arms around her, it caught her by surprise. He drew her against him and everything inside her screamed that she should pull away and start running, but she couldn't. It felt so good for him to hold her, to hear the strong, steady beat of his heart, that she brought her arms around him and for long moments, they stood in the shade and fragrance of the pines, hugging each other.

And suddenly, all her repressed desire for Sheppard came roaring to the surface, and he felt it and slid his fingers through her hair, tilted her head back, and kissed her. A soft, tenuous kiss at first, then deeper. His hands slid to the small of her back, to her waist, up under her shirt, and against her skin and her breasts. Desire sprang from every pore in her body. The rest of the world fell away from her. She forgot where they were, the weeks of loneliness, everything but the physical sensations of Sheppard's hands against her.

They stumbled until she was backed up against a tree, in the deep shade of the pines. His mouth went to her throat; they fumbled with zippers. Her shorts slipped down her thighs, the fabric rustling like dry leaves against her skin. She was breathing hard; blood rushed and pounded with the fury of a stormy ocean surf inside her head. The trunk of the tree scratched and clawed at her shirt, but the waves of intense pleasure that coursed through her obliterated everything else.

Distantly, a horn blared, and the sound of it snapped her back into the here and now. She pressed her hands to Sheppard's chest, pushing him back. "Wait," she said hoarsely. "What's this mean? Why're we doing this?" She jerked her shorts back up, straightened her tank top. "This doesn't solve anything. I'm still the thing that goes bump in the night."

Sheppard stepped away from her, fumbling with his clothes, tucking his shirt in. He looked disconnected, rattled, like a man emerging from a dream so real that he couldn't quite figure out where he was or what had happened or why. "I didn't mean to . . . aw, fuck it," he spat, and all his walls went up, she could almost see it happening. When he spoke again, his voice was controlled, cool, all business.

"Do you want a ride or not?" he asked.

"That's *it*?" she burst out. "*Do I want a ride?*"

"What do you want me to say, Mira?"

Now that his walls had gone up, she couldn't reach him. "What just happened? Was this a booty call, Shep? Is that it?

You're horny, so you followed me into the woods? Just what do you want from me anyway?"

"I don't know."

"Well, good luck figuring it out."

She jerked the bike up from the ground, hopped on it, and pedaled madly downhill, the bike's wheels banging against roots, rushing through pine needles and leaves.

11

The DVD

The early afternoon heat shimmered against the black asphalt and beat down against Finch's head, heightening his awareness of the tiny, hard ball of discomfort at the base of his neck. A remnant of the migraine. A reminder, he thought, that at any moment an explosion of pain could bring him to his knees. Under the baseball cap, his scalp was sweating. Beads of perspiration rolled down the sides of his face. Another half hour out here, he thought, and he would look like he'd gone swimming with his clothes on.

He pedaled his bike along Mango Hill Road, aware that he was doing exactly what experts contended that criminals often did—returning to the scene of the crime. But he had something to deliver. The DVD rested snugly in one of this pockets. That aside, he enjoyed wading into the swelling throngs of press and paparazzi that swarmed across the road, sharks in a feeding frenzy because of something *he* had done. It made him feel like a god, something he'd never felt in Hollywood.

In the unlikely event that he ran into anyone he knew, he doubted he would be recognized. He looked like a nerd out for his constitution. Baseball cap, sunglasses, olive-green shorts, a pale green T-shirt with a Chinese symbol on it that meant *Go with the flow.* Early on, he had learned the art of disguise—how to look and behave like a good kid, a model student, a preppie, whatever a situation required. When you changed schools every several months, you learned to act in order to survive.

For as long as Finch could remember, his old man had sold used cars and hadn't been able to hold down a job longer than four or five months because of his excessive drinking. So whenever he got fired, they would pull up stakes and go on the road again to the next town and the next and the next. And at each place, Finch would attend a new school, if he attended school at all. He rarely made friends. What was the point of friends when you knew that in a few months you would move on and never see them again?

By the time they reached Seattle when Finch was four-teen, he had lost count of the schools and towns and was largely self-educated. At fifteen, he took the GED, passed it, and enrolled part-time at a junior college. He worked thirty hours a week in an electronics shop, saved his money, and bought his first used Radio Shack computer for a thousand bucks and his first car for another thousand. He refurbished it, rebuilt the engine, and for a year after that, he and his old man shared little more than living space in the trailer.

His old man hated Finch's independence, hated that his old tactics for keeping Finch in line no longer worked. His verbal abuse rolled off Finch without touching him. On the rare occasions when his old man had come after him with fists, Finch had stood up to him. And because he was taller, heavier, and no longer afraid, his father had backed down. When Finch was sixteen, he moved into an apartment with a friend. His old man had threatened to report him as a run-away, but he never had. He was glad to be rid of him.

Six months or so after he'd moved out, he returned to the trailer one night to pick up the rest of his belongings. Unfortunately, his old man was there, blasted, and had come after Finch with a broken bottle. He was so drunk that when Finch had leaped to the side, his old man had stumbled and knocked himself out. Finch set fire to the trailer and never looked back.

Fire: the universal purifier.

He felt a sharp flare of pain at the base of his neck, vestiges of the migraine, a warning. Finch cut off thoughts about his old man.

In the eighteen years since the migraines had started, Finch had become something of an expert in the affliction. Migraines affected more than twenty-five million people in the U.S. alone, tended to run in families, and were three times more common in women than in men. They could last from several hours to several days, often began during adolescence, and certain triggers could bring on an attack. Fatigue. Stress. Foods containing nitrites or MSG, aspartame, chocolate, aged cheeses, and alcohol. Caffeine withdrawal, menstruation, and weather changes were also blamed.

His major triggers were stress, chocolate, and weather changes. During Danielle, when the barometer had fallen so precipitously, he'd been reduced to a throbbing, blurring mass of pain for at least ten hours. The onset of a severe thunderstorm could do it, and so could sudden temperature extremes. But the biggie was stress, always stress. Sometimes, the migraines came on suddenly, with no aura or warning at all. He would be brushing his teeth, for instance, and his peripheral vision would vanish. He would be unable to see the hand that was brushing his teeth and one entire side of his face would disappear from his vision.

Other times, he was free of migraines for weeks. During his first several years in Hollywood, he'd had a migraine maybe once every eight or nine months. In the six years he'd worked in Silicon Valley, he'd had three straight years without a single migraine.

During those years, he'd loved his job, made a lot of

money, felt successful, and had a stable relationship with a woman who also worked in the computer industry. Then she ran off with her married lover and the migraines started up again. Since he'd started watching the Nicholses a year ago, the migraines had gotten worse. A pretty clear message, but he didn't want to think about it.

Before he rounded the curve in Mango Hill Road, he saw the first of the press vans, their satellite dishes glimmering in the hot light. They were lined up on either side of the road, one after another, extending along the curve and then beyond it, nearly as far as he could see. Hundreds, he thought. People congregated, some of them filming news segments, others just standing around with their bottles of Perrier and Evian, waiting for whatever might happen next.

For a moment, a kind of wild urge came over him and he felt like waving his arms and shouting, *Hey, morons, I'm in your midst!*

As he neared the Nicholses' home, the vans and cars multiplied like rabbits. He figured there were at least seventy-five people jockeying for space on the sidewalk directly at the bottom of Mango Hill, all of them with video equipment aimed at the house. Waiting for the next sighting. Salivating for the big bonus, the big promotion, the treasure at the end of the rainbow.

No one paid any attention to him. He simply navigated his way up the street.

Just beyond the house, a man stood outside a van with TELEMUNDO written across the side in bold blue. His tripod and camera, set up on a patch of grass in front of the van, were aimed at the house. Finch leaned forward on the bike as he passed, making sure that he was well below the camera, and stopped on the other side.

"Hey, man, what's going on?" he asked.

"You haven't heard? Suki Nichols lives there." He had a slight Hispanic accent. "Her son is missing, the housekeeper was murdered."

"Yeah, I know all that. But my God, there're hundreds of people here."

The guy laughed. "She's big news. This is big news. The rags pay major bucks for close-ups on shit like this. Then you toss in cable news, network news, Internet blogs. Everyone's scrambling for the inside dope."

"You know anything about the woman who found the body?"

"Local businesswoman, Mira Morales, supposedly a psychic."

"I hear she's the real thing. But I'm still wondering how she found the body. I mean, what was she doing in the house? Is she, like, a friend of the family or something?"

"Don't know. There're a lot of questions about all this and everyone out here's looking for the answers."

"Well, I'll tell you one thing. I've been in that house. I know the layout. And the weakest point is that utility-room door. That's how the intruder got in."

The man suddenly took a renewed interest in Finch. "You live on the island?"

"Been here for years."

The man stuck out his hand. "Enrique Ruiz, with Telemundo. Good to meet you, Mr. . . ."

"Jones. Jim Jones."

"You're kidding. Jim Jones? Like the Kool-Aid guy?"

Shit, bad choice of names. "Blame my mother."

"Well, my mother named me *Punto* Ruiz. Try going through life with *that* name, right? *Point.* I finally changed Punto to Enrique, which got whittled down to the English version, Ricky." He stuck out his hand. "Nice to meet you, Jim. So you know the Nicholses?"

"Just socially. I used to install security systems in houses, right? And that utility-room door of theirs was vulnerable from the get go. Couple that with no power, no parents at home, an aging housekeeper, no ferocious guard dog, most

of the perimeter fence down . . . anyone could get in there."
And do what I did.

"So are the rumors true?" Ruiz asked, leaning closer to
Finch. "That Paul Nichols screws around?"

Finch laughed, a low, conspiratorial laugh. "What do you
think? Guy like that, tons of money, famous director, women
around him all the time . . ."

"Yeah, but c'mon, man, if you have Suki Nichols in your
bed, you don't need to look any farther. They said there hasn't
been any ransom demand, so what do you think this guy
wants?"

"Beats me." He thumbed the air over his shoulder. "One
of your buddies down there a ways asked me to give this to
the guy at the Telemundo van." He slipped the DVD from his
pocket, held it out.

"What is it?"

Finch shrugged. "He didn't say. Hey, maybe it's that lot-
tery ticket photo, right? Good-bye Telemundo, hello Tahiti."

Ruiz laughed. "Then no one in this crowd would pass it
along. Can you point out who gave it to you?"

Finch craned his neck, pretending to scan the crowd.
Ruiz's cell purred, saving him the pretense.

"Excuse me," Ruiz said.

The moment he turned his back to take the call, Finch
pedaled away, smiling to himself, then laughing out loud.

The afternoon heat seemed to bear down against Sheppard
like some massive, invisible hand. The quicker he tried to
move along the line of cars that snaked from Old Post Road
into the dock's parking lot, the greater his need to find an air-
conditioned room, a cold shower, even a patch of shade. The
breeze that usually blew in off the bay between Tango and
Key West had died twenty minutes ago. The air stank of ex-
haust from the fifty or sixty press vehicles that idled in line,

waiting to turn in their passes and be cleared for the ferry trip back to Key West.

Sheppard and one of Cordoba's men worked the line for the four-thirty ferry, and Goot and another Cordoba lackey worked the line for the five o'clock ferry. There would still be two more lines for two more ferries before the six P.M. curfew for the press. He didn't know if he could stand it that long. Let the mayor get out here and do this. Better yet, bring Cordoba out.

As each press pass was returned, the names were checked off on an alphabetized list that had been issued by Mayor Dawson's office. Invariably, people griped about the bureaucratic red tape and asked where they were supposed to pick up tomorrow's passes. All the hassle, Sheppard thought, would put a dent in tomorrow's press turnout and that could only be a good thing, especially for him and Goot.

A man with a press pass around his neck trotted over to Sheppard, huffing and puffing, his face bright with sweat, his cheeks flushed from the heat. He looked like he was on the verge of a stroke.

"Excuse me. Are you Agent Sheppard?"

"Yeah." Sheppard glanced at the man's press pass— *Enrique Ruiz, Telemundo*—and figured him for one more guy looking for special privileges. "What can I do for you?"

"I, uh, need to pass along some information."

"About what, Mr. Ruiz?"

"A guy named Jim Jones."

"Jim Jones." Yeah, okay.

"Not that Jim Jones," Ruiz said quickly, and his story spilled out.

As soon as Ruiz related that "Jim Jones" had said the intruder had gotten into the Nicholses' place through the utility-room door, Sheppard's internal alarms went off. That fact intentionally hadn't been released to the press. Suki's statement about Adam being taken out of his bedroom window implied the kidnapper had entered that way too, a deliberate ploy on their part to keep certain facts hidden. How would an alleged local resident know about the utility-room door without inside information? Sheppard could count on his fingers the number of people who knew it—half-a-dozen law enforcement personnel, Tina Richardson, the Nicholses, and Mira. None of them would release that kind of information to the press.

"Would you be able to describe this man, Mr. Ruiz?"

"Sure. But . . ."

"To a police artist?"

"Absolutely. Except for his eyes. I never saw his eyes. He wore really dark sunglasses. What I wanted to tell you is that—"

"What would you say is this man's most distinctive physical feature?"

Ruiz's expression hardened. "Hey, can I have a couple seconds here before you bombard me with more questions?"

"Uh, yeah. Of course. Let's sit in my car, where it'll be cooler."

Once they were inside the Jetta, Sheppard turned the AC full blast. Ruiz brought out a portable DVD player and a DVD. "This Jones guy said one of the other press people asked him to give this to the Telemundo guy."

He turned on the DVD player and Sheppard stared in horror at the little screen, his mind racing, sucking in the details. The lighting. The music. The voices. Neither he nor Ruiz said a word until the sequence ended.

"I haven't said a word to anyone about this, Agent Sheppard. I've got kids. I know how I would feel if this boy were mine."

How differently this might have turned out, Sheppard thought, if "Jim Jones" had given the DVD to a reporter who lacked scruples. "Look, Mr. Ruiz. I appreciate what you've done, coming forward like this, and I know what you're thinking right about now, that here goes your story. I'm asking you to keep all of this confidential and in return, you'll be the first person I call with tips on progress in the investigation. We'll put you up for the night and cover your expenses."

Sheppard quickly called Goot to let him know what was going on. "I'll get one of Charlie's men to fill in for you," he said. "And I'll meet you at forensics in an hour."

Once they were en route to the forensics building, Sheppard dug his cassette recorder out of the glove box, turned it on, and asked Ruiz to relate everything that had happened. It was immediately apparent that Ruiz had an excellent memory for details.

"I thought the whole thing was pretty strange and on impulse, I turned my camera around and taped him as he pedaled on down the road."

Sheppard leaped on this. "You still have that?"

"Sure. I didn't get much, just his back."

"That's great." Better than great. No telling what sort of magic Tina and her people would be able to conjure. "We'll run it through forensics."

"And I get it back, right?"

"When we're done with it."

Ruiz suddenly snapped his fingers. "I just remembered something else. He asked me about the woman who found the body and said he'd heard that she's good, as a psychic, right? But he was wondering how she'd found the body—in other words, how she happened to be in the house."

Ever since the press conference this morning, Sheppard had wondered how the press had gotten Mira's name. But he'd been so insanely busy that he hadn't had a chance to think about it. Now here it was again and he knew he had better pay attention. The people who knew that Mira had discovered Gladys's body were the same group who had known about the utility-room door. But there were some probable additions to the list—like Ace and Luke. They revered Mira, though, and wouldn't do anything that might harm her. So forget them, forget everyone, he thought, except for Charlie

Cordoba and Paul Nichols, the two people he trusted the least in all of this.

A few minutes later, Sheppard turned into the parking lot of the forensics building. He let Ruiz off in front, then drove off to find a parking space. As soon as he was alone, he called Mira's cell number. When he got her voice mail, he hung up and called Ace.

"Yeah, man," Ace said. "What's happening?"

"Ace, are you interested in a part-time job?"

"Right now part-time is my full name. What do you have in mind?"

"Sticking to Mira like Velcro."

Ace snickered. "So now I'm Elliot Ness?"

"Only if you still have a permit to carry a gun."

"Still got it. Define Velcro."

"CNN identified Mira as the woman who found the housekeeper. A supposedly random guy on a bike got into a conversation this afternoon with a reporter from Telemundo and Mira's name came up."

Silence on the other end, then: "You're asking for a quantum leap here, Shep, but if I'm hearing you right, you think this random guy is *the* guy and may be looking to have a little chat with Mira?"

"That's the gist of it."

"C'mon, you know what you're asking me to do here, Shep? It'd be easier to stick to the dog like Velcro than to Mira. She won't even accept my offers of a ride to the store. I try to stuff food down her throat so she's not so skinny and she complains that she's going to die of obesity. Please. And when she, Luke, and me are together, weird shit happens and we all get freaked. I don't know if I can do this. Besides, she'll pick up that I'm hiding something from her."

"What weird shit?"

"Poltergeist weird shit. Last night. In the trailer. And on top of it, Tom supposedly paid her a visit. You know, dead hubby Tom. *That* Tom. And he took her to see Adam, so she could see the kid was alive. Then Suki Nichols shows up and hires her for six figures."

Six figures? Mira never had been paid that kind of money for her psychic work. Never. Talk about pressure. It explained why Mira had said what she had when they were out in the woods. *I'm working for her, not you.* "Just do the best you can, Ace. Drop by the office tonight so I can pay you."

"Right. And I'll bring some Velcro," he murmured, and disconnected.

Ace was as close to Mira as anyone could get, he knew how to shoot the gun he owned, and he wouldn't hesitate to use it to keep Mira safe. Sheppard would pay him. In cash. No record, no paper trail, no proof. That way, Cordoba or any other bureaucrat like him wouldn't be able to toss it back in his face someday.

The Tango Key forensics lab couldn't compare in scope or size with the Bureau's main forensics facility in Quantico, Virginia. But whenever Sheppard needed something yesterday, when he needed efficiency, precision, and insight, the Tango lab provided it. Its facilities handled DNA analysis, trace evidence, computer/Internet fraud, and latent prints, Tina Richmond's baby. In addition to latent prints, Tina's unit also handled photographic analysis and sketch art.

Sheppard and Goot were in her office on the second floor of the building that housed the lab, standing in front of a 24-inch computer monitor, watching the seven-minute film for the third time. It unfolded in slow motion now so they could take a closer look at each frame.

"He obviously edited the film," Tina said. "And was very careful about removing anything that might give a clue about his location. But it appears that Adam is being fed and that he has a lot of stuff to keep him busy—books, a laptop, an Xbox, and an environment that's comfortable."

"The lighting is consistently artificial," Sheppard remarked.

"Except for here. . . ." She paused the film, then moved forward and paused it again. "And here. Streaks of natural lighting."

"He never shows a window," Goot said. "Why not?"

"Because we might see something identifiable," Tina replied.

"Or because there are hurricane shutters on the windows and that's why we see just a few streaks of natural lighting," Sheppard speculated.

"A lot of places in the Keys still have shutters on the windows," Tina said. "But a lot don't. That would help us to narrow down the possibilities."

"The music selections," Sheppard said. "What do they tell us?"

Tina brought up a separate window on the computer. "They're all snippets of musical scores from films. We've identified music from six of the eight films. *The Fugitive, One Flew Over the Cuckoo's Nest,* and *Hollow Man* share themes of alienation and isolation. *Death Wish, Fatal Attraction,* and *Dirty Harry* are revenge movies."

"Okay, so he feels alienated and isolated," Goot said. "That's not news. Most sick pups feel that way. And he's saying that revenge is his motive? Sure, that's possible."

"In the three alienation-theme movies, the protagonist was a good guy caught in difficult circumstances," Sheppard said. "In *The Fugitive,* Dr. Kimble didn't kill his wife, but everyone thought he did so he had to go on the run. In *Cuckoo's Nest,* we all know McMurphy wasn't nuts, but the establishment thought he was. In *Hollow Man . . .*"

"That character isn't as clear-cut," Tina interrupted. "But if we look a little deeper, to the poem that inspired the film . . ."

"T. S. Eliot," Sheppard said.

"You got it." She flipped open a folder and took out copies of Eliot's poem.

It had been years since Sheppard had read Eliot. But as soon as he read through the poem, an excitement bubbled up inside of him.

"Between the idea and the reality," Tina said quietly, reciting the poem from memory, "between the motion and the act, falls the shadow. For Thine is the Kingdom." She paused. "He *is* the shadow. And the shadow is God, at least in my understanding of this poem."

"A man who thinks he's God." Sheppard nodded. "It fits."

"So what's God look like?" Goot asked. "We have anything from the police artist yet?"

"Well, this artist's sketch is based on Ruiz's description of Jim Jones." She played the keyboard. "We've gone this route before, guys, when Annie was kidnapped. The technology has improved a lot in a year. But this time we've got just a sketch to play with rather than actual photos, so it's trickier." Her fingers played the keyboard and the artist's final, colorized rendition of "Jim Jones" came up on the screen.

A Caucasian between the ages of thirty and forty. Slender, elongated face. Narrow chin. Full, expressive mouth. His eyes remained a mystery. He appeared to have a scar above his left eyebrow. His dark hair was conservatively cut.

"Based on the images in the DVD and the video clip Ruiz provided, we know that Jones is probably six feet or a little taller," Tina explained. "His legs are muscular, suggesting that he's in good physical shape. Maybe he works out. I ran this sketch through our database, using an updated version of the software that helped us identify Annie's kidnapper. It searches for certain matching facial characteristics."

"With those shades, he looks like Tommy Lee Jones in *Men in Black*," Goot remarked.

Tina laughed. "Funny you should say that, Goot." She brought up a photo of Tommy Lee Jones as Agent K in *MIB,* and enhanced his face. "Same sunglasses. I think the resemblance is intentional."

Sheppard made a mental note to check local gyms and video stores.

Tina hit several more keys and a lineup of mug shots appeared. "Here are the eight closest matches that the program found."

A quick glance told Sheppard that none of the eight was an exact match. But two looked eerily close to the final sketch. "Numbers four and six," he said.

Goot agreed. "What've we got on them?"

"Number four." Tina brought up a larger version of four's mug shot. "This guy did three years for armed robbery in Miami and before that, he did time for grand larceny. He was released two years ago, did parole in Jacksonville, completed it, and his present address is unknown."

"A guy who thinks of himself as God doesn't steal."

"Unless he demands a ransom," Goot added.

"If he demands a ransom, then I'm going to have to rethink my gut feelings," Sheppard said. "What about number six, Tina?"

"Meet Spenser C. Timble, age sixteen or seventeen in this photo. He lived with his father, Ray Timble, in a trailer outside of Seattle, left after he got a GED, apparently moved in with a friend. The trailer burned, the old man died of smoke inhalation. He apparently had been drinking pretty heavily. Anyway, the son came under suspicion, but was never found and nothing was ever proven."

"Then why's his photo even in a database?" Sheppard asked.

"Because if we fast-forward several years, we meet Spenser C. Wickett." She brought up another photo, an older version of Timble. "During the nineties, he spent six years in Silicon Valley and made a fortune off stocks. Charges were brought against him for attempted vehicular homicide—he apparently tried to run over an ex-girlfriend. But she dropped the charges and not long afterward, he sold his stock hold-

ings and left California with five or six million. He hasn't
been heard from again."

"He died?" Goot asked.

"No death certificate was ever filed. According to the
IRS, he paid his 1999 taxes in March of 2000, but that's the
last the IRS ever heard of the guy. I ran his Social Security
number, checked with Ma Bell, property records in South
Florida, the credit bureaus, customs . . . and hit dead ends at
every step of the way. No Wickett."

"Damn," Sheppard murmured. "You did our work for us."

Tina shrugged. "You know how I am. Once I catch a
scent, I can't let go of it. The Silicon Valley firm he worked
for started out producing business software, but has expanded into other areas. We use some of their products in
forensics." She handed Sheppard a folder. "Everything I uncovered is in here, including fifty copies of the sketch."

"What did he do between Seattle and Silicon Valley?"
Sheppard asked.

"Unknown. He probably had another identity."

Sheppard gave Tina a quick hug. "Thanks for all your
help."

"You going to release the sketch to the press?" Tina asked.

"Not yet." Sheppard looked over at Goot. "I think it's
time we worked the phones and hit the sidewalk with copies
of this sketch."

"Sounds like a plan, amigo."

Outside, Sheppard and Goot paused on the front steps.
The brutal sun was releasing its hold on the sky and slipping
down behind the trees to the west. By nine P.M. tonight,
Sheppard thought, it would be only a few degrees cooler,
maybe in the high eighties, and the generator at Goot's place
wasn't powerful enough to keep the AC running. That meant
Sheppard would be sleeping on the futon in his office again.

"How wide a net are we casting here?" Goot asked.

"Every gym and video store from Tango Key to Big Pine."

Goot whistled softly. "Let's take it island by island. And first we need lists."

"There's only one gym on Tango and three video stores. But based on what Mira said, I think it's unlikely this guy is on Tango. Let's save some time here. We'll do Tango tomorrow and start in Key West this evening and work our way north. The Barnes & Noble there has power, sandwiches, coffee, and wireless access, so we can download the names and addresses for gyms and video stores."

"I'll drive."

As they strode across the parking lot, Sheppard slipped a quarter from his pocket, thought a moment. "Tails is yes, heads is no," he said aloud.

"This looks like a Mira technique."

"Actually, it's an Annie technique. Quick divination, she calls it."

"What's the question?"

"Is Spenser Wickett/Timble holding Adam on Tango Key?" He tossed the coin, caught it, slapped it down on the back of his hand. "Heads."

"So he isn't." Goot frowned, eyeing the coin with suspicion. "And this works?"

"Nine times out of ten."

"Let me try it." He brought out a quarter. "Is Wickett Timble whatever his name is our man?" A big toss. The coin landed tails up on the ground.

"A resounding yes," Sheppard said.

"Unless this is the one time out of ten when the toss is wrong."

"Yeah, there's that."

But for the first time since Adam's disappearance, Sheppard felt certain they were on the right track.

12

In the Woods

The workmen had left, Mira had turned off the generator, and, for the first time in hours, she was alone in the bookstore, standing in the center of the blissful silence. A soft evening light filtered through the front windows, providing enough illumination for her to see the newly laid floor. Progress, she thought. The walls and the floor were now finished and the roof was supposed to be done within the next two weeks. With any luck, she would be ready to reopen in the fall, in time for the tourist season.

If there *was* a tourist season this year. Unless Tango Key was brought fully back onto the grid, nothing would be happening at her store or anywhere else on the island. And so far, the power company had given only rough estimates about when full power would be restored.

She locked the front door, shrugged on her pack, and hurried back through the stifling emptiness to the yoga room. The only damage in here had been from water that had seeped under the door from the main part of the store, and it wasn't serious because the floor was tile. The roof had held, the walls hadn't leaked or blown down. Maybe the word

Nadine said at the end of each yoga class had protected this room: *namaste—the light in me greets the light in you.*

The tap of her sandals against the floor echoed and she felt an acute pang of nostalgia for the months before the storm. At that time, her bookstore sales were at an all-time high, Nadine's daily yoga classes were jammed, Annie was in a good space, Sheppard had moved into her place, life was good.

And now?

Pity party, whispered that scolding inner voice.

She stepped out the rear exit, into the alley, and locked the door. Not that there was anything to steal inside. She just didn't want to come in here tomorrow and find homeless people camped out on the floor. She probably would feel so guilty about it she would allow them to stay or would decide to forgo books entirely and open a soup kitchen.

As she climbed onto her bike, an eerie sensation crept through her, the kind of thing that made her skin prickle and raised the hair on the back of her neck. She glanced quickly around. Shadows pooled along the edge of the alley, where an overflowing Dumpster verged on the edge of collapse. The stink of garbage suffused the air.

On the other side of the Dumpster, a thicket of trees, bent and twisted by Danielle's winds, looked like a group of arthritic old people struggling to escape the bogeyman. But she didn't see anything human.

For just a moment, though, movement in her peripheral vision caused her to look quickly to the right. Something—someone—was materializing there in the shadows. Tom again? Cordoba's jodhpur-wearing ghost, Graham? The woman from Adam's room? The nanny? Suki's father? Hepburn? Mira glanced away, refusing the contact.

She pedaled up the alley between her store and the restaurant next to it and headed for the Tango park. Here, the bike trail would take her half a mile north, then she would have to cut along a dirt road to get to her side of the island. Even though she had a flashlight mounted on the bike's handlebar, she wished she had left the store earlier or had accepted Ace's offer of a ride.

Mira touched her pocket and felt the comforting shape of her Motorola phone, complete with a camera, e-mail, and Internet browsing. A compact little world, she thought, and wondered if the technology had evolved out of the crash at Roswell, New Mexico, in July 1947. The theory was hardly new. Conspiracy nuts had been talking about it for years and there were hundreds of blogs these days that dealt with all things alien. Mira, like Fox Mulder, always had sensed there was truth to these theories, so that wasn't anything new either. The big question was why she should think about all this now.

She pedaled faster, crossed the street to the park. In the first two weeks after the hurricane, the bike trail had been impassable, blocked by fallen trees and debris left behind by the waters that had flooded the downtown. Most of that debris had been hauled off—while most of the debris piled in front of homes had not. The county claimed that the storm had created two years' worth of refuse and that they simply didn't have the manpower or the money to haul it all off in a month. And yet, on her daily walks, she had ventured into the mayor's neighborhood and noticed that *his* streets were totally free of debris.

The trail started a gradual climb uphill. Just a few cars passed in either direction. Not much was happening downtown after five. Eight or nine restaurants and bars were open after dusk and all but two of them were running on generators. Most people she knew didn't eat out now. They saved their cash for essentials.

Headlights coming up behind her illuminated the deserted trail ahead and threw the trees on her right into a surreal relief, exposing the new growth on the branches, tiny leaves that looked like green fuzz. Mira kept expecting the car to pass her, but it chugged along behind her, as though it

didn't have any power on this incline. She looked back and
the driver clicked on the brights, forcing her to look away.

"Bastard," she muttered, and abruptly swung the bike into
a sharp U-turn and pedaled back in the direction from which
she'd come. Mira caught a brief glimpse of the car as it
passed, still moving in the opposite direction—small, sleek,
some sort of sports car. She pedaled quickly across the road,
unease tap-dancing across her heart.

The cross road she'd hoped to take to the west side of the
island still lay another half mile up the hill. To disappear
here would mean plunging into a densely wooded area
where many of the trees had been stripped bare by Danielle
and were, only now, showing new growth. Unfortunately,
new growth wasn't enough to hide her.

Another glance at the road. The sports car had turned
around and was headed back this way. So had the driver
made a wrong turn? Realized he was on the wrong road? Or
was this something she should be worried about?

She didn't pick up anything one way or another. She
rarely could when it involved just her. But she didn't intend
to take chances. Mira leaped off the bike, pushed it into the
trees, and ran alongside it, moving deeper and deeper into
the woods. It was quickly apparent that she couldn't keep
pushing the bike. The ground was too uneven, riddled with
roots and fallen branches. And forget riding the bike, she
thought, and quickly slid the flashlight out of the holder, set
the bike down in the leaves, and took off on foot, the flashlight's beam aimed at the ground.

She worked her way toward the heart of the woods, where
the trees were larger, had leaves, and grew more tightly together. The squeal of brakes pierced the stillness and Mira
broke into a run, crashing through the underbrush, certain
now that the driver was coming for her.

And that it was Adam's kidnapper.

Because I opened the door.

Mira weaved around piles of dead branches, leaped over

fallen trees. Despite the fact that she was in good physical
shape because of all her walks, blood pounded in her ears
and sweat rolled into her eyes. She tripped once and went
down on her hands and knees. She remained like that for
long, uncomfortable moments, straining to hear anything
besides the buzzing of mosquitoes that swarmed around her.

Whack, whack, pause, *whack, whack.* Machete? *Jesus
God, run like hell. Or hide.*

Hide where?

Just ahead, moonlight spilled into an area of fallen pines.
Bordering it stood a clutch of banyan trees, their massive
trunks and long, twisted arms reminiscent of the Ents in
Lord of the Rings. Maybe these trees would talk and move
and carry her home.

Whack, whack.

She ran along the edge of the clearing, keeping to the
shadows, and stopped close to the banyans. Six of them,
growing in an erratic semicircle. A seventh banyan, uprooted by the storm, lay on its side, a pathetic, dying giant,
its leaves brown, shriveled, thin, and as fragile as some ancient parchment. Two of the others had lost most of their
leaves, had branches like broken arms, and seemed to be
leaning the way the wind had been blowing. The three trees
in the center had gone bald at the very top, but in the middle,
the branches and leaves were thick, exuberant.

Struggling against a rising swell of panic, Mira turned off
the flashlight, clipped it to a belt loop in her shorts, removed
her sandals, and slipped them into her pack. Then she
climbed onto the fallen tree and scrambled several yards up
the massive trunk. She rolled onto the balls of her feet and
grabbed onto the lowest branch of the closest banyan, lifted
her legs, and brought the soles of her feet to the trunk of the
tree.

She started swinging, harder, faster, and moving her feet
higher and higher on the trunk until they found a groove in
the branches. Mira scrambled up, up, up into the thickest

leaves, where smaller branches curved and twisted, providing ample handholds, footrests, places to lean against.

She found a secure foothold when she was in the bushiest
part of the tree, and wrapped her arms around the trunk,
hugging it so tightly that the odor of moisture and antiquity
inundated her senses. The muscles in her arms ached from
the sudden exertion; her eyes and throat flashed dry. It was
as if his proximity were sucking away her body's moisture.

Now she heard him moving through the woods with all
the subtlety of an enraged giant, the whacks of the machete
rhythmic, echoing.

If he looked up and saw her, if the branch on which her
feet rested suddenly cracked and gave way, if her cell phone
rang . . . No, she had put it on vibrate, she clearly remembered doing that. One thing in her favor.

*Keep going, guy, keep moving, don't look up, leave me
alone.*

Somewhere distant, a motorcycle revved its engine. Closer
in, she heard the *whacking* sound again. Then it stopped.
Everything went still, except for her heart, slamming around
in her chest like a tennis ball. It made so much noise she was
afraid he might hear it.

"Mira, come out and play," he called.

Goose bumps exploded along her arms, fear coiled in her
belly. Exactly what he intended, she thought, and pressed her
cheek against the sweet-smelling trunk, praying that he
would move on. Willing him.

Whack, whack. Then: "I know you're here, Mira. I found
your bike. You're not that fast on your feet. You hiding under
here?" *Whack.* "Oops, was that your leg? Nope. Too bad.
But it's not your leg I want, you know. I want what's in your
head. They say you're good." *Whack, whack, whack.* "They
say you're the real thing. Worked with cops, the feds, the
whole nine yards. I looked you up on the Internet. They say
you found your husband's killer. Never mind that it was five
years after the fact. You found him. That's impressive. Yes in-

deed. I'm impressed." *Whack.* "She hired you, didn't she? Suki Nichols hired you to find her son." *Whack, whack.* And he started laughing. "But I'll find *you* before you find the kid. Trust me on that."

Mira's head pounded, she squeezed her eyes shut. His voice flowed through the clearing and up through the soles of her feet like a hot liquid, connecting them. Images flashed through her—of the house she'd drawn at Suki's, of Adam in that shuttered room.

Then she had a vivid image of his face, but it wasn't human. It looked like the alien popularized by Whitley Strieber's book *Communion,* a gray face with huge, black wraparound eyes, two little black holes for nostrils, a dash for a mouth, skin as smooth as a baby's. Metaphor. But what did it mean? That he felt *alienated*?

Whack, whack.

"Here's the thing," he went on, and moved into her field of vision, a madman in the moonlight wearing some sort of mask—*an alien mask, that's it, that's why I thought of Roswell*—and shaking his machete like some wacko shaman who, any second now, would turn into something else, a wolf, a coyote, a giant bird. "I know who you are. I know where your store is. I know your grandmother lives with you, that you have a daughter about the same age as Adam, and that your husband, Tom, died when your daughter was three. I know more about you, Mira, than you will ever know about me." *Whack.* "And if you keep up with this bullshit, I'll plunder your life and make you wish you were dead." *Whack.* "Are we clear?" he shouted.

Then: silence.

She breathed in the smell of the banyan and talked herself through a mounting panic. Annie and Nadine were in Miami. No way this man could find them. Her home number was unpublished—and at the moment, inoperable. He wouldn't find her address through the reverse phone directory. But in the event he located her house some other way, she shared a trailer with two men who owned guns and wouldn't hesitate to use them.

And while all of that was great and certainly in her favor, it didn't do squat for her immediate situation. She was stuck forty feet up in a tree, in the middle of a wooded area flanked by Old Post Road, relatively untraveled in the post-hurricane world at night. If he realized where she was and came after her with the machete, she had nothing in her pack with which to defend herself.

But she had something better than a weapon. His location. And he was too arrogant to see how he had exposed himself by coming after her. Mira slipped her phone out of her pocket, sent Sheppard a text message.

Kidnapper followed me. Am hidden 40 ft up in banyan between e/w old post wooded area. He has machete.

A response returned within seconds:

Stay till I text u. Did u c his car?

Mira typed:

Sports car

But as soon as she wrote this, Mira sensed something wrong about the car, but couldn't pinpoint it any more than that.

On our way.

Whack. "I'm like Jack Nicholson in *The Shining,* Mira. Still here. You thought I'd left. But I'm a patient man. I can wait."

His voice drifted on the currents of heat, the waves of

stillness. In lieu of touching him or something he had touched, Mira sensed she could read him through his voice by tuning into a frequency of sound rather than of touch.

She carefully slipped her cell phone back into her pocket and began to alter her breathing. She suddenly felt like Schrödinger's hypothetical cat in the quantum world, both alive and dead, here and not here, and understood that many possible versions of these events existed.

If she went back to where it had all begun, that day in May when Suki had come into her store, then there was a version of events where Mira hadn't read for her, where the door between her and this man never opened. And there was another scenario where she never stumbled upon the Nicholses' house that morning, never had the vision that had prompted her to enter the house.

More recently, reality had split off at the moment she'd left her store. In one possible version of events, she had accepted Ace's offer for a ride back to the trailer and gone home without incident. In a second version, the man had come up behind her while she was on the bike and had snatched her. In yet another scenario, the man had caught her on the ground and she hadn't made it into the tree. In a fourth version, she fell out of the tree, and in a fifth, she got out of this mess. There might be dozens of other possibilities, but only one that mattered, escaping.

She allowed herself to sink into his voice, to tune into its frequency, then opened herself up a little at a time, hesitant to take in too much at once. She saw a little conch house, two people making love, and then a boat of some kind, blurred, hazy, as though she were seeing it in a dream. She sank deeper. . . .

They speed through the desert, the man and the boy, the old rusted heap of a car spitting out air that is barely cool.

The boy is sweating, nauseated by the heat, the speed, the blurring landscape of sand and cactus. "I'm gonna be sick," the boy says, and suddenly doubles over, vomiting on the floor of the car.

The man swerves to the side of the road, the tires shrieking and whining against the hot pavement, and slams on the brakes. "Jesus God, what a fucking mess you made. Clean it up." He smacks the boy's head with a roll of paper towels. "Now."

"I . . . I . . ."

The man leans across the boy, hurls open the door, and shoves him into the heat. "Finish puking out there."

The boy stumbles forward, then falls to his knees and gets sick again. The man marches around to the passenger side of the door and punches the boy in the side of the head. He falls to the right and just lies there, groaning. . . .

A screeching siren severed the connection.

Two minutes after Sheppard and Goot arrived, more choppers swooped in out of nowhere, bright, burning lights spilling across the wooded area and the roads that surrounded it. A dozen cruisers converged on the area, sirens blaring, lights spinning, brakes screeching. Doors flew open and men in SWAT gear leaped out, Charlie Cordoba among them. A little Hitler, barking orders, directing his men this way and that.

"I told you it was a mistake to call that asshole for backup," Goot muttered.

"I told him *backup,* surround the woods, and I told him *quiet.* I didn't mention choppers, SWAT teams, a goddamn production. Check out the sports car before Charlie's men get to it, Goot."

"I'm on it."

Sheppard hurried over to Cordoba, his blood pressure soaring. Before he could say a word, Cordoba spoke.

"Shep, the place is surrounded. The fucker is trapped."

"The fucker is *gone*, Charlie."

He looked indignant. "You don't know that."

Sheppard threw out his arms, a gesture that encompassed the whole glaring mess of lights and noise and bullshit. "You blew it. We could've had him and you blew it. Call your men off. Now."

"I don't take my orders from—"

Sheppard grabbed Cordoba by the front of his miserable shirt, and jerked him forward. "Yeah, you do. If you want to be in the loop, Charlie, you take your orders from me."

Cordoba's eyes turned homicidal, he wrenched back. His glare was filled with contempt, rage, and a myriad of other emotions that Sheppard had no intention of deciphering. He finally touched the mike on his lapel. "Hold your positions." He covered the mike with his hand. "Where do you want them?"

"Fanning out toward the dock, south toward the nearest marina, and anywhere within a mile of here. Since he needs a boat to leave, the choppers should sweep out across the island, alert for any vessel heading away from Tango."

Cordoba gave a curt nod, issued his instructions, covered the mike again. "You say he's gone and you're basing this on what?"

Sheppard held out his cell phone, showing him Mira's last text message: *He's gone.*

"Yeah, I figured it was something like that," Cordoba spat, and turned away in disgust.

When the first siren had torn apart the stillness, Finch had known it was for him, that Mira must have called or e-mailed or sent a text message to the cops. Stupid of him not to think of that. But then, he hadn't planned for Mira the way he had planned for Adam.

Finch hurled the machete into the trees and took off, sprinting through the woods to where Mira had left her bike. The sports car, now abandoned by the side of the road, had been stolen from the ferry parking lot, where some schmuck had tucked his keys in the visor, secure in his certainty that no one would dare take his pretty little car. So the cops would find the car—but no prints—and that would distract them for a while.

He pedaled madly away from the woods, the alien mask tucked in his back pocket. The bike sped up and down side roads that would lead him into downtown Tango and to the cove where he had tethered his skiff. Now, distant but closing in fast, he heard the *whoop, whoop* of choppers. Best to lay low, he decided, and detoured into the alley behind Mira's store. He hopped off the bike and pushed it quickly into the stand of trees behind the overflowing Dumpsters.

Finch was winded and stood for a moment in the shadows, catching his breath, scanning the alley. Due to the damage to downtown Tango Key, nothing within four blocks of the ruined pier was open at night. Good thing. He would get into the store and stay there until an hour or so before curfew began. What better place to lay low than inside her store? No one would think to look for him here.

He set the bike on the ground, shrugged off his backpack, unzipped it, brought out his flashlight and a small packet of tools. Just in case. Flashlight on, he darted across the dark alley and stopped at the building's rear door. No handle, just a lock. No problem. He had it picked within twenty seconds.

He entered a large room with mats stacked against one wall. Against another wall stood cartons of books, dozens of them, maybe hundreds. Posters of flexible women in an array of yoga postures decorated the other walls. Just looking at their postures made his back hurt.

He went through another door and into a huge room with

empty bookshelves. The floor was new. The walls had been recently plastered. And the roof, he thought, dropping his head back, still sported blue FEMA tarps.

Nothing to steal in here. The only possible reason for locking the door was to keep people like him out.

His sneakers squeaked against the floors, the noise echoed. The flashlight's beam swung from left to right, exploring, penetrating into the dark recesses. He passed the curved counter, an empty display case, everything new, waiting to be filled with books once the roof was done.

To the far left, he spotted another door. It was locked. He picked it in even less time, slipped inside, shut the door behind him. He shone his flashlight around. An office. A bit too warm, but snug, safe. He opened the rear exit door and saw a generator tucked away in a vestibule, then the loading dock beyond it.

He was tempted to turn on the generator, worried that it might be heard, but dismissed the thought. No one was around to hear it. He turned it on, plugged in a light, the fan, and Mira's lonely PC. Then Finch made himself at home in the comfortable leather chair, booted up the computer, and rubbed his hands together like a gleeful kid who knew he was getting away with murder.

"Right here," Mira said, pointing at the spot where she had left her bike. "This is where I dropped it and started running."

The powerful hurricane lanterns that Sheppard and Goot held cast a wide swath of light across the ground. "You're sure?" Sheppard asked.

"Positive."

"That explains how he got outta here," Goot said. "I'll alert Cordoba that we're looking for a guy on a bike."

Mira suddenly realized why something about the sports

car had bothered her earlier. "The car he drove. It was stolen."

"So he either left his car at the Key West dock and came over on the ferry, or he came on his own boat," Sheppard said. "Goot, make sure Cordoba has people posted at the dock and at every marina on the island."

"I thought we told him that."

"We need to keep reminding him. We're moving in on curfew, so if this guy is still on Tango, he may try to get off in the next fifty minutes. And pass out those sketches from forensics."

"Right."

Goot hurried off, leaving Mira and Sheppard alone. He asked, "You feel up to showing me where you hid?"

What she really wanted was to shower, eat, sleep, and not necessarily in that order. But in the last several minutes, it had occurred to her that she was in the process of reinventing herself. She hadn't climbed a tree since she was six and yet, she had scrambled up a sixty-foot banyan and managed to stay hidden for more than an hour. She had tuned in on the man who had terrorized her and done it without touching him or anything that he had touched. Although that had happened before, this time it had happened spontaneously and not because she had willed it. Even more curious, she had tuned in on him without taking on any of his physical ailments. Then there was the value a client had placed on her abilities. Two hundred thousand dollars. And even if it never happened again, it had forced her to see herself in a new light.

Sleep, food, and a shower could wait. "Sure. You have an extra flashlight?"

He dug one out of his pack, handed it to her. As she retraced her path through the woods, something nagged at her, something about the vision she'd had of the young boy in the car speeding through a desert. But she couldn't isolate it.

"When did you realize you were being followed?" Sheppard asked.

Mira explained her unease upon leaving the store. "But I wasn't really sure until the car doubled back."

"Ever since your name was released to the press, I've been afraid something like this would happen."

Mira thought she detected something else in Sheppard's voice, something he wasn't saying. "Let me guess. You asked Ace to keep an eye on me. That's why he called and offered me a ride home. That's why he and Luke canceled their trip up to the preserve."

"I didn't realize they'd canceled anything."

"I'll take that to mean you're guilty as charged."

"Never try to fool a psychic," he muttered.

"I appreciate the effort, Shep, but rather than paying someone to protect me, let's just find this shit before he finds me or kills Adam."

Moonlight now filled the clearing. A slight breeze had risen that strummed the branches of the trees, creating a kind of hum, an eerie music. Night sounds she hadn't noticed earlier now suffused the darkness—the chirr of crickets, a chorus of frogs, and the haunting hoot of an owl.

Mira stopped under the banyan where she had hidden, glanced around, and walked over to the approximate spot where the man had stood when she actually had seen him. "Here. He stood right about here."

"Let's take a look around."

As they searched the immediate area, Sheppard questioned her for specifics, details. She cut to the chase. "He taunted me while I was hiding, threatening to wreck my life if I didn't leave this investigation alone. He guessed that Suki had hired me. He said he wants what's in my head, my ability. He's searching for something, Shep, and figures a psychic can help him find it."

"Searching for what? Do you have any idea?"

She started to say no, but suddenly realized that the desert vision held the clue. "Maybe something he can't remember or figure out about his childhood."

"Look."

Sheppard's light impaled an upright machete, the blade sunk deeply into the ground, a dark twin of Excalibur, she thought. "You won't find any prints on it. Or in the sports car."

"We'll check just the same."

He snapped an evidence bag over the handle and started to pull it out of the ground. "Wait," Mira said. "Let me. It's the first thing we've gotten that he's held."

Sheppard stood aside and swept his arm toward the machete. Mira stepped over to it, hesitated, her breathing already deepening. *Give me the rest of it,* she thought, then brought her hands to the evidence bag and the wooden handle that it covered.

The bright light glints from the shiny blade as it rises and falls, hacking away at a mass of tangled trees and vegetation. The manual work is oddly satisfying, the evidence of progress immediate. Already, he has chopped the fallen trees in the side yard into manageable pieces that he'll haul to the curb and pile on top of the other debris.

The screen door bangs open and shut. "Hey, hon, how about a cold beer?"

He straightens, wipes his arm across his forehead, and flips the machete away from him. The blade lands upright in the ground. Then he turns toward the woman now standing on the porch in tight denim shorts and a halter top. As always, he's struck by her beauty. All that copper hair, the dash of freckles across her cheeks, the glow of her pale skin.

He joins her in the porch hammock, a colorful weave that swings gently in the heat, and tips the beer to his mouth. Then he rolls the chilly bottle across his face.

"Hey, if you want to cool off, I can connect the AC to the generator for a while."

It isn't air-conditioning that he wants. He wants her. He turns toward her, slides his fingers through her hair, drawing her face toward him, and slips his other hand inside her halter top, cupping her breast, freeing it from the fabric, and she laughs softly.

"Someone's going to see us."

"No one's around." He murmurs the words with his mouth against her breast and his other hand now sliding between her legs.

Suddenly, light explodes in his peripheral vision. He breaks away from her, gripping the sides of his head as the agony bites through skin, bones, and starts sucking him dry. And then he is elsewhere, in a car, and his small fingers claw at the glass and his mouth opens wide in a silent scream and . . .

Mira jerked back from the machete, her horror as extreme as the hard, relentless pounding in her temples. "A redhead." She kept stumbling back until she tripped over something on the ground and went down. "His girlfriend's a redhead. I think she lives in a little conch house here in the Keys. She's a knockout and he's crazy about her. Sexually crazy about her. I'm not sure about his real feelings aside from the sex." She massaged her temples, rubbed the back of her neck. "There's more. The boy in my vision yesterday on the Nicholses' property."

"The kid in the car?"

She nodded, knuckled her eyes.

Sheppard dropped into a crouch beside her, the machete forgotten. "What about him?"

Her hands dropped into her lap. "Shep, he grew up to become the man who took Adam."

PART TWO

Mile Zero

Go on till you come to the end; then stop.
—Lewis Carroll

13

Suki & Paul

Suki, stretched out on the bed in Adam's room, watched the
hands of the battery-operated clock click along until it was
four minutes past midnight. The hot, stagnant air felt like a
tremendous weight against her. She still held the Ambien
that she had dropped into her hand twenty minutes ago. She
didn't want to take it, but craved the oblivion that it promised, the dreamless sleep.

The door to the room was shut and locked, to keep Paul
out. She didn't feel like talking to him, seeing him, interact-
ing with him about anything. At a time when they should be
drawing comfort from each other, her feelings were a pathetic commentary on their marriage. But there you had it,
she thought, the raw truth.

The feds who were monitoring the phones stayed out of
her way and, thanks to the mayor's edict, the media had been
gone since dinner. The generator had been turned off for the
night, so the only noises that reached her through the open
window were night sounds—a distant rumble of thunder and
closer in, the chorus of insects and frogs and the hoot of the
burrowing owls that lived in the field behind the house. The

sounds of the owls comforted her, offering an odd kind of continuity between when she, Adam, and Paul had moved into this house and now.

During the hurricane, she had worried about them, hoping they had left and that they would return. Three days after Danielle had moved on and the saturated ground was starting to dry out, the family of owls had returned to the field and begun building a new home.

The owls had what she needed—resilience.

She lay here, flashlight aimed upward. The light spilled thinly across the ceiling and parts of the walls, and glinted off the wings of the model airplane that hung in the middle of the ceiling once again. Had Paul replaced it? Had she? Suki couldn't remember.

Several years ago, Adam had dreamed that he was a tiny boy, a Tom Thumb small enough to fit into the cockpit of the plane. He had climbed behind the wheel and taken off, soaring through their apartment in New York, and out the window, out into the darkness and over Central Park. His interpretation? That he felt small and insignificant in the presence of his famous parents. She remembered telling him that she felt small and insignificant in *his* presence and honored that he had chosen her as his mother.

I chose you? Really? Is that how it works?

She didn't have an answer then and didn't have one now. And Adam, she knew, had kept chewing at the central questions ever since: *Is everything we experience random? How much is destiny? How much is free will?*

Years ago when she was still in her teens, she and her mother had gone to see *Ordinary People*. The impact of the storyline—the suicide of a troubled teenaged boy and its impact on his family—and the depth that the actors had brought to their roles had devastated her. And it had raised the same issues for her that her remark to Adam had raised for him. For days afterward, she had sifted through the events of her young life, trying to find the hand of destiny in her own experiences. She decided she wouldn't have children because if she lost a child, she wouldn't survive it.

Recently, her agent had handed her a book called *The Lovely Bones*. He wanted to know if the story grabbed her enough to play the part of the mother. It began with a dead girl talking about her rape and murder and the impact it had on her family. Every paragraph was so painful, every page so wrenching, that by the end of it she was sucked dry and a kind of superstition seized her. If she played a role in the movie, then the events might happen to her just as they had happened to Christopher Reeve, whose last role before his accident was as a paraplegic in a wheelchair. She had told her agent she wasn't interested, but ultimately, it hadn't made any difference. Another version of her worst nightmare had happened anyway.

She pressed his pillow against her cheek and squeezed her eyes shut, fighting back tears, despair, the utter blackness her life would be without Adam. She wished that the room would explode with inexplicable movement, as it had yesterday. At least then, in some weird way, she would feel closer to her son because Adam had talked about the spirit. *Friend.* But the room remained silent, stifling, hot.

The glass in the window that had shattered during yesterday's freaky events had been repaired, every piece of furniture returned to its proper place, just like the model airplane. Even the bed had been remade. Paul didn't make beds, didn't move furniture, didn't repair windows. She was too tired to figure it out.

The police believed Adam had been taken in the early morning hours of July 27. She had chosen the arbitrary time of four A.M. as the zero hour. The meant Adam had been missing for slightly more than forty-four hours.

And all I can do is lay here, waiting, marking time until— what?

As if in response to the question, her cell rang. Suki snapped upright, glanced at the number in the ID window.

John Gutierrez. "John." Her voice sounded breathless, ridiculously hopeful. "Any news?"

"We've got a couple of leads that're going to take some research. We could use some help, if you're willing."

A lifeline. "Just tell me where."

"Ross Blake will pick you up. He's got a curfew pass. We're working at the Bureau office, which has power. Bring your laptop."

"What else?"

"Make sure you're comfortable. It may be a long night. He'll be there in a few minutes."

"I'll meet him at the gate."

Her first stop was Adam's bathroom; she dropped the Ambien in the toilet and flushed it away. At least the toilets had never stopped working, she thought. At least the water had continued to flow from the faucets, even if it wasn't potable. Small things for which she was immensely grateful. She splashed water on her face and hastened out of the room, moving quietly past the door to Paul's study, where the light shone under the door. She could hear him on the phone. With who now? Her manager? Her agent? A producer? A director?

Paul, wheeling and dealing at midnight, pitching loglines. *Son of famous director and Oscar-winning actress is kidnapped.* Paul wouldn't include the rest of it in his pitch, that the director and actress were on the verge of divorce, that the director couldn't keep his pants zipped, that their lives had unraveled completely.

Suki raced upstairs, through the darkened house, to the master bedroom. Thanks to the generator, the light in here was dim, maybe sixty watts, but sufficient for her purposes. She peeled off her jeans, put on shorts, slid her feet into sandals, ran a brush through her hair. She slipped a few essentials into her handbag, then picked up her flashlight and went into an adjoining room, a small office where the desk was stacked high with scripts, faxes, e-mails, phone messages, much of it accumulating since before the hurricane.

Her career room. The Oscar and a Golden Globe sat on a shelf midway up the wall. To either side of it hung photos of her, Paul, and Adam on various shoots, of her with directors, fellow actors, people whom she loved and admired. Her most prized possession was a framed letter from Nelson Mandela, one of her heroes, thanking her for her help in a charity function. But really, right now, did it mean anything? The instant Adam had disappeared, everything else in her life had stopped.

She zipped the laptop into its case, scooped the memory stick off the desk and pocketed it. Anything else? Anything she was forgetting?

"Suki?"

Shit. She turned. Paul, silhouetted in the doorway, clasped his hands behind his back and stretched his shoulders, rolled his neck, made it clear through body language that he'd been working so hard—at something—that his shoulders were tight, his neck ached. She was supposed to comment on this, maybe rub his neck, coddle him somehow.

Right.

"What is it?" she asked.

"I just got off the phone with Harvey."

Like she was supposed to know who the hell Harvey was. "Harvey who?"

"Weinstein."

That Harvey. "The answer's no." She strode right up to him, the laptop case gripped in her right hand, her handbag over her left shoulder. "Excuse me."

"Wait a minute. Christ, give me a few minutes here, Suki."

She glared at him. "For what? Your pitch?"

"To tell you what this involves."

She stood there, a hand on her hip. "Shoot." *You've got sixty seconds, Paul.*

"We're going to find him, Suki."

"Wait. I thought this involved Weinstein."

"Well, yeah, it does, but—"

"But what, Paul? But, oh, gee, let's sell our story to Miramax, to Touchstone, to—"

"Jesus, Suki. Calm down. You're not the only one in pain here."

"Really? You're in pain, Paul? And just where do you hurt? *Where?*"

He looked as though she had kicked him in the balls, his liquid eyes bulging, shadowed, dark.

"Here?" She pressed her palm to his chest. "Does it hurt *there,* Paul? Huh? Does it?"

He knocked her wrist away from his chest. "I can't talk to you when you're like this."

"And why is that exactly? What's your excuse this time? Because I have PMS? Because I'm hysterical? Because Adam's been taken? Explain it to me, Paul. Tell me why you feel compelled to wheel and deal what's happened to us. I really need to know that."

He lifted his hands, a barrier. "Hey, all I was trying to say is that Weinstein called. So did Spielberg, Rob Reiner, Ron Howard, Penny Marshall. . . ."

The names rolled off his tongue with a kind of arrogant familiarity. *See me? I'm a big shot. Hear me? I know all the greats.*

"They called for what exactly?"

"To offer condolences and support . . ."

"And then you butted in about a possible deal that would involve what's happened to Adam. Sounds like a goddamn Lifetime movie to me. Yeah, I get the picture, Paul. I *fucking get it.* So let me make my position clear. Our son's disappearance is NOT for sale."

Their eyes locked.

His body still blocked her exit.

"You disgust me," she spat, and pushed past him.

But he grabbed her arm, hard, and she swung the laptop case and it struck him in the shoulder.

He stumbled back. "What the fuck's wrong with you?" he shouted. "I'm trying to talk to you about—"

"Did you release Mira's name to the press? Did you release Adam's photo? Huh? Did you? Is this just a publicity stunt for you, Paul? To kick-start your directing career?"

He looked shocked, shaken, suddenly uncertain.

"I want you out of here," she hissed, conscious of the feds down the hall. "Go to a hotel. Go to your girlfriend's house. I don't give a shit where you go, but I don't want you here when I get back. We are done, you and me. We are fucking *history,* Paul."

She yanked her arm free of his grasp and swept past him.

"Where're you going?" he shouted after her, almost as if it were an afterthought triggered by the sight of her laptop, her handbag.

"To find Adam." But she didn't say it loudly enough for him to hear.

My God, what had she ever seen in him? How had she managed to sleep in the same bed with this man for fifteen years of marriage and—what? A year before that? Two years? What had she needed back then that she'd believed he could provide? Where was the chemistry? Who the hell was she when she'd thought she loved him? How had it come to this travesty?

When she reached the bottom of the driveway, an old station wagon waited there, engine humming, headlights off. The passenger door swung open and she scooted inside.

"Thanks, Mr. Blake. I appreciate this."

"My pleasure," he said. "And the name's Ross."

"You saved me. I was feeling useless and stupid and debating about whether I should take an Ambien so I could sleep."

Blake regarded her with an odd expression. "I never figured that you would feel useless and stupid about anything. You seem so . . . self-sufficient."

"That's movies talking."

He laughed and turned on the headlights. "Not for me. I've never seen any of your movies." He sounded embarrassed. "I guess that's like admitting, I don't know, like I've never seen *E.T.* or *On the Waterfront.*" He quickly added, "I've seen both of those."

She couldn't remember the last time she had met anyone who hadn't seen at least one of her movies. "You don't go to movies?"

"I fly," he replied, as though that explained everything. "And when I'm not flying, I read. And when I'm not reading, I'm running my business. And when I'm not doing that, I guess I'm diving into the other stuff that interests me."

"Which is?"

"The weird, the strange, the inexplicable. Easter Island. Stonehenge. The Egyptian pyramids. The Mayan ruins. Machu Picchu. The planet itself seems to be filled with mysteries." He laughed again, put the car in gear, and backed into the road. "I guess I need a couple of lifetimes just to explore everything."

Her eyes went to his left hand, where the little finger was missing. "What's the most recent movie you saw?"

"You mean, like a movie separate from TV movies?"

"Yes."

He thought about it. "*Harry Potter and the Prisoner of Azkaban.*"

"My son's favorite of the Harry Potter books and movies." She paused. "But I sense hesitancy, Ross."

He laughed, a quick, quiet laugh. She liked the sound of it. "Complicated," he said.

"Harry Potter?"

"No, not Potter. Well, yes, Potter, but that's not what I'm talking about." He drove slowly along the main road through downtown Tango Key, silent and deserted at this hour, and suddenly lifted his hand from the steering wheel. "I lost this finger in 1968, I was born in 1985. But I'm fifty-three years old."

Huh? "Granted, I'm no math whiz, but you've really lost me now."

"You need some background information, Suki, so you have some idea of the kind of people you're dealing with."

"Which people are we talking about? The good guys or the bad guys?"

"Good guys."

He then proceeded to tell her how in 1997, when he was twelve years old, he was abducted by a man named Patrick Wheaton and taken through a black water mass that had formed off the coast of Tango Key—and back in time to the 1960s. For the next six years, he'd lived in that time as Wheaton's adopted son.

Then in the summer of 2003, Mira's daughter, Annie, was abducted by this same man, taken back to 1968, and Blake—as a teenage boy in that time—had helped her through the "time sickness." Mira had pursued her daughter, and ended up in 1968 too. Sheppard had figured out that the mass was nature's wormhole and gone through the black water to find them.

"I don't expect you to believe any of this," he said. "And the only reason I'm telling you any of it is because if you *do* believe it, then you'll understand these people aren't ordinary. If anyone can find your son, they will. They won't do it in any conventional sense, Suki, but they'll do it."

Suki didn't know whether to laugh, pat him on the back, and placate him about his delusion, or lunge out of the car and run like hell. Instead, she did nothing. She had known plenty of bullshit artists in her decades in the movie industry—she was *married* to one of the masters of bullshit—and felt certain that Blake wasn't in that category. But if he wasn't, then what the hell was he?

"So in this scenario that you're describing, you chose to stay in 1968 while Mira, Annie, and Shep returned to their time. That would mean that you aged as though you had been born in the early fifties."

"Yes. There are still a lot of details we don't understand about what happened and about the repercussions. Shep developed acute claustrophobia. Annie seems to have become more psychic. Those effects may just be the surface. And we aren't sure yet about Mira. Based on a couple of remarks she has made, I think her abilities may be changing somehow. But she doesn't talk much about it."

"So these repercussions are because of this time sickness you mentioned?"

"Maybe. It could have been caused by a virus, like herpes, and once you catch it, the virus never leaves your body. It's just there. Or it could be related to something else entirely. We just don't know enough."

"What happened to Wheaton?"

Blake rubbed his jaw and shrugged. "A younger version of Wheaton escaped. The version of Wheaton that I knew, who took Annie, died."

"How is that possible?"

He shrugged and didn't answer immediately. "*Sliding Doors*. Did you see it?"

"One of my favorites. Gwyneth Paltrow makes a choice and that choice results in two different probabilities."

"It was the same thing with Wheaton, except there were a lot of choices, a lot of possibilities. Shep and Mira cite quantum physics when they're explaining it. The Many Worlds Theory. But me? I just think about *Sliding Doors*."

"Why did you stay back in the Sixties?"

"I wasn't about to go back to my family. My old man was an abusive alcoholic, my childhood was pretty bad. I was Wheaton's heir—and he had plenty of money, property, goods. I had quite a bit of knowledge about the future of the stock market, land, that kind of thing, so I made a lot of money through the years."

He touched her arm, a soft, almost hesitant touch, yet it electrified her skin. "Tango Key is . . ." He paused, struggling to find the right words, the right description. "An anomaly. Inexplicable, mysterious, both a riddle and an answer. Mira, Shep, Annie, Nadine, Goot, their circles of friends . . . all of them are part of whatever's happening here. And now you and Adam are part of it too. You're connected to the island's magic. You can deny it, you can rant and rave and even leave. But in the end, it always comes back to this place. It's like myth. It grabs hold of you and won't let go."

They were in a parking lot now, the engine silent, the windows open to the humid summer air. And right at that moment, she felt as if she had been inducted into some secret society, a circle of alchemists or ancient magicians, a weird X-File that even Scully and Mulder had failed to decipher.

"Your thoughts?" he asked after a few moments.

Surrounded by the surreal, the inexplicable, the ridiculous, she started laughing. She laughed until tears coursed down her cheeks. She laughed because she didn't know what else to do, and Blake laughed too. At some point during all that nervous, silly laughter, she grasped his hand, the hand that was missing a finger that had been cut off in 1968, even though he'd been born in 1985, and clung to it like a drowning woman clutching a rubber ducky in the middle of the Pacific Ocean.

14

Research

In the weeks since Sheppard had moved out of Mira's place, his office had expanded into the staff room and now looked like a small apartment. Two couches, a fridge, a two-burner stove, sink, shower, TV, and a conference table for six, each spot with a wireless Internet connection.

With a pot of fresh Cuban coffee and a platter of snacks to fortify the group—Mira, Suki, Blake, Goot, and himself—he brought Suki and Blake up to speed on the investigation and the night's events. He also passed out copies of the police artist's rendition of the man known as Spenser Wickett and Spenser Timble.

Suki stared at the picture, the blood drained from her face, and she suddenly said, "I've seen this guy. In April, I think it was, I was in the grocery store. It was crowded. I came around the end of an aisle and this cart slammed into mine. It jarred me and I . . . I glanced up and there he was. Just staring at me. In this picture, his eyes are all wrong. He has really intense, piercing eyes. They creeped me out. He creeped me out. Anyway, he apologized and then hurried on past me."

"Do you remember seeing him at any other time?" Mira asked.

Suki shook her head. "Not after that. I'm not sure about before April. But even when he ran into me in the grocery store in April, I knew I'd seen him before. I just can't remember where or when."

"Maybe it will come to you as we move along here," Sheppard said. "Our guy was on the island yesterday afternoon. He gave a DVD to one of the reporters outside your house, Suki. It's a home video of him and Adam. If you prefer not to see this, I . . ."

Her face went hard. "I want to see it."

Sheppard dimmed the lights, turned on the DVD player, and the TV screen lit up. The seven minutes and seven seconds of video seemed to pass with an agonizing slowness. At one point, Suki asked him to pause it. She got up and walked over to the TV screen, studying one of the clearer images of Adam and his kidnapper.

"There's something so eerily familiar about this guy, but I . . . I can't place it. Can you make prints of this image, Shep?"

He said he would, and she sat down again and watched the rest of the DVD without saying anything. When he turned the lights back on, Mira looked at him strangely, frowning. He didn't know what it meant.

Sheppard flipped the chalkboard around so they could all see it. "We're about to do something in here that's outside of Bureau protocol. So what happens in this room has to stay in this room. Each of you will have access to every database the Bureau has at its disposal. With five of us working various databases, we're going to find what we need much more quickly. And here it is in a nutshell." · -

He pointed at the chalkboard. It held two lists: every component of information that they needed and the database and password where it might be found. "We know that Spenser C. Timble or Spenser C. Wickett is the man we want. That's not his name now, but we need everything we can find on him when he was these two people. We need the history of Suki's house and who lived there when there was a fire. The Mango Hill house is old, built around 1940, so we have a lot of years to cover. But those years can be narrowed somewhat.

"Mira believes this guy is between the ages of thirty and forty and that he was four to six years of age when he was taken from the Mango Hill house. That would put us somewhere between 1964 and 1974. Let's extend it a couple of years on either side, say from 1962 to 1976, just to be safe. Once we know who owned the house when our guy Spense lived there, we'll have more information to go on.

"We know he'd been watching the Nicholses for quite some time, learning their routines, their habits. We're fairly certain he used a boat to take Adam from Tango to someplace else. But his scrutiny of the family was seriously compromised by Danielle, so I think it's pretty safe to narrow our boat search to vessels that have been in the Tango marinas since Danielle. We need the type of vessel and owner."

"What about coves?" Blake asked. "There're a lot of boats in the coves around the island. They're unregulated."

"If you drop anchor within three miles of the Tango Key coast, you're required to register with the county. That law has been in effect since 9/11."

"Just because he's supposed to register doesn't mean he would," Goot remarked.

"I think he tries to follow rules as closely as he can without endangering himself," Mira said. "That's how he has stayed off the grid for so long. Given his history with names, he probably uses several names in his life now. Maybe he has one name for his license and registration and another name for the title to his home, to pay his property taxes, that kind of thing."

"How do we know he owns his home?" Blake asked.

"I got an impression of a two-story house, on water," Mira replied. "He owns it. I'm sure of it."

Blake nodded. "I'll do the search for boats."

"I'd like to research the house history," Suki said.

"I'll do the search for Wickett Timble," Goot said.

"And I'm going to play with this artist's software," Mira said, "and come up with a likeness of the redhead I saw him with."

"Great." Sheppard nodded, pleased they had each found a niche. "I'll check on every house purchase between Tango Key and Big Pine for the last year. Somewhere in all this information, we'll find connections, links. Help yourselves to food, more coffee, or a couch if you need to rest. It's going to be a long night."

Recently, Sheppard had read an interview with legendary physicist John Wheeler in which he speculated that information was at the root of all existence. He contended that the essence of anything—from a stone to a star to an atom—lay in the information it contained. Wheeler was referring to the notion that the universe is participatory, that it adapted to man just as man adapted to the universe. In much the same way, Sheppard believed that the key to finding Spenser Wickett Timble, or whatever name he used now, was to immerse themselves in the flow of information he had generated over the course of his lifetime—and then to interact with that flow.

Sheppard decided to start his search with the first six months of 2003. Based on Mira's impressions, he eliminated Tango Key from his search criteria and requested a list of waterfront-home purchases from Key West to Big Pine Key. To narrow the search, he asked for cash purchases only. The list was absurdly long. Where had all these people made their money anyway? In the illicit drug trade? The dot-com boom? Inheritances? Politics? Lobbying? Oil?

He copied the list into another program and broke it down

four different ways—alphabetically, by date, by island, and by purchase price, and printed everything out. He brought up detailed street maps for each island and placed the homes at their appropriate addresses. He automatically eliminated homes in gated developments; it seemed unlikely that their guy would invite the scrutiny of security guards, cameras, passes, and the other types of scrutiny that gated communities used. Also, docks in gated communities wouldn't be very private.

Even if Spenser had cleaned up financially during the dot-com boom, as Tina Richardson had said, would he spend a million bucks on a home? He had survived all these years by maintaining a low profile. However, given the price of real estate in the Keys, Sheppard doubted there were *lots* left in the Keys for less than a million, never mind *homes*. So even if Spenser had bought a home in the million-dollar range, it wouldn't be out of step with what was normal for real-estate prices here.

Sheppard scanned the printout of homes listed by price: They ranged from $450,000 to five million. He began at the lower end, 450K to 750K, and paused, wondering if he should eliminate the corporate owners. If a lot of the home owners were involved in illicit activities, then they might be hiding behind offshore corporations. He decided to keep the corporate owners and run searches on them later. He now had over two hundred homes, a staggering number. And where was he supposed to go from here?

It would take days to run a check on every corporation, address, owner. And they didn't have days.

Until he had another block of information, he had reached a dead end.

He printed out five copies of the list and passed them out. "This is as far as I can go with what we've got," he said.

"I've got something," Suki exclaimed. "Maybe this will help. May 17, 1975. Here come five copies." She passed them around as they slid from the printer.

Local Boy Still Missing,
Mother in Coma

TANGO KEY. No one knows what happened to Spenser Longwood, 6, or to his mother, Joy Longwood, 30, a math teacher at Tango Key High. She lies in critical condition in the burn unit at Jackson Memorial Hospital in Miami. She was found unconscious by firefighters yesterday morning, May 16, in the driveway of her home at 243 Mango Hill Drive. She was airlifted to Jackson and hasn't regained consciousness. Her son, a student at Tango Elementary School, is missing.

According to Detective Glenn Kartauk of the Tango Key Police Department, the cause of the fire that destroyed several rooms in the Longwood home hasn't been determined yet. "At this point, we don't have any leads about the whereabouts of Spenser Longwood. We are hopeful that Mrs. Longwood will regain consciousness and be able to provide details about what happened."

If you have information concerning the events at Mango Hill Drive, please contact Detective Kartauk at 305-555-9862.

Included in the article were photographs of Joy and Spenser Longwood.

"Oh, my God," Mira said softly. "This is the presence I saw in Adam's room. And the detective's name . . . how would you all pronounce that?"

Sheppard grinned and snapped his fingers. "Car talk. That was the phrase you picked up. This guy is *car talk*. Now we just have to track him down."

"I'll do that," Goot said, and went to work.

"Wait, there's more," Suki added. "Joy Longwood died on May 19, 1975. In an article several months later, the *Gazette* ran a follow-up on Spenser's disappearance. Kartauk was still on the case, but nothing had turned up. A year later, there was another follow-up. The boy was still missing. No mention of Kartauk."

Sheppard took it all in, filing the facts away in his head. "Suki, we need to know when Joy bought the house, where she came from, anything and everything that's pertinent. Newspaper databases are good. We subscribe to a dozen archives. All the passwords and log-ins are on the board."

While she worked the archives, he went into the Social Security database and entered Joy Longwood's name and date of death. While the search engine churned away, he glanced through the house-purchase list for Longwood, found nothing, and did a property records search for Longwood in both Tango and Monroe counties. No Longwood. Too easy.

But the SSA was more helpful. Her DOB was listed as February 3, 1945, place of birth New Haven, Connecticut. Armed with that information, he got her Social Security number and ran it through every database to which the Bureau had access, and through some federal databases he had access to only because his boss had arranged it years ago.

From 1970 to 1975, Joy Longwood filed taxes as a single mother, with one deduction for her son, C. Spenser Longwood. But between 1968 and 1970, she had two deductions—Spenser and another son, Lyle, both boys born on the same date, August 27, 1969. *Twins.* What happened to Lyle? And who was the father?

Sheppard ran the names and dates of birth of the sons through *ancestry.com,* one of the bureau's subscription services, but only Joy Longwood was listed as a parent. When he searched for a death entry on Lyle, nothing turned up.

Another dead end?

"Okay, here's the deal on Kartauk," said Goot. "It looks like he left Tango Key in the early eighties to teach criminology at the University of Florida. He was involved in the search for Adam Walsh, acted as a consultant on John Walsh's TV show, and that subsequently led to a consultant position on CNN."

"So as a result of the Longwood case, he became a recognized expert in criminal law," Blake remarked.

"Looks that way. And then he went on to teach at the University of Florida. Here's his e-mail address and a department number." He ticked it off. "But it's summer, so who knows where he is?"

Just as Sheppard finished dashing off an e-mail to Kartauk, there was a knock at the door, then: "Hey, Shep. It's Charlie Cordoba. You going to unlock the door or what?"

Everyone exchanged glances. Sheppard rolled his eyes and spoke quietly. "We share, but not everything. Not about Kartauk."

They all nodded in agreement.

"Hold on, Charlie," Sheppard called, then unlocked the door, opened it wide, and grinned. "Busted."

Cordoba's eyes swept around the room. "What the hell? My men are out there busting their butts in overtime, and you five are mighty cozy in here, in the air-conditioning." He pinned Sheppard with his dark, weasel eyes. "What's going on, Sheppard?"

"Pull up a chair, Charlie, and we'll fill you in."

"Got a list of boats and owners for every single marina on Tango and for all the vessels that have dropped anchor in the coves in the last six months," Blake announced.

"Great. Print out six copies. Suki, anything else?"

"She bought the house in 1970, went to work for the school system the same year. I still can't find anything on where she came from." She flashed a smile at Cordoba. "We've made headway, Charlie."

"Wonderful," he drolled.

Sheppard prepared a folder for Cordoba that included everything except information on Kartauk, and handed it to him. "Here you go, Charlie. See if you can come up with anything else along these lines. I think we're calling it a night here. Good work, people."

But Cordoba didn't get up. He opened the folder and started paging through the material. Sheppard ignored him. "Goot, is eight too early for you in the morning?"

"No, amigo, I'm cool."

"Excuse me, but my men have been on duty all night, keeping an eye on the docks and the marinas," Cordoba said.

"You have more staff than we do," Sheppard said.

"They'll be on rotating shifts until the curfew's over at six A.M. Then it's your turn."

"We'd need a small army out there to watch every marina plus the docks," Sheppard said.

"Tough," Cordoba replied with a smirk. "I'm sure a bright guy like you will figure it out, Shep."

Sheppard snatched the folder out of Cordoba's hand. "Then find your own leads, Charlie."

His nostrils flared, anger burned in his tired eyes. He got slowly to his feet. "At every goddamn step in this investigation, you've tried to exclude me, Sheppard. Tonight, I filed an official complaint with the FBI's southeast division that you and Goot are running a rogue outfit here that has no regard for the rule of law."

Goot snickered. "No regard for the rule of law? Look who's talking."

Cordoba puffed out his chest like a rooster strutting its stuff. "And exactly what the hell's that supposed to mean?"

"Well, let's see, Charlie. For starters, we figure you're the one who released Mira's name to the press and also you're the guy who jumped the gun on the release of Adam's photo."

"What bullshit. Even if I had done something like that, it doesn't have anything to do with the *law*."

"You need to brush up on *your* law," Sheppard told him. "The abduction is *federal* domain. So if you prematurely released information related to our investigation, Charlie, then you interfered with a federal investigation. It's enough to get your ass fired."

Cordoba looked flustered—and confused that the tables had been turned on him. "We're talking about *your* rogue outfit, Sheppard."

"Yeah, yeah. So go do what you gotta do, Charlie."

"Fuck off, Sheppard," he barked, and marched out of the room, slamming the door behind him.

"Jerk," Goot muttered.

Mira shot Sheppard a warning look. "Be careful, Shep. Charlie can throw a wrench into the direction we're moving in this whole thing."

Yeah, yeah. Been there, done that. And with more formidable adversaries than Cordoba.

Deserted roads. Clouds thickening in the sky. No stars, no moon. Just darkness and silence. Sheppard welcomed the silence in the night, but not inside the car, where Mira sat stiffly in the passenger seat, her face turned toward the window.

"We made headway tonight," Sheppard said. "We have huge blocks of information on this guy and all we need to do now is connect everything."

"I hate to burst your bubble, Shep, but I don't think it's that simple."

"Sure, it is. If we dig deeply enough, connect what we don't know factually with what you know psychically, we can find this guy."

"Not without something else happening."

"Such as?"

"I don't know. I can feel it, but I don't know what it is. I guess I'm too beat to intuit much of anything. I wish you had shown me that DVD earlier."

That explained the odd look she'd given him. "Tina and her people were still working with it."

"I think he could have been involved in some facet of the movie industry, Shep."

"You picked that up while you were watching the DVD?"

"No, it wasn't a psychic feeling. Just . . . one possibility. It's almost like he really wanted Suki and Paul to see what an excellent little movie he'd made."

Sheppard thought of the section of the T. S. Eliot poem that had struck him viscerally. "Between the desire and the spasm, between the potency and the existence, between the essence and the descent, falls the shadow."

He felt her eyes on him—hot, burning, as if she were actually seeing him for the first time. "Goddamn, Shep. T. S. Eliot? What's he got to do with our boy Spenser?" Then she snapped her fingers. "The music from *Hollow Man,* right?"

"Tina made the connection. But I think she's right. Spenser sets things in motion, then watches how everything unfolds. He's like the shadow Eliot wrote about."

"He likes playing God."

"Exactly."

She ran her fingers through her hair and turned her face to the rain-speckled window. "We're doing what he wants us to do, analyzing every goddamn detail of that tape. He's playing with us. This whole thing is *orchestrated.*"

"Yeah, but what's it *mean*?"

Mira threw out her hands, exasperated. "Eliot felt like shit when he wrote that poem, his marriage was going down the tubes, he was finding religion. The poem became an *event* and critics and scholars have been analyzing it to death ever since. Our guy Spenser creates an *event,* the media dissects it, the cops analyze it. But people are suffering because of what Spenser has done. *No* one suffered because of Eliot's poem."

Sheppard lifted his hands from the steering wheel. "Hold on, okay? I'm just saying that 'The Hollow Men' symbolizes Spenser's feelings about himself."

Mira pressed her fingertips against her eyes and massaged them. "Yeah, it fits."

It started to rain before he reached Mira's street, a soft, gentle summer rain that released the wonderful scents of rich earth and salty sea, of an island struggling to recover from the ravages of Danielle. Somewhere out there, Sheppard thought, fruit trees rebounded—papayas, grapefruits, oranges, fields of strawberries. Even the damaged trees exhibited new growth, as though spring had finally arrived.

By the time he pulled up in front of the trailer, the rain came down in earnest, with a strong, steady wind out of the east hurling it against the sides of his Jetta. The windows of the trailer were dark. No cars in sight.

"Didn't you talk to Ace tonight?" he asked.

"Yeah, I told him I was going to be working with you and Goot at your office. I guess he figured he was off the hook and decided to join Luke in the preserve. He must've taken Ricki with him."

"Shit," Sheppard murmured. "I don't like this."

"Oh, gimme a break." She sounded irritable. "I don't need an armed companion, okay? I'll lock the doors and in few hours, it'll be light."

"I'll stay here," he said, and killed the engine.

"Excuse me, Shep, but even in the best of times, you didn't have the right to boss me around. I'll be fine." She threw open the door, grabbed her bag, swung her legs out. "Thanks for the ride."

Before he could say anything, Mira dashed through the rain toward the trailer.

Sheppard sat there for about two seconds, then got out and opened the trunk. He grabbed a backpack that held extra clothes, toiletries, and some computer supplies, and darted toward the trailer. He burst through the door just as she was turning on her flashlight. "I'll sleep on the couch," he said.

She shone the flashlight at him. The beam slipped down

his body to the spreading puddle of water on the floor in front of him. "Only if you dry off first. There're towels and an extra toothbrush and other stuff in the bathroom. I'm going out back to start the generator."

When she returned minutes later, the lights were on and cool air poured through the ceiling vents. They had both changed clothes. Mira wore gym shorts and a tank top that hugged her breasts. Her hair hung loose, damp, and long, brushing her shoulders. He had made up the couch and was fixing mugs of tea laced with strong shots of rum.

"I hope those FEMA tarps hold. Otherwise I'm going to have a flood in the house and in the store," she said.

"They'll hold as long as it's not another hurricane." He held out a mug of tea. *"Salud."*

They clicked mugs. "What're we drinking to?" she asked.

"Whatever you want to drink to."

"Eight hours of sleep," she said.

Sheppard chuckled. "Sounds fine."

"And finding Adam before this Spenser guy hurts him."

"He won't hurt him yet. He still needs him."

"Hmm. For more media events." She sipped and made a face. "Damn, this is Mamajuana, from the Dominican Republic."

"It's strong and smooth."

"And allegedly an aphrodisiac," she added.

He didn't know what to make of that remark, so he let it pass.

"You really didn't have to do this, Shep. But I appreciate your concern." Then she yawned, gulped down the rest of her tea, set the mug on the counter. "I've got to sleep. Lock the front door, okay?"

He nodded, and she turned and went into the bedroom. He felt mildly encouraged that she didn't shut him out completely by closing the door.

Sheppard went over to the couch, sat down, and sipped at the tea and rum, listening to the rain as it hammered the trailer. He considered fixing himself another drink, minus the tea this time, but instead, turned off the light and slipped between the sheets. They smelled of Mira, of the soap she used, of her shampoo, her perfumes, her essence. He flipped onto his side and found his gun and cell phone and slipped them under the pillow. He lay there with his eyes wide open, his desire for her thickening like smoke, memories pushing at him, eating him alive.

"Fuck," he murmured, and sat up.

Rain smeared the trailer's windows and drummed the roof with a soft, rhythmic music. He thought of the events in that wind-blown clearing a month ago, of him and Mira in that wooded area only yesterday. He thought and thought and finally got up and went into the bedroom, his cell and gun in hand.

She didn't move. He could tell by the way she breathed that she was sound asleep. Carefully, trying not to wake her, he got into bed beside her, slipped his gun and cell phone under the pillow, then pulled the blanket up over his body. He rolled onto his side, draped his arm over her waist, and fitted his body against hers so that they lay like spoons in a drawer.

He wasn't sure what woke him, maybe a change in her breathing, maybe the wind and rain. But as soon as he opened his eyes, he knew that she too was awake, listening, adjusting to the presence of his body, pressed up against hers.

"What're we doing, Shep?" Whispered words, almost desperate.

"I'm sorry about what happened that night," he whispered back, and brought his mouth to the curve of her neck. "I'm sorry for what I said to you when I was talking about seeing that mermaid. Jesus, Mira, I miss you."

For what seemed the longest time, she didn't say anything. But she brought her hand to his, covering it, and gradually moved his hand up under her tank top, across the silken smoothness of her skin, to her breast. He pressed his body closer to hers. His feet sought her feet, his toes greeted hers, and she turned onto her other side, facing him, her hands sliding up the sides of his face.

"I hate my life without you in it," she said. "But I can't be something I'm not, Shep. I see the weird, the strange, the invisible. It's not something I ask for. I don't encourage or nurture it. It just happens to me. It's what my life seems to be about. I know this makes you uncomfortable and I know you wish it were different, but it's not. This is what I am."

He didn't know what to say. He had nothing to say. He knew all this. And at some level, he also knew that whatever Mira was would conflict always with what he was. But it didn't matter anymore. Life with her at whatever level that meant was preferable to life without her.

He cupped her face in his hands and kissed her. Her mouth opened against his, her tongue as soft and familiar to him as the pillow that held his head. The days and weeks of uncertainty fell away. They made love quickly, almost violently, as if to reclaim what they had lost that night in the clearing, and in the aftermath, they held hands tightly, the sheets tangled at their feet, the rain outside pounding against the trailer.

She fell asleep in his arms, her breathing soft, even, deep. He adjusted his body to hers and finally let the rum take him away.

15

The Artists' Colony

They were back. The media vans. The paparazzi. They had
begun trickling in shortly after the first ferry had docked at
6:40, and now there were probably fifty vehicles crowded in
the street, with more arriving by the minute. Suki, standing
at the kitchen window with a mug of coffee, watched them
gathering in the rain like buzzards at roadkill. Their colorful
umbrellas bobbed up and down as they moved around, jockeying for the best view of the house and property. But she
was ready for them.

When Blake had brought her home around four this
morning, he had told her he thought he could track down
more information on Joy Longwood and that he would pick
her up around eight. Promptly at 8:05, her cell vibrated and
Blake's number appeared in the ID window. Suki hurried out
onto the patio so that she could answer the call without being
heard by anyone in the house. The feds. Paul. He hadn't left
last night, but she suspected he would leave now that the
curfew had ended for the night. She didn't much care where
he went, as long as it was away from her.

"Hey," she said softly into the cell phone. "Where are you?"

"Almost there. I'll meet you at the edge of the woods."

"Okay." She slung her pack over her shoulder, shrugged on a poncho, and stepped outside, where the electric cart waited.

The cart was loaded with wood and rolls of wire mesh that stuck out the back of it. Even though part of her route would be visible to the press, the rain created a shimmering curtain that even powerful lenses would have trouble penetrating with any clarity at all. But in the event that any of the media people got a good look at the person in the cart, they wouldn't see Suki Nichols. Instead, they would see a handyman in a poncho, coveralls, and heavy boots, unloading fencing materials along the side of the property.

She drove the cart as fast as it would go, rain dancing against the canvas roof. Suki stopped at the edge of the property where the pines began. She started unloading the wood, wire mesh, a shovel, and began digging a hole for the first beam. After a few minutes, she dropped the shovel and simply walked into the trees. Blake waited in another electric cart, silently laughing at her disguise.

"Pretty convincing," he said.

"You think?"

"Take my word for it. Did you get any sleep?"

"A couple of hours. You?"

"The same."

Once they were in the pines, Suki shed the poncho and coveralls. Underneath, she wore denim Capri pants and a turquoise T-shirt. She folded the coveralls and slipped them inside her pack, then exchanged the heavy boots for sandals, and tugged on a baseball cap. "Voila," she said.

"That must be an acting trick."

"Theater, with quick costume changes."

He brought out a thermos and two ceramic mugs with his company logo on them. "Do us the honors."

"Gladly. So where're we going exactly?"

"Well, I was living on Tango when Joy Longwood lived here. Granted, I didn't know a whole lot of people, but I know a woman who did. She got me—and Mira and Annie—through the time sickness."

"Wait, tell me more about this time sickness."

"Before you travel to a foreign country, you get inoculations. Before you travel through time, you should do the same thing, but no one except Wheaton knew that. It's why he had to bring back five kids before he found the one strong enough to survive the sickness. Annie."

"But you survived too."

"Yeah, but I was different. He adopted me. Wheaton hired Lydia to treat these kids he brought back through the mass. I guess she was the equivalent of today's alternative healer. Anyway, she knew Joy Longwood."

"Lydia treated her?"

"No, she knew her because Joy was an aspiring photographer and took classes at the Tango Artists' Colony, where Lydia was a cleaning woman. Today, Lydia pretty much runs the place."

Suki and Adam had visited the colony shortly after they moved here. They had lunch, she remembered, beneath a giant banyan tree on the outdoor patio, and spent a long time in the gift shop, selecting pieces of island art for the house.

They took the cart as far as Tango Sea and Air, then transferred to Blake's car and drove into the hills at the northeast corner of the island. He turned off Old Post onto a gravel road and a hundred yards later, they passed under an arched wooden sign that read: TANGO ARTISTS' COLONY. The gravel road twisted through a wet forest of pines, banyans, and acacia trees. Here and there, trees had fallen or been stripped by the storm. But for the most part, the forest seemed to have emerged relatively unscathed by the hurricane.

The colony, located on fifty acres of prime real estate, was financially self-sufficient. "All its revenue comes from donations and from what the artists produce, the gift shop, theater, the workshops and seminars and summer programs, and so on," Blake explained. "They recently started a film program, and I suspect that's going to be a major money-maker in the near future. There are forty cabins now where interns live and work. Most of their power is solar-generated."

"Sounds like they're light years ahead of what the rest of the country is doing."

The road emptied into a clearing where a dozen concrete buildings, a few in various states of repair from the hurricane, stood in a half-moon circle, each one painted a different color, with some sort of mosaic or tile design on the front. Each building had a name connected to the island's history and mythology: Rum Runners, Pieces of Eight, Sirena, Pirates Lair, The Pod. They pulled up in front of Rum Runners, the administration building.

Adirondack chairs lined the wooden porch deck, inviting visitors to kick back and chill. Several people had done exactly that. At one end of the porch, a woman stood in front of an easel, painting. Off to the right, a film crew was shooting in the rain. As he and Suki got out of the car, someone in the crew called out, "Hey, Mr. Blake. Lydia said to tell you she's in the archives."

"Thanks," Blake called back.

They went inside the administration building. Suki wasn't sure what she'd been expecting, but knew it wasn't this—an explosion of color, shapes, and textures. Just being in this huge room, bright despite the rain outside, brought a smile to her face and a tidal wave of warmth to the center of her chest. All kinds of art and photographs covered the walls. Rain drummed the pair of skylights overhead. The tiled floors were inlaid with tropical designs—flamingos, lush green mango trees, seagulls so realistic that she wouldn't be surprised if they suddenly lifted from the floor and flew away. A fountain in the center of the room seemed to grow upward from the floor as though the entire room were something organic, living, sentient.

"This is amazing," she breathed.

"This is just the beginning," he said with an amused smile. "The archives are back here." They went down a wide hall painted in eye-popping psychedelic colors and decorated with dark wood carvings. The hall curved gently to the right and ended at a pair of steel doors. "We could take the stairs, but let's do the elevator." Blake slid a plastic card into the slot, the light on the panel turned green, the doors opened to an elevator. "Now we go thirty feet down."

The doors clanked shut and the elevator shot downward so fast that her stomach was left up where they'd started. Seconds later, they emerged in a windowless room the size of a three-car garage. Rows of filing cabinets and bookshelves filled half the room; high-tech equipment and desks took up the rest of it. The scent of fresh roses and gardenias, arranged in a hand-blown glass vase on the conference table, perfumed the cool air. Music played from one of the smaller rooms off the archives.

"This is where most everyone at the colony rode out the hurricane," he explained, then called: "Hey, Lydia, you've got company."

The music stopped, a door opened, and a tall black woman hurried out, her short, wiry hair threaded with gray, a pair of granny glasses riding low on the bridge of her nose. She looked to be about sixty. A sleek black cat darted out ahead of her and curled between Suki's legs.

"You don't need to be yellin' down here, Ross. I'm not deaf yet, you . . . "Her eyes settled on Suki. "Holy shit," she whispered. "You're . . ."

"Suki Nichols, this is Lydia Santos," Blake said.

"Oh, my God, I am so deeply sorry about your son." She took Suki's hand and held it in both of hers, patting it. "But honey, believe me, Shep, Mira, my buddy Ross . . . they're the best. They know what they're doing."

"I know they do. Thanks."

"You devil," she said to Blake. "You didn't tell me you were going to bring a movie star here."

"You wouldn't have believed me."

"You got that right." She peered at them over the rim of her glasses. "So let me get this straight. You think there's a connection between the kidnappings of Spenser and Adam?"

"Actually, Lydia, we think Joy's son took Adam."

Her dark eyes widened. "Spense? I used to stay with him when Joy had faculty meetings or a date. He seemed like a regular kid. Sort of quiet and solitary, though. And he liked to fiddle with gadgets."

"The evidence points at him," Blake said.

Lydia, now seated across from them, spoke softly, as though she were afraid she might be overheard. "I'd like to say that it's because his old man ruined him. Ray Connor, that was his name back then. Bastard sadist, ex-cop from up north somewhere. I think he used to beat up on her. She was always looking over her shoulder, the way abused women do, you know what I'm saying? No telling what the hell he did to Spenser after he took him."

Lydia stabbed her long finger at the air. "But I don't buy that horseshit that the childhood environment sculpts the person. If it were true, I'd be out there murdering people right and left. So if Spenser grew up to do what was done to him, then it's because there was some evil within when he was born and whatever he endured with his old man just made it blossom. So let's see what, if anything, like that shows up, huh? I'll show you what I found down here in the archives."

"Who was Joy dating?" Suki asked, her eyes following Lydia as she stood.

"Don't know. She confided some things, but not that. You got to understand. In those days, I was the cleaning lady around here. Only reason Joy and I got to know each other is because I was cleaning up the photography lab one afternoon when she was in the darkroom. She showed me some photos she'd taken of her son, the house, and we got to talking. After that, we'd have lunch or dinner together, and then I started staying with Spenser when she was going out. Let me get this stuff. Be right back."

Suki's cell phone rang. She slipped it out of her back pocket, saw Paul's number, and didn't answer it.

"The signal won't be strong enough down here anyway," Blake told her, as if he knew it was Paul and was trying to make her feel less guilty about not taking the call. "Not only are we underground, but the walls are probably twenty feet thick, solid concrete with reinforced steel."

"Was this intended as a bunker or something?"

"That's my guess. It was built right around the Cuban Missile Crisis."

Lydia returned with half-a-dozen legal-size folders and lined them up side by side on the conference table. Suki saw that five of the folders were neatly labeled JOY LONGWOOD and covered a period from February 1970 to late April 1975, shortly before the fire that had killed her. The last file was labeled SPENSER LONGWOOD, 1972–1975.

"This was everything I could find. In the early days, people who were interested in studying here had to audition to get in. The board was real picky. The people who got chosen lived in the cottages for next to nothing and in return, they agreed to give the colony copies of their work so we could stock the archives. Joy never interned here, but she gave me copies of her stuff and asked me to get it into the archives. Then she asked me to keep Spenser's best things too. For the longest time, I kept this stuff in a box under my bed." She gestured at the folders. "Go ahead, take a look."

Suki and Blake opened Joy's folders and fanned the photos across the table in vertical rows, arranged by year, with the left row the most recent. It struck Suki that their minds worked in a similar fashion, seeking a pattern in what amounted to random chaos. As Blake stood to get a better look at everything, she opened Spenser's folder.

No photographs, mostly finger paintings, watercolors, awkward charcoal sketches. The paper was now decades old and had begun to yellow. Even so, the age of the paper didn't diminish the violent colors, the odd shapes and textures, the strangeness of his young mind. Most of the time, she didn't know whether she was looking at a house or a field, people or an upside-down sky. Everything was exaggerated, too large or too small, swirls of brilliant color overwhelming shapes or shapes overpowering texture. No balance. Some of the finger paintings reminded her of Rorschach inkblots, thick with meaning that she couldn't decipher.

Joy's photos, taken in an era before digital technology, had that same surreal quality, filtered through senses that didn't see the world in the way that other people did. A wet road lit up by streetlights became an exercise in terror when you realized that the lone silhouette in the foreground belonged to someone who pursued a solitary figure in the background. A field of bright purple Mexican heather was broken up by a massive, amorphous shadow over the field. Was it a thundercloud? A jet? An extinct bird? A UFO?

Suki turned this photo over to see if an exact date had been printed on the back. No date, just a faint scribbling in pencil. "Something's written on here in pencil. It's almost too faint to read."

Lydia handed her a magnifying glass. "See if that helps."

Suki tilted the photo to the right, so that it caught the light, and held the magnifying glass over it. "I think it says, *'This is how Spenser makes me feel at times.'*"

"Like a big shadow," Blake said. "Maybe this is why." He picked three photos out of the middle row.

They looked as if they'd been taken within moments of each other, with a telephoto lens, through the glass of the sliding patio doors at the house. They had captured Spenser watching a toad, then hunched over it, then trapping it against the ground and tearing off its legs.

The horror of it seized Suki viscerally. The toad became her son and the boy torturing the toad became the man who had taken Adam. *The evil within,* as Lydia had said. But equally horrifying was that Joy Longwood had stood at the sliding-glass doors and shot the sequence of photos as her son had tortured the toad.

"Jesus," she whispered. "I'm going to be sick." She shot to her feet and stumbled toward the nearest door. Instantly, Lydia was beside her, hurrying her to the next door, turning on the light, and then holding her head as she threw up in the toilet.

Her head spun, everything in her peripheral vision went fuzzy. The next thing she knew, she sat against the wall, with Lydia holding a cold towel to her forehead and another to the back of her neck. "Breathe," she said. "Breathe real deep."

Suki breathed. Her hands went to the towels, holding them in place. She kept her eyes shut.

"What do you need, Lydia?" Blake, his voice coming from the doorway.

"In my office. Second shelf. A dark blue bottle." Lydia crouched next to Suki. "What you saw in those pictures happened thirty years ago, girl. Don't go thinking he's doing that to your son, okay? He needs your boy alive."

Suki opened her eyes. "We still don't know what he *wants.*"

"Maybe *he* doesn't know. Maybe that's what he's trying to figure out."

Blake reappeared. "Here you go, Lydia."

"Thanks, hon." She unscrewed the bottle, filled an eye-dropper, handed it to Suki. "Squirt this under your tongue. It'll take care of the nausea."

"I heard about your alchemy." Suki attempted a smile, squirted the stuff under her tongue. Tasteless, but cool. "How it saved Ross's life. And Annie's."

Lydia's eyes widened. "Ross told you about that?"

"She needed to know that the investigation is in good hands," Blake said, as if defending himself.

"Well, then you're now a member of a very different club." Lydia rocked back onto her heels. "Feeling better?"

"Like it never happened. Thank you, Lydia."

"Then let's get some breakfast and go back to work."

Blake reached out and pulled her to her feet. In the moments before he released her hands, something passed between them. She felt it, an electrical current, an attraction so powerful that it astonished her. Never mind that it was premature, that the timing was wrong, and that her life was too complicated to get involved with someone as genuine as Blake. It was just good to know she could feel anything like this at all.

16

One World Books

She woke to Sheppard nibbling at her ear like a small, hungry fish. "You awake?" he whispered.

"Hmm. I am now."

Awake to the delicious sensations of his hand and mouth against her skin and the hard, insistent noise of the rain. Rain meant that no one would be working on her store today. It meant she could sleep in, that she and Sheppard could stay in bed all day and make love until her body ached.

Well, not exactly.

She rolled onto her side, facing him, and slid her fingers through his beard. "You may be the horniest guy I've ever met."

He laughed and linked his fingers through hers, pinning her hands against the mattress. "I'm making up for lost time."

His mouth burned a path from her throat to her breasts and belly, his tongue inscribing a trail of secret symbols that he could follow, like bread crumbs, through the wilderness and home again.

The theme song from *E.T.* brought her back. Sheppard's cell ringing.

"You're kidding," he muttered.

"Don't. Let it ring."

"Maybe it's about Spenser."

She drew his face toward hers, kissing him hard, and felt the rapid beat of his heart against her. Suddenly, she saw the face of a plump man with liquid blue eyes and heard a now familiar phrase—*car talk.* "It's him," she said. "Kartauk."

Sheppard rocked back, slipped his cell out from under the pillow, and swung his legs over the side of the bed. "Agent Sheppard . . . Yes, Mr. Kartauk. Thanks for returning my call so promptly."

He walked out into the front room. Mira pulled the sheet over herself and watched the rain washing across the windows. Even without the workmen at the store today, she needed to be there to make sure the roof tarps weren't leaking. To sift through her thick and messy files. To continue her inventory. She needed to read Suki's house again, to sift through the material they'd collected, to earn the exorbitant amount she'd been paid. She was obligated to go to the end of the line with this. Or, as Key West conchs were fond of saying, all the way to mile marker zero.

"Kartauk has a home here," Sheppard said as he hurried back into the bedroom. "It's where he comes when classes are out. He came down after Danielle to tend to repairs and broke his leg falling off a ladder. I'm going to meet him."

She pushed the pillows up against the headboard and sat up. "Damn, you look good without any clothes on, Shep."

He grinned and dived back onto the bed again. "I told him thirty minutes. Now where were we anyway?"

Sheppard offered to drop her at the store, but it was still early enough to fill the van with gas before the station ran dry for the day. So they headed out at the same time, Sheppard promising to call her as soon as he left Kartauk's.

At the station, the line had formed already, but it wasn't long yet. She waited, the engine on, and the windows shut against the rain. The windshield wipers whipped back and forth across the glass, an even, mesmerizing sound that acted like a drug on her brain, releasing endorphins or something else equally pleasant. This substance, whatever it was, seeped through her body until her relaxation was so extreme she thought she might fall asleep before she reached the pump.

As she leaned forward to break her torpor, the gas station suddenly vanished.

Wind drives the rain into her eyes like nails. She can barely see as she stumbles across a driveway toward a towering wooden gate. Her sandals are gone, she lost them somewhere, and the gravel slices into her bare feet. She doesn't dare look behind, is terrified that if she does, she will realize how hopeless this is. She reaches the gate and frantically struggles to open it. But it's too heavy and now it's too late, her time is running out, she . . .

"Hey, lady, move forward, you're holding up everyone else!"

An angry man pounded his fists against her window, his bulbous nose and the broken veins in his fat cheeks a testament to a lifelong problem with alcohol. She quickly lowered her window.

"Calm down," she snapped. "And while you're at it, get your liver and heart checked. You're about an inch away from a heart attack and even closer than that to cirrhosis. And by the way, your father-in-law won't lend you the money for your business. Have a great day."

She raised her window, put the car in gear, drove up to the vacant pump, and got out. She was so irritated by the man's behavior—and so puzzled by whatever had come over her—that she didn't realize the man had marched up to her until he spoke. "You're Mira Morales."

Mira, pumping her gas now, gave him a dirty look. "Sorry, pal, you've got me mixed up with someone else."

"Nope." He raised a digital camera and snapped pictures of her. "You're working on the abduction of the Nichols boy."

Mira turned her back on him and finished filling her tank. But the man came around in front of her, still talking away and snapping photos, introducing himself as a reporter with a cable news channel and would she like to tell him where the investigation now stood?

Mira looked as him as if he'd lost his mind. Then she snatched her receipt, got into the van, and the relentless reporter leaned in close to her window, snapping photos through the glass. She flashed him the bird and sped away, hoping that his need for a tank of gasoline was greater than his need to follow her.

Psychic makes obscene gesture to reporter after refusing to answer questions. Great new cable fodder, she thought, and continued to check her rearview mirror. It seemed the reporter had chosen a full gas tank.

Question: Why had she attracted that sort of confrontation?

Sheppard would call it random. Her name and picture had been linked with the disappearance of a celebrity's child, the reporter had Googled her name, found her photo, recognized her. Simple. But Mira knew better. Everything in her life was connected to everything else. She thought it was like this for Nadine and Annie too, but didn't have any idea how it was for other people. The confrontation, coming so quickly after her vision, was a warning.

But about what? That she should back out of this whole thing and return Suki's money? Frankly, she would like nothing better. Yet she felt obligated now—to Suki, and to Adam most of all.

Her cell rang and an unfamiliar number in the 305 area code came up. "Mira Morales," she said.

"Mom. You sound so formal."

"Annie. I didn't recognize the number."

"I'm calling from someone else's cell. Nadine and I have been watching the stuff on the Adam Nichols disappearance. Is it true that you're working on that?"

"Why, did you place a bet with someone?"

Annie laughed. "Yeah. Twenty bucks. I said you were. 'Cause a kid's involved."

"You win."

"Is the house finished yet? The store? Is there electricity?"

"No, no, and no." Mira braked for a light.

"Mom, when can I come back to Tango? It's, like, so incredibly boring here. Nadine's friends sit around and play bridge or dominoes all day or they do their weird Santeria rituals and everyone is asleep by eight at night and the cats are driving them crazy. One lady is allergic to them, and the other lady is afraid of them, and I'm starting to lose it bigtime."

"Give me a couple of days, Annie. I'll come up and get you."

"Tomorrow's Friday. Can I take a bus then?"

"No. We're still under curfew, there's only one gas station open and it's dry before breakfast, and most of the kids you know have gone elsewhere." *And things with Shep have taken a new turn and I need some time.* "We're making progress on the Nichols case, honey. Just a couple more days."

"I'll call Shep. He'll come and get me."

Testing her, Mira thought. "Shep's living in his office, Annie, and the Nichols case is his."

"So you're working together?"

Mira heard hope in her voice—hope that Sheppard would

return to their lives, that everything would be as it had been before Danielle. "Yeah, but I was hired by Suki Nichols."

"Wow. Is she as cool as her movies?"

"Cooler."

"If I wait till you can pick me up, will you introduce me?"

"Absolutely."

"Will you introduce me as your bright and talented daughter who kind of has acting aspirations of her own but who also has written a script? Would you?"

"You're working on a script?"

"It's called *Doppelganger.*"

"That's fantastic, Annie. How'd this come about?"

"Nadine sent me to this acting camp. They have a screen-writing course. There were, like, seventy submissions, and mine was one of the two chosen. We're shooting a movie of it. So when you pick me up, it'll just be for the weekend. I have to be back for the rest of the shoot next week."

Hardly bored then, Mira thought with a smile. "Well, I'll be sure that I introduce you as my talented and beautiful daughter, who has written this incredible script about a dop-pelganger."

"*Eu coosi dao,* Mom."

In their secret language, than meant *I love you.* "Ditto and bigger than Google."

An acting camp. A script. A movie of *Doppelganger.* Nadine might be misguided where Sheppard was concerned, but she was right on target with Annie.

Mira pulled into the alley behind her store, parked, and dashed through the rain to the rear door. She got out her keys, but as she slipped the key into the lock, realized the door wasn't locked. Odd. She was pretty sure she'd locked it last night, but she'd been spooked, rattled by a feeling that she was being watched, so maybe she hadn't turned the key all the way.

And even if it had been open all night, so what? There

was nothing to steal inside. Even in her office, what could anyone possibly want? Her PC? She had backup files.

She pulled the door open and stepped inside, out of the rain. The dry, quiet yoga room comforted her. But the boxes of books stacked against the wall did not. They were a constant reminder of everything she needed to do before she could open for business again. But by fall, she hoped the entire store would be like this room, as snug as a womb, fortified against the elements, everything rebuilt to the standards established after Hurricane Andrew.

Her sandals clicked and echoed against the new floors. Tile floors. The tile had cost her a small fortune, but it would last longer than she would. She stood in the middle of the huge room and looked upward, at the blue FEMA tarps that still covered holes in the roof. She didn't see any obvious leaks and there didn't appear to be any water on the floors. She walked around to make sure, though, and checked the windows while she was at it. Here and there, she placed her palms against the walls, searching for cool, damp spots.

Nothing. Everything had held.

Maybe her life was on an upswing now.

If she could just locate Adam, she would be in great shape.

She unlocked her office door and went inside, intent on getting the generator started so she could turn on lights, the fan, her computer, and get down to work. She would work a couple of hours, then head over to Suki's to see what else she could pick up on Adam.

She felt uneasy as she crossed the room; her heart rate picked up, perspiration sprang from the pores in her palms. The same feeling she'd felt last night in the alley swept through her again and she spun around.

Nothing there.

Natural light from the other room spilled through the doorway. Dust particles floated in it. She listened, didn't hear anything. Disgusted with her paranoia, she hurried over to the rear exit. It opened to a stoop, where she kept the generator, and a loading dock. Rain streamed off the roof, creating a shimmering veil between her and the dock. She started the generator, and the racket it made caused her to wince. She picked up the extension cord and set it on a pair of old plastic crates so it wouldn't get wet from the rain. She backed toward the door, the remaining part of the cord in her hands, and twisted it around the knob as she stepped back into her office.

She turned—and there, at her desk, sat a man with a gun. Square jaw. White teeth like luminous Chicklets. Cool, beautiful eyes.

"The great Mira Morales." He brought the gun up, aiming it at her. "What a pleasure to meet you at last."

It was moments before she found her voice. "And you must be Spenser C. Timble or Wickett or whatever name you go by now."

He lifted his brows, an expression of surprise, and it threw his forehead into a chaos of lines. "Hey, I'm impressed. You found bits of my past. Just call me Spenser. So here's the deal. We're going to walk to the back of the store, through the yoga room, and out into the alley to your car."

"I'm parked on the street out front."

He laughed and shook his finger at her. "It's not nice to lie, Mira."

He pushed to his feet. She'd guessed from the DVD that he was slightly taller than six feet. He wasn't quite Sheppard's height of six four, but was certainly taller than she was.

"Take off the pack and drop it on the floor. And no heroics. The safety is off and I'm an excellent shot. Especially at this distance. Do you know anything about guns?"

"That they kill." And that six months ago, she'd taken a gunshot to her thigh and it had taken several surgeries to repair the damage. She shrugged off the pack, dropped it on the floor. Her cell phone was in her back pocket. Her shirt covered it.

"A sense of humor. How charming. And I bet you're a hardcore fan of *Bowling for Columbine* and cheered when Fatso Moore reduced the great Charlton Heston to a blithering idiot."

It sounded like he'd broken in here to talk about movies, the NRA, and gun control. "I actually thought that scene was pretty sad."

"But you're anti-NRA and guns."

"And you're not."

He smiled at that, a smile that would dazzle, she thought, if the circumstances had been different.

"Too bad we're on opposite sides when it comes to guns," he remarked.

"I think we're probably on opposite sides on just about any issue."

"Well, this beauty is a Walther P99. Think *Die Another Day*. You know, the 2002 James Bond movie with Pierce Brosnan. It weighs slightly over a pound, has a ten-round magazine. It's a single-action trigger pull. Nice weapon, very accurate. Especially from this distance, which is about the distance from which I shot the Nicholses' housekeeper."

"That's something to be proud of. Shooting a sixty-nine-year-old woman."

"I told her to just turn around and leave the room. If she'd done that, she'd be alive. Instead, she tried to interfere. Kick the pack over here to me."

She nudged it with her foot.

"You can do better than that, Mira. A hard kick. C'mon."

Mira crouched and pushed it across the floor toward him. He dropped to a crouch as well and for moments they were eye to eye, his as hard, beautiful, and intractable as stones. She had a sudden image of these eyes on a movie poster and wondered what it meant.

He pulled her pack toward him, grabbed the strap, slung it over his shoulder. "Stand slowly," he told her, and she did.

"I love cooperative women."

"I detest bullies."

"It's all a matter of perception. I'm really not such a bad guy."

"Pardon me while I gag. You shot a defenseless old woman and snatched a kid. And back in Seattle, you were a suspect in your father's death. Then there was a young woman, an ex-girlfriend in Silicon Valley who claimed you tried to run her over. Just how does that fit into not being such a bad guy?"

He twitched, as though his shirt had shrunk, and a muscle twitched under his right eye. She thought he was about to lunge for her and she flinched, drawing her arms in closer to her body, and felt herself shut down psychically.

"Car keys," he snapped.

"They're in the pack."

Without taking his eyes from her, he set the pack on her desk, unzipped it, and dug around inside. Out came the keys.

"Cell phone."

"It's in my car."

His eyes locked with hers. "Empty the pockets in your shorts. Fast."

She turned the side pockets inside out. Change clinked as it hit the floor. A couple of dollar bills drifted down.

He strode over to her, jammed the gun up against her head, and leaned in so close to her she could feel the warmth of his breath against her face and smell the toothpaste he'd used. She recognized it as the organic toothpaste in the bathroom off her office.

She suddenly knew he had hidden in her office last night when he'd fled the woods, had used the generator, had fallen asleep in here, and that her arrival had surprised him. He hadn't planned for it. He had hoped to be out and gone by sunrise.

His fingers closed around her throat. "I think you've got back pockets, Mira, and that the phone is there. Or maybe it's here." He ran his hand over the front of her T-shirt, across her breasts. "Oops, there's something here, but not a gun. No bra either. I like that. I like women who don't wear bras. It's sexy, especially with tits like yours. Bet your skin is real soft too." He thrust his hand up under her shirt.

She held her breath, didn't move. The urge to squeeze her eyes shut nearly overwhelmed her. But she knew if she showed fear or horror or any of the other terrifying emotions she felt just then, he would shoot her. She was expendable. His presence here was about last night. He was proving that although she had escaped him then, it hadn't made any difference at all, now had it?

"Nice skin, soft, just like I thought." He reached behind her, patting the back pockets of her shorts, and pulled out the cell phone. He wagged it in front of her face. "Just like I thought. I'm really very disappointed in you, Mira. I sort of equate psychics with, you know, spiritual types. And spiritual types don't lie. But you lied." He stepped back, away from her, and pocketed her cell phone. "So what'd you pick up on me?"

That's what the touchy-feely was about? Good God. She had figured this guy all wrong. "Nothing. I can't pick up anything when a gun's jammed to my head. I shut down as soon as I saw the gun."

"You have control over it that way?"

"It's automatic. I see a gun, everything shuts down." She didn't intend to tell him too much, just enough to keep herself alive. "Fatigue, illness, guns: Those are some of the triggers that turn me off. It's like someone yanks the power cord and I don't have a battery backup."

"How long's it take for you to power up again?"

"I don't know. I haven't had a gun pointed at me that often."

"Well, then. We'll go with the original plan." He motioned toward the door with the gun. "Move. We're taking your car."

"Taking it where?"

"You're the psychic, tell me."

"Like I said, I've been unplugged."

On their way out of the office, he grabbed an umbrella hanging from a hook on the wall. And while he was distracted, she removed one of her earrings, a delicate pearl Sheppard had given her, and dropped it on the floor.

"You're going to drive," he said.

"You won't get off the island. People are looking for you."

"People." He snorted. "What people? Cops? Feds? Give me a fucking break. They don't know anything. They're so inept they didn't figure the obvious, that I came here last night, that I hid here." He patted his pack. "That I have your hard drive. You're going to get us off the island, Mira, because Adam's life depends on it."

On their way through the store, Mira slipped out the other pearl earring. At the first opportunity, she let her hand brush a shelf and left the earring there.

"Just for the record," he said. "What did you think of *Fahrenheit 9/11*?"

So now they would have a conversation. Okay, fine, she could play this game. "That it was ironic Ray Bradbury got all huffy about the title. Even if it had been the exact title, it wouldn't matter, since titles aren't copyrighted."

He laughed. "That's clever. You give an opinion without answering the question. That's what journalists do these days. C'mon, answer the question."

"It was a documentary, angry and biased, shot through the lens of Moore's opinions and beliefs. But at the end, I cheered. Happy?"

"Personally, I think that *Fahrenheit* and *The Passion of the Christ* captured the schizophrenia of the country right now."

She felt Spenser's hunger for discourse, and wondered what he and his redheaded girlfriend talked about. The price of condoms?

"So, as a psychic, who do you think will win the election in November?"

"Not you or me."

"You're playing with me, Mira."

"It's the other way around, Spenser." *Keep him talking. Distract him.* "You don't really want answers to questions."

"Then what do I want?"

"Publicity? Revenge?"

No snappy comeback. He jabbed the gun into the small of her back and she pushed through the door of the yoga room.

Before they stepped out of the rear door and into the alley, he opened the umbrella and dug the gun a little harder against her spine. "If I pull the trigger, you'll be a cripple. Got it?"

"Got it," she murmured, and they stepped out into the alley and the driving rain, the umbrella obscuring their faces from any security cameras.

Once they were both inside the car, Mira in the driver's seat, he pressed the gun to her temple. "Let's test your movie skills, Mira." His voice slipped around and through her, a cool, seductive liquid. "This is the decisive question. If you don't answer it correctly, I pull the trigger."

Beads of perspiration erupted on her forehead, her upper lip. The pressure of the gun against her temple became more intense. Unbearable. She could hardly swallow, much less speak. "It's like the Taliban. You're both interrogator and judge."

"Fuck the Taliban. Right this second, Mira, I'm God. Okay, here's the question. 1987, vampire film, directed by a woman. What was the film?"

Panic. She rarely watched vampire movies. "Can't you give me a little more information? I'm not a vampire fan."

"One of the stars, who played a character named Severen, was also in *Titanic* and *Mighty Joe Young.*"

Her mind had emptied. She and Annie and Sheppard had seen both movies, but she couldn't remember who had acted in either of them. It was the ultimate game of Trivial Pursuit.

Stall for time. "I . . . I can't remember." Maybe she imagined it, but the pressure of the gun against her temple seemed to ease. "Why those movies?"

Spenser leaned toward her and whispered in her ears, his breath warm, putrid. "Why not? I know the answer and you don't. And you're the psychic. You're supposed to have access to that kind of information."

"I access emotions."

"And I'm emoting."

"And I'm unplugged, remember?"

"Watch the clock on the dashboard, Mira." The pressure against her temple increased as he leaned in closer to her. She felt the warmth of his breath against her cheek, smelled the mint that he now sucked on. "Tick-tock. You have thirty seconds."

Where were all these helpful spirits when she needed them? Where was Hepburn? Tom? Joy Longwood? *Hey, hello, someone help me out, please.* "I don't know if I even saw that movie."

"Tick-tock," he whispered, and ten seconds had vanished.

Her tongue slid along her lower lip. "The game. That's your adrenaline kick. The God game."

"Wrong answer. Tick." He paused and breathed, "Tock. Ten seconds."

"I . . . I don't know the answer."

". . . seven . . . six . . ."

"I don't know the fucking answer." She nearly choked on the words.

The pressure on her temple eased and Spenser laughed and laughed. "And *that* was the right answer, Mira. The movie was *Near Dark,* directed by Kathryn Bigelow. Bill Paxton played Severen."

Mira turned her head toward him, aware that sweat beaded her face, that her throat was dry, that she looked as shocked and terrified as she felt. He seemed inordinately pleased with himself, and she suddenly understood that the whole purpose of *this* little game was to drive home the point that he could end her life at any second, that for her, right now, he really was God.

"Now drive," he said.

17

Revelations

The shimmering curtain of rain made Glen Kartauk's modest Spanish-style home in the Tango hills resemble a bastion of peace. It sat on a secluded acre that backed up to woods, its broad front windows bordered by dark blue wooden shutters. The only obvious signs of damage from the hurricane were a collapsed wooden fence at the sides of the house, trees stripped of leaves, and missing tiles at the right front corner of the house.

"This neighborhood seems to have fared better than Mira's," Goot remarked.

"Probably because of the hills and the woods," said Sheppard.

"Frankly, amigo, I'm starting to think it was all the luck of the draw. You know, karma or something."

Given his reconciliation with Mira, Sheppard figured his karma was on the rise. But then, his karma had been so bad lately that it had nowhere to go but *up*.

As Sheppard started to ring the bell, the door opened, and a plump, jolly-looking man stood there, leaning on a crutch, his right leg encased in a cast that reached just above his knee. He wore a shorts and a Minnesota Vikings T-shirt and was barefoot. Sheppard pegged him to be about sixty.

"Heard the car." He thrust out his hand. "Glen Kartauk."

"Wayne Sheppard, John Gutierrez. Thanks for seeing us, Mr. Kartauk."

"My pleasure. Please, come on in."

"You have air-conditioning," Goot exclaimed as they walked up a tiled hall.

"Only because the house has an in-ground generator that comes on within moments of lost power. Wonderful invention. The tank holds propane and if this power outage lasts much longer, I imagine the tank will be scraping empty and then it's good-bye creature comforts. Let's go into the kitchen, it's cooler. Don't know if you gentlemen have had breakfast yet, but my housekeeper made us some fresh coffee and pastries."

The table had been set. The pastries reminded Sheppard that he hadn't eaten anything before he'd left Mira's trailer, and the coffee smelled great. Once they were settled, Kartauk said, "If you hadn't called me, Mr. Sheppard, I would've called you today. Yesterday morning, I was on a ladder, replacing screen on the back patio, and I had the TV on. Heard about the disappearance of Adam Nichols from the Mango Hill house. It shocked me, I lost my balance, fell off the ladder, and broke my damn leg. They wouldn't release me until this morning."

"Shocked you because?" Goot asked.

Kartauk's bright blue eyes went to Goot. "I dislike coincidences, Mr. Gutierrez. Another boy disappears from the Mango Hill House, the two crimes separated by nearly thirty years." He shook his head, slipped on a pair of Ben Franklin reading glasses, and slid a thick file across the table to Sheppard and Goot. "Here's everything I collected on the abduction of Spenser Longwood. It covers the three years I pursued Ray Connor and everything I knew about the case. I lost his trail in Arizona."

"How do you know Ray Connor took Spenser?" Sheppard unzipped his laptop case, removed the file that contained all they'd found on the Longwoods, and set it on the table. An information exchange. "We didn't find any definitive evidence about that."

Kartauk opened Sheppard's file and stared at a photo of Joy Longwood. "This picture doesn't do her justice." He raised his eyes. "Look, this is a long and complicated story. Let's start with Friday, May 16, 1975. Joy didn't feel well that morning and called in sick to work. Spenser didn't feel so great either, so Joy figured they'd caught the same bug. She let him stay home from school. I know this because she called me around seven that morning. We talked most mornings. I told her I'd stop by the house that afternoon to bring her chicken soup and groceries or anything else she needed. I should have just gone over there and taken care of her and Spenser."

"I didn't realize you knew her." *Or knew her as well as it sounds like you did.*

"We were close. Had been for a long time. I was, uh, still married and was trying to get out of it gracefully." He smiled ruefully. "Big mistake. I made a lot of mistakes in those days. The instant I met Joy, I was crazy about her. You're lucky if you get a chance like that once in your life. But I was bogged down in obligations, responsibilities, wife, kids. . . ." He shook his head again. "Hell, I'm a Pisces and we feel guilty about everything."

Sheppard laughed. He liked this guy already. "So she called you at seven. And the fire trucks and paramedics arrived when?"

"Around nine. At some point during those two hours, someone came into the house, there was a violent confrontation, and Joy was knocked out. The person set fire to one of the downstairs rooms and snatched Spenser. Like I said, that person was Ray Connor, who Joy had lived with up north. I pursued him for the next three years, following a few leads

and my instincts. Then I lost track of him. By then, I'd re-
signed from the department, my marriage had collapsed, and
I had run out of money. I was forced to give up my search."

"You mentioned leads," Sheppard said. "What kind of
leads?"

"Eyewitnesses who saw Ray Connor with a young boy. I
had photos that I took on the road with me."

"Fill us in on Ray Connor, Mr. Kartauk."

He removed the photo of Joy Longwood from Sheppard's
file and ran his fingers slowly—lovingly—over the surface.
"They met when she was doing graduate work at Yale. Her
room got broken into or something. I'm a bit vague on these
details. Anyway, the New Haven cops were called. Ray
showed up. He was a beat cop in New Haven in those days.
They were lovers for a couple of months, but he was a big
drinker and she broke it off. He didn't like that. He started
stalking her, making her life miserable. She got a restraining
order and for a while, he left her alone. Then she found out
she was pregnant and dropped out of Yale and moved back to
Norwalk with her mother.

"Ray pursued her, harassed her, threatened to hurt her
mother if Joy didn't give him a chance. She was seven
months pregnant by then and worried that he would make
good on the threat against her mother."

"Pregnant with twins," Sheppard said.

Kartauk's brows lifted, pushing the wrinkles on his forehead into his hairline. "You've done your homework. I'm
impressed. I thought cops and journalists had lost the art of
homework."

"Not all of us," Goot said.

"Joy moved in with him. He supported her, waited on her
hand and foot. He wanted to marry her so the twins would
have 'proper parents.' She refused to marry him and in her
eighth month, her mother had a fatal accident. She fell down
her cellar stairs. Joy went into early labor, probably because
of the emotional trauma." He sipped from his mug, helped

himself to one of the pastries. After a moment, he went on. "Fast forward a few months. Joy sold her mother's house and opened a separate account with that money that Ray didn't know about. She was terrified of him, especially when he'd been drinking.

"Anyway, one night while Ray was working late, she packed the kids into her van and left him. He found her two days later in Delaware, beat her up, and told her she could leave, but he would keep the twins. She refused. They made it another few months. Then one of Ray's cop buddies told him Joy had filed half-a-dozen charges against him. I guess ole Ray realized the shit was hitting the fan and decided it was time to cut his losses and run. So he took Lyle with him. Joy fled with Spenser and eventually ended up on Tango.

"She bought the house on Mango Hill with money from the sale of her mother's place. The high school was always on the lookout for qualified math teachers and she got the job within a couple of weeks of moving here."

"Any idea where Ray went with Lyle?" Sheppard asked.

A darker mood clamped down on Kartauk. His expression seemed to be veiled in shadow. "North Carolina, around Raleigh. Ray apparently worked as a security guard at a local college. In December of 1974, Lyle was hit by a car. He died."

Kartauk stared into his mug for so long that it was as if his soul had left the room altogether.

"The wheels in Ray's fuzzy brain must've started turning and he set out to find Joy and Spenser. Ray didn't have the benefit of the Internet, but it didn't take him long to find her, to claim his other son. I urged her all the time to change her name to something else, but she never did. Maybe if I pushed her harder, she would still be alive and we wouldn't be sitting here now." His voice turned thick with regret. "Five months later, Ray nabbed Spenser, torched the inside of the house, and Joy died." He rubbed his hands over his face. "Now the boy has returned as a man and done to some-one else what was done to him."

This was the same thing Mira had told them, was what the photos had proven, and now Kartauk was saying it. How much more confirmation did they need?

"How can you be so sure?" Goot asked.

Kartauk's hands dropped away from his face. "You mean, you didn't know?"

"Yeah, we knew." Sheppard opened his file and removed the juvenile photos of Spenser Wickett Timble and the artist's sketch that had been made based on the reporter's de-scription of the man on the bike. He placed them side by side and gave Kartauk the brief version of the juvenile record and the vehicular homicide charge. "We got lucky."

Kartauk stared at the two photos, then tapped the eyes on both. "It's right there. The eyes tell everything. A face is smooth at seventeen, gets crow's-feet by thirty-five, wrinkles by fifty, and looks like parchment by eighty. But the eyes never change. It's Spenser. I'd know those eyes anywhere."

"Do you think he remembers being abducted?" Goot asked.

"I doubt it. The mind has a way of closing off painful memories, especially those that happen when we're young. And I think it's part of what drives him."

"He hasn't demanded a ransom," Sheppard said. "The only contact he has made is a DVD of himself and Adam that he gave to a Telemundo reporter." As Sheppard ex-plained, he brought out a copy of the DVD and set it on the table. "I'd appreciate it if you would take a look at it when you can and call me."

"Sick fuck," Kartauk murmured, turning the case over in his hands.

"Other than some deep psychological thing about doing what was done to him, what do you think his motive is for taking Adam?" Sheppard asked.

"Did you ever read *A Boy Called It*?"

Mira had given him many books over the years and he often had trouble remembering what he'd read, skimmed, or set aside. But this one had stuck with him. "Dave Pelzer. Child abuse. Supposedly true story. Written by the guy who lived through it." Parts of the book had been so horrific that he'd felt physically ill. "You read it, Goot?"

"One chapter. I couldn't get beyond that."

"Well, here's the curious thing about human nature," Kartauk went on. "Given what Pelzer went through, he might have grown up to become a serial killer. A rapist. Or a child abuser himself. But that's not how his destiny unfolded. I don't doubt for a second that Spenser went through some of the things that Pelzer did. Ray was an alcoholic sadist, a twisted fuck. Spenser was six when Ray took him and— what? Sixteen or seventeen when the trailer fire happened?"

"Seventeen," Sheppard said.

"That's eleven years of extreme abuse, during an era when people looked the other way. If it had been me, I would've tried to kill the bastard. I don't have Pelzer's capacity for forgiveness." He sat forward, fingers laced together. "I'm betting that the only happy years Spenser has known were between the ages of one and six. And because the mind is such a curious thing, because it can compartmentalize and rationalize and be duped into forgetting, I don't think he has a conscious clue. Except I think a part of him remembers the house. The house as a symbol of when he was happy. He may not verbalize it in that context. He may not consciously know why he took Adam. In that sense, he could be reenacting what happened to him. But I'm pretty damn sure that what he wants is the house."

The *house*? Sheppard rolled that around, testing it against some inner standard that had developed during his two decades in law enforcement. *I want what you have.* That was one of the motives Tina had mentioned on the beach. Moments ticked past. No one spoke. He felt Goot doing the same thing that he was. They looked at each other. Kartauk looked at them.

"And how would taking Adam get him the house?"

Kartauk shrugged, palms facing the ceiling. "Who the hell knows? I'm just giving you my best theory."

Sheppard felt that the psychological impact of abuse was probably true, but he didn't buy Kartauk's theory about *I want your house.* "We're missing six years of Spenser's life," Sheppard told Kartauk. "From around 1987 to 1993, between when he left Seattle and ended up in Silicon Valley. Until we know what he did during those years, I don't think we have the final answer about his motive or what he intends to do with Adam. And on a whole other level, there's the glaring coincidence that both he and the Nicholses have lived in the Mango Hill house."

Kartauk nodded. "Yeah, coincidences really beg for interpretation, don't they? Kind of makes you feel that there's a design in the universe that we'll never understand."

"Any idea what Spenser may have done during those six years?" Goot asked.

"Not a clue," Kartauk replied.

After Ross Blake dropped Suki off at the back of the house, she made sure that Paul was gone—to where? A hotel? His girlfriend's place? Then she collapsed on the couch in the living room and dozed fitfully. She dreamed, but the dreams were as disjointed as her life, like snippets of colorized movies.

In one, Judy Garland in *The Wizard of Oz* sang like Elvis Presley, shaking her hips and practically making love to the microphone. In another, Robert De Niro as the bad doctor in *Godsend* assured her he could clone Adam, no problem, and Nicole Kidman, looking like the pale ghost mother in *The Others,* warned Suki not to trust him, then ran around the room, jerking the black curtains across the windows. Suki bolted awake, sheathed in sweat, the air noisy with the hammering of rain against the roof.

She wandered into Adam's room and crawled onto his bed, clutched the gray Fids bear to her chest, and wept. It disgusted her. Served no purpose. Got her nowhere. Bottom line? She no longer knew her direction, her location, her place in the larger scheme of things. It was as if she had misplaced the compass of her life.

Shower, she thought. A shower would wake her up, wash away the heat, get her moving. She turned her cell back on and set it on a shelf above the toilet in Adam's bathroom. It was as tidy in here as it was in his bedroom. The towels were fresh, the soap was new, unscented Dove, the only kind he used.

Stacked on the back of the toilet were half-a-dozen books that ranged from the latest Harry Potter to books on theoretical physics by Michio Kaku to Oriah Mountain Dreamer's *The Invitation*. It occurred to her that she didn't know what Adam thought about what he read. She knew he had tried to talk to her about it—in the car, on their occasional bike rides together, sometimes at breakfast or dinner. But her mind usually had been elsewhere, or she and Paul had been arguing, or the phone had been ringing, or they'd had guests. It must have seemed to Adam that he fell somewhere behind the trash collector in his mother's priorities.

Gladys, surrogate mom, friend and confidante, had known more about Adam's thoughts and feelings, hopes and dreams, than she did.

Her cell beeped repeatedly, signaling that she had received dozens of messages. She ignored it and stepped into the shower, under the cold, unforgiving spray. The needles stung her spine, her face, her eyelids. She pressed her palms to the wall, zipped herself up inside her son's skin, and saw the accretion of her betrayals, the subtle messages that must have told him to butt out, that he was an inconvenience, a postscript, that he didn't count.

She stood in the stall, not moving, waiting for self-disgust to work its way out and away. Her cell rang repeatedly, then fell silent. When she finally turned the shower off, the stillness in the stall seemed deafening, eerie. Yet she felt calmer, more accepting of her monumental flaws, her numerous camouflages, her bullshit. She thought it might be time for her to get out of the movies, leave while she was at the top of her game and before she lost her soul completely.

Some women in this business—Streep, Sarandon, Lange—seemed to be able to hold onto their intrinsic selves, their families and private lives, without compromising themselves or their children. But she wasn't like them. Her compromises had begun fifteen years ago, when she had married the wrong man and hadn't told him that Adam was not his son.

She stepped out, wrapped a towel around herself, picked up her cell phone, her umbilical cord to the larger world. Suki clicked through the messages—her agent, her manager, her PR person, two directors, a producer, several journalists. She deleted all the numbers, put on clean clothes that she kept in the linen closet in the hall, combed her hair, and went into Paul's study.

What did he do in here all day? In the weeks before the hurricane, he had spent eight and ten hours a day in this room, typing away on his computer, supposedly working on a new book, a new script, and creating new material for his courses this fall. But she hadn't seen anything he had written. He had shut that door a long time ago.

In the early days of their marriage, they had spent long, intimate hours brainstorming for stories, characters, plots. In those days, they had been partners in the truest sense of the word. Paul had screened the scripts that had arrived, covered them with notes about how she could play this or that character if this detail or that plot device were changed. He'd had the eye. And she had done the same thing for the scripts that crossed his desk.

Then things had started to go wrong. They had faltered in their attention to each other, to the marriage. But perhaps the attention hadn't been there to begin with. Maybe it had been a sham, just another layer of camouflage. For the last several years, she had screened her own scripts. *Acid Trip,* her Oscar movie, was based on a script Paul had rejected. *Hate it,* he'd written in the margin. *Ridiculous. Do this one at your own peril.*

And she had selected the script because that "peril" had appealed to her.

She plugged his PC into the extension cord in the hall that connected to the generator. Granted, she was no computer nerd. Programming was beyond her skills. But thanks to her son's expertise with computers, she knew enough to search for what bothered her. And after poking around for a while, she found it in a hidden file, e-mail exchanges between Paul and a woman who called herself "paradise."

There must have been hundreds of exchanges, spanning a period of at least fourteen months.

> I wish I could write something cool, but I still feel u inside me, hot and wet and forever. You must, absolutely must, finish your script. U are on the right track, I really feel it, and oh please, Paul, come 2 me tomorrow or the next day or the day after that.
> luv,
> paradise

> Hon, have five scenes that I love, a million other scenes that suck. You give me courage. Will call u this week.
> Loving u
> Paul

Hon. When was the last time Paul had called *her* hon? As Suki clicked through the e-mails, she counted dozens of exchanges like these. Then there were dozens more concerning arrangements—where they would meet, when, the lies and cover-ups. More recently, in the last several months, the exchanges sounded different on his part, more reserved, as though he were pulling back, getting tired of her, bored. But he couldn't quite break it off.

Will call.
Can't call.
Can you meet me in Miami?
Stop pressuring me!
Am horrendously busy.

Did Adam know? Had he poked around in Paul's computer?

Probably. *Oh, baby, I'm so sorry.*

She suddenly felt like taking a bat to the monitor, the tower. Smashing them, destroying them. But her practicality kicked in. Her attorney would want to see these e-mails, the first tangible evidence of Paul's infidelities. They could save her millions in the divorce.

Suki went into his Outlook Express folder, clicked through it until she found a folder called *Identities,* opened it. Five identities. *Five.* Why did he need so many? Was he conducting multiple affairs? Visiting porn sites? *What?* She clicked through them, copying the folders onto her memory stick, one after another, until she had copied everything. Then she printed out dozens of the most lurid e-mails, stapled them together, and put them in a folder.

She poked around some more and found another curious item. The networking box was checked. Was it checked on her computer too? Was he monitoring her e-mail? Her files? She unchecked it, then poked around some more, looking for other anomalies.

Suki was so involved in what she was doing that she didn't

realize Paul had come home until he was standing in his office doorway, his face bright red, shiny with sweat, as if he'd been running.

"What the hell are you doing in my office?" he demanded.

She pocketed the memory stick, picked up the folder, stood. "What I should have done a long time ago."

"What the hell does that mean?"

Rage seeped up from the center of her being, then rushed into her chest, her neck, her face. And when she finally met his eyes, he must have seen it because he flinched. "I wish I could write something cool," she said, reciting from one of the e-mails. "But I still feel you inside me. Hot and wet and forever."

Blood drained from his cheeks, he opened his mouth to speak, but nothing came out.

"Jesus, Paul. So what number is she? Eight or eighteen? *Paradise.*" She spat the word. "That's who you were with the night Adam was taken. So go be with her."

Suki started past him, but Paul grabbed her arm. "Suki, wait. Please. Hear me out."

She spun around. "Hear you *out*? *Again*? Is that all you can say? What do you want me to listen to? How you whispered sweet nothings to this woman and then came home and fucked *me*?" She nearly choked on her own words. "I'm outta here. And when I come back, I want your stuff gone. Do you understand? *Gone.* I told you last night that I wanted you gone, but you didn't get it. From now on, we communicate through our attorneys."

"You can't *throw* me out," he snapped. "This house is also mine."

"There's one name on the deed, Paul. *My* name. It was paid for in cash, from my accounts." With that, she wrenched her arm free of his grasp and the folder that contained the e-mails slipped from her hand and hit the floor. The sheets of paper scattered across the den.

Paul stared at them. Suki crouched and quickly gathered them up and stuck them back in the folder. *"You printed my e-mails?"* he burst out. "My God, what kind of . . ."

"Evidence, Paul. You fucked around, I'm divorcing you, getting full custody of Adam, and you won't get a cent."

She slammed the study door as she left and ran for the stairs, taking them two at a time, the folder tight in her hand now. In the bedroom, she shut the door, locked it, leaned against it, and squeezed her eyes shut, the folder tight against her chest.

Please return my son to me. . . .

She opened her eyes. Muted light spilled through the windows and across the king-sized bed. It cast long, narrow shadows against the floor and the movie posters on the walls. She stared at the posters, trying to make sense of them.

In the poster for *Acid Trip,* a solitary woman in hippie clothing moved down a country road, where a pewter sky hung low with thunderheads. In the poster for *Connections,* where she played a healer, a pair of silhouetted hands against bright light looked magical, ethereal. She didn't have a clue what it told about the story, but the image was compelling. The box office take had been the best until she'd won the Oscar.

In a third poster, for *American Dream,* she and her movie children looked like the American dream, bright and smiling and beautiful. And yet, the image had nothing to do with life as most people lived it. It was a lie. It disgusted her.

Suki rubbed her hands over her face and pushed away from the door. She forced herself to cross the room, to go into the closet, to pull down a small gym bag from an upper shelf. She dropped it on the floor at her feet, jerked clothes off hangers, scooped up shoes, dug out an extra cell phone charger. She went into the bathroom, grabbed essentials, stuffed them down inside the bag. She slipped the folder down inside it, zipped the bag shut, slung it over her arm. She would go to the bookstore, find Mira, stay with her.

Ironic. Out of all the people she knew, her trust lay with a woman she barely knew, whom she had hired to find her son. Yes, there were plenty of people she could call who would listen, sympathize, offer to hold her hand. But most of them would want something from her in return. Most of them were like the flight attendant on the plane who had lent Suki her cell. Her face, her name, her presence, represented an opportunity, a doorway, nothing more.

Banging on the bedroom door. Paul shouting at her to open it. She vaguely wondered what the feds monitoring the phone thought of it.

She glanced quickly around the room for her cell phone, didn't see it. Had she left it downstairs? She patted the pockets of her shorts. There. Back pocket. She wasn't quite as out of it as she'd thought. Encouraging.

Suki pulled out the cell, punched out her home number. The answering machine came on. "This is Suki Nichols. I'm calling from my bedroom. My husband has become violent and abusive. Could you please restrain him until I leave the house?"

Click, click, then a hushed voice: "This is Agent Ellis, ma'am. Please stay in the bedroom. We'll restrain Mr. Nichols. Are you, uh, pressing charges?"

"I just want to get out of here."

"We're on it, ma'am."

She snapped the cell shut and stood at the door, waiting. Within moments, all hell broke loose on the other side of the door. Paul shouting. The agents threatening. Then Ellis's voice: "You can open the door, Ms. Nichols."

She unlocked the door, cracked it open, peered into the hall. The two agents held Paul against the wall. His nostrils flared. He looked homicidal. But he wasn't about to argue with guns and a pair of feds.

Suki slipped out into the hall and hurried down the stairs and out onto the back porch. She raced into the woods on foot, the gym bag banging against her ribs, the rain pouring over her.

It didn't take her long to reach Mira's bookstore. Only a few people were out and about in the rain, umbrellas hiding their faces. Now and then, a car sped past her or someone whizzed by on a bike, hunched over the handlebars. With her baseball cap pulled over her face, the rain pouring over her, she was just another pedestrian.

The front door of One World Books was locked. Suki hurried to the loading dock and walked quickly up the ramp to a dry spot under the eaves, where Mira kept the generator. It was silent. The door to her office wasn't shut all the way and when Suki nudged it with her foot, it swung open slowly, creaking on its hinges.

"Mira?" she called, and slipped inside.

Light seeped in through the open door, a thin, pale stream that flowed across the floor, strewn with dollars bills and loose change, like vestiges of a rich kid's broken piñata. Farther along, near the door to the rest of the store, she spotted a pearl earring. She started to pick it up, thought better of it, and called Mira's name again, her voice echoing. She quickly crossed the office and went out into the rest of the store. The empty shelves. The smell of new wood. The cacophony of the rain against the roof tarps.

The money on the floor. The earring.

Frowning, she whipped out her cell, called Mira's number, reached her voice mail. Suki didn't leave a message. She disconnected, turned slowly, and looked around, goose bumps rising on her arms, the skin on the back of her neck tightening.

Wrong, wrong. Something had happened here.

She punched out Sheppard's number.

18

Unplanned

Finch felt trapped on the ferry. The van was wedged tightly in a middle row on the lowest deck, all exits blocked until the ferry stopped and people drove off the other side. Despite the steady rain, the inside of the van was hot, muggy. He couldn't run the AC; every engine had to be turned off once the ferry got under way. Even if he ran the AC off the battery, it wouldn't cool the car enough to make a difference.

If he lowered the windows, it would be too easy for Mira to shout for help. If she shouted, he would have to shoot her, then fire randomly into the crowd to create enough chaos so he could escape. The only escape route lay over the side of the ferry and into the water.

Forget chaos. All he wanted to do was get home, tend to the kid, put Mira somewhere safe. In with Adam? Probably. Adam's room was secure. He would let her rest, eat, commiserate with the kid, and then he would demand that she read for him. *What's in my immediate future? Tell me about my early years in the Mango Hill house. Are the Nicholses suffering as much as I did? Or do I need to kill Adam to really bring the point home?*

It occurred to him that maybe none of these questions mattered, that maybe it all boiled down to what Mira had said earlier—the kick, the unmitigated power. Perhaps that was the best psychic information she could offer him. She'd claimed she wasn't plugged in when she'd told him this, but how did he know if she was telling the truth?

She sat behind the wheel, her head resting against the seat, eyes closed, fingers flexing against the steering wheel. "So what do you want from me, Spenser?"

"I want you to sit where I'm sitting. We're going to trade places."

"Besides that."

"We'll discuss it later." He squeezed back between the bucket seats and kept the gun on her as she moved into the passenger seat. The child locks were engaged, he'd made sure of that, so she couldn't lunge suddenly out the door. He slipped into the driver's seat, suddenly grateful for the rain, a kind of curtain between them and the rest of the cars on the deck. He pulled her seat belt over her, snapped it into place, then unzipped his pack and brought out a roll of electrical tape.

He tore off a long strip, wrapped it several times around her wrist, then around the seat belt. He repeated this with her other arm. He grabbed a wrinkled beach towel from the backseat and spread it over her hands, covering them.

She didn't say anything. She just stared at him, beads of sweat rolling down the sides of her face.

"I'm going to lower the back windows, so we can get some air in here," he said. "If you shout, if you try anything at all, I'll shoot you."

"And then what? You don't have a silencer on that gun. Everyone would hear it."

"Except you. At point-blank range, a bullet in your side would tear through your chest cavity, puncture your heart and lungs, and you would die before the noise of the shot even registered."

"But you'd be fucked. You'd have to fire into the crowd, inciting chaos so you could dive over the side of the ferry."

"Actually, Adam would be fucked. See, I would leap over the side and I might or might not survive it. Even if I survived, I'd be in a world of shit and wouldn't be able to go back to my place. Right now, Adam is in a sealed room. He can't escape. There's a cooler with some food in it, but how long will that last? Before he's found, he would die of hunger. In the end, the kid you've been hired to find would die and it would be your fault."

Her expression didn't change; she was good at keeping her face impassive. But her eyes revealed what she felt and he knew he'd won this round of repartee. She recognized that everything he had said was possible. Threatening Adam would keep her in line.

"So it's better for Adam if you don't make trouble, Mira."

"Have you sexually abused him?"

"Jesus, what kind of question is *that*? I'm not a pervert."

"You nab a kid, kill an old woman, burn down a trailer. . . ." She shrugged. "I figure sexual perversion isn't such a stretch."

He was starting to hate her and struggled not to shout at her, to reveal the depth of his rage. *It's a role,* he reminded himself, so when he spoke, his voice held only a sharp edge. "You don't know shit about me. How could you? You had a perfect childhood. Ms. Popularity. Cheerleader. Prom queen. Straight A's in college. Had every advantage. Born with the proverbial silver spoon. Mira Morales, perfect citizen." He snorted. "You don't have a fucking clue how it is for other people." People like him.

"Cheerleader? Prom queen? Ms. Popularity?" She burst out laughing. "Try class nerd, introvert, bookworm. In elementary school I was so sensitive to other people's energy that for a long time I couldn't sit in the cafeteria filled with kids without taking on their symptoms, their moods, their bullshit. And if by silver spoon you mean money, Spenser, we were comfortable, but not rich. My parents worked all the time. I was raised by my grandmother. And, good thing for me, she understood what I was about. So you don't know shit about me either."

It was the most she had said to him—and certainly the most personal information she had related about herself— since she'd found him in her office. And yeah, okay, so she hadn't been a cheerleader or a prom queen. She still didn't know what it was like to have lived *his* childhood, with *his* old man.

She rested her head against the back of the seat, closed her eyes. Shut him out. He sat there and stewed. His head began to ache. He couldn't tell if it meant another migraine was headed his way or if it was just an ordinary headache. He gobbled a couple of meds anyway.

After a few minutes, she said, "So let me get this straight. Because you had a shitty childhood with an abusive father, your psyche is warped, so you do to others what was done to you? Does that about cover it? Is that what this is about? I think there's more. I think the whole goddamn thing is about revenge. But for what, Spenser? What did these people do to you that could possibly warrant kidnapping their son?"

If they weren't trapped on the deck of the goddamn ferry, jammed among other vehicles, with so many people nearby who might, at any second, peer through the van's windows, his arm would become a club and that club would smash her nose back into her brain. Instead, he leaned toward her and slipped his arm around her shoulders, like a man about to nuzzle his lover's ear. He curled his fingers through her hair and jerked hard, forcing her head to tilt toward him.

"I could just maim you. Remember that."

He released her hair, shoved her away from him. Tears rolled from the corners of her eyes. Good.

The ferry churned its way toward Key West. The air got warmer, the rain came down harder, the inside of the van grew more and more uncomfortable. The meds he'd taken nibbled at the ache in his head but didn't banish it. He needed food, a shower, sleep, silence.

The theme song to *Butch Cassidy and the Sundance Kid* suddenly burst from the pocket of his shorts. His cell. He dug it out, saw Eden's number in the window, turned off the phone. Later. He would deal with her later.

"A woman," Mira said.

"What?"

"On your cell."

"None of your goddamn business."

"Actually, it's very much my business. When you broke into my store, it became my business. When I first read for Suki, her stuff became my stuff. That's how it works, Spenser."

"Shut up."

"She's a redhead."

His chest tightened.

"Since the beginning, I've been puzzled about how you knew when to make your move for Adam. How you knew he was there alone with the housekeeper. The redhead is the connection. It makes sense. You watched the Nicholses, followed them, so you knew about Paul's lady friend and thought maybe you could use her to keep tabs on the family. Something like that. Then it became a sexual relationship. That must be really difficult for you, Spenser. Trying to maintain a relationship when you've got so many secrets."

"You talk too goddamn much."

"You helped saw up the trees on her property after the hurricane."

Shit.

"Thing is, if I figured it out, the cops will too."

He suddenly hit the lever at the side of her seat and it snapped back, into a nearly reclining position. She made a startled noise, but shut up. He unzipped his pack again, brought out the roll of electrical tape, and used his pocket-knife to slice off a length of it. He pressed one end to the door of the glove compartment.

"You say another word and I tape your mouth." Mira looked at the tape, at him, then turned her face toward the door.

The silence that followed was somehow worse, a subtle torture in which her words replayed themselves a thousand times in his head. *If I figured it out, the cops will too.*

As the car splashed through puddles, Finch's head pounded and ached. Sharp pains stabbed through his eyes. He kept leaning forward toward the windshield, swiping at the foggy glass with his hand, trying to clear enough of it so that he could see where he was going. It had been one goddamn thing after another—the bad weather, the tardy ferry, the snarled traffic out of Key West, and now the rain and wind sweeping across the two-lane highway with a ferocity that shook the van.

Where had the traffic come from? Were tourists pouring into the Keys? Were conches finally evacuating Key West for places that had electricity? What the hell was going on? He felt as if the universe were conspiring against him.

Mira hadn't spoken a word since he'd snapped the passenger seat back. He couldn't see her face. She had turned her head toward the window and he wondered if she had fallen asleep. Even though he had secured her with the seat belt and tape, she could jackknife her legs. She could throw her body into his. She could make any number of moves while he drove. But bottom line, he knew she wanted to see if Adam was alive and figured the best way to do that was to remain passive, cooperative.

He began to wonder if he had taken on more than he could handle.

Ridiculous. He had handled situations more impossible

than this one in his life. He, like the Mad Hatter, flourished under pressure. And it always came back to playing the game—*the role*—fully immersed in the character. That was how you won.

But what was the role? A week ago, it had been clear to him. Now he wasn't so sure.

I am Spenser Finch. Like God, I hold the power of life and death.

Just look at the actors who had played God. George Burns in *Oh, God!* Gene Hackman in *Two of a Kind,* Val Kilmer in *Prince of Egypt,* Morgan Freeman in *Bruce Almighty . . .* and that was just the short list. Now, Spenser Finch as God.

But even God could use a few insights into the future. And if Mira provided a few glimpses, he would have some indication about his next move. And the next.

How would he know if she was telling the truth? She already had lied about the cell phone.

He would hold a gun to Adam's head. That would force her to tell him the truth. And he would test her somehow, tell her to predict something that could be proven within ten or fifteen minutes. Like the call from Eden. How had she known the call was from her? Did Mira know her name? *And if I'm God, how come I don't know my own future?*

As he slowly drove the final stretch to his house, he scrolled through the address book on her phone. When he found Sheppard's cell number, he typed out a text message that made him smile, and placed it in the draft folder. One man to another. Sheppard would understand that.

His own cell rang as he turned onto his street. When had he turned it on again? He couldn't remember. A reflexive action. He reached into his pocket. Before he could look at the ID window, Mira said, "It's her again. The redhead."

Finch looked over at her. Her huge blue eyes regarded him with such pathos—not contempt, but *pity,* for Chrissakes— that his arm snapped away from him as if with a mind of its own.

She whipped her body to the right, as if she'd seen the blow coming, and his arm glanced off her shoulder. She made a choked, raw sound, then threw her body into his, and the van swerved to the right, the cell slipped out of his hand, and she sank her teeth into his arm.

He bellowed and tried to jerk his arm free, but she held on like a shark. Finch slammed on the brakes, hurling them both forward. His forehead struck the steering wheel, stars burst in his eyes, his head spun. The engine died, the thundering noise of the rain filled him. The next thing he knew, the passenger door stood ajar, wind blowing the rain inside, and Mira was gone. Flaps of electrical tape remained on the seat belt.

Finch threw open the door and leaped out, rain pouring over him. He saw her just ahead, stumbling along like a cripple. *Jesus, the neighbors.* What neighbors? Most of them had left before or after Danielle.

Most, not all.

He loped after her, gnomes pounding hammers against the inner walls of his skull. She veered into a field on the right, tripped, moved faster. Faster. A bubble of hysterical laughter surged in his throat. The road was a peninsula, water on three sides. Her only recourse was to leap in and swim, but only if she didn't hit the rocks first.

Finch hurled himself at her, but at the last instant, she feinted to the right. He struck the ground and rolled. Dirt and bits of grass splattered his face and jammed up under his fingernails. Royally pissed now, adrenaline raging through him, he scrambled to his feet and tackled her a foot short of the seawall.

They slammed to the ground, Mira shrieking, grunting, kicking, fighting. Then he pinned her down, her chest heaving, her body still. For seconds, no more than that, he stared down into her fathomless eyes—and saw her horror of him.

But I'm God. You can't feel that way about God.

Something snapped inside him. He heard it, a noise like

twigs cracking underfoot. And his arm became a club and the club slammed against the side of her head. Her eyes rolled back in their sockets. She went completely still.

His head pounded and screamed. His skull threatened to split open. He wanted to just stay there, the rain dancing against his spine, his face buried in the wet, sweet hollow of her shoulder, and breathe in the fragrance of her skin, her hair, the earth, salt, sky. But he was exposed. Someone might be watching. There could be witnesses. A nosy kid. A crazy woman out walking her poodle. Some window voyeur.

Finch pushed up on his hands, rocked back onto his heels. He lifted her by the arms, hoisted her over his shoulder like a bag of mulch or sod, made his way back to the van. Fatigue seeped through him. His head kept shrieking. The migraine would be a mother, all right, and he wasn't sure he could make the two hundred yards to the gate of his house without curling up in a fetal position and passing out.

But he would. He had to.

And he suddenly found himself in that trailer in Seattle, saw himself before he was taller and stronger than his old man, and felt that first agonizing blow from his old man's fists.

And so he somehow got her into the back of the van, slammed the hatch, drove to the gate. His cell rang and rang, the hideous noise echoing inside the van. He stumbled out, opened the gates, drove inside. He could barely see now. The peripheral vision on his right side was completely gone. His drenched clothes clung to him. He desperately wanted to rest his head against the steering wheel and shut his eyes.

Somehow, he left the van again, trudging out into the sharp, relentless rain, and shut the gates. *Now. Quick, stay focused. Yes, okay, back to the van, open the hatch, grab her ankles.*

Finch made it up the stairs and into his kitchen and nearly collapsed from the exertion. Not much farther, just down the hall to the kid's room. Uh-huh, uh-huh, he could do this. He had to do this. If he surrendered now, he was fucked.

To the bone, boy.

"Shut up, you sack of shit," he hissed at his old man, and made it to the door of the kid's room. The remote. He couldn't see the keypad and had to punch in the code by touch.

The door clicked and he kicked it open, prepared to dodge a booby trap, but nothing happened. He blinked, clearing his vision. Lamp on. Bed made. Cooler lid open. Shower running. Bathroom door shut. Good, that was good. The room listed to the right. He quickly set Mira on the floor, then lurched back into the hall, shut and locked the door, and weaved toward the kitchen.

He didn't make it. His stomach heaved, a blinding agony gripped his skull, he vomited, his knees turned to dust. As he went down, his hands flew out, seeking something to grab. Then, deaf and blind, he fell into a black hole so vast and deep that he was unconscious before he hit the floor.

19

The Looking Glass

Sheppard walked through the store, up and down the aisles of empty bookshelves, his senses blocked to the people and noises around him. He didn't know what he was looking for, but knew he would recognize it when he saw it.

And then, toward the back of the store, his gaze fixed on a white object on an empty middle shelf. The mate of the pearl earring that Suki had found on the floor of Mira's office. Sheppard picked it up, held it tightly in his hand, and turned slowly, orienting himself to the store as it had been before the hurricane. Was he standing in what had been the young adult section or bibliographies? Politics or history? This should have been as clear to him as his own name, but he couldn't remember. Yet the spot where she had put the earring might be important. Might tell him something.

And you could be grasping at bullshit.

He shut his eyes, trying to visualize the sections of the store as it had been when there were books on these shelves, life in these aisles, the aroma of fresh coffee in the air. He had to step through the looking glass into Mira's world to do this, but he stepped eagerly, hopefully.

This was the young adult section. So what's the message?

Maybe nothing. Maybe this was just the place where Spenser Longwood or whatever the hell name he went by now had been distracted and Mira had seized the moment. Then again, if there were no accidents, as Mira constantly said, then the message pointed to information in Spenser's early life that might be relevant. *Young adult, early life.* And since Mira hadn't been at Kartauk's, she couldn't possibly know any of what he had told Sheppard and Goot unless she'd picked it up psychically. And for her to do that, Sheppard thought, the bastard probably had touched her.

"Shep, you got a minute?" Tina Richardson's voice startled him.

His eyes snapped open. Tina stood in front of him, her soft eyes skewed with worry, triumph, anxiety, determination. "We got print matches on the bike out in the alley with our man Spenser."

"Do they tell us where he is now?"

She cocked her head, sort of smiled. "Uh, no, Shep. We're good, but we're not that good."

He held out his hand and opened his clenched fingers, revealing the other pearl earring. "Found it here." He gestured at the shelf. "Tell me about Hansel and Gretel, Tina." He knew that Tina heard the pain in his voice.

She gently rubbed his shoulder. "Stop beating yourself up, okay? Hansel and Gretel were just a couple of screwed-up kids with dysfunctional parents who followed bread crumbs through the woods. This guy's leaving us a lot more than bread crumbs. It's Mira's bike out in the alley, with Spenser's prints all over it. He's getting sloppy, Shep. He hid here last night." She threw out her arms. "Mira's store. The asshole hid in the most obvious place and we didn't get it. That's part of his MO, okay? To do what we least expect. Her car is missing and it shows up on the security feed for the nine A.M. ferry, which left way late and didn't get into Key West until around eleven."

And then? The cameras didn't extend beyond the dock's parking lot. "Yeah, great. And he's got more than a hundred miles of highway beyond it that lead to Miami. So where'd he take her?"

The question hung in the air, one more conundrum. The peal of his cell punctuated the silence. It took him a moment to recognize the number.

"It's Annie," he murmured.

"And you're the dad," Tina said. "That's how you need to play it." With that, she walked away from him.

The dad. Sure. The *absent* dad, who technically hadn't been even a stepdad. The guy who, right now, was just the ex-live-in boyfriend. "Annie the granny," he said in the most cheerful voice he could muster. "What's going on?"

"Can you talk, Shep? I mean, is this an okay time?"

"For you, it's always an okay time." He kept walking toward the back of the store. "What's up, kiddo?"

"Shep, I spoke to Mom really early this morning, she was on her way to the bookstore. We were talking about me coming to Tango. Anyway, after we talked, I started feeling uneasy and I kept calling her cell to tell her I was going to come today. But she didn't answer her cell. Is she with you?"

Sheppard combed his fingers back through his hair and struggled with his conscience. If he told Annie the truth, she and Nadine would be down here by nightfall, both of them eager to help and in the way. Nadine would have the usual chip on her shoulder and would blame him for what had happened. Yet he loved Annie like a daughter and, at the least, owed her the truth.

"Shep?"

"Yeah, can you hear me all right?" He now stood in the empty yoga room, staring at the door through which Mira and Spenser had left the building. "I'm inside."

"I can hear you." She paused. "You're stalling, Shep. Something's happened, right? Something with Mom."

He heard the sharp rise in her voice, the soft tremor of fear beneath it. Of course she would know. She had been here before. Sheppard pushed open the rear door and stepped out into the alley. The rain still fell. He huddled under the eave and started talking, but kept it simple and brief, like an article in *People* magazine, something you could grasp before you jumped in the shower. And in the ensuing silence, Annie's quick intake of breath sounded like wind through a tunnel.

"I knew it," she whispered. "I knew something wasn't right."

"I'd appreciate it if you kept this to yourself. I don't want Nadine to worry."

"You don't want to hear her shit."

He smiled at that. "Yeah, there's that. We'll find her, Annie. And I want you to stay where you are."

"Can I call you? Like, when I feel panicked or something?"

"Always. And I'll keep you posted."

Silence, then: "I have your word on that?"

"Annie, have I ever lied to you?"

More silence. He paced back and forth under the eave.

"No. But you never said good-bye either, Shep. How come? How come you didn't at least talk to me about what was going on when you moved out?"

The easy answer was that Mira wouldn't let him talk to her or see her. But the truth was more complex, it always was. "I was angry. I felt . . . ashamed. I felt like I had failed you, your mom. I thought it would be easier for you if I just got out. I don't know. It's complicated, Annie."

"So do me a favor, okay? From here on in? Just be up front with me?"

"You got it."

"Are you and Mom . . . you know, like getting it together?"

"I think so." *Hope so.* "Yes."

"Like, well, how together? Are you moving back into the house?"

"We haven't gotten that far yet, Annie."

"But things have improved, right?" *You've slept together.* That was what she really was asking.

"Vastly improved."

She was silent for a few moments and he could almost see her, intense Annie, pacing, squinting, trying to sink between the lines to read what he wasn't saying. Finally, she spoke. "Listen, Nadine picked up a word related to all this. *Eden.* Does it mean anything to you?"

Eden. As in the garden of? Was Eden a street? A name? A place? What? "That's it? Just Eden?"

"Just the word."

"It might be connected to something. If you or Nadine pick up anything else, call me. Hell, call me even if you don't have squat, Annie."

"Love you, Shep."

"Love you too, kiddo."

But she already had disconnected.

Mira came to on the floor, with a blurred face hovering over her and a cool, damp cloth pressed to her forehead. The side of her head throbbed and ached, as if she were suffering from a massive hangover.

"You're Mira. I saw your picture on TV."

Her vision swam into clarity. "Adam." She tried to lift up on her elbows, but her head spun.

"Take it easy." He slid a pillow under her head. "Just stay still for a few seconds. He must've hit you pretty hard. The side of your face looks nasty. I'll get you some water."

Mira stayed still, eyes shut, her mind stuck back in that open field where he had tackled her, the last thing she remembered.

"I heard the car drive up, so I turned on the shower, shut the bathroom door, and hid in the closet. I could see him through the slats in the door. He left as soon as he set you down on the floor, stumbled outta here. Migraine, that's what I figure." Adam crouched beside her, lifted her head gently. "Take a sip." He touched a bottle of water to her mouth.

Mira sipped eagerly at the cold, soothing water.

"He looked really bad," Adam went on. "Like he does when a migraine hits him. I heard him puking on the other side of the door, then there was a crashing sound. I think he passed out in the hall."

Mira took the cloth away from her forehead and managed to sit up without too much dizziness this time. "Are you okay? Did he hurt you?"

"Lots of threats." He rocked back onto the soles of his feet and wrapped his arms around his knees. "Sometimes he grabbed my hair. He was . . . gone a long time, since yesterday. I didn't think he was coming back and was trying to conserve the food and stuff in the cooler. All the ice melted." His eyes suddenly brimmed with tears and when he spoke again, his voice was a hoarse, choked whisper. "I'm sorry he brought you here, but I'm so glad to see you, I'm not sorry." The tears spilled over and he looked quickly down at the floor, embarrassed.

Mira slipped her arm around his hunched shoulders, hoping to comfort him. Instead, the contact catapulted her into the rushing flow of Adam's youthful energy and she caught glimpses of what he'd endured since he'd been snatched from his bedroom.

Whispering: "Listen, Adam. We're going to get out of here. But you need to tell me everything you've learned about him. And while you do that, we're going to search this room for a way out and . . ."

"There's no way out." He pulled back, rubbing at his eyes. "But now that there are two of us, we might be able to rig something, to trick him. He's really strong, so I don't think that even the two of us could take him physically." He leaned over, his cheek flat against the floor, and peered under the crack in the door. "The same dark shape is there," he whispered. "He hasn't moved." He pressed his ear to the door, listening. "No sounds. Maybe he had a stroke or something. You think he's dead?"

Dead? Mira's senses moved away from her like tentacles, probing the space beyond the door. "He's not dead. He's somewhere else." *But not indefinitely.* She sensed something else forming in the field of energy around the man, something he didn't expect, but couldn't define whatever it was. She kept seeing a small bird too, like a sparrow or a finch. How did that fit?

She pushed unsteadily to her feet and Adam caught her arm. "You okay?"

"I'm good." But her skin tingled where Adam's hand held her arm and images popped into her mind of Adam cowering on the bed in this room as the temperature plunged. As frost formed on the windows. As the man hurried over to the thermostat to check the temperature. "Adam, tell me about the woman you've seen. The one who makes the temperature drop. Tell me about her."

He looked surprised. "I . . . uh . . . how'd you know?"

"I've seen her too. Her name is Joy." Mira told him what had happened in his room at home when she'd read it—the way the furniture moved crazily through the room, even what she had seen after his mother had fled.

"What'd my mom say after all this happened?" he asked.

"She understands now that what you call Friend is a ghost." Mira now sat at the edge of the bed. She ran her hand over the right side of her face. The skin felt hot, swollen. She drank from the bottle of water again.

"Mom never believed me before. She just thought I had an active imagination. And my father . . . well, he wanted to take me to a shrink." He sat beside Mira. "So Friend is a poltergeist?"

"No. Not really. She . . ." Mira hesitated, uncertain of how much to say now, how much to tell him. "Died in your house in 1975. Now she watches over you. When did you first see her?"

"I . . . I think I first dreamed about her a long time ago, like when I was seven or eight. I had just gone into the gifted program at a new school in New York and I hated the teacher. She didn't like me because my parents were in the movie business. Or maybe she just didn't like the movies my parents did. I don't know. Anyway, Friend used to come to me in dreams and advise me on how to deal with the teacher."

Interesting, Mira thought. Spirits often appeared to children in the dream state. Sometimes they just conveyed messages or comforted; other times they seemed to pave the way for physical manifestations. Occasionally, both purposes were served and the spirit's presence in the child's life hinted at some deeper connection at a future time. That seemed to be the case with Adam.

"Then, not long after we moved into the Mango Hill house, I started seeing her. In the beginning, I thought I was imagining her, like I was asleep and dreaming or something. But then I would wake up in the middle of the night from a nightmare and she . . . she would suddenly be there. And the room would be colder."

"Can you hear her?" Mira's eyes moved quickly around the room now, taking in the details, looking for possible exits, weaknesses, weapons. "Can you carry on a conversation like we're doing now?"

"Yeah, most of the time." He rubbed his hands over his bare thighs. "Shouldn't we be coming up with a plan or something?"

"Yes." Mira forced herself to get up, to move around the room and inspect everything closely. But she didn't touch anything, not yet. She wasn't ready for any tactile impressions. Adam hurried alongside her, as though he were terrified she might get too far from him and vanish. "What do you talk about with her?" Mira asked.

"Music, books, movies. She's really interested in computers, so I show her stuff on the computer sometimes."

"So you understood all along that she was dead?"

"Yeah. Sure. I didn't like thinking about it, though, because it made me feel like the kid in *The Sixth Sense* and the whole thing spooked me too much to even try to talk about it with anyone." He paused. "Gladys knew. She saw me talking to Friend one day. I mean, all she saw was me talking to myself, right? Anyway, she asked who I was talking to and I told her the whole thing."

"What'd she say?"

"That I should, like, tell Mom. Or Dad. I didn't want her blabbing about it to them. I was afraid Dad would send me to a shrink and that my mom would be freaked. So I lied and promised Gladys that I'd tell them."

Mira paused in the bathroom door, eyed the rain-smeared skylight. She thought Adam was probably right, that there wasn't any exit from the room. That would have to try something else. She turned and looked at Adam, who now leaned against the wall, rubbing a pair of apples against his shirt. "You know who she is?" Mira asked.

He met her gaze, held out one of the apples. "This is the last of the fruit. We could starve to death in here before he comes to."

"We'll be outta here long before we starve to death." She sounded more certain than she felt. But more to the point, was he avoiding the question? "Are there any dry clothes in here?"

"There's stuff in the drawers. What do you need?"

"Just a T-shirt. My shorts are almost dry."

"I'll see what there is."

Assigned a task, he got right to it. Mira turned on the water in the sink and avoided looking at herself in the mirror. She knew it would be bad. The throbbing ache on the right side of her face had spread down through her jaw and up toward her ear. The skin there now felt as if she had lain in the sun for eight hours.

She splashed cold water on her face, jerked a towel from the rack. She soaked it in the stream of water and held it against her face. When she finally raised her eyes, her reflection exceeded Adam's description of *nasty*. She looked as if she had been beaten up and discarded as trash. The skin from her temple to her jaw was as purple as a grape. Dried blood bloomed in the corner of her mouth like a rosebud. It seemed miraculous that Spenser hadn't broken her jaw. Or bones in her cheek. Or her chin.

My arm's a club, boy, and don't you forget it.

She heard the voice, felt the fury, and wrenched herself out of the flow of Spenser's childhood by dropping the towel. She used toilet paper to blot her face dry. No images surfaced. Why had she picked up something from the towel but not from the metal faucets when she'd touched them? Metal was generally a better psychic conductor than cotton.

Frowning, she brought her hands to the faucets again. Nothing. Maybe their captor used the towel more often than he did this bathroom.

"Mira, I found some clothes." Adam hurried into the bathroom with several T-shirts draped over his arm. "One of these should fit you."

"Thanks." She ran her fingers over the fabric first, testing it for any emotional residue. But the shirts apparently hadn't been worn for some time. She took them. "Let me change and I'll be out in a jiffy. Any noise in the hall?"

"Not in the last sixty seconds. But I'll check again."

He shut the bathroom door as he left and Mira stripped off her soggy T-shirt and draped it over the towel rack. She selected the smallest of the T-shirts Adam had found, plain white with COMPUTER NERD written across the front in vivid blue letters.

As she pulled it over her head and the fabric settled

against her skin, a terrible weight and sadness came with it that had nothing to do with her and Adam's present situation. These feelings were linked directly to Spenser Longwood, to who he had been and who he was now. The emotions were so vast and deep they nearly overpowered her. She started to pull the shirt off, but suddenly found herself in complete darkness, surrounded by loud, clanking pipes in an enclosed room. It hurt to breathe.

A cool autumn night. The flicker of lights inside the trailer. TV lights. His old man is probably six sheets to the wind, passed out in front of the television. Good. He can get in and out with the rest of his things and his old man won't know the difference until he's sober enough to see that the smaller bedroom has been cleaned out.

He raps softly at the door, no one answers, so he slips inside. The TV volume is soft, some old movie playing. He sees his old man slumped low on the couch, feet propped on the coffee table. The air here stinks of smoke, booze, burned food, an undercurrent of violence. His throat tightens, a chill licks its way up his spine. His body remembers what it was like to live here.

Quick now. Up the hall. Into the smaller bedroom. His old room. He turns on the bedside lamp, the buttery circles of light spilling across the worn quilt, the ugly throw rug, the bureau from some thrift store way back when. Over the bed hangs the huge crucifix that haunted his childhood.

His boxes are still pushed up against the east wall, but they are no longer sealed. The masking tape has been slit, the contents dug through as though rats had been released inside. The fucker prick has violated his personal things, picked out whatever he thought he could sell, and put it all in several other boxes against the closet door. But because he's such a hopeless drunk, the boxes are still unsealed, unlabeled, the items just stuffed inside.

He stares. His hands curl into fists. The light seems to ebb until he stands in darkness. He blinks against it, struggling to detect light, any light at all, but the blackness is complete, a lunar eclipse, no stars, no moon, nothing at all. And then the rage seizes him.

He jerks the crucifix off the wall and marches into the kitchen. He flings open the door under the sink, grabs the huge container of lighter fluid, a box of kitchen matches. He squirts the lighter fluid over the stove, the tacky throw rug in front of it, and backs slowly and carefully into the living room, saturating everything in his path until he reaches the shoddy living room.

His old man's body has slipped to the side, shoulders resting on some pillows, mouth open, his snores loud, erratic. An empty bottle of rotgut wine sits on the coffee table. Next to it is an ashtray heaped with cigarette butts. A pack of Kools sits next to it, a lighter on top of it.

Yeah, Mr. Fucking Kool.

He squirts lighter fluid over the crucifix, saturating the ancient wood, and squirts it over his old man's slippers and up his hairy legs and gym shorts and shirt and into his hair, over his skin. He strikes a match, touches the flame to the crucifix, and sets his father's slippers on fire. The flames race up his legs, his shorts catch fire, and suddenly he leaps up, awake, sober, shrieking, and slapping his hands against the flames that are consuming him.

Spenser lurches back, emptying the can on the coffee table, the rug, and lighting more matches. When the can is empty, he jams it into his pocket and spins around, lurching for the door. He explodes through it and races for his car.

Good-bye, fucker, good-bye, and good riddance.

Mira tore the shirt off over her head and threw it across the bathroom, ending the vision. Doubled over on her knees, she gasped for breath, her body slippery with sweat, stomach churning, bile surging in her throat. She yanked her own shirt off the towel rack, wrung it out, pulled it over her head.

Soft, urgent raps at the door. "Mira? His cell's ringing."

Cell, ringing.

Trailer, burning.

Old man, burned to death.

Focus, focus.

She threw open the bathroom door, stumbled out. Adam caught her. Supported her. "Dear God," she whispered, and clutched at the boy as if he could save her.

The cell abruptly stopped ringing. She heard groaning outside the door. Stumbling, then silence.

How much time do we have before he comes to?

Not enough. Not nearly enough.

20

Persons of Interest

By four that afternoon, the sketch of the redhead that Mira had made last night and the image of Spenser as he might look now had been circulating in the media for roughly three hours. Sheppard was pleased with the results. Calls and e-mails had been pouring in at a frantic rate, mostly from places north of the Keys, where there was power.

Fortunately, he and Goot had plenty of help to field both—Kartauk, Blake, Suki, Lydia, and a couple of her trusted cronies from the artists colony. He suspected that Charlie Cordoba would show up sooner or later, demanding to be included, but for the moment, his absence was a blessing.

Shepard, Goot, and Kartauk had put together a guideline sheet that helped to cull additional information and details from the calls and e-mails. This enabled them to sift genuine tips from the nutcases. But at the moment, the nutcases outweighed everything else. Sightings came from as far away as Hawaii and Alaska, from religious and conspiracy freaks, and even from alleged alien abductees who claimed that

Adam Nichols had been snatched for hybridization experiments by reptilians from the Pleiades.

Sheppard's head ached and all he could think of was Mira, deliberately placing her pearl earring on an empty bookshelf. He pushed away from the conference table and went into the staff room in search of Advil. Moments later, Suki joined him.

"Shep, I need to show you something." She set her laptop on the table, brought a memory stick out of the pocket of her shorts, slipped it into a USB port. "Paul was with his girlfriend the night Adam was taken. That's why he never made it home. I'm sure Mira told you that much."

He nodded.

"Well, here's the proof," she went on. "And while I've been out there, taking calls and answering e-mails, I keep thinking *suppose*. Suppose Paul's girlfriend knows something about Adam's disappearance."

"Knows because she was involved?"

"Yes."

"So she and Spenser are partners?"

"Right."

Goddamn. "So go on."

"I was trying to look at all the angles and it occurred to me that maybe she's working with Spenser and her job was to act as a decoy, to keep Paul from getting home that night, so it would be just Adam and Gladys at the house."

Sheppard felt a sudden excitement about the possibility. "But how did she and Spenser meet? And what's their motive?"

"I don't know. We're working on assumptions. Okay, now take a look." When the files had copied, she clicked on a folder called *e-mails from paradise.*

Sheppard's headache abruptly backed off as he scrolled through the e-mails. Was this woman who called herself *paradise* the *Eden* that Nadine had picked up? Or was Eden a place, street, or just a word that would lead to some other, deeper layer? Regardless, he now had sufficient cause to bring Nichols in for questioning. One way or another, he would get the woman's name, address, everything Nichols knew.

"Why do you think she refers to herself as *paradise?*" he asked. "Is it some private little nickname? An inside joke?"

Suki glanced him. "Maybe it's a subtle way of reminding him that she's paradise. Or it's what he claims he feels when he's with her? Jesus, who the hell knows?"

Sheppard thought about it. "How far back in time do the e-mails go, Suki?"

"Fourteen or fifteen months."

"Then consider this. In all the time that Spenser watched you and your family, Paul was involved with this paradise woman. Suppose Spenser discovered it and decided that he could use paradise to keep tabs on the family? So he met her. Got involved with her."

She looked stricken and when she spoke, her voice seemed riddled with pain. "It's as possible as anything else."

Sheppard gave her arm a quick squeeze. "We're closer," he said softly. "You have to believe that."

She bit at her lower lip, looked away from him.

"Is Paul at the house now, Suki?"

"He better not be." She told him what had happened earlier, when Agent Ellis had to restrain Nichols so that she could leave the house. "I told him I wanted him gone by the time I got back."

Sheppard punched out the Nichols house number and reached a recording. "Agent Ellis, this is Agent Sheppard."

A click on the line. Ellis immediately picked up. "Yes, sir."

"Is Mr. Nichols in the house?"

"Downstairs. He left for several hours after there was a, uh, domestic disturbance. He returned a while ago, pulled his car around to the back of the house, and now appears to be loading things into it. I'm watching him from an upstairs window, sir."

"I'd like you to bring Nichols in for questioning. Bring him here to the office."

"It could get ugly, sir."

"Then you arrest the prick. Do whatever you have to do."

"You got it."

"Any activity on the phones there?"

"Nothing."

"Okay, call me when you're headed this way with Nichols."

Sheppard disconnected from the call. "Would you mind if I put these e-mails on my laptop?"

"Put them on and keep the memory stick."

"Once Paul is brought in, Suki, there's going to be a media circus in front of your house again. So while Paul's being questioned, I think it'd be a good idea if you went home and packed whatever you need for a few days. I'm sure Glen Kartauk would be delighted to put you up. The press doesn't know about him. You won't be bothered there. What do you think?"

"You think he'd mind if I brought Dolittle with me?"

"Dolittle?" Who the hell was Dolittle?

"Our cat."

Sheppard suspected that as far as Kartauk was concerned, Suki could move into his place and bring everything she owned. "I'm sure it'll be fine."

Just then, his cell beeped, signaling that a text message was coming through. When he saw the number in the window, his heart seized up. A text message from Mira's cell. He opened it.

Tough luck, Sherlock.
She's one gorgeous babe.
Over & out.

Sheppard felt as if his insides had been poured through a meat grinder.

Suki, reading the e-mail over his shoulder, asked: "Are you going to answer him?"

He shook his head. "That's what he wants. So he can gloat. I'm going to come down hard on Paul, Suki."

"He isn't easily intimidated."

"We'll see."

And just in case he changed his mind about answering Spenser's text message, he quickly wrote Fuck u and stored it under Quick Notes. Pointless, but it made him feel better.

That feeling lasted only until he went out into the front lobby to wait for Agent Ellis—and Charlie Cordoba barreled through the front door. John Wayne on the warpath. Sheppard figured he'd seen the photos on the Internet and had come here to demand that he be included in whatever would go down. Either that or Nichols had called him. Sheppard leaned against the counter as Cordoba made a beeline toward him.

"What's up, Charlie?"

"What's *up*? What's fucking *up*? You know damn well what's *up,* Sheppard. You're trying to cut me outta the loop again. Those photos on the Internet . . . the phone banks . . . The homicide is mine. I've got a right to know what's going on."

"I thought we had this conversation earlier this morning, you know, long before the sun came up, Charlie. And you had filed an official complaint with the Bureau. We *did* have that conversation, right? I didn't dream it, did I?"

Cordoba huffed and puffed like the big bad wolf, but buildings didn't topple, roofs didn't fly off. He seemed, in fact, pathetic and powerless. "I didn't get any satisfaction from you then and it's obvious I'm not getting it now."

"I'll give you satisfaction, Charlie, but with one condition."

"Fuck your conditions."

"Then no satisfaction and you don't get beyond the lobby."

He whipped off his shades. Pursed his mouth. His eyes narrowed to small, dark slits. "What's the condition?"

"That you take your orders from me."

"Yeah, right." He gave a quick, clipped laugh. "And exactly why would I consent to that?"

Sheppard slipped his cell from his pocket, brought up the text message, and held it close to Cordoba's face. "That's why. He got Mira. He hid in her store last night when he fled the woods. That makes it *my* game. So you either play by our rules, or you're out of the loop for good."

Cordoba went through his usual facial contortions, but knew Sheppard had him. "Okay, we'll play it your way."

"Even if our next stop is interrogating Paul Nichols?"

Cordoba's eyes widened, questions swirled through them. But he had the sense not to protest or to ask what the hell was going on. "Even that."

It had taken him hours to crawl out from under the mother migraine that had struck him down. But he'd done it. He'd gotten to the other end. Now the shadows against the balcony were longer, the rain came down harder, and there were probably a hundred messages from Eden on his cell phone.

First things first, right? So the very first thing he had done was send Sheppard the text message from Mira's phone. Let the poor schmuck's imagination run wild.

Now he loaded up the cooler and carried it down the hall to Adam's room.

Finch set the cooler down in front of the door to the room, raised the lid, and scooped his weapon off a container of strawberries. He didn't intend to take any more chances at this point in the game. Mira had nearly escaped once and he didn't intend to let it happen again. The clip was loaded, the safety disengaged.

He shut the lid and turned the cooler so that one end rested against the door. He didn't hear any sounds inside the room. It could be a trick, the two of them waiting for him behind the door, ready to tackle him, knock him out, something. He pressed the button on the remote-control clicker, heard the telling click as the lock disengaged, and shoved the door open with such force that it slammed against the wall.

No one was hiding behind the door, but the reverberation tugged at the last vestige of his migraine, a small pulsing knot at his temple. He pushed the cooler into the room with his foot, so that it would hold the door ajar, and slipped in behind it, back to the wall.

He nearly laughed out loud at his commando antics. Neither of these two would ever be a physical threat to him. The woman lay stretched out on the bed, a cloth covering her eyes and forehead. The kid was at the computer, playing Free Cell. A rollicking duo.

"Adam, bring the empty cooler over here." He gestured with the Walther. "And then push the new cooler over to the wall."

The kid swiveled around in his chair, his face expressionless, except for the burning hatred in his eyes. "I ran outta food." He got up. "My clothes are dirty. This room stinks. And then you bring her here. What's wrong with you anyway? You don't know what you want, what you're doing. You're losing it big-time."

"Shut up and do what I told you to do."

Adam folded his arms across his chest and sat down. "Go fuck yourself."

Goddamn shit. Finch's arm snapped to the right and he fired at the bathroom door. It blew a hole in the center of it and splinters of wood flew away from it. Mira snapped upright, Adam wrenched back, and Finch turned, aiming the gun at the woman. "She takes the next one, kid."

Adam raised his hands like shields. "I'm exchanging the coolers."

"Very wise." Finch kept his eyes pinned on Mira, who looked as if she had swallowed a softball and might, at any second, choke to death on it. The entire right side of her face was swollen from where he'd hit her when his arm had become a club. But her eyes were as clear and bright as glass and never left his face.

While the kid exchanged the coolers, an odd thing started happening to Mira's face. The ugly bruise began to fade, turning a lighter blue, then a sickly yellow. The swelling seemed to go down. He thought it was a trick of the light or of perception, that the migraine continued to impair his vision. He blinked, but the bruise still seemed to be fading.

"Something's happening to your face," he blurted out.

Her hand went to the side of her face, sliding along the skin, as if feeling for what he knew was happening to it. And then she spoke, her voice soft, quick. "May 16, 1975. You were—what? Five? Six? You and your mother were living in the house on Mango Hill. The house where Adam lives now. A man came to the house, knocked your mother unconscious, set fire to the room where she lay, and kidnapped you. Her name was Joy Longwood. She died from burns and smoke inhalation. I wish I could tell you that your father was completely responsible for damaging you beyond repair, but it just isn't true."

Horror seized him, paralyzed him. He couldn't swallow, couldn't blink, couldn't control the trembling of his hand. The hand that gripped the weapon. And she knew it, saw it. Glaring at him, she swung her legs over the side of the bed and when she spoke again, her voice rose in pitch until she was shouting. "And if you shoot that gun again, if you threaten Adam, if you don't get out of here *now,* I won't tell you another goddamn thing."

Her shouts echoed, stabbing at his skull, waking up the remains of the beast that had crippled him hours ago. He stood there for what seemed like forever, his temple throbbing, and struggled to put what she'd said into some sort of context. But it didn't fit logically into what he knew about himself, didn't fit in a reasonable, linear way. And yet . . . it resonated. In some strange and inexplicable way, he felt the *rightness* of what she said.

And it infuriated him.

He lurched across the room, grabbed her by the hair, jammed the gun up under her bruised jaw—*even now that bruise is fading, going away, impossible, what the hell is this woman?*—and leaned in close to her, hissing, "You want me to shoot the kid? Is that it? Is that what it comes down to? You tell me the rest, you tell me or . . ." And his arm snapped upward again and he fired and the shot took a chunk out of the wall. "Or there goes Adam's head."

Instead of cowering, she made a sharp, strangled noise, her eyes rolled back in her head, she went limp. He let go of her hair and she toppled sideways against the mattress. He didn't know if she had passed out or if she was faking it.

Finch leaned over her, tapped her cheek. "Hey, Mira. Cut the shit. I know you're . . ."

"You killed her, you killed her!" the kid shrieked.

As he spun around, the desk chair slammed into his legs, sending shoots of pain through his kneecaps, and Adam tore toward the open door. Finch shoved the chair away and stumbled after him. Adam leaped over the cooler with the nimbleness of a deer and Finch, not far behind him, pulled the cooler out of the way, so the door would shut behind him, and raced down the hall.

By the time Finch reached the kitchen, Adam was scrambling frantically around like a cornered rat, jerking on the handle of the remotely controlled front door, racing from window to window, struggling to get one of them open. Finch fired at the floor in front of him and the kid whipped around, eyes the size of hubcaps. He backed up to the door and pressed against it as though he hoped he might melt right through it.

"Go ahead, just shoot me!" Adam shouted. "Get it over

with. I've seen your face, I know what you look like, so just get it over with."

"Shut the fuck up." And his arm became a club and the club slammed into the side of Adam's head, knocking him sideways into the couch. After a moment, the upper part of his body slipped off the couch to the floor.

"Christ." Finch tucked the gun into the waistband of his shorts and hurried over to the kid. Crouching, he touched his neck, seeking a pulse. Strong, steady. Good. He wasn't ready to get rid of Adam yet.

Finch picked him up, carried him down the hall. Remote control out. *Click* and the door unlocked. Just in case Mira planned to ambush him, he kicked the door open and it banged against the wall as before, allowing him to see the entire room. Mira stood by the bed, startled, but no more a threat now than earlier. Finch carried Adam over to the bed, set him down.

"My God, what the hell did you do to him? He's bleeding."

"He tried to escape." Now that he was closer to her, he realized that the bruise on the right side of her face was almost gone. But that was impossible. Either his vision had been wacked earlier or there had been shadows on her face.

"He's bleeding a lot." She grabbed the pillow and pressed it to the side of Adam's head. "He needs a doctor."

"Sure, I'll get right on it. Maybe I can find one who's discreet and makes house calls." His cell rang. He ignored it. "Those things you said . . ."

"I don't remember what I said." She removed the pillow from the side of Adam's head. "He's still bleeding. Can you at least get me a first-aid kit?"

"In the closet, top shelf. You won't find anything inside that you can use as a weapon, though. How can you not remember what you said?"

"That's how it works."

"Well, it'd better start working differently once you've

got the kid fixed up. You're going to read for me. You aren't unplugged. That was all lies."

"I can't read on demand."

"Bullshit."

"Look, I'm going over to the closet to get the first-aid kit."

He brought out the Walther. "Go ahead. You read for people when they come to your store. How's this any different?"

"You're a smart guy. It should be obvious."

"Explain it."

She picked up the first-aid kit in the closet and turned. "You really don't get it, do you?" She opened the kit, checked the contents, snapped it shut. "Okay, Spenser, I'll spell it out. I'm in a hostile situation, with a wounded boy, and the kidnapper is holding a gun on me. And that's just for starters. The psychic part of me turns off."

"I don't believe you. You said plenty of stuff before, you were reading me then."

"I was telling you what I know about you. What I learned from research." She set the kit down on the bedside stand, opened it, removed what she needed. "And since you're such a computer whiz, why didn't you do a search on the Mango Hill house? You could have found out what I just told you."

He didn't have an answer other than the fact it hadn't occurred to him. It suddenly seemed that he might not be such a meticulous planner after all, and that pissed him off. Who was *she* to point out weaknesses in *him*?

"The only psychic things I've seen are what happened to you the day you were kidnapped in 1975," she went on. "And I saw that the day I was out for a walk and found Gladys's body."

"You know what? I think you're a fraud. I don't think you're any more psychic than I am."

"Whatever."

He hated that she now ignored him and fussed over the

kid. He fired at the floor less than a foot to her right and her head snapped up. It gave him enormous satisfaction to see the fear coiled in her eyes. "Tell me something about myself that no one else knows."

"I already have. I told you about the redhead."

"That doesn't count. Tell me something else."

"I can't. I can't do it while you've got a gun on me."

He turned slightly to the right and aimed the gun at Adam. "Okay, now the gun is on him. Go ahead. Tell me something."

"You cell is about to ring. It'll be the redhead."

"You have to the count of three to tell me any single fact about my self that no one else knows, Mira. Otherwise I shoot the kid in the foot. Next time, I'll shoot him in the knee. And after that . . ."

His cell rang. Mira just stared at him.

Finch reached into his pocket, glanced at the number, turned off the phone. "That's hardly psychic. She calls every two seconds."

"You went into your father's trailer one night and soaked him with lighter fluid and held a match to him."

It was as if she had punched him in the stomach. Air exploded from his mouth, his eyes flashed dry, drums pounded inside his skull. "He . . . he was drunk and . . . and came after me. I had to defend myself."

"He was passed out on the couch. You got pissed that he'd gone through the boxes of your things. You found lighter fluid, soaked a crucifix with it, squirted the stuff all over your father, lit the crucifix, and set him on fire." She paused, then rushed on. "You have a selective memory. You remember yourself as a victim, so that it justifies what you do and—"

"Shut up!" he screamed, and fired at the floor again.

Mira wrenched back. Finch, breathing hard, stepped toward her, the gun still aimed at Adam. "You want me to shoot him, Mira?" The words hissed from his mouth. "Is that it? Is that why you're lying? My old man was a vicious sadist. He—"

"Yeah, he was a sadist. But the night you set him on fire, he was just an old guy who'd passed out from too much booze. Defenseless. And you were playing God again."

"You aren't unplugged." He now stood less an arm's length away from her. "So read me. My future."

"I have to touch something you've touched or I have to touch you in order to tune in."

"You weren't touching me seconds ago."

"I picked all that up earlier. I have to touch you."

The expression on her face made it clear that touching him appealed to her about as much as touching a tarantula. "When you do, notice my aim, Mira. Notice the tension in my arm, my hand, my fingers. If you try anything, I shoot first and think about it later. The way I figure it, the shot will enter Adam's left foot and tear upward through his leg, probably severing an artery. It's a hollow point, you know what that means?"

"No, but I have a good imagination, Spenser."

She brought her hands hesitantly to his shoulder. A light touch, barely a touch at all. He heard the shift in her breathing, then a gasp, and when he stole a glance at her, he saw that her eyes were shut and her eyeballs rolled from side to side beneath the lids, as if she were dreaming.

"I'm . . . I'm a computer whiz. Everyone loves me." She spoke quietly, evenly, in an odd voice. "I fix problems. I create and develop software. I'm incredibly good at my job. I have a lover, a redhead." She paused. "She thinks you're brilliant."

Holy shit.

Moments ticked by. Adam sat up, one hand holding gauze against his bleeding temple. He watched silently, warily, listening.

"I'm young," she finally said, reverting back to the first person, as though she were seeing the scene from within someone else. "Three, maybe four. Mommy tells me what beautiful teeth I have. She shows me how to floss, to brush, and when I smile for her, it's always a big smile, so she can see how I take care of my teeth."

Jesus God.

"I'm a little older now," she went on. "Five or six. There's a toad on the patio, jumping toward the water. I don't like toads. Mommy tells me I shouldn't hurt any living thing, but toads are disgusting. Mommy is inside the house on the phone. She can't see me. I trap the toad and it squirms under my hand and I hate the way it feels, all damp and bumpy and sticky. I want to hit it with something, but I can't find anything close by, so I pull off its legs and . . ."

Mira made a harsh, choked sound and wrenched back from him, her eyes bright with horror.

Something stirred deep inside Finch—and a crack opened in his memories, widening just enough to let an image surface: of a young boy on the patio of the Mango Hill house, crouched down with a toad trapped under his hands. The memory was so real he could smell the hot air, the freshly mown lawn, the chlorine in the swimming pool.

"Go on. Tell me more."

Mira shook her head. "I can't." A whisper. "It'll make me sick."

"Stop doing that," he snapped. "You're looking at me like I'm a monster."

You are *a monster,* her eyes shrieked; then she leaned over Adam again and pressed two Band-Aids over the gauze at his temple. She didn't look at him, didn't speak.

"Hey, all kids do shit like that," he said.

"Right."

"Get off your moral high ground, Mira. I'm sure that even you held lit matches to ants' nests when you were a kid."

Silence.

"Hey, I'm not a monster," he said. "I'm not Ted Bundy or Jeffrey Dahmer or Richard Speck or Hitler or . . ."

"If I were you, I'd give plenty of thought as to why you chose those people as your measurement for monsters."

"Don't you dare judge me. I . . ."

"Kismet." She spun around, eyes wide, pupils as large and shiny as wet, dark stones. "And *bluff.* That's what your God game is all about."

Startled that she was still tuned into him, that she had found the two words that unlocked the biggest failure of his life, he stammered, "You . . . you . . ."

"Kismet was the name of a production company my parents had," Adam burst out. "And *Bluff* . . . that was the antiwar film they did. It . . ."

"Shut up," Finch hissed.

Mira rushed on. "The lost years. Between 1993 when you left Seattle and 1999 when you left Silicon Valley, you were in Hollywood, Spenser. That's what none of us could figure out. Where you'd been. C'mon, give me your hand, Spenser. Or let me touch your shoulder again. Let me get the rest."

He backed away from her. She kept right on talking. "You auditioned for a part in that movie. You didn't get it. There was a woman. Her name starts with a T. No, with a P. Patricia? Portia? No, no, that's not quite right. Priscilla. You blamed Priscilla. You stalked her, cut her tires, and . . ." Mira suddenly stopped, the coin dropped from her hand, clinking loudly against the floor. "Revenge. It's all about revenge."

"I don't care about the past. Tell me about the future, Mira. Let's see if you can read the future as well as you can the past." He grabbed her wrist.

She wrenched free and moved away from him, rubbing her wrist, shaking her head. "I can't. I need to eat first. To rest. To . . ."

He moved the gun through the air, toward Adam. "You have . . ."

His cell rang. Eden, again. If he didn't take the call, she would keep right on calling.

"You've got fifteen minutes," he said briskly, and

slammed the door as he left. He locked it, pressed the *answer* button on his cell, hurried up the hall.

"Hey, I was just going to call you, hon. What's going on?"

"Spense." Breathless. "Paul's been taken in for questioning. It's on CNN right now. How could they think he would kidnap his own son?" Her breathlessness rose to near-hysteria. "I've got to go in there, explain that he was with me that night, that he . . . I'm his alibi and. . . ."

He tuned her out, squeezed the bridge of his nose, backed up to the wall. The solid coolness of the wood against his spine, the faint residue of cooking scents in the air, and her goddamn whining, hysterical voice. Paul, Paul, Paul, always about Paul. Finally, he said, "You need to do it in person. I'll drive you over there. I'll be at your place in about twenty minutes."

"Really? You'll drive me? Oh, my God, thank you, Spense. I . . . I just don't think I could live with myself otherwise. I'll be ready when you get here."

She disconnected and he remained against the wall, clutching the cell, struggling against a terrible weight in the center of his chest. Twenty minutes.

And then?

He would talk her out of it.

Clean clothes, car keys, hurry.

Mira and Adam would have to wait.

21

Sex, Lies, and Videotape

It was just like the movies, Sheppard thought, with the suspect pacing through a small, windowless room equipped with an old wooden table and a couple of chairs. In the days before smoking was banned inside state and federal buildings, there would have been an ashtray, matches, and a pack of smokes on the table, probably Marlboros, the cigarettes of choice for restless loners, con men, cowboys, and famous directors in their waning years. Now, there was just a bottle of water on the table.

In the old days, the suspect was watched through a one-way mirror; now, hidden security cameras and mikes recorded the suspect's every move, mutter, breath. The cameras could zoom in or out and noise could be filtered, enhanced, wiped out. Now, it was all about the magic of technology. The bottom line, though, was the same. Getting information.

"So what's our agenda, amigo?" Goot asked, jamming his hands into the pockets of his chinos. "We don't have anything solid on this guy. He has a girlfriend and was apparently with her the night his son disappeared. That's not a crime."

"My thoughts exactly," Cordoba said.

We're not asking for your thoughts, Charlie. "Mira saw both Nichols and our perp with a redhead."

Cordoba rolled his eyes. "Last time I checked, psychic information doesn't stand up in court."

"We're not going to court. We just want information," Sheppard snapped.

Kartauk leaned heavily on his cane. "Fuck court. Our job is to find out who the woman is—name, address, employer, the works. And I doubt if the good-cop/bad-cop routine is the way to go. Mel Gibson and Danny Glover kind of exhausted that one."

"I thought Bruce Willis did it in," Goot said.

"Hey, Crockett and Tubbs squeezed it dry during *Miami Vice,* and that was a long time before any of the *Lethal Weapon* movies," Sheppard said.

"This isn't a goddamn movie," Cordoba muttered.

"Ha," Kartauk said. "It's *Sex, Lies, and Videotape.*"

"We have *videotape*?" Cordoba exclaimed. His hungry eyes said it all: The voyeur in him was hoping, perhaps, for a glimpse of famous Paul Nichols screwing his even more famous wife or, if not that, his lover. "How come I haven't been told about *that*?"

Sheppard rolled his eyes. "For Chrissakes, Charlie. *Sex, Lies, and Videotape* is a movie."

"So how do we play it?" Kartauk asked.

Sheppard wagged the folder that held the e-mails Nichols and his lady friend had exchanged. "We go for the jugular and play the rest like Stanislavsky."

Kartauk chuckled. "Great idea, Shep."

"Who's Stanislovsky?" Cordoba asked.

Kartauk answered that one. "A Russian acting coach who believed that an actor has to take his own personality into the portrayal of a character. If you're playing a role that involves fear, then you have to remember something frightening and try to act in the emotional space of fear that you once felt.

Emotional memory, Charlie. Immersion." He apparently felt compelled to explain how he knew this bit of information. "Acting in college," he said.

"And which emotional memory are you playing here, Shep?" Goot asked.

An image of Mira's earring, just sitting on that bookshelf, came to mind. "Rage, Goot."

"And Glen and I will be your calming influence?"

"I'll calm him," Kartauk said. "You restrain him. And we enter at just the right moment."

"Our own little passion play," Sheppard remarked.

"What part do I play?" Cordoba asked.

"Spectator," Sheppard replied, and left before Cordoba could protest.

Moments later, Sheppard threw open the door of the interrogation room. It banged against the wall, startling Nichols, who paused in his restless pacing. "I have the right to call my attorney and I'm demanding a phone right now."

"Sit down, Mr. Nichols."

"I said, I—"

"I heard what you said and I'm telling you to sit the fuck down."

Color burned in his cheeks, but Nichols jerked the chair out and sat down, his large hands flat against the table. Then his fingers started drumming the surface. "Okay, I'm sitting. Now what the hell am I doing here? Am I being charged with something? Am I under arrest?"

Sheppard pulled out the other chair, whipped it around so the back faced the table, and straddled it. "You're not under arrest. You're here to answer some questions."

"So I'm under suspicion for something?"

Sheppard didn't bother answering that question. "It's come to our attention that you have information regarding someone who is involved with the man who took your son, Mr. Nichols." He slapped the folder down against the table, opened it, picked up the top e-mail, and started reading aloud. Before he gotten out more than two sentences, Nichols snatched the paper out of Sheppard's hand.

"You have no right to . . ."

Sheppard shot to his feet and leaned so close to Nichols's face that he wrenched back. "While you were fucking your brains out on Big Pine Key, the woman you were with was acting as a decoy so that her partner could get into your house and take your son." Theories, nothing more. But Nichols didn't know that. "I want her name and address, Mr. Nichols, and if you don't give it to me, I'm charging you with accessory to kidnapping."

Nichols looked stunned. His mouth dropped open, his eyes widened, he didn't exhale. Silence gripped the room. Then Nichols breathed out and scooted his chair back, putting distance between himself and Sheppard. "That's . . . that's impossible." No shouting. No threats. Just denial.

"Her name."

"I . . ."

Sheppard grabbed another e-mail from the folder and read it aloud. "*'I miss you so much and dream of the moments when you'll be inside of me again. Paradise.'* Or how about this one?" Sheppard reached for another e-mail.

"I know what they say!" he yelled, and lunged across the table at Sheppard.

Sheppard jerked back, his chair tipped and crashed to the floor, the file flew out of his hand. Then he and Nichols were locked together and rolling across the floor, the scattered e-mails. The stink of testosterone filled the air. Nichols grunted and snorted like a wild hog and tried to get a tight grip on Sheppard's throat. But Sheppard saw red; his knees snapped up and sank into Nichols's balls. Sheppard threw Nichols off as he bellowed and howled and struggled to his feet. Sheppard leaped up and went after him.

The door flew open and Cordoba and Goot rushed in, both of them shouting. Cordoba waved his arms like a referee and Goot thrust himself between Sheppard and Nichols. "Back off, Shep, back the hell off."

"So much for immersion and Stanislavsky," Kartauk drolled, limping into the room on his crutch.

Sheppard's arms swung to his sides and he shook his head to clear it. "He refuses to divulge the woman's name. That makes him. . . ." Sheppard stabbed the air with his index finger. "An accessory to kidnapping."

Nichols's shiny red cheeks puffed out like a squirrel's and he huffed, "I didn't . . . have anything to . . . do with Adam's disappearance." He had backed up to the wall. Blood dribbled out of the right corner of his mouth, his right nostril. He wiped the back of his hand across his mouth. "I'm suing your ass for assault."

"If I were you, Mr. Nichols," Kartauk said in a quiet, even voice, pointing the end of his crutch at Nichols, "I would stop threatening federal agents. There are three witnesses here who saw you make the first move on Agent Sheppard." He walked with an uneven gait over to Nichols and aimed his crutch at the nearest chair. "Have a seat."

"I'm fine right here," Nichols spat.

"Suit yourself. As I was saying, there are three witnesses who will testify that Agent Sheppard was defending himself. So at the moment, we have several charges against you: accessory to kidnapping, assault on a federal officer, interfering in a federal investigation. . . ."

"I want to call my attorney."

Nichols, a broken record, Sheppard thought, and suddenly *knew* that Eden wasn't a street or a place. It was his lover's name. "Eden who? What's her full name?"

Shock seized Nichols's face. He rolled his lips together, made his way to the chair, and sat down heavily, as though the weight of his own body were suddenly too much to bear. "I . . . I . . ." Nichols stammered. "How . . . I mean . . . Jesus." He ran his hands over his face. "Her name's Eden Thompkins."

He took a deep breath, as though it were a relief to finally have said it, to confess. Then he spoke fast. "I don't know where she lives, I swear. I never went to her house. We just met at motels."

"Where's she work?" Goot asked.

"In Key West. At a restaurant."

Kartauk snapped his fingers in Nichols's face. "For Chrissakes. Get with it, man. The name of the restaurant, we need the name."

"Pepe's. Pepe's Bar and Grill."

"Lock him up, Charlie," Sheppard said, and was already on his cell as he hurried from the room.

It didn't take long to find out that Pepe's had no phone service or power. It would take him and Goot forty minutes to get to Key West on the ferry and five minutes on either end to get to the dock and then to the restaurant. Call it an hour. Ross Blake could get them there faster by seaplane. But if Eden wasn't at work, he would have to get a home address and no telling where she lived. They would need a car.

"What's the plan?" Goot asked, catching up with him as he headed toward the conference room.

"Even though word's gotten out that Paul was brought in, call the Telemundo guy. We owe him a favor. Confirm that Nichols was brought in and tell him we have two persons of interest. No names. Then tell Charlie to hold a press conference, same information, no names. We need time to get to Key West and track down Eden Thompkins."

"The press conference will put Charlie right where he wants to be, in the spotlight. It'll keep him occupied. How about if we ask Ross to fly us to Key West and have someone from the Bureau there meet us at Pepe's with a car?"

Sheppard grinned at Goot. "Great minds and all that. You talk to Ross, get the others in the conference room up to speed, have them keep fielding calls and e-mails just in case we're on the wrong track here. I'll meet you and Ross in the parking lot in five minutes. I need to speak to Glen."

He found Kartauk in the hallway outside the restrooms, eyeing the vending machines. "Is this coffee any good?" Kartauk asked as Sheppard approached.

"No."

He laughed. "Now that is a refreshingly direct answer, Shep."

"Have Suki drive you over to the Cappuccino House on Pirate's Cove. They've got electricity, their coffee's to die for, and they have terrific Greek food. Tell Joe, the owner, that Shep sent you. He'll give you a discount."

Kartauk looked puzzled. "Suki?"

"She needs a haven for a few days, Glen. Can she stay with you?"

"Are you kidding? What man in his right mind could say no to a request like that? I'd better call my housekeeper. There're dust balls under the couch, the guest room needs clean sheets, the . . ."

Sheppard touched his arm. "Hey, relax. She doesn't give a shit about dust balls right now, okay? You're her refuge from the press. And she needs to bring her cat."

Kartauk blinked, then laughed, his fleshy jowls trembling. "Her cat, her furniture, whatever. Christ, I've lived alone too long."

"Naw, it's that Pisces thing and guilt."

"Yeah, yeah," he said with a quick grin. "Where is she now?"

"Probably on her way home." Sheppard ticked off Suki's cell number. "Call her. Offer her a refuge, a sanctuary, great coffee, company, and peace, Glen."

"Jesus, should I ask her to marry me too?"

"She's not divorced yet, Glen." Besides, Sheppard was pretty sure that Blake had designs of his own. "I'll be in touch."

Mira sensed that Spenser had left the house and would be gone longer than fifteen minutes. But just in case she was wrong, she and Adam spoke in hushed voices as they went through the freshly stocked cooler. Now that her jaw no longer ached and the swelling had gone down, her appetite had come roaring back. From the looks of it, Adam was hungrier than she was.

They split up the sandwiches, helped themselves to fruit, containers of juice, bottles of cold water. Once they had fortified themselves with food, she thought, they could try to figure out a way to escape. Adam's break for freedom sure hadn't worked.

"Is he really gone or is it a trick?" Adam whispered.

"I think he left to tend to the redhead."

"Eden. Her name's Eden."

"He told you that?"

Adam nodded, unwrapped a sandwich, examined it, and bit into it. "He tried to hurt me by telling me that Eden and my dad are having an affair. I found some photos of them together."

Mira sat beside him at the edge of the bed and bit into a tuna fish sandwich peppered with radishes and bits of celery. "I'm sorry you had to find out this stuff about your dad, Adam."

He shrugged. "It isn't the first time. It doesn't matter. He isn't even my real dad."

Interesting. Suki had told her that no one else knew this fact. "How do you know that?"

"I found my birth certificate in Mom's things. Only Mom's name was listed under parents. If Paul Nichols were really my father, his name would be on that birth certificate."

Mira wondered what to say. Adam took care of that for her.

"You already knew, right?" he asked.

"I picked it up when your mom hired me to find you."

"I just wish she'd told me."

"Parents try to do what's best for their kids, Adam, but sometimes we screw up."

He shrugged, accepting. "How're we going to get outta here, Mira?"

"I don't know yet."

Already, she was on her feet, moving restlessly around the room, touching this and that, seeking more information on Spenser. Given the size of the room and the number of objects and surfaces she touched, she uncovered surprisingly little that was new. Either he hadn't spent much time in here, or his emotions had been as dormant as a bear in winter when he'd been in here.

Many homes seemed to have rooms like this, spaces the residents entered rarely if at all, places where books, boxes, and dust devils accumulated and nothing much of interest happened. This room felt like the guest room at her parents' home or like a model home, as though people tiptoed around inside it, never raising their voices, making love, laughing, crying, or expressing much of anything at all.

"The room's a problem, isn't it," Adam remarked, shadowing her as though he were afraid that if she got too far away, she would vanish. "I mean, for the way you work."

"I can't find much of him in here."

"I think that's why Friend has only appeared once since I've been here."

"Do you know who she is, Adam?"

Mira thought he might avoid answering the question, as he'd done earlier. But this time he nodded. "His mother. He looks like her. Has her mouth and chin, but not her eyes. Her eyes are, like, kind and warm. But his are the dark side of the moon. Since she couldn't protect him, she was trying to protect me. Except her efforts to protect me suck big-time."

"Tell me about his migraines."

"They come on without much warning. When Friend— Joy—made the room cold, a migraine drove him outta here. The night he took me, he was in a lot of pain and it got worse the closer we got to . . . wherever we are. Then he had another one today. Maybe he has a brain tumor or something."

Maybe, but she didn't think so. She was pretty sure she
would have picked up something like that in her contact with
him. "I think his migraines are connected to what he can't
remember about his own kidnapping and to the things he has
done over the years. What do you know about the casting director for *Bluff?*"

"Not a whole lot. Mom had some articles she'd saved
about her death. She supposedly drove over the side of a cliff
because she'd been drinking. That was the official verdict. I
think it happened a couple of weeks into the shooting of
Bluff. So he did all this to get back at my mom because he
didn't get the male lead?"

"Basically, yes. But it's a lot more complicated than that.
I think his father made him feel like a failure at everything.
Once he was older, I think he started fighting back to prove
to himself that his father was wrong about him. He was apparently a success in Silicon Valley, but he failed in Hollywood,
and he never forgot it. It ate away at him."

"Then why am I still alive? Why hasn't he . . . killed me?
That would be the ultimate vengeance against my mom."

"I'm not sure, but my guess is that he likes playing God.
It makes him feel that he succeeded at what he set out to do."

"Can I ask you a, uh, personal question?"

"Sure."

"When he brought you in here, your face was so bruised
the skin on the right side was almost black. I could tell you
were in a lot of pain. But now you seem okay and the swelling
is gone and the bruise has nearly faded. How's that possible?"

She appreciated the way he phrased his question. Instead
of exclaiming that it was *impossible,* he asked *how* it was
possible. "It's one of my body's peculiarities. But this time it
took a lot longer than usual." Hours.

"But how's it work? I mean, it's like, incredible, okay?
I've never seen anything like this."

Sheppard had asked her the same thing many times over

the years. *How's it work? Explain it to me. What's involved?* These conversations usually plunged into chaos quickly because, bottom line, all she had were theories patched together from books, conversations with Nadine, and her own experiences. She didn't have a simple answer. And while Adam was a bright kid who probably had read many of the same books she had, this wasn't the time or the place for a discourse on quantum physics. Movies could explain it just as well.

"You saw *Carrie,* right? And *The Fury?*"

"You're saying it's a kind of telekinesis?"

"That's my theory."

"Like Ellen Burstyn in *Resurrection.*"

"Similar. Burstyn healed herself and then was able to heal others. I can't heal other people. I mean, sometimes it happens because I inadvertently take on their symptoms, their aches and pains, and my body transmutes them. Right now, for instance, I have a headache from working on you." She rubbed her temple. "Right there. And here." She touched the spot between her eyebrows. "Just like you. But it's not like I can put my hands on someone with cancer and they're healed. It's more like self-protection."

"Suppose you're stabbed? Or shot? Or you get MS or cancer or AIDS or something like that?"

"I got shot last Christmas and my body couldn't handle it. I flatlined briefly and ended up having several surgeries." She pushed up the hem of her shorts and showed him the scar on her upper thigh. "And I don't know about disease. I've never had a disease."

"Do you get colds?"

She laughed. "Yeah, and sinus infections and I go to the dentist. I had my tonsils and appendix taken out when I was a kid. This isn't like *X-Men.*"

He rubbed his hands over his thighs, nodding, pensive. "So you're an anomaly."

"Exactly. For lack of a better word, that's what I am."

"You ever read Colin Wilson?"

In all her years in the book business, no thirteen-year-old had ever asked her about Colin Wilson. She suddenly saw Adam in a much different light. "Yes. Have you?"

"*The Outsider, the Occult, Mysteries* . . . Those are my three favorites."

Mira had read *The Outsider,* Wilson's 1956 classic, when she was a year older than Adam, and it had explained more about who she was than anything Nadine ever told her. She *was* the outsider, the weirdo, the factor X that Wilson had written about. The fact that Adam apparently identified with Wilson in the same way made her realize she had underestimated him. His body might be thirteen years old, but his mind, his spirit, his very soul were ancient. Like her, he straddled two worlds. He was psychic and didn't realize it and his raw talent probably surpassed hers. She guessed he'd been seeing the dead long before Joy Longwood had appeared to him and that in the cosmic scheme of things, the kidnapping was his wake-up call. His initiation.

Her head ached now in a way that had nothing to do with Adam's discomfort or their situation. Lights burst inside her skull, an explosion so brilliant that if it were physical, it would blind her. She shut her eyes, her breathing shifted. The brilliant light gradually faded enough so that she could see several of the myriad paths that would open to him as a result of this experience.

If he survives.

And that was her job. To make sure that he escaped, that he survived, that he went on to achieve his potential. There was a message here for her too, but she didn't know what it was. Even as she thought this, she could feel a block of information pressing against the edge of her consciousness, but couldn't quite seize it.

"Adam, I need to know what's coming up for us. The easiest way for me to find out is to read you. Would that be okay with you?"

"Mom swears by you."

Hey, how encouraging. She had done such a great job of finding Adam that she had to be snatched to do it. "I'd like you to start talking about everything that has happened to you since you were taken, okay? And at some point, I'll take your hand."

"So it's like downloading music or information."

A psychic download. "Yeah, something like that. Start with the night he took you."

He began to talk, his voice quiet, even, steady. Mira shut her eyes. She used the alternate breathing technique that Nadine had taught her when she was too young to understand that it brought both hemispheres of the brain into sync with each other. When the shift in her awareness occurred, she flowed into the slipstream of Adam's voice.

His world, for all its access to privilege, wasn't like the movies. It wasn't the world of Spielberg or Lucas. It wasn't *Wayne's World*. Adam had grown up with a huge rift between him and Paul, the result of several past lives in which Suki had been central to their hostility toward each other. Their relationships to Suki in these other lives had been vastly different—in one, she was a man and Adam and his father were sisters who loved him. In another, the three of them were siblings. In yet another, Adam had been Suki's father and Paul had been Adam's daughter. The intricate web quickly became confusing, and she pulled back from this path of information.

She was seeking a deeper connection between Adam and Spenser and it didn't necessarily originate in a past life. She suspected that before Adam had been born, his soul had agreed to experience something dramatic and emotionally wrenching that would alter the course of the lives within his immediate family and open him psychically.

That Spenser had lived where Adam was living now, in the Mango Hill house, wasn't enough of an attractor. But suppose Spenser, like Adam, had never known his birth father. Suppose the man who'd taken Spenser believed the boy was his son, just as Paul Nichols believed that Adam was *his* son? And suppose Spenser's kidnapper, like Nichols, was oblivious to the truth? It was the kind of pattern that could act as an attractor, she thought, but she didn't have any idea if it was true for Spenser and the man who had kidnapped him.

And how the hell did *she* fit into this picture? Why had *she* attracted this sort of experience?

Because it involves a child.

Yes, that was part of it. But the deeper pattern—paternity—didn't apply to her. The man she knew as her father—a science-fiction writer who, like her lawyer mother, was largely clueless about Mira—was her blood father. Of course he was. Her parents had been married for forty-four years, since her mother was a twenty-year-old college student and her father was a twenty-one-year-old graduate student in the engineering department at the University of Miami. Her mother had turned sixty-three in July; her father would turn sixty-four in August. There was no mystery here, nothing hidden from her.

Or is there?

"Mira?" Adam whispered.

She opened her eyes and realized she was gripping Adam's hand.

"I'm sorry, I didn't mean to clutch your hand so . . ."

"The room's getting cold," he whispered.

The temperature plummeted just as quickly as it had in Adam's room at home, minus the poltergeist activity. Nothing moved, the air seemed to be sucked free of sound. Frost gradually formed on the windows. Mira pulled the quilt off the bed and pulled it around herself and Adam as they lowered themselves to the top of the cooler. Static filled her head, she could see her breath now, and moments later two forms began to take shape in the middle of the room. "Can you see this?" Mira whispered.

"She's not alone," Adam whispered back.

If either of them had been wearing watches or there had been a clock in the room, Mira knew that the hands would be spinning or stopped altogether. Instead, the lightbulb in the floor lamp blinked off and on. The computer went dead and whirred to life again. The static in her head abruptly ceased and a man and a woman materialized like characters in *Star Trek* beamed from elsewhere, their images wavering, strange, then gradually solidifying so they looked almost real.

"Holy shit," Adam breathed. "It's never been this . . . this real before. This clear. Who's the guy?"

"My dead husband." Mira didn't move as Tom and Joy came over to them. Her heart ached at the sight of him, but she was angry that he only showed up in time of stress and crisis. "Unless you're here to open the door, Tom, you and Joy can leave."

"I don't just show up in a crisis, Mira," he said. "I'm with you more than you realize, but you block your awareness of me when life is good."

Emotion swelled in her throat, she swallowed it back. "Then what do you want, Tom?"

Joy Longwood spoke, her voice surprisingly soft, feminine, melodic. "To apologize for the trouble I caused in Adam's room. I only wanted to show Adam's mother that I'm not an imaginary playmate. And I need to apologize to you, Adam, for not protecting you the way I had hoped."

"You should've told me the whole story," he said.

The closer they came to Mira, the more electrified the air became. The hairs on Mira's arms now stood up, her skin tingled and tightened, as if she had outgrown her own body. She felt strangely uneasy and sensed there was another layer to all this. She got to her feet, interposing herself between Adam and Joy, and held out her hand. "Give me the truth," she said to the woman.

Joy glanced at Tom, as if asking for his permission or advice. Joy had been dead much longer than Tom, Mira thought, but seemed to understand far less than he did about what was allowed.

"It's okay. She's done this before."

Joy raised her right hand, as if to pledge her allegiance to truth or country. Mira raised her right hand as well and Joy touched her palm to Mira's.

The touch wasn't like that between two living people. There was no warmth, no grasping of fingers, no sliding of flesh against flesh. The sensation that tore through her was unlike anything she'd experienced before, as if lightning ripped into the top of her skull and blew it off completely. She couldn't wrench free of it. Images poured into her, shocking in their clarity, intimacy, agony, and horror. Her nervous system short-circuited; she thought she smelled smoke and the stink of her own flesh burning. When she couldn't stand it anymore, her brain went into lockdown, all her psychic doors slammed shut, and she fell away into darkness.

22

Fatal Attraction

Thanks to the already soggy ground, the rain had turned many streets in Old Town Key West into shallow rivers. Finch didn't want to risk having the car stall out, so he parked three blocks from Eden's, on a street that was more elevated. He trekked barefoot through the rain, his umbrella slanted into the wind, and went over what he would say to her. He knew that he could convince her to see things his way. It was just a matter of playing the part of concerned lover and friend, as he had in the beginning of their relationship, when he listened for hours to all the intimate details of her affair with Paul Nichols.

Her apartment was the back of a wooden two-story house built in the days before Key West had become a tourist travesty. It was 750 square feet, with a tiny porch that looked out upon a garden the size of a potted plant and a small wooded area beyond that. The single bedroom was no larger than a stamp, the plumbing in the cramped bathroom leaked, the kitchen was barely large enough for two people to move around in comfortably. But at nearly a grand a month, it was considered a steal.

As Finch turned onto her block, the flooded sidewalk was lit here and there by lights from apartments powered by generators. The steady, noisy chug of the machines created a grating undercurrent of sound to that of the rain, like a garage band competing with an orchestra.

Finch was struck by the sight of her building just ahead, barely a silhouette in the rainy dark and yet somehow menacing, as though it held unimagined horrors. He suddenly felt that he should immediately turn around and walk fast, very fast, back to his car, return to his house, pack up, and disappear. He actually stopped right where he was, ankle deep in water, and considered it. But that wasn't how the game was won, he thought, and ran the remaining distance to Eden's building.

He hurried along the side of the building and onto her porch. The door was open and Eden stood just inside, fussing with her purse, her raincoat. In the glow of electric lanterns, she looked old, used up, ravaged. Her lustrous copper hair was wild, frizzy, exploding from the sides of her head with a kind of wild abandon. "There was nowhere to wait for you outside without getting drenched," she said, and tossed him a hand towel so he could dry himself off.

Finch set the umbrella against a small bamboo cart that held fresh fruit. "I had to park three blocks away. Let's wait a few minutes until this downpour lets up." He shut the door with his foot and rubbed the towel vigorously over his face and arms.

"I can't tell you how much I appreciate this, Spense."

"I'm not so sure it's a good idea, Eden. Once it gets out into the press—and it will—it could jeopardize his son's life. It may be just what the kidnapper's waiting for."

"Why do you say that? He may be dead already, for all we know."

"I don't think he's dead. That isn't what Paul wants."

"What's that supposed to mean?"

He pulled out a chair for her, then one for himself, and sat down. "Let's talk about this for a few minutes."

She remained standing. "I want to get going."

It irritated him that she wouldn't sit. He stayed where he was, making it clear that he wasn't budging. "Consider this, Eden. It's possible that Paul arranged the kidnapping of his son as a publicity ploy, to revive his career and . . ."

"*What?* That's totally ridiculous. Paul loves Adam, he would never do . . ."

"Yeah, he loves him so much he was screwing around with another woman on the night he was supposed to be home because his wife was out of town. C'mon, his career took a nosedive years ago. Why do you think he's teaching about directing instead of actually directing? No one wants to hire him. He's a has-been, for Chrissake, but all this publicity could change that for him."

"I'm not going to stand here and listen to this bullshit. It's . . ."

"Let me finish," he snapped.

She looked stunned that he spoke to her with such sharpness.

"If I'm right about Paul and you go in there claiming to be his alibi, then it's possible the police will consider you an accessory."

Her frown threw her forehead into a chaos of lines, pinched her eyes at the corners, and turned her mouth into a parody of itself. It was obvious that none of what he'd said had occurred to her. Finch, certain he had dented her resolve, rushed on.

"It makes sense, Eden. Think about it. Think about how devious he is, how often he had to lie just to be with you. There's even another, worse scenario. You go in there claiming to be his alibi and he turns the tables on you, swears that *he* ended the relationship with *you* and that you got back at him by taking his son."

She threw her arms out. "You see a kid here, Spense? I didn't do a damn thing to Paul or to his son."

"*I* know that, but the cops won't."

Tears gathered in her eyes, she sank into the chair with a kind of tragic resignation, and the tears spilled. "I . . . I just want to do the right thing."

"The right thing is to protect yourself by staying out of it."

She rubbed her hands over her face, her nails bright red against her soft skin. "I feel so stupid." A hesitant smile, unbearably sad. "What would I do without you, Spense?"

"I can think of one thing you can do *with* me," he said, touching her hand.

"I'm really not in the mood for that right now."

"I'm not talking about sex. Pack a bag. We'll go somewhere."

What am I saying?

"You mean, like, on a vacation?"

"No. We'll move somewhere together." *Really? Am I ready for this?* "We'll go on my boat. There's nothing to keep you here."

"The houseboat?"

"I've got another boat, with a cabin. It's comfortable, we can go anywhere. Do you have a current passport?"

"Yeah, but . . . Where would we go?"

"Wherever you want."

Eden looked as if her fairy godmother had just told her that with one sweep of her wand, any wish she had would be granted. "New Zealand. I've always wanted to go there. Is that too far?"

He laughed. "It'll take forever, but it's not too far."

She considered it for about five seconds, then threw her arms around his neck. "Spense, oh, Spense," she said softly. "But. . . ." She pulled back. "What about your job?"

"I can sell computer stuff anywhere. Or I can just quit. I've got enough money to last a long time."

"And you really want to do this? With me?"

"I can't think of anyone else I'd rather do it with. I'm tired of Florida anyway." Tired of all of it. "It's time to move on." As soon as he said it, he knew it was true.

She ran her nails through his hair, kissed him, knuckled her eyes, and looked slowly around the cramped kitchen. "There's not much here I want to take. Most of it's junk."

"Pack a couple of bags. I'll go get the car. Your street's pretty flooded, but maybe I can get as far as the end of the block."

"There's an old alley on the other side of the trees out back. Take that road. It hardly ever floods. I'll meet you there, by the edge of the trees."

He got up, anxious to get moving. "We'll stay on the boat tonight and get an early start tomorrow."

"Where's your boat?"

"Sugarloaf."

"What about my rent? The stuff in the fridge? My job?"

"We can mail your landlord the last rent payment, pack the fridge stuff in a cooler, and fuck your job. They cut back so far on your hours they don't deserve any advance notice."

The longer he talked, the more inevitable it became. His boat, the Flybridge, was docked behind a snowbird's house a short distance from his place. He would bring it to his own dock, he and Eden would stay there for the night, and when she was asleep, he would torch the house, ending all of it, just as he had with his old man. Eden would never know about Mira and Adam.

Eden went to the door with him, hugged him again. "Hurry back," she whispered.

If it hadn't been the dead of summer, in the aftermath of a category-five hurricane, the shoreline of Key West would have been filled with boats, Sheppard thought, and unfit for the landing of a seaplane. But Blake was able to take them within a quarter-mile of shore, and the Zodiac raft carried the three of them the rest of the way.

They put in at the dock nearest to the restaurant. As they got out, a heavy bouncer-type in a yellow rain slicker hurried over and informed them the slip was reserved and to get the hell out. He had teeth as bad as his attitude and a beer belly that made him look six months pregnant. Sheppard flashed his badge and slung his arm around the man's shoulders, walking him up the pier a ways.

"You were saying?"

"Hey, man, stay as long as you want."

"Excellent choice," Sheppard replied. "Now point us toward Pepe's."

As soon as Sheppard saw the place, he recognized it, a landmark from another life, another Sheppard. The name had changed, that was all. The year? He wasn't sure, could no longer remember. It had been during his first stretch with the Bureau, before Hurricane Andrew, and he and his wife had come here for dinner. They'd had too much to drink, he remembered, and all sorts of weird shit had come to the surface. She did *not* want kids, they would interfere with her legal career, she was going places, and they could go places together. But not if he really wanted kids. Uh-uh, no way. And in the end, their different needs on this single issue had ended the marriage.

He hated the place just on principle.

Inside, the lights ran on a generator, the air was hot and sticky, and the booths were nearly empty. But the covered bar in the patio area was full. The thin, tanned hostess came over to him and Goot. "How many?" she asked.

Sheppard held up his badge. "Where's the manager?"

"Oh." Breathlessness, Key West–style, then, more softly: "Shit. Hold on."

She hurried off and Goot remarked, "It smells funny in here."

"Mold," Sheppard said.

"Uh-huh, I knew it," Goot replied. "First marriage. Bad night."

"Most of the nights were bad then."

The manager was a chunky guy with a weathered face. He looked like he suffered from a terminal disease. "What can I do for you, gentlemen?"

His phony smile grated on Sheppard, who held up his badge. "Eden Thompkins. Is she working this evening?"

"Eden?" Blink, blink went his eyes. "Uh, no. Her hours were cut back."

"Then I need a home address."

The manager folded his arms across his chest. "I can't just give out my employees' addresses. What's this about?"

A petty bureaucrat. It seemed that every facet of American society was filled with them, from the guy with bad teeth out on the dock to this little shit in front of him to Charlie Cordoba and on up through the ranks of government. The irony was that from where the manager stood, Sheppard was the petty bureaucrat. Well, so be it.

Sheppard leaned into the man's personal space and in a quiet, tight voice said: "What it's about, my friend, is all over the news. And if you don't give me her home address, you'll be charged as an accessory to kidnapping. Any other questions?"

Two blinks, one blink, two again. Like some sort of archaic code. "I . . . I need to, uh, look it up," the man stammered.

Sheppard glanced at Goot, who nodded and accompanied the manager through double doors. Blake touched Sheppard's shoulder. "I'm going to make sure we've got a car out front. Breathe, Shep. We'll get there."

Right. Breathe. The zen of the moment and all that. But just being inside this place was like time-traveling. He could see his former self with his ex-wife, seated at that table out in the patio, under the thick, woven branches of the banyan tree, their disagreement deepening with every glass of wine they drank.

Sheppard squeezed the bridge of his nose. His cell rang. Kartauk's number came up. "Yeah, Glen."

"Suki and I are at my place, Shep."

"Great." *And what's your real reason for calling, Glen?* "Thanks very much. I appreciate your helping us out here."

"Have you seen the news in the last fifteen minutes?"

I've been in a seaplane. I'm now standing in a restaurant that's running on a generator. Nope, sorry. "No, why?"

"Cordoba blew it. The prick gave names, Shep. He did everything he was told not to do."

"He gave *Eden's* name? In a press conference?"

"Eden, Spenser and his aliases, said that Mira is missing, the whole nine yards."

"Christ." *Damnshitfuck.* "Thanks for the tip, Glen. Keep me posted."

"Did you find her yet?"

"Almost."

"Keep me in the loop, Shep."

"You bet."

The manager emerged from the double doors and, judging from his avid hand gestures, was arguing with Goot. And Goot lost his temper, shoved the manager up against the wall, and snatched a scrap of paper out of his hand. Then he hurried over to Sheppard, wagging the paper.

"Got it. We're outta here. She lives on Elizabeth Street."

The manager ran after them and caught up with them on the sidewalk. "You think you can just barge in and intimidate people and shove them around?" he shouted. "This is America. We have laws, we have . . ."

Sheppard got into the passenger seat of the waiting cruiser and slammed the door, cutting off the sound of the man's voice. Once Goot scooted into the back, Sheppard

said, "Make it fast, Ross," and gave him the address on
Elizabeth Street in Old Town Key West.

Eden waited for Finch at the edge of the woods, where
the trees bent over the alley, huddled together like kids in-
specting roadkill. She had a suitcase on wheels in one hand,
a backpack in the other, and a raincoat thrown over her head.
She wore Capri jeans, a cotton shirt, flip-flops. A woman
who traveled light, he thought, and in that moment she reminded him of Suki in *Acid Test*. He knew he had made the
right decision.

He pulled the VW wagon alongside her and she tossed
everything into the backseat and slid in beside him. "It's
really happening, isn't it," she said, and gave him a sloppy
kiss on the cheek. "What will you do with your car?"

He shrugged. "Leave it."

"Really? You can afford to do that?"

"It's just a car. We can buy another car."

"And you have a boat you never told me about. What else
don't I know about you, Spense honey?"

He glanced at her, grinned, winked, and drove on to the
end of the alley. As he turned out onto the road, he jammed
on the brakes, barely missing the police cruiser that swerved
to avoid hitting him, its horn blaring, blue lights spinning.
Time shrieked to a crawl, then stopped altogether. In a
frozen moment of utter clarity, Finch knew the tall man in
the passenger seat was Wayne Sheppard.

Time slammed forward again, the cruiser sped around the
corner, and Finch sat there paralyzed, hands gripping the
steering wheel, the roaring rush of blood pounding in his
ears.

Spense, Spense, Spense . . .

His neck felt stiff as he turned his head, looking at Eden.
"Yeah?"

"That goddamn cop nearly hit us," she exclaimed.

And now they're nearly at your place. He could barely swallow.

"Spense, the engine stalled."

Sweet Christ. He put the wagon in park, turned the key, the engine fired up. *Drive. Fast.*

He made a U-turn in the middle of the road and sped off in the opposite direction, swerving up and down back streets, alleys, trying not to imagine what was going on at Eden's. *Paul talked.* "Those cops are headed to your place, Eden," he said finally. "Paul must've told them about you."

"How can you possibly know where they're headed?"

Because I recognized the fed in the passenger seat. "It makes sense. Paul told them where you live."

"Paul doesn't know where I live. He'd never been to my place. He never even asked where I live."

"Then they must've gotten your address from work."

Eden fell into a moody silence, her head turned toward the window. The road out of Key West now stretched before them, shiny, dark, as straight as a needle. Finch took the VW up to seventy, the car slammed into a pothole, the front tires skidded. Slow down, he thought. He had to slow down.

But how long did they have? Minutes? An hour?

No, no, no. The cops didn't have any idea where Eden was, how could they? She might be at a friend's place, visiting family, shopping, bar-hopping; they would have to wait at her apartment until she showed up. And despite what Mira said the feds knew about him, his past, it didn't matter. They didn't know about the Sugarloaf house, the Flybridge, the kind of car he drove. They didn't have enough basic information about him and his life *now* to find him.

"Well, I hope Paul feels like shit when he gets my letter," Eden said finally in a small, stubborn voice.

"What letter?"

She ran her hands over thighs, making a soft, brushing sound. "The letter I left in my mailbox for the postman to pick up."

Finch slowed and struggled to keep his voice controlled, quiet. "Tell me you didn't really do that, Eden."

"What difference does it make? By the time he gets it, we'll be gone. I just wanted him to know that—"

"What?" He sounded desperate, tried to tone it back. "What could you possibly want him to know?"

"That . . . that even if he doesn't want me, someone else does and that we're going to sail halfway around the world and good riddance to him and his miserable little life and that if he really did take his son, then he's more fucked up than I thought." She spoke rapidly, urgently, paused. "I think that about covers it."

"You're sure?"

"You sound a little jealous, Spense." She leaned into him and nibbled at his earlobe, whispering, "I think I kinda like that."

"I just don't want the cops pursuing you and trying to implicate you in Paul's mess."

"I didn't *do* anything. But I should've. I should've told him I wanted money or I would go to his wife and tell her about our affair." She shrugged. "But I couldn't bring myself to do it."

Finch doubted the cops would look in her mailbox. Even if they did, the letter wouldn't tell them anything. By the time the letter made its way to Paul Nichols, it wouldn't make any difference to him or Eden. They would be long gone.

Calmer now, he enjoyed the few moments of silence, Eden's head on his shoulder, the future already unfolding the way he envisioned it. Then he realized the gas light was on, that the car was running on empty. He pulled into a gas station three miles later, the only one between here and Sugarloaf that had gas. Five bucks would do it. He wouldn't be using the car again after tonight.

The pump's credit card slot was broken, so he had to go inside to pay. The tall, scrawny kid at the register had his feet on the counter, a Coke in front of him, and was staring at a small TV. "Five on pump two," Finch said, and handed the guy a ten.

While the kid was looking for change, Eden came in and headed for the restroom. "Hon," she called, "can you get me a pack of gum?"

Finch nodded, didn't see any gum at the front. "Where's the gum?"

"Halfway down aisle two," the kid said.

As he hunted for gum in aisle two, Eden came out of the restroom, went over to the refrigerator, looking for something cold to drink. Finch still didn't see any damn gum, but he selected a couple of bags of trail mix. Then, from the TV, Finch heard: "This afternoon, director Paul Nichols, married to Oscar-winning actress Suki Nichols, was brought in for questioning concerning the kidnapping of the couple's son, Adam. He and two other people are now considered to be persons of interest in the kidnapping. If you have any information about either of these individuals, please call . . ."

Finch didn't hear the rest. He had raised his head and saw sketches of himself and Eden on the TV screen. They were good enough so that Eden had recognized herself and was backpedaling from the counter, looking around frantically, and the kid was stealing glances at her, at Finch, then looking back at the screen.

Finch had left his weapon in the glove compartment.

He moved quickly up the aisle. As the kid reached for the phone, Finch broke into a run and Eden spun around, her eyes widening, and he suddenly knew that she had pieced it all together.

He scrambled over the counter, his arm became a club, and the club slammed into the side of the kid's head. He let out a squeal and toppled sideways, his arms flung outward, hands grappling for something to grab. He fell into the register, his head struck the edge of the open drawer, and he was dead before he hit the floor.

Finch whirled around just in time to see the door closing shut behind Eden.

He went after her, his shoes slapping the hard, tile floor, the TV voice droning on behind him, and burst through the door, into the rain that sliced across the dimly lit pumps and the lot around them. No Eden.

Finch ran over to the VW, certain she would be behind the wheel, fumbling with the key in the ignition. But she wasn't. He got in, started the car, hit the brights, made a slow circle through the lot—and saw her pop up from behind the large black garbage can between the pumps. She grabbed the hose from the pump where he'd been parked and gas spewed out. He realized the guy inside must have activated the pump when Finch had handed him the ten bucks.

She shouted at him to stay away from her and danced around, the hose in front of her, gas gushing everywhere, the stink of the fumes rising into the wet air. "You used me, you fucker, you used me for information about Paul and his family, that was it from the get-go. Right?" she shrieked. "Isn't that right?"

Finch opened his car door, stepped out, held up his hands like a man with a gun against his spine. "You've got it all wrong, Eden. Let go of the hose, c'mon, you're freaked out, that's all. I didn't do anything to you. To anyone."

She hesitated; gas no longer spewed from the hose. "You have him, Spenser, I know you do. You have the kid. I . . . I did some research. I found clips from that old TV series and it was you." She aimed the hose at the garbage can. Gasoline spewed forth. "And in my letter to Paul, I told him to take a look at all that stuff and to call me. I left him my backup cell phone. I . . . I was going with you to find Adam. *I was using you, shithead!*"

And then she dropped the hose and stuck her hand in the pocket of her Capri pants and wagged a pack of matches in the air.

Finch stopped and backed toward his car, certain she intended to immolate herself. "Don't do it, Eden." His voice rang out, but she didn't seem to hear it.

She lit a match, held it to the matchbox, and tossed it toward the garbage can.

Finch ran toward his car, threw himself inside, and was still racing in reverse when the garbage can ignited. Flames sped along the trail of gasoline, bright and hot, and then the pumps blew, a fireball hurtling upward, lighting up the wet darkness.

He spun into a U-turn and raced toward the road—then saw her flying into the trees on the other side like some enchanted being. Finch jammed the accelerator to the floor, the tires spun, shrieking against the wet pavement, and tore after her. The wagon slammed down over the shoulder of the road, into pebbles, coquina rock, dirt, dead trees. Rain drummed against the car; the wipers whipped back and forth, creating half-moons of thin mud against the glass.

The car bounced through the trees. Eden dodged left, he swerved after her. She cut to the right, he spun the wheel in the same direction. Behind him, a series of explosions sundered the air.

She vanished between trees growing so narrowly together he was forced to go around them, but he went faster, faster, and shot toward her. Eden leaped upward and the car crashed into the tree where she scrambled like a terrified monkey. The impact knocked her down and she landed on the hood of the VW, her cheek mashed against the glass, eyes wide with horror, blood pouring from her nose. The wipers slapped her face, blood mixed with the mud on the windshield.

Distantly, like sounds in a nightmare, he heard more explosions.

Eden suddenly reared up on her knees and, like some mythological Amazon, grabbed the wipers with her hands and bent them back. Enraged, Finch threw the car into reverse again and crashed into something behind him. Eden tumbled to the ground.

The engine died.

In the glare of the headlights, he saw her limping away, pathetic in her terror, hardly worthy of someone like him. But she deserved to die. He started the car, tore forward, and crashed into her from behind.

Her body catapulted up, up, and vanished somewhere above him, in the rainy darkness, in the embrace of the broken trees. He turned abruptly and raced back toward the road. He supposed her body had struck the ground already, bones broken, spine fucked, the life leaking from her. *God has spoken. Your time is up.*

He swerved onto the slick asphalt. Flames from the gas station licked at the plumes of black smoke that billowed through the rain. Sirens wailed through the darkness. They were close.

Too close.

He raced up U.S. 1, the stupid, twisted wipers whipping through the air, the windshield so thick with mud and rain he couldn't see anything. He lowered his window, slowed the car to a crawl, and leaned out, swiping at the glass with an old towel. He grabbed the wiper and twisted it back toward him until it brushed the glass.

Not great, but it would do.

He didn't know how he made it the last seven or eight miles. The wiper on his side squealed and complained and hit the glass every second or third pass. The car rattled and coughed, the side mirror fell off, he was pretty sure he lost part of the back fender.

When he finally stopped in front of his gate, he was so tired, so completely spent, his body folded over the steering wheel and he pressed his cheek against the warm plastic and shut his eyes.

It could've been so different.

At some point between Eden's place and the gas station, he had seen just how wonderful it might have been for them, the two of them taking off into a sunrise, headed toward New

Zealand, his need for vengeance sated. Paul would be in jail, Suki would be distraught, their marriage would be destroyed. All of that would happen regardless, except that he didn't get Eden. He didn't get the girl because she had turned on him.

Finally, he hauled himself out of his car and pushed the heavy wooden gate open and drove inside. Get the Flybridge, bring it to this dock, load it up, do whatever he needed to do with Adam and Mira. Then he would split. That was the plan.

It sucked as a plan, but it was the only one he had.

He had reached the end of the line, mile zero.

PART THREE

End Game

*Of course the game is rigged. Don't let that stop you.
If you don't play, you don't win.*
                              —Robert Heinlein

23

Lay Lady Lay

The inside of Eden Thompkins's apartment looked as if she had left in a hurry—and that she planned to be away for a while. The closet was nearly empty, dresser drawers hung open and had been cleaned out, hangers littered the closet floor. Sheppard didn't find any makeup, shampoo, conditioner, or hair dryer, or any of the other items that women usually included on their toiletry list.

Several pairs of shoes were on the mat just inside the kitchen door. A torn umbrella, still damp, stood in a corner. Her generator had been turned off when they'd entered the house, but the AC unit in the bedroom still felt warm and the coffeepot still held hot coffee. She hadn't been gone that long.

According to what Goot had found out from the manager of Pepe's, Eden didn't have a car. It seemed unlikely that she had set out on foot with a suitcase, and the taxis in Key West were about as rare these days as rain in the Sahara. So how had she gotten out of here? A friend?

A friend like Spenser?

Sheppard suddenly thought of the car they had nearly hit on their way in here, tried to remember the make, model, color, something, but drew a blank. He was pretty sure, though, that two people had been inside.

He hurried into the living room, where Goot and Blake were going through some of Eden's belongings. "That car we nearly hit," Sheppard said. "Do either of you remember what it looked like?"

"I think it was a VW," Blake said. "But I wouldn't swear to it."

"Our guy was in it, with Eden," Sheppard said. "I'm almost sure of it."

"I'll put out an APB," Goot said. "But what color? Model?"

"Not a Bug," Blake said.

"And not a van," Goot added.

"Then put out an APB for any VW except for those two models," Sheppard said. "My guess is they're headed out of Key West."

"So she was screwing Paul and Spenser and he used her to get info on the family," Goot muttered. "Do I have that about right?"

"That's how it looks," Sheppard replied.

"It makes a weird kind of sense," Blake remarked. "It would explain how Spenser knew Paul wouldn't be home that night and that Suki was out of town."

"I'm going to knock on a couple of apartment doors, find out if she told anyone she was leaving and where she was going."

Outside, the rain continued to fall, a shimmering curtain in the glare of his flashlight. He stood for a moment on the porch, wondering if Spenser intended to take off with Eden and leave Mira and Adam where they were or if he would kill them before he left. If the man's past was any indication, Sheppard suspected the latter. He seemed to be the sort of man who tied up his loose ends. How would it end? Bullets? Or fire?

How long do they have? Minutes? Hours?

Anxiety ripped through him as he hurried along the side of the building, where the ground was like sponge, and climbed the creaking stairs to the front door of the building. Inside, the hot, humid hallway stank of mold and old cellars. Mailboxes, two rows of three each, were lined up on the wall, each with a doorbell next to each box and an intercom above the rows. The bells wouldn't work without power, so he would have to go door to door. But before he did that, he thought, he wanted to take a look inside Eden's mailbox.

It was neatly labeled E. THOMPKINS, and required a key— or a warrant—to open it. Fuck both, the clock was ticking. He brought out a small leather case from his pack, unzipped it, and removed the handiest tool he owned. It looked like a dentist's pick. He slid it into the lock, worked it hard and fast, heard the telling click, and the little metal door swung open.

The package inside was about half as tall as a bottle of water, slightly thicker. A trick? Some perverted little calling card from Spenser? He hesitated, then picked it up. It was addressed to Paul Nichols.

Sheppard sat down on the bottom step of the stairs, set his flashlight beside him, and tore open the package. A cell phone, a handwritten letter.

Dear Paul,

By the time you get this, I'll be on my way to New Zealand, on Spense's boat. I've been seeing him nearly as long as I've been seeing you. I figured that since you're married, why shouldn't I have someone else too? Since there's nothing for me here, it's time to get out.

Spense believes that you arranged the kidnapping of your son for publicity purposes. As he puts it, you're a faded memory no one will hire and what better way to revive your career than a publicity pity ploy?

I have some trouble with this theory, but you definitely are a liar and a cheat, so maybe it's not a stretch that you would do something as awful as kidnap your own kid for the publicity. Then again, I'm kind of uneasy about my honey Spenser Finch. Maybe I just have lousy taste in men.

See, I was going through my old videotapes, trying to decide which ones to take with me, and ran across a copy of a short-lived show called Long Hours. The male lead was a guy named Scott Connor, who looks an awful lot like Spenser, but younger. I asked him about it once, early on in our relationship, but he claims he was never in Hollywood.

Anyway, if that name means anything to you, please use this cell to call my regular cell. It's the backup I got right before the hurricane hit.

Well, I'm off to Sugarloaf and then to New Zealand. I kind of hope I don't hear from you. That would mean that Spenser was right about you and he couldn't possibly be the cutie on Long Hours.

Spenser at least enjoys being with me.

Eden

Sugarloaf. Spenser Finch's boat was on Sugarloaf. But which Sugarloaf? It consisted of two islands, known as Upper and Lower Sugarloaf, had a population of over six thousand souls, more than four thousand homes. Water everywhere. Boats everywhere. At least two marinas and countless coves and nooks where boats anchored. And it was dark. And raining. Could it get any worse?

He stepped out onto the porch, where a wet breeze cooled him, and scrolled through the numbers on the cell's phone book. He found an entry for *main cell* and one for SF—had to be Spenser Finch, he thought—and called Eden's cell first. He got a recording and hung up.

If Finch's cell was on, they could track him. It might take longer than usual because so many cell towers were still down due to the hurricane. He called the office and Lydia Santos answered.

"It's Shep, Lydia. His name's Spenser Finch. I need you to run a cell number. Got a pencil?"

"Shoot."

Sheppard ticked it off, noting that it was a 305 area code—Miami. "I need to know the mailing address for the bills. Tell Agent Ellis we need to triangulate that number, if possible. Also, I want the last ten numbers he called."

"I'll call you back as soon as I've got something."

He disconnected and stood there a moment, his mind racing through his options. The air smelled thick, viscous, the way it had in those long, nightmare hours as Danielle had moved on. He felt that if he raised his hand, hooked his fingers into claws, and raked them down through the darkness, he would rip open the fabric of space and time.

His cell rang and Goot's number came up. "Shep, I just got a call from Cordoba. There's been an explosion as a gas station just outside of town. Thanks to the rain, the station didn't burn and there're troopers there now. They say they have Spenser and Eden on the security videotape."

Bingo. "I'll meet you at the car."

Finch turned the Zodiac raft down a canal just east of his house. The engine chugged noisily, and the raft bobbed like a sick fish in the rain-pocked water. His destination was the fourth house on the right.

For months now, he'd kept the Penn Yann Flybridge tied up at the dock of an elderly woman who came down here only in the winter. He paid her handsomely for the privilege, and always included a personal note with his money order, playing up his role as a friendly neighbor who reminded the lady, of course, of her son.

But she and her bridge buddies weren't around now, and even if any elderly folks remained in the houses along here, they probably were too deaf to hear the engine. He drew the raft up alongside the seawall, right behind the Flybridge, turned off the engine, and tipped it back inside the raft. He tied the raft to the back of the Flybridge and scrambled onto the seawall, alert for movement, lights, people. But nothing human moved out here. The rain fell softly, a soothing, gentle sound. Now and then, a gust of wind blew through, rustling trees along the canal, and stirring the water so that it slapped against the sides of the Flybridge.

The boat wasn't large—just thirty feet long, with twin Mercruiser engines. It had an anchor pulpit, swim platform, a small kitchen with a microwave, fridge, stove, and a mahogany futon couch. The head was hardly the lap of luxury, and barely large enough to accommodate one person. But the toilet and shower worked, there was hot and cold running water. It would do.

Within minutes, the Flybridge was headed through the rain, back into the lagoon, towing the raft behind it. The wet air cleared Finch's head. He had clothes and other personal items already on the Flybridge. In the storage closet on the porch of the house, he kept a supply case packed and ready. The food in the house refrigerator would go into a cooler; he would take his PC, his laptop, a few personal items. Everything else would burn. In the years since he'd fled Seattle, he'd learned that if necessary, he could live with few possessions.

He tied up at his dock, plugged in the boat so he could have lights and power without turning on the engine, and lowered the plank that would make access to the deck easier. He loped up to the house, still wrestling with the end game.

Kill Adam? Take him? What? Would the ultimate revenge in terms of Suki and Paul Nichols be their son's death or that he was missing indefinitely?

Closure, he thought. There was a lot of be said for closure. It freed you.

He didn't intend to free the Nicholses. Okay, so Adam would stay alive for a while, but he would crank up the anxiety level.

And what about Mira? She was excess baggage, but might prove useful with Adam. A mother figure and all that. Down the road a piece, he might be able to use her as leverage too.

Then again, she irritated him—the way she looked at him, the things she said, the way her eyes rolled back in their sockets when she picked up something especially *awful* about his past. Holier-than-thou Mira. Who needed it? However, if she could see his future—and if he could trust what she said. . . . Too many *ifs*?

He unlocked the storage closet, slid the storage box out, removed the wheelbarrow, and set the box inside it. He put his bike and tire pump inside too, and pushed the wheelbarrow out to the boat. He felt a sudden, inexplicable loss as he pushed the wheelbarrow across the plank and onto the deck. Eden was supposed to be here. *It could've been so different.*

Finch unloaded everything and sank onto the cooler, his exhaustion as abrupt and extreme as this mystifying feeling about Eden. If they hadn't stopped for gas, would she be here now? Would she be laughing, eager, loving? He wondered if what she'd said to him at the end was true, the horrid, hurtful things about how she was using him.

And did she really leave a letter for Paul or was she just testing his feelings for her? What was real?

She's dead. That's real. Get over it.

But he was having a few problems getting over it. With his old man, with Priscilla Branchley, he'd felt like God when he had ended their lives. But he hadn't felt that way when he'd struck Eden with the car. He'd felt empty. It was as if, at that moment, he had lost his taste for the God game.

He pressed his fists into his eyes, then forced himself to stand, to move, to finish the task.

Several days from now, Sheppard and his boys would find the house. Or its remains. If he didn't torch the place, what would they actually find? The power and water would be off, the fridge cleaned out, the beds made, the dishes in the cabinets, two cars in the driveway, a bedroom still boarded up, and everyone gone. Forensics would sweep in, dusting for prints, taking hair and dust and fabric samples. The forensic shrinks would go through his books, photo albums, DVDs, CDs, and eventually would cook up a theory about who he was, what made him tick, and where he might be headed and why. They would be wrong about all of it.

Only two things were certain right now: He would not be heading to New Zealand and, once again, he would be alone.

The stink of smoke and ruin blanketed the station and the surrounding area. The stench had seeped into the back room where Sheppard and Goot watched the video feed from the security cameras inside the station. What struck Sheppard most about the images was the moment when Eden Thompkins apparently recognized the sketches on CNN and turned with a wild, terrified expression and looked around for Finch.

And then, in yet another image, caught by a second camera, there was Finch's expression. Astonishment, shock. Sheppard suspected it was the turning point: Finch had realized that Eden knew the truth. Instead of tending to her, though, Finch raced toward the kid behind the counter, who was reaching for the phone. By the time he remembered Eden, the clerk was dead and Eden was out the door.

The feed switched to the outside cameras and carried the drama until the seconds before the garbage can ignited.

Sheppard asked the officer to go back through these final images a frame at a time. An instant before the garbage ignited, there was a flurry of movement to the left—Eden, he thought, racing away from the station.

Had she made it? Was she alive?

While Goot remained to get copies of the video feed, Sheppard went outside, into the stink and the diminishing rain, past the barrier of police cars, and stopped on the other side of the road. He called Eden's cell number; her recording came on after just two rings.

Flashlight on, he headed into the trees. The rain released the sweet scents of pine and earth and pretty soon, those smells overpowered the ones from the explosion. The fallen pine needles and wet earth cushioned his footsteps and a beautiful silence settled through the trees. Sheppard pulled out Eden's backup cell phone and called her regular cell number. If she was in here and the phone was on—and not on vibrate, with the ringer loud enough for someone to hear—then he would hear it here.

One ring. Two. He held the phone slightly away from his ear and strained to hear something. Anything.

On the fourth ring, he heard it, a refrain from an old Bob Dylan song, "Lay Lady Lay." If anything typified what he knew of Eden's life, this song was it, he thought, and moved toward it. He stopped when her message came on. He disconnected, shone the flashlight to the left, right, and noticed that the ground here was torn up, as if a car had raced through. He called the number again, waited for the song, heard it, and moved sharply to the right.

He found her up against the trunk of a tree, her body twisted grotesquely—one arm bent behind her, her right leg at an impossible angle against the ground, her head at a forty-five-degree angle. Her eyes were wide open, her clothes were soaked, and the end of a branch protruded from her throat.

Sheppard knelt beside her and gently shut her eyes. He

glanced around slowly, looking slightly to the left or right of whatever he saw. Mira had taught him to do this whenever he was in the presence of someone who had just passed over. *The spirit stays close to what is familiar and what's more familiar than your body?* He didn't see anything, but just the same he leaned close to her and whispered, "Help me. Help me find this fucker before anyone else dies. Please."

Could she hear him?

Did spirits hear anything?

This is nuts.

He went through the pockets of her Capri pants, found her cell phone, a copy of the letter she'd left for Paul Nichols, and some cash in her back pocket. Had she been carrying a purse? A pack? He stood, shrugged off his raincoat, and spread it over her. Then he called Goot, told him what he'd found.

Sheppard moved around through the trees, his flashlight probing into this shadow, that crevice. He found the pack hundreds of feet from her body, unzipped it. A few items of clothing. More cash. A videotape, neatly labeled *Long Hours.* An address book. A pocket calendar. Sheppard went through the address book, but there was no entry for Spenser Finch. Hell, she probably didn't know that he lived on Sugarloaf. The pocket calendar wasn't helpful either.

He returned to where she lay and while he waited for Goot, Lydia called. "No signal, Shep. His cell's off. The only calls he's made—or received—in the last two months have been from Eden Thompkin's cell. The bill is sent to a PO box at the Sugarloaf Key post office. I tried contacting the postmaster there, to see if there was a home address, but the guy's on vacation and his stand-in doesn't know squat. What do you want me to do?"

Find me a miracle. "I don't know. Just stand by. Be there, Lydia. Just be there."

"I'm here, hon, for as long as it takes."

Sheppard stood in the rain-soaked silence, staring down

at Eden's shrouded body. Should he tigthten the pressure on
Finch by sending him a text message? Or would additional
pressure increase the risk to Adam and Mira? He thought a
moment, brought out Eden's cell phone, and typed:

takes more than that to kill me, spense

He pressed send and prayed he'd make the right decision.
Goot appeared in the trees with a couple of paramedics
who had a stretcher, and gestured for Sheppard to hurry up,
Blake was waiting. They were headed to Sugarloaf.

24

Final Destination

Noises pierced her awareness and Mira bolted forward, disgusted that she'd nodded off. Listening, she thought the sounds were coming from downstairs. When Adam had gotten as far as the kitchen much earlier, he'd told her the house was on pilings, so *downstairs* could be a carport, a porch, a storage area.

She withdrew her arm from Adam's shoulder, lowered his head to the pillow, slipped off the bed. In the middle of the room, she got down on her hands and knees, pressed her ear to the floor. She strained to hear the sounds.

Movement. It was nothing violent, nothing like pounding or hammering, but something more subtle and ominous. He was moving objects from one place to another. From a closet or storage to—where?

The dock.

A boat at the dock.

But what, exactly, did it mean? Would he burst in here, puffed up with his own importance, threatening them, making demands? Would he set the house on fire? That seemed to be one of his favorite ways to close unpleasant chapters in his life. Or would he just leave them here?

Mira rocked back on her heels, alternated her breathing, placed her palms flat against the floor. *Let me see.* The images flashed through her in vivid color, a glaring difference from when she had blundered onto Suki's property and seen everything in negative images, black and white. Spenser, loading things onto a boat. Sheppard, closing a dead woman's eyes. Cordoba, ranting. Goot, racing through wet trees. Smoke, fire, destruction. *But where? Where is this happening?* Or had it already happened? She didn't know what any of it meant, where it belonged in time. She could see things, but couldn't put any of it into a context that would help her or Adam.

Frustration washed through her and right behind it came its dark cousin, despair. Suki had paid her an enormous sum to find her son—and she'd done it, she had—but to what end? Had she saved Adam? No. Had she figured out what the hell was going on? Yes, bits of it here and there that included some weird psychic download from Joy Longwood that she couldn't recall. A lot of good she was doing here.

Louder sounds down there, beneath her.

"We are so fucked," she whispered.

No, you're not.

A woman's voice, clear, crisp, close. Mira looked around and saw a vague shape, as insubstantial as a shadow, pass through the wall. Then the shape solidified. A redhead, the woman in the photo Adam had shown her. Eden.

You need to know the layout of the house and there isn't much time.

Mira took it in, all of it, all of her—the wild red hair, the freckles, the clothes, and suddenly understood the image she'd seen of Sheppard closing a dead woman's eyes. *Finch just returned from killing her.*

Eden seemed to be aware of her thoughts. She nodded and said, *Your friend asked for my help.*

Sheppard, *her* Sheppard, asked a dead woman for help?

He understands more than you give him credit for. Now listen closely. Once you go through this door, turn right. There's another bedroom at the end of the hall. It has a latch on the door, that'll buy you some time, and a door that opens to a wraparound porch. It's not controlled electronically. The stairs are on the other side of the porch, to your right. If you can get to the stairs before he does, run for the wooden gate or for the dock, where the boats are. You'll see them as you go down the stairs to the front yard.

Might, maybe, what if. It seemed that Eden didn't know any more about the immediate future than Mira did. That worried her. It meant that nothing beyond this point was certain for her and Adam.

There's a cell phone on the desk, his backup. Grab it. And then run like hell. I'll do what I can do help you, but there's only so much I can do . . . from here. Hurry now. Wake Adam and go through with your plan.

Eden didn't fade away—she simply winked out like a candle. Mira hurried over to the bed and woke Adam. "It's time. Get in the cooler." Then she repeated everything that Eden had told her.

Adam frowned. "How do you know all that, Mira?"

"A friend told me," she said.

Suki tiptoed from the guest bedroom, past Kartauk snoozing on the living room couch, and went into the kitchen. She had slept for a couple of hours, and now she needed coffee and a bite to eat before she headed over to the makeshift command center. She couldn't just stay here, waiting for news about Adam. At the center, she could at least field calls and feel that she was doing something useful.

She turned on a small desk lamp, started a pot of coffee, and helped herself to a container of fruit yogurt. Dolittle appeared and wound between her legs, meowing softly for attention, food, or both. Suki picked him up and pressed her face into his soft fur. He purred and drew his rough, warm tongue across her cheek. Ever since they'd gotten here, the cat had stuck close to her, as though he were afraid she might desert him, as Adam had done.

As Suki fed him from the supply of cat food she'd brought with her, she remembered that her car was at her house, where she'd left it when Kartauk had picked her up. Either he would have to drive her into town or she would have to borrow his car. She hated to wake him, to ask him for yet another favor. Besides, she knew he would try to discourage her from going into town. He would tell her to wait for Sheppard's call. But Sheppard hadn't called.

Suki filled a mug with coffee, then scribbled Kartauk a note. *Didn't have the heart to wake you. Went to Shep's office. Call me if you want me to pick you up!*

She went in search of his keys and ended up in his office, a large, comfortable room crowded with books, old newspapers, maps on every wall. Stacks of books stood on his floor, papers and folders were strewn across his desk, and off to one side of the desk was what looked like a manuscript, the pages neatly stacked. She remembered that Kartauk had had a number of books published on criminology.

Suki glanced at the title page: *The Face of Evil.* She turned to the introduction and started to read. Ripples of shock shuddered through her. She became so absorbed in it that she didn't become aware of Kartauk until he cleared his throat, startling her.

Her head snapped up. Kartauk stood in the doorway, leaning heavily on his crutch, his eyes puffy from sleep. "I wrote the introduction after talking to Shep and Goot for the first time."

"My God, Glen," she breathed. "He's your *son*? Spenser is your *son*?"

"Yes." He whispered it. "November 1968. Vietnam. Hippies. Drugs. Janis Joplin. Hendrix. Protests. I was twenty-four years old, involved with a woman I didn't love but who I figured I should marry. I went to Cape Cod to clear my head—and met Joy the first day I was there." He raised his eyes. "I was in a bar. Saw her across the room, standing at the jukebox. And as corny as it sounds, the instant our eyes met, I knew she was it. I didn't know at the time that she was on the run from Ray Connor."

Emotions skittered across the curves of his face—pain, elation, regret.

"It was the single most intense ten days of my entire life. It was as if we both knew that what we'd found was doomed and we made every second count. I had gone up there for a long weekend, but kept extending my stay. So did she. Her mother got sick, my girlfriend kept calling, but we kept pushing the rest of the world away. By the time we both knew we had to leave, we had started talking about the future."

He fell silent and shifted so that he now leaned against the door frame. He looked so bereft, so lost, that she wanted to put her arms around him and pat him on the back and assure him that it would be okay. But it wasn't okay. Events that had happened more than thirty-five years ago were as fresh and vibrant in Kartauk's mind as today. As right now. Even though Joy Longwood was long dead, Kartauk's struggle and guilt continued.

"So what happened?" Suki finally asked.

"She went back to Ray, discovered she was pregnant, I got married, he threatened and then killed her mother, and eventually she fled, just like I told Shep. I didn't know about the twins until she showed up here on Tango. By then, I had two kids with my wife and I couldn't just . . . just leave her. So I divided my life between my wife and Joy. I kept telling myself that as soon as my kids were old enough—whenever that was going to be—I would divorce my wife and Joy and I would live happily ever after." Another pause. "What horseshit. You can't postpone happiness, Suki."

It was as if he'd spoken these words specifically for her, for her situation with Paul. "But you had five years together here on Tango," she said.

"A difficult five years in which I lived two distinct lives."

Like Paul and his affairs. Except that none of his ladies had been the love of his life, she thought. He was too caught up in himself to love anyone the way Kartauk had loved Joy Longwood.

"What I learned is that we're amazingly adaptable creatures, we humans. We can rationalize almost anything. Then something happens that throws all those neat rationalizations in our faces and suddenly, we're fucked." His eyes locked on hers. "That's how I felt the day she died."

"And Spenser? How did you feel about him?"

She saw immediately that it was a difficult question for him. He hobbled into the den, picked up a Magic Marker, crossed out the title, and beneath it scribbled: *Spenser: The Face of Evil.* He dropped the marker, stared at what he'd written.

"I'm supposed to be an expert on the criminal mind. But in all these years of studying people like Dahmer, Speck, Hitler, Bundy, Manson, and Susie Smith and Aileen Wournos, I've found only one consistent truth. DNA, upbringing, your parents, abuse . . . all those things are symptoms, not causes. Some people are just born evil." He paused and met her gaze. "I think Mira probably would say that evil is one of the roles the soul agrees to play before it comes in. But I can't buy that. It would mean that in terms of humanity, Hitler, for instance, would represent a collective spiritual lesson. And people like Bundy would represent the same thing, but on a much smaller scale."

Suki looked at the manuscript pages that she held and set them back on top of the pile. She didn't know what she believed about evil. "I don't know shit about Hitler or Dahmer or Bundy. I just want my son back, Glen. And right now, I need to go to Shep's office. May I borrow your car?"

"You need a curfew pass."

"There's one on your car."

"I'll take you there."

She looked at his crutch, his cast, and reminded him that she had driven from her house to his.

"And I got from Shep's to your place on my own," he said, and slipped his hand into the pocket of his shorts and brought out his car keys. "Let's get moving."

Suki convinced Kartauk to let her drive his Mini Cooper. But it quickly became apparent that Kartauk's cast wasn't the issue; the weather was. The rain kept falling and every time they went through a puddle, she worried that the Mini would stall.

She called the command center, hoping to find out what, if anything, Sheppard had discovered at Eden's home. "FBI Tip Line. How may I help you?"

"Ace? It's Suki. What're you doing there?"

"Lydia called Luke and me about Mira. We had some car trouble, so it took us a while to get back here. We're relieving Lydia and the others."

"What've you heard from Shep?"

"When did you last talk to him?"

"Right before he, Goot, and Ross left to track down Eden's address."

"Oh, uh, well, I don't know how much I'm supposed to pass on. But what the hell," he added, and the details spilled out.

Suki switched to speakerphone so that Kartauk could hear the conversation too. Sugarloaf. He had her son somewhere on Sugarloaf. And it was—what? Just thirty miles from here? It might as well have been three thousand miles. She had no way of getting there. The ferries had stopped running at midnight, no planes could take off or land. A brief, almost crippling despair welled up inside her.

"How the hell are they going to find one house on Sugarloaf, Ace?" Kartauk asked, leaning close to the phone.

"Beats me, sir. They, uh, haven't advised me of their strategy. But I think they're trying to locate him through his cell phone."

A beep sounded, indicating she had a call coming through. Maybe it was Sheppard. "Ace, I've got another call coming through. Glen and I will see you shortly."

She took it without looking at the number. "Hello?"

Static, breathing, then: "Remember Priscilla Branchley?"

That voice, that name. She swerved to the side of the road, braked. A violent shudder whipped through her and then it all made sense. "Scott Connor." She could barely say the words.

He went on in a soft, insidious voice. "Very good. You at least remember my name."

"You played the rotten son in that TV show that lasted nine or ten episodes. *Long Hours*. You auditioned for the male lead in *Bluff*."

He gave a small, chilling laugh. "What a memory. Too bad I had to call you before you remembered. You know, that night I got Priscilla alone, she had her casting notes and showed me your comments on my audition." He clicked his tongue against his teeth. "Let me see if I can get it exactly right. '*Suki says he has homicidal eyes, Paul thinks he's unhinged.*' Is that about right, Suki?"

She didn't answer. She didn't know what to say. But if she kept him talking, maybe his location could be triangulated. Her thoughts raced. Kartauk tapped his watch and mouthed, *Keep him talking*. Then he entered a text message into his cell—to Sheppard, she hoped. "You were brilliant in your audition. You brought exactly the right edge to the male lead. But Priscilla thought you were too young for the part." True. "The guy who got the lead was five or six years older than you."

"I could've made myself look older. That's not any reason to reject me. And just think how different everything would be if I'd gotten that role. Priscilla would be alive, I'd still be working in Hollywood, you wouldn't know about Paul's silly affairs, and you would still have your son. The penalty for our past decisions is often very harsh, don't you think?"

Tears leaked from her eyes. Kartauk was busy text-messaging, but gestured for her to keep up the dialogue. "What about the penalty to you for killing Priscilla and taking Adam?"

"Loneliness," he said, his voice quiet. "Despair. No roots. I've been so many people since those days in Hollywood that I'm not even sure who I am anymore."

"You don't even know who your father was," she rushed on. "Ray Connor wasn't."

Kartauk glanced up, mouthed, *Yes, keep him talking.*

"You don't know shit about my father."

"I know that your mother got pregnant on Cape Cod, where she went to get away from Ray, who was an abusive drunk. She met a man, fell in love, they went back to their respective lives to try to tie up loose ends, but that didn't work. She tried to get away from Ray several times, but he beat her up, threatened to kill her mother, succeeded, and she gave birth to twins. She fled one night, but Ray found her. He eventually took your twin, Lyle, and she fled to Tango Key with you. And she moved into the Mango Hill house. You lived there until you were six. By then, Lyle was dead. He got hit by a car. So Ray came looking for you. He still believed you and Lyle were his. And he took you away. Do you remember that? Your real father was a cop and he looked for you for three years. He's still looking for you. Would you like to speak to him? He's here in the car with me."

Silence, then an explosion of rage. "That's horseshit. You think I don't know what you're doing, trying to keep me on the line with some goddamn story like that? You could say anything, but you don't have proof. Kiss your fucking son good-bye, Suki, he's . . ."

"You have a scar over your left eye, Spenser," Kartauk said quickly. "You know how you got it?"

"Who's this?" he demanded.

"Glen Kartauk. I was the guy on Cape Cod. That scar over your eye is from an accident you had when you were four. You tripped out by the pool and hit your head against a ring of stones around a little garden. Your mother and I took you to the ER and you had to have five stitches. You used to call me Uncle Glen."

"Sorry, none of that rings any bells. Ding-dong, the witch is dead and we've run out of time."

"Wait," Suki burst out, sobbing now. "Please. Let me have Adam back. I . . . won't contact the police, I swear. I . . . just want my son." She tried to stifle her sobs, but failed.

"Hurts, doesn't it," he said, his voice now slippery and insidious again. "All that wanting."

"Let's make an exchange," Kartauk interrupted. "Me for Adam and Mira."

"Two for one? And for what purpose? I don't know you."

"You'll recognize me as soon as you see me," Kartauk said. "Blood always knows blood. It's in the cells."

Spenser howled with laughter. "Yeah, right." He disconnected.

Finch stood at the kitchen counter, breathing hard, the cell clutched in his one hand, the fingers of his other hand tracing the faint scar above his left eyebrow. Was it true? Was any of that true?

Does it matter?

Yes, it did. He didn't know why it should, but it did.

His cell jingled. He hadn't realized it was still turned on. He glanced at the window, saw that he had a text message, but the number it had come from didn't show. He pressed *read:*

takes more than that to kill me, spense

"No way," he whispered, and switched off the phone. He had seen her body hurled into the air, had felt the impact in his own bones. But he hadn't stuck around to see her hit the ground or to check to make sure she was dead, so maybe it *was* possible.

Equally possible, though, was that the police had found her and Sheppard had used her cell phone to send him a text message.

Maybe this, maybe that. Maybe Uncle Glen was his true father, maybe he wasn't. Maybe Eden was dead, maybe not. Maybe he should make a trade—and maybe not. Maybe he should cut his losses, get his ass moving, and leave. Nothing ambivalent about that.

Finch stepped quietly into the room, a small pillow tucked under his armpit. Shoot them, then torch the house. He didn't turn on any lights, didn't have to. The bathroom door was shut, the shower running, and the glow of light from under the door was enough for him to make out the shape in the bed. To his left was the cooler.

He pressed the manual override on the clicker, so the door wouldn't lock automatically, and slipped the clicker into his back pocket. He gripped his weapon more tightly, held the pillow in his left hand, and approached the end of the bed. He held the pillow out in front of him, pressed the gun against it, and fired, muffling the noise so that whoever was in the bathroom wouldn't hear it. Then he started toward the bathroom, hoping it was Mira in the shower. He had never killed anyone who was naked.

He wasn't sure what tipped him off—a soft whisper of noise, a stray scent, an inexplicable stirring of air. He spun around, but it was too late. She came at him like a six-wheeler without brakes on the downward slope of a steep hill. She crashed into him so hard that it jarred him to the core and he stumbled back, firing wildly into the air as his arms pinwheeled for balance. He slammed to the floor, the air rushed from his lungs, and his ears rang with the echoes of the gunfire.

He heard her screaming for the kid to run, run, and he

struggled upward and aimed at the door and fired over and over again. He didn't know if he hit either of them, he couldn't see enough of the door from here. But then she wasn't screaming anymore and he scrambled up and lurched forward.

As the cruiser raced up U.S. 1, Sheppard played the laptop's keyboard and brought up a map of the two keys that comprised Sugarloaf. With Goot repeating the coordinates that Agent Ellis gave him from the triangulation of cell towers, Sheppard was able to narrow Finch's location to an area of about one square mile, somewhere on Lower Sugarloaf Key.

"It's too large an area for just the three of us, in one car, to cover," he said. "And we don't have a boat."

"Check how many waterfront properties there are within the triangulation areas," Blake suggested. "Mira had said the place had water on two sides, right? A canal and some sort of bay or lagoon."

"Okay, there's Lower Sugarloaf Sound and a bay between two peninsulas. We're looking at two main roads off of here— South Point Drive is the first one, then Sugarloaf Boulevard. There are eight or nine streets off of South Point and other dozen or so streets off of Sugarloaf Boulevard, all on the water. Even if we just select the homes at the end of streets that are on canals and the sound, we're looking at dozens of places. Dozens. We don't have that kind of time."

"We need the fucker to turn on his phone again."

"Okay, we're approaching Lower Sugarloaf Sound," Blake said. "Tell me what to do."

Sheppard looked up from the laptop screen. The bright headlights exposed the horizontal rain, gusting across the road as they passed a cluster of mangroves. He began to despair, to believe they had reached a dead end, that unless Finch turned on his cell or they got another piece of information, they were at the end of the line.

Then he saw something just ahead, at the right side of the road, but couldn't tell what it was from here. Visibility wasn't good enough. "What's that?" He pointed. "You see it? Off to the right there?"

"I don't see shit," Goot said.

"Me either," Blake said.

Sheppard leaned forward, wiping frantically at the glass. "Slow down," Ross."

"I still don't see anything, amigo." But as soon as the words were out of his mouth, he snapped forward. "Wait. I see her. A hitchhiker."

As Blake slowed and they neared the woman, goose bumps exploded across Sheppard's arms and the back of his neck. It wasn't just a woman. It was Eden Thompkins, her thumb stuck out, a hitchhiker, hoping for a ride.

"Holy shit," Blake breathed, and slammed on the brakes a yard away from her.

They all leaped out, but it was Sheppard who ran toward her, Sheppard who understood what it meant, that she had heard him.

The rain didn't seem to touch her, but it lashed his eyes, making it difficult to see her clearly. He kept wiping his arm across his face, and saw that she was stabbing a thumb toward the street that ran to her right. He glanced up at the sign. Sugarloaf Boulevard. When he looked back at her, she was starting to fade like some old photo worn yellow by time.

Sheppard whipped around and ran back to Blake and Goot, who just stood there, gaping in disbelief. "C'mon, fast, he's down Sugarloaf," Sheppard shouted, and they piled into the car.

25

Meltdown

The room, the porch door. It was just as Eden had described, and now Mira and Adam tore across the porch, the rain driving against them from the west, the boards slick beneath their bare feet. They skidded around the corner, clutching each other's hands, and raced toward the stairs. Not much farther. They were going to make it, Mira thought.

The first thing she saw was the boat tied up at the dock, its deck lit up like a carnival. It cast light into the yard, where she could see two cars, trees, bushes, and a wooden gate. But where was the raft Eden had mentioned? Panic gripped her, bile surged in her throat. Maybe it sat too low in the water to see from here.

They reached the stairs and broke apart, Adam in the lead, Mira slightly behind him, the rain pouring over them. She tripped over her own feet and grabbed onto the railing to keep from falling . . .

 . . . *and she and Adam speed across the canal in the Zodiac raft, a distance of perhaps ten yards. Trees bend over the ground on the other side, there's a house back there, people who can help. But Spenser fires at them and the first bul-*

let tears through her right knee and brings her down. She screams for Adam to run, run, but he hesitates, and hurries back to help her, to pull her farther up the shore, into the trees. The second shot hits him and he lurches back, hands flying to his chest, and is dead before he hits the ground. She . . .

. . . let go of the railing, a gasp exploding from her mouth, her feet moving faster, faster. Adam reached the bottom of the stairs first and glanced back at her. "Where? Gate or dock?"

Mira pointed frantically at the dock. Eden had been right about everything else, so why not about this too? Adam took off, his thin body leaning into the rain and wind, moving as quickly as time. Mira loped after him, her bare feet slapping wet, cold sand, coming down hard against gravel, sliding across the slippery, splintered wood. And she saw the raft, bobbing in the water like an engorged cork. *You were right, Eden, thank you, thank you.*

It was tied up behind the larger vessel, its engine tipped forward, and it was filling rapidly with water. "There's too much water in it," Adam said, his voice thick with anxiety. He kept wiping at his face, trying to clear the rain from his eyes. "We need to pull it out and tip it over."

"No time. Just get in. I'll get the rope."

Adam swung around and eased himself over the side of the dock and into the raft. Mira fumbled with the tight, wet knot that held the rope to the dock's railing. . . .

. . . *the car slams across stones, branches, stumps, aimed straight at her. In the moment when her head snaps around, her copper hair wild, flying through the air, her face looks as plump as a pumpkin, bloated with fear. . . .*

Mira jerked her hands away from the rope, horrified that to untie the knot, she would have to endure the visions of Eden's last moments on the planet. She rubbed her hands fast against her wet, slippery thighs, trying to rid herself of Spenser's energy, of the emotional residue the rope had retained.

"Mira, shit, hurry, I think I see him," Adam called. "Up here on the porch."

A breath later, bright security lights blazed from the aves just under the roof, exposing them like tumors on an X ray. And then Finch opened fire, and Mira threw herself to he dock, craving the cover of darkness. The first two shots lew wide, the third struck the dock just behind her, and the ourth was so close she heard it whistle through the air aches above her head.

She shot upward, clawing again at the knot, struggling to llow the violent images—of the car, Eden—pass through er. The knot loosened. She glanced back; Spenser raced own the porch steps, a madman. Then the knot gave way, ae tossed the rope into the raft, and practically threw herself ato it.

"Go, go," she screamed, and Adam opened the engine ide and the raft swerved away from the dock, around the oat. The water inside sloshed around, so much of it that hen Mira was sitting on the floor, it covered her legs. "Can move any faster?"

"It's open all the way," Adam shouted back. "Pretty soon ere's going to be so much water in here it'll just sink. hich direction? Where should I go?"

Anywhere except the other side of the canal. "Just get us vay from here fast."

As the raft shot toward the open lagoon, the lights from enser's home lit the way. She grabbed onto the handholds, d in her mind's eye saw Spenser firing on them from the rner of his property, and one shot puncturing the raft.

"Turn left," she hollered. "Do it now."

He turned the raft abruptly and sharply to the left. Low-nging branches raked across the top of Mira's head, the ft slammed through the water, rising up, up like a balloon, en slamming down hard. Over and over again. "Move ay from the shore," she called. "Find a canal. Maybe we n get onto a seawall and run like hell."

It wasn't much of a plan, but it was the only one she had.

As they sped away from the house, farther out into the lagoon, the darkness clamped down around them, a sweaty fist so tight and suffocating that Mira could hardly draw a breath. She knew that Adam couldn't see anything at all. Worse, she didn't have any idea whether the tide was high or low. They were traveling blind and going much too fast.

She shouted at Adam to cut back on the power, but the wind swallowed her voice. She started crawling back toward him, through the rapidly rising pool inside the raft, and the weight displacement pushed the rear of the raft down. The engine suddenly died, water poured over the sides, and Adam yelled, "Go back to the front, Mira, you're sinking us!!"

She scrambled backward on her hands and knees, her hands sinking so deeply into the center of the raft, into its soft, watery belly, that it felt as if they were being swallowed whole. Water rose to her armpits, over the backs of her thighs. The raft was going down and she didn't have any idea how deep the water was, how far they were from shore, or worse, where Spenser was.

And then, rising over constant noise of the rain and the sucking sounds the water made as the raft started sinking in earnest, she heard the noise of an engine, *his* boat, coming for them. Adam splashed toward her and she reached out and grabbed his hand. "Let's not get separated."

He was treading water and thrust something at her. "A life jacket. There was just one inside, but we can hold onto it so we don't get worn out. Maybe pretty soon our eyes will adjust to the dark and we'll be able to figure out how far we are from shore."

Mira grasped one side of the life jacket, Adam held onto the other. No images rushed into her. She doubted that Spenser had ever worn the life jacket. She let her legs rest for a few minutes, then treaded water again. Rest, tread, back and forth until she fell into the rhythm.

"Mira?"

"Yeah?"

"Do sharks come in here?"

Only the human variety, she thought, listening to the approaching clatter of a boat engine. "No."

"I just heard something splashing off to my right."

Shit. "Start kicking, Adam. We're going left. I think that's where the shore is."

Sheppard was hanging out the window, hoping for another sign of Eden, when he heard what sounded like gunfire, echoing eerily through the dark, rainy silence. "It came from just ahead," he shouted.

The tires screeched as Blake took a corner down one of the side streets. Too quiet, too dark, Sheppard thought, and told Blake to back up and take the next street. And the next. And the next. On Wahoo Lane, he heard a boat's engine, something larger than that of a raft or a canoe, but couldn't tell exactly where it was coming from.

"Pull up here, Ross."

Sheppard and Goot ran between two houses, both of them all shuttered for the hurricane season, and stopped at the edge of the canal. The blazing lights of a place on the other side seemed to light up the rain from the inside out, as though it were some huge, weird Halloween lantern. And then something popped out of this weird lantern—a boat, a large boat—and raced off to the left.

Sheppard and Goot whipped around at the same time and back toward the car. Blake raced up the road and hung a right onto Flying Fish Lane. At the end of the street, the lights they'd seen from across the canal now burned like a miniature sun. Blake screeched to a stop at a tall gate; Sheppard thought it looked like something out of ancient Italy, the rain pouring over it, the wood glistening in the brilliance of the headlights.

"Get the gate open, Goot, I'm going to bang on doors. We need a boat."

"Got it, amigo."

Sheppard ran to the house next door, but it was obvious no one was home and hadn't been home for weeks. Maybe months. It was the same thing at the next house. Then, two houses farther up, on the other side of the road, a shirtless guy with a beer in his giant paw and a tan belly hanging over his belt opened the door.

"FBI." Sheppard flashed his badge, quickly explained what was going on, and the guy grinned.

"Yeah, man, I got a boat at the dock. Small, but fast. Out back. Which way did he go?"

"Left."

"Well, the only way he'll get out of there is by circling around. There's no exit to the Atlantic in that direction. You'd think he'd know that, living here and all. He'll have to head out under the bridge to the gulf."

They were outside now, by the dock. "What mile marker is that bridge at?"

"Between sixteen and seventeen."

His first call was to Goot. Sheppard told him to be waiting at the corner of the seawall, they would be picking him up, and could he get Sheppard's backpack from the car? And Blake, he said, should follow them on the roads as far as he could.

His second call was to Charlie Cordoba. "Cordoba here."

"Okay, Charlie. I need a marine block and a roadblock between mile markers sixteen and seventeen and I need them now. We've nearly got him."

"What? How? Why—"

"Just fucking do it," Sheppard snapped, and disconnected.

Within minutes, he and his new best buddy had picked up Goot and sped out into the lagoon, the boat's searchlight burning through the rain. But the large vessel was no longer in sight. Either Finch was navigating without any lights and they couldn't hear his engine over the roar of their own, or he had ducked into one of the canals, hiding until they passed.

Finch spotted them by accident—a faint bit of color in an otherwise colorless landscape. Shades of *Pleasantville,* he thought, when the world had gone from black and white to color because the characters had attained some sort of conciousness.

In terms of *this* drama, maybe it meant that Mira and Adam had realized their time was up, it was their turn to die regardless of what they did. Maybe it meant nothing at all. He didn't give a shit one way or another. Except for Hollywood, he always finished what he started and he intended to finish this.

He aimed his searchlights at the bit of color and hit the switch. Despite the rain, he saw them clearly, both of them clinging to the bright orange life jacket that had been in the aft. They were treading water fifty yards away, rats whose ship had sunk.

As soon as the light hit them, they kicked frantically, fighting to distance themselves from him. It was pathetic, comical, and he started laughing, and slammed the engines into high gear and raced toward them. For long moments in the glare of the light, they simply stared, shocked into paralysis, their faces frozen in time, like snapshots taken at a moment of intense trauma. And then they did the unexpected; they released their hold on the life jacket and swam in opposite directions, forcing him to choose.

But it wasn't really a choice at all. Relative to his speed, they moved like molasses, and even when he went after one, the other wouldn't get far enough away to make a difference. Mira was doing the valiant thing, trying to lure him toward her to save Adam. So Finch aimed toward the kid.

Adam saw him coming and dived.

Not enough, kid. He would have to come up for air in about twenty seconds, thirty if he had good lungs, maybe ninety seconds if his lungs were in terrific shape. That was fine. Finch could spare ninety seconds. He cut back on his power, waiting for the kid, biding his time.

And then an extraordinary thing happened. Mist seemed to appear out of nowhere, rolling in through the rain, across the water, enveloping the spot where the life jacket now floated, supporting no one. In seconds, the jacket was no longer visible. Finch leaned forward, searching for Mira, the kid, but the mist only thickened.

He took the engines up to their maximum power, plowing straight through the mist. The jacket got sucked under his boat, he saw it, the damn thing vanishing like yesterday. His boat struck something. He didn't have any idea what the hell it was, but it caused the engines to sputter, strain, shriek. He cut back on the power and in the glare of the searchlights, could make out a massive flotsam of debris wrapped around the front of the boat—tangles of leaves and branches, plastic containers, pieces of fencing, wire mesh, junk left over from the hurricane. It probably had been floating out here for weeks.

Then, farther out, slightly to his right where the mist was thickest, something huge emerged, causing the flotsam to part like the Red Sea. Dolphins, dozens of them, fifty, a hundred, who the hell knew? They spread out across his path, dark shapes in the thickening mist, arching, diving, surfacing, again and again, forming a tighter and tighter and tighter chain across the water, through what now looked like fog.

Finch slammed the engines into maximum speed, whipped the wheel to the left. The Flybridge pitched sharply, its right side lifting out of the water, hurling everything that wasn't nailed down to the opposite side of the boat. He would plow through the fuckers.

"I don't think this is going to work, Spense."

Finch didn't have to look very far to see the source of the

voice. Eden stood just to his right, as calm and poised as the Dalai Lama, hands clasped in front of her. She wore the clothes she'd been wearing when he'd last seen her, those denim Capri pants that hugged her hips, that feminine cotton shirt that accentuated her beautiful breasts. Her clothes were stained with blood, but she looked solid, real. He wasn't hallucinating.

"Jesus God," he muttered, and leaped to the left, away from her, his hands now free of the boat's wheel, and the Flybridge flew free and wild. "You're dead."

"And you're in deep shit." She threw her head back and laughed and flung out her arms, a gesture that took in everything—fog, flotsam, dolphins. "You don't have a chance against magic."

His entire being slammed into meltdown. He felt it happen, every horrible, agonizing pain—the pressure that seized his skull, the abrupt loss of vision in his left eye, the sour taste of vomit in his throat, the utter emptiness of Spenser Finch.

He lunged for her, but she just laughed and faded away and the shoreline rushed toward him, a jetty of tall, thick rocks. Panicked, certain he couldn't bring the boat around in time, Finch leaped over the side of the Flybridge seconds before it crashed into the rocks.

Mira shot to the surface for air and saw the boat fold up like an accordion against the rocks, wood and metal flying away from it. Moments later, its propane tanks exploded, throwing black smoke and fireballs that lit up the sky and hurled the stink of gas across the water.

"Adam," she shouted, and suddenly felt the water beneath her heaving, rising, and then she was out of the water, her body lifted up by a pod of dolphins.

Tossed around like a beach ball, she grappled for something to hold on to. Her fingers clamped shut over fins and she gripped them as the dolphins raced forward. Images flowed into her, fluid, bright, in bold, crayon colors, and she didn't understand any of them. They were as foreign to her as words in Latin or Greek. But she allowed herself to surrender to the strangeness, the unknown, the exhilaration of this alien world.

And then she was dumped, unceremoniously, into water so shallow that when she slipped off the pod, her hands and feet sank into seaweed. She gasped, she felt like a baby bird tossed out of the nest because it was deformed, genetically unfit, and she started to cry. For just a moment, she felt something against her leg, something soft, almost human, and a hand grasped hers. A webbed hand.

Images crashed over her, music flowed into her, she was transported, transformed, she got it. *I am here. Here is home. Go home. Home is love.* And when this too was gone, when she felt the webbed hand slipping away from her, she crawled to shore and collapsed against the sand, her cheeks pressed into a mound of crushed shells, seaweed, and the rain falling gently against her spine.

She opened her eyes and found herself staring into Adam's face, pressed against the same sand and crushed shells, his breathing hard. He moved his arm until his fingers touched hers. His mouth moved.

"Oh, my God," she whispered, her voice hoarse.

"The dolphins. And the mermaid. Did you see her?"

Mira moved closer to him, flung her arm over his body, and pulled him next to her. Strands of seaweed were woven through his hair. He smelled of salt, rain, sand, high summer, and childhood's end. "We found the magic," she said softly.

Sheppard crouched next to Mira, Adam. He pressed his hand to her forehead, her cheeks, ran his knuckles the length of her arm, then touched his fingers to her neck, checking for a pulse. Strong, steady. Beside her, Adam breathed.

Sheppard ran his fingers through Mira's hair, pushing it

off her face, and her eyes opened slowly, reluctantly. "Shep," she said.

"It's okay," he said. "We'll have you out of here in no time. Are you hurt? Is anything broken?" Stupid, his words sounded stupid and inadequate. He rocked toward her.

"Bruised. Exhausted." She extended her hand and he pulled her to a sitting position.

"We fished him out of the water." Finch, handcuffed, was lying on the sand no more than thirty feet away, and even though Sheppard gestured in that direction, Mira didn't turn her head. She kept looking at Sheppard. He handed her a bottle of water and she drank, then passed the bottle to Adam, who was also sitting up now.

"Shep."

"What?"

"I saw her. I saw your mermaid. She grabbed my hand."

Sheppard rocked back on his heels, his knees digging into the crushed shells, and held her hand tightly, nodding. Dolphins, mermaids, ghosts, the weird and the strange, all the things that went bump into the night and onto into daylight, 24/7. Mira's world. He was okay with it. And maybe, in time, he would learn to embrace it.

26

August 3

Mira and Sheppard stood in front of the one-way glass, watching Spenser Finch fidget at the table where he sat alone. His leg chains rattled, his handcuffs glinted. He drummed his fingers against the tabletop. In the wash of fluorescent light, his face looked chalky, Mira thought, and the circles under his eyes were like bad bruises.

"It's kind of unusual to do this, isn't it?" she asked.

"I think Glen deserves the opportunity after nearly thirty years."

Two cops stood behind Finch, and another opened the door to admit Kartauk. He limped in, leaning heavily on his cane. Finch's fingers went still.

"Who the hell're you?" Finch barked.

"Not your attorney," Kartauk replied, and limped over to the table.

The door to the viewing room whispered open. Suki and Adam slipped inside and joined Mira and Sheppard at the one-way window.

"So you're another cop?" Finch asked.

Kartauk pulled out the chair and sat down. "I'm your father."

Finch sat back, studying Kartauk. "I don't see the resemblance."

"I do," Adam whispered.

"And here's what you don't know about the first five or six years of your life," Kartauk went on, and started telling him how he'd met Joy Longwood on Cape Cod all those years ago.

As he spoke, three vague forms began to take shape in the room, at opposing ends of the table. They swirled like mist, then fog, then shadows, then smoke, and at each level they looked more real, more solid, more recognizable. Joy Longwood, Eden Thompkins, and a kid who looked exactly like young Spenser. His twin, Lyle.

"My God," Adam whispered. "You see them, Mira?"

"See who?" Suki and Sheppard asked simultaneously.

Mira and Adam shared a commiserating glance and she gave his hand a quick squeeze, an acknowledgment of their passage through Spenser Finch's nightmare world.

For long moments, the dead remained, watching and listening just as Mira and Adam were doing. Then the three of them joined hands and started to fade.

"I need to pick up Annie at the ferry," Mira said.

"Let's all go," Suki suggested.

"Great idea," Sheppard agreed.

Mira—and then Adam—took one last look into the room where Finch and Kartauk sat. But the ghosts already had disappeared.

In fall of 2007,
Pinnacle Books will be delighted to present
a terrifying new thriller from
T. J. MacGregor.
Please turn the page for a preview.

The sudden shriek of tires against the pavement distracted Nora. She glanced quickly toward the street, but the dozens of customers waiting along the patio wall for seats blocked her view. Then two officers marched onto the patio as though they owned the restaurant, the man moving with a macho swagger, the woman a few brisk steps ahead of him. Waiters and waitresses hurriedly stepped aside, customers slid their chairs out of the way. Nora's body went stiff, her eyes turned dry, a pulse beat at her throat.

Like when they took Mom.

The male officer was the same guy with whom she had collided on the street, but he looked much taller now, at least six feet four, with thick, muscular arms. She stole a glance at Jake, to see if he recognized the man as well, but he was huddled in on himself, as if he hoped to vanish, his eyes glued to the menu, hands gripping it. He looked terrified.

The feds moved slowly and deliberately among the tables, scanning the faces around them. On the sleeve of the man's shirt were letters and numbers: T6747. For the briefest moment, his eyes caught hers, then darted to Jake.

"Mr. McKee?" the fed said. "Professor Jake McKee?"

Distantly, the sounds of traffic punctuated the silence that now gripped the balcony. Everyone watched them.

"Mr. McKee?" the fed repeated.

Jake suddenly shot to his feet, overturning his chair. He grabbed the edge of the table, overturning it. The bottle of wine, ice, glasses, silverware, everything crashed to the floor. Pandemonium erupted on the balcony, the two feds lunged for Jake, but he was gone, racing between tables, knocking over empty chairs, leaving an obstacle course behind him. Then he leaped over the low wall that separated the patio from the street.

Nora jumped up and tried to shove her way through the crowd. She finally found an opening, vaulted the wall, and tore after Jake and the feds.

Her shoes pounded the sidewalk, her breath exploded from her mouth. Despite the chill in the air, sweat poured down the side of her face. Jake tore a ragged path through the shoppers and tourists on the other side of the street. Pedestrians scrambled out of Jake's way as soon as they saw the officers, as if the bitter-chocolate-colored uniforms were an archetype synonymous with the bogeyman. They scrambled and then gawked or turned away, pretending they hadn't seen anything.

Nora loped up the street after the feds and Jake. As the tall guy closed in on Jake, she spotted a possible escape route off to the left, but knew that Jake didn't see it. Adrenaline coursed through her, she drew on reserves she didn't know she had, and sprinted toward Jake and the fed. A heartbeat after the bastard tackled Jake, Nora slammed into him from behind, knocking him forward. His arms flew out to break his fall, she heard bone smacking concrete when his knees struck the sidewalk.

Nora grasped Jake by the shoulders, tried to pull him up. *"C'mon, Jake, get up, run, fast—"*

Blood streamed from the corner of his mouth, his eyes

looked dazed. *"Leave,"* he said hoarsely. "While you can. Glove compartment. Leather case. Parked five blocks south."

The female fed shoved Nora roughly to the side and swung, punching Jake in the face. He fell back, grunting with pain, blood pouring from his noise, and the woman handcuffed him. Nora scrambled to her feet.

"Where's your warrant? What're you charging him with?"

"Section fourteen, code three," the male fed barked, waving a document that he pulled from his jacket pocket. "Now back off, Mrs. McKee, before I arrest you for assaulting a federal officer and interfering with an arrest."

"Who the hell are you? What's your name? I have a right to know who's arresting my husband. And what's section fourteen, code three? What's that mean in plain English?"

He looked—bored? Pissed off? "You don't have any rights, ma'am. And since you're guilty by association, my advice is to go home and call your attorney."

Guilty by association? "Where're you taking him?"

"Call your attorney."

He pushed past her, but Nora shouted, "Hey, you jerk, that isn't good enough." She grabbed his arm. "I'm entitled to an answer."

He wrenched free and spun around, his face seized up with a kind of primal rage, as if no one had challenged his authority before now. He stabbed his index finger so close to her face that she leaned back, breathless, terrified.

"I'll say this only once, Mrs. McKee. If you touch me again, if you continue to interfere, I'll charge you with assault and handcuff you and haul your ass off this street and out of this town and you won't be able to help your husband."

With that, he turned away and pushed Jake into a car that had pulled up to the curb. Then T6747 slid into the passenger seat and Nora just stood there, powerless, arms clutched against her body, tears coursing down her cheeks, Jake's bloody face against the window, mouthing, *Run, Nora, run.*

More Thrilling Suspense From

T.J. MacGregor

More Nail-Biting Suspense From Your Favorite Thriller Authors

More Thrilling Suspense From Your Favorite Thriller Authors

f Angels Fall y Rick Mofina	0-7860-1061-4	$6.99US/$8.99CAN
Cold Fear y Rick Mofina	0-7860-1266-8	$6.99US/$8.99CAN
Blood of Others y Rick Mofina	0-7860-1267-6	$6.99US/$9.99CAN
o Way Back y Rick Mofina	0-7860-1525-X	$6.99US/$9.99CAN
ark of the Moon P.J. Parrish	0-7860-1054-1	$6.99US/$8.99CAN
ead of Winter P.J. Parrish	0-7860-1189-0	$6.99US/$8.99CAN
int It Black P.J. Parrish	0-7860-1419-9	$6.99US/$9.99CAN
hick Than Water P.J. Parrish	0-7860-1420-2	$6.99US/$9.99CAN

Available Wherever Books Are Sold!

Visit our website at **www.kensingtonbooks.com**